Mirrors & Smoke

A NOVEL

ADRIENNE
STEVENSON

adriennestevenson.ca

Mirrors & Smoke © 2023 Adrienne Stevenson

First Equae Books Publication August 2023

Front cover photo © Credit: Teacherdad48; Stock photo ID:473675306
Cover Design © 2023 Crowe Creations
Interior design by Crowe Creations
Text set in Garamond; headings in Clarity Gothic SF

Equae Books
ISBN: 978-1-7782233-5-8

Mirrors & Smoke captivates from the start and delivers a moving tale of perseverance in the face of tragedy. Rebecca Plummer is a healer, midwife, and caregiver to women whose strength has been diminished by childbearing, near starvation, and abuse. In 1812, when the United States invades Canada, Rebecca's dedication to healing is put to the test. Told from multiple perspectives, the reader is given interwoven views of the war, and contrasting perceptions about Rebecca and her life. Based on real people and historical events, this fictionalized account is told from the Canadian perspective and presents a rarely seen view of life in war-torn, rural Canada.—Donna D. Conrad, award-winning author of *House of the Moon: Surviving the Sixties*

Mirrors & Smoke tells the remarkable story of Rebecca Plummer. Life is not easy for a healer and midwife in Upper Canada in the early part of the nineteenth century, especially one who wants to improve the lot of women. Inevitably, such desires bring her more enemies than successes.

Adrienne Stevenson presents us with an oh so realistic, yet fictionalised, account of those turbulent times from the perspective of a woman living in Niagara in Upper Canada. With more enemies than friends, Rebecca navigates the anti-feminist repression of the time with intelligence, determination and a capacity for hard work. The chaos brought by the US invasion in 1812 multiplies her problems. Her skills must turn from saving the lives of injured soldiers to saving her own family as the turmoil causes both friend and foe to reveal their true nature.

As I read on, I became more and more involved with Stevenson's artfully crafted characters. It was a jolt to realise the author had not actually lived through those times, although she must have immersed herself in every last detail. Stevenson brings a light and poetic touch to this important subject matter without hitting us over the head with the underlying serious theme.

It is refreshing to see a book about the war of 1812 that reveals the wider effect on the people of the time and how a woman might achieve her goals against her political adversaries and the agonies of war raging, albeit slowly, around her.—Brian Wyvill, author of *The Second Gate* series

To my parents, who started me off
and to Jim, who keeps me going

"The present rearranges the past. We never tell the story whole because a life isn't a story; it's a whole Milky Way of events and we are forever picking out constellations from it to fit who and where we are."—Rebecca Solnit

"plus ça change, plus c'est la même chose"
—Jean-Baptiste Alphonse Karr

PART 1
Family Affairs

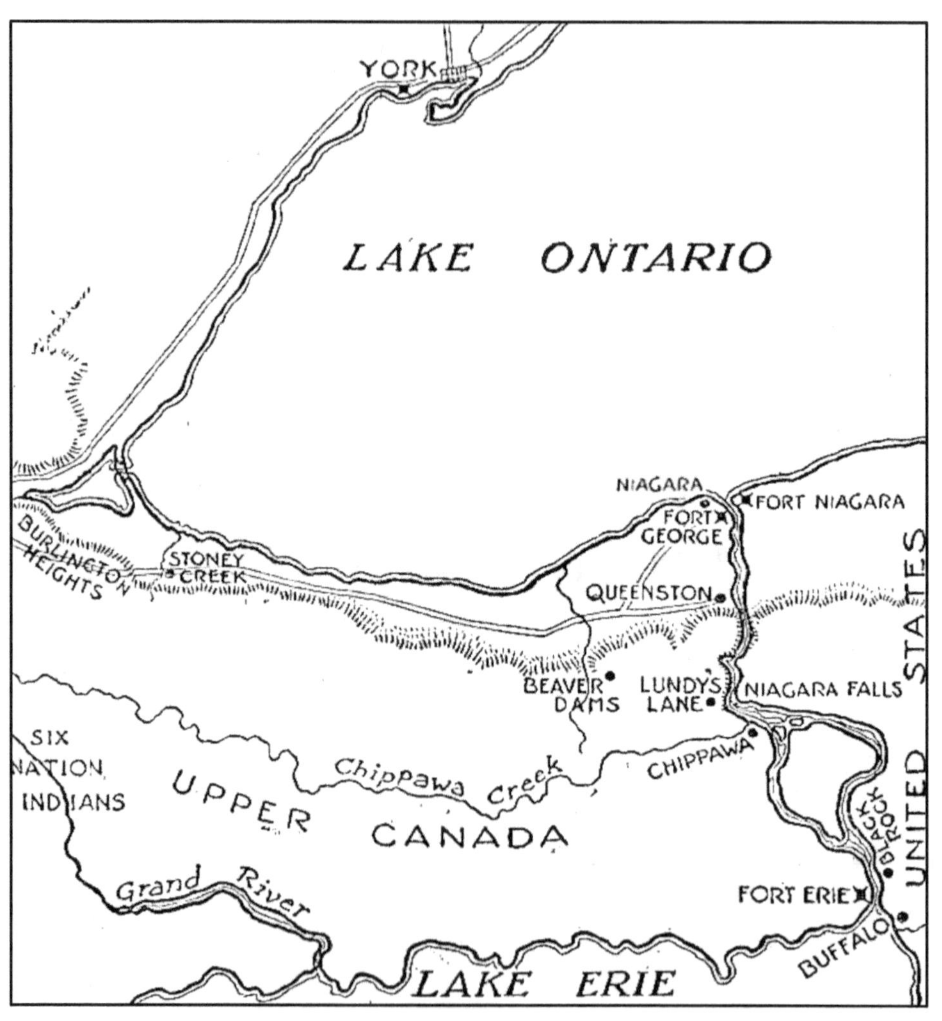

YORK
LAKE ONTARIO
NIAGARA
FORT NIAGARA
FORT GEORGE
QUEENSTON
BURLINGTON HEIGHTS
STONEY CREEK
BEAVER DAMS
LUNDY'S LANE
NIAGARA FALLS
SIX NATION INDIANS
Chippawa Creek
UPPER CANADA
CHIPPAWA
UNITED STATES
BLACK ROCK
Grand River
FORT ERIE
BUFFALO
LAKE ERIE

1809

"In every age there has been a stream of popular opinion that has carried all before it, and given a family character, as it were, to the century."—Mary Wollstonecraft

"Men and women must be educated, in a great degree, by the opinions and manners of the society they live in."
—Mary Wollstonecraft

June

Rebecca

My stillroom faced north, a sanctuary in an uncertain world. Its multi-paned windows spilled light onto my workbench, but there remained enough dark corners where cooking and medicinal herbs could cure properly, and my decoctions rest secure. In one corner cupboard, bearing the only lock in the house, lay our precious stores of salt and tea. I took a deep breath, reveling in the scents—basil, marjoram, thyme, mint—still fragrant after winter storage. I sorted through last year's stock, keeping one ear cocked for my young cousins' footsteps.

Eliza and Maryel had gone to gather spring herbs and greens from the countryside. I hoped to include fresh foods in our evening meal. They should have returned by now. Since the news of their mother's death in England came with the first spring letters, they had taken to disappearing together, I believed to grieve in private. Even then… they were never gone this long.

I stepped onto the stoop, my eyes watering at the sudden glare. To the east, Fort Niagara loomed across the river's mouth on the American shore. I heard the drumbeat that signaled soldiers drilling there. To the northwest, the stone lighthouse guarded the Upper Canadian lakeshore. No sign of the girls. Perhaps the house was blocking my view. As I rounded the corner, I could see along the Niagara River. Nobody there, either.

Maryel was nineteen, and Eliza twenty-five. No longer girls, but young women. I had brought them out to this frontier town, Niagara, Upper Canada, when their father sent for them to join him in his mission to the Mohawks, some fourteen years ago. Eliza found the colony's wildness as intimidating as I did then, at twenty-seven. Maryel had known little else, and sometimes scoffed at our fears. But I could never quell my uneasiness over the dangers in this wild place, to which all women were vulnerable. Wolves, bears, men… I remained on edge when foraging or midwifery took me out of sight of the town.

I hastened along the river path toward Fort George. A wooded hill obscured my view, but I heard shouting. Some commotion was underway. My breath quickened along with my pace.

As I crested the hill, the common ground between town and fort spread before me. Below, near Navy Hall, men ran, chased by a red-coated officer. A small group huddled near the riverbank. Two more redcoats, and—yes, two women, one standing and one prone. My girls!

I pelted down the hill, skirts clutched high, with no thought of modesty. "What's going on? What happened?" I cried.

Eliza clutched her shawl around her, and stood a wary distance from one redcoat, darting him furtive glances. Tear-tracks smeared her dirty face, signs of vomit stained her bodice, and her fair hair had fallen askew. Maryel was wrapped in an officer's red tunic, her skirt beneath it torn and ragged. Her honey-colored hair had come unpinned and straggled wildly. Her pupils were so wide they nearly obscured the blue irises. She tried to rise, but her left foot could not support her, and she collapsed back onto the grass. Neither spoke, though Maryel groaned when her foot landed. I touched each girl's face briefly. Their skin was chilled and covered in a sheen of sweat.

I bent to check on Maryel. "Tell me, dear, are you injured? Where does it hurt?" Maryel's arms tightened around herself; her mouth opened, but no sound emerged. She gave the tiniest of nods

I looked up at Eliza, saying "are you all right?" She nodded.

Shock. I must get them home immediately.

"You men, will you help?"

The shirt-sleeved officer sketched a rough bow. "Ensign Stevenson at your service, ma'am, and Ensign Dawson, of the 100th Foot. Your daughters, Mrs....?"

"Miss Plummer. My cousins, but in my charge. Come—we should hurry."

Eliza walked on her own, avoiding the assistance offered by Ensign Dawson, but Maryel leaned heavily on Ensign Stevenson and me. Our progress was slow, but steady. As we walked, my thoughts teemed with a thousand possibilities, none of them good. Had they been violated? Would there be consequences? Would I be forced by circumstance to make an unthinkable decision? I would steel myself to do so if necessary, being all too aware of the stigma attached to a "ruined" woman. And the consequences—but perhaps I was worrying to no end.

Our sorry little group straggled to the house, set a little off from its neighbors. For a wonder, nobody appeared in the street, and no twitch of a curtain betrayed a prying eye. Better if Reverend Addison's daughters could be shielded from gossip. I hoped these young officers would not spread their story.

Eliza sank into a fireside chair in the parlor, while Maryel collapsed onto the settle. Both immediately burst into tears. I would ask them for details when they were calmer. None of us was capable of intelligent discourse just then.

I sent Ensign Dawson to the well for water, leaving Ensign

Stevenson standing in the doorway, while I darted into the stillroom for some clean cloths and my medicine case. When I returned, Dawson was hard on my heels, the bucket sloshing water over the side.

After handing Eliza a damp cloth for her face, I turned to Maryel, who had fainted. Ordinarily, she had the stronger constitution of the sisters, so she must be badly hurt. I manipulated her foot. "Thank God, it's but sprained, not broken." Her eyes opened and looked calmer. "We'll get this cleaned and bound up. It should be fine after a few days' rest." I looked at the officers. "Now, sirs, if you would explain…"

Ensign Stevenson took the lead. "We heard screams and came upon the young ladies under attack by some drunken ruffians. Part of a work detail from our regiment got their hands on some illicit grog, sorry to say." He scowled. "They'll be severely punished."

"But," I turned to the girls, "why were you so close to the fort? You know it's unwise to venture there."

Stevenson interjected. "Ma'am, perhaps it's best we take our leave. We must return to duty. Your cousins are safe at home." He smiled down at Maryel. "Miss, if I may have my coat?"

Maryel blushed scarlet and held her arms tightly crossed over her bosom. I held a length of towel to shield her. "Hand me the coat, my dear, and cover yourself with this. And give these men your thanks for what appears to have been an heroic rescue."

The young officers, too, were now as red as their coats. They backed out of the room, muttering excuses, and made swift tracks to the door. After it closed behind them, I took a deep breath, choking back the harsh words that so often follow relief from fear, and stood looking at my bedraggled young relatives.

"Well?"

"Oh Rebecca," said Eliza, "I've never been so frightened. Not even when wolves howled under our windows last winter."

Maryel gulped, and wiped her eyes on the toweling, exposing most of her breast. "Those awful men…" She turned her head away.

"Eliza?"

"The breeze along the river was cool, and there was mint and sorrel on the bank, and young nettles for cooking. You said something about running low on willow bark and blue cohosh, so we were looking for new shoots. I didn't realize we were so close to the fort." Her lip trembled. "And then… and then… those horrible men."

"Calm yourself, Eliza. Take a deep breath, that's right."

"They appeared out of nowhere and grabbed us." She shuddered. "I dropped the basket." Tears welled in her eyes.

"Never mind the basket. What did they do? They didn't…?"

Eliza shook her head. "Not me. They were interrupted. But oh, Rebecca, their filthy hands were all over us, ripping and grabbing and squeezing. They stank of liquor and tobacco. One of them pushed me down in the mud and another stuck his hand down my dress. I threw up all over his shirt. He cuffed me around the head and I rolled down the bank. Right into a cowpat." She giggled weakly.

I breathed a little easier. "And Maryel?"

"My back was to her. All I know is they ripped out the front of her dress." She turned to her sister.

Maryel sniffled, resorting to her towel for support. Her face gave nothing away. What if…? Curbing my impatience, I prepared bandages for her foot, and looked through the medicine box for arnica and wintergreen, to ease the sprain. The odor of wintergreen was soothing to the spirits, too.

After a few moments, she spoke. "I just want to forget it."

"The memory will fade faster if you share it. Better than stewing over it alone."

"I can't. I just can't." Her voice shrilled, cracking. Great sobs wracked her slight frame.

I hugged her close and rocked her a little. "Shh, shh." She calmed a bit when I stroked her hair.

"Eliza, hand me my work basket, please." I wound bandages around Maryel's injured foot so tightly that she protested.

"Ow!"

"Think yourself lucky it isn't worse. You'll have to keep it raised, and stay at home for a few days, but otherwise, it'll do. Your arm will bruise, but your sleeves will conceal it.

Eliza joined us on the settle. I felt her shivering. "Can we lie down for a bit? I don't feel well."

We helped Maryel upstairs, and I tucked the coverlet round her. Eliza crawled into the other side of their bed.

"I'll come for you in an hour or so to help you clean up before your father returns."

I controlled my shaking hands long enough to close their door and stumble down the stairs. My skin felt fragile, as if it could shatter and peel away. Please, God, let all be well with them.

✳

When I went back upstairs, it was to find both of them calmer. Eliza had changed her dress and helped Maryel into a clean shift. I could hope for the best, but I must get the full story.

"Now…" I waited.

She spoke in almost inaudible tones. "It was hot… cool breeze so tempting…"

Eliza interrupted. "We cut some river willow and were searching for blue cohosh. We didn't notice the rough gang until they were upon us."

Maryel nodded. "The one that grabbed me was covered in tattoos. Anchors all along his arms. His shirt was open and he pressed my face into his hairy chest." She shuddered. "It was horrible. He was fat and sweaty and stinking. Another man came up behind. They crushed me between them." Another pause. "They ripped my dress.

A man with a scraggy beard stood watching… laughing."

She choked on her words. I patted her leg. The suspense made my stomach roil, but I mustn't upset her further. Not until I had the full story. "Eliza, please ask Hannah to make tea." She nodded and left us. "Go on, my dear, you're doing fine. Tell me how your ankle came to be injured."

"Their hands were all over me—my buttocks, my breast—they squeezed everything they could get hold of. I cried out, but the fat one clamped his hand over my mouth and another got his hand round my throat." She swallowed hard. "I struggled, but couldn't get my arms free. The bearded one rucked up my skirt… fumbled with his trouser buttons. I raised my knee to his vitals as hard as I could. And screamed. All I could think of was not to go down without fighting."

"Good girl." All might yet be well…

Tears threatened, reddening her eyes and the tip of her nose. Eliza returned with Hannah and the tea tray. I spooned sugar recklessly into our cups, pouring the hot, fragrant tea over it. Sugar for shock, tea for comfort, and water for cleansing. They were all I could offer right now. Healing the injury to their spirits would take time. I handed Maryel a cup, and she sipped at the hot liquid.

"That's good." She swallowed about half the cup, then continued her tale. "When I fell, my ankle twisted under me. I heard something crack and thought it was my leg. It hurt, but it must have been a branch." She gulped. "I thought I was done for when he grabbed me between my legs. Oh, cousin, he poked his fingers inside me and twisted." The wild look came back to her eyes, but she took another sip of tea and calmed again. "Then his hands came off me. I heard shouting and the sound of running footsteps. All I could do was lie there and shake." She clutched my hand as to a lifeline.

Thank all the powers that be! I was sure as I could be I wouldn't need my special decoction to bring on her courses. If he had penetrated her, she would have said. It was clear from their stories there hadn't been time for more than rough handling. Which was bad enough.

When I thought her calmed sufficiently, I spoke again, as gently as I could manage.

"You'll need to be more cautious now the garrison is so enlarged. You should be wary even of the officers. They're as likely to take advantage as the regular soldiers. Many will have left wives and families at home and merely be seeking comfort here. These two young officers…"

Eliza spoke first. "They were most gentleman-like. The one who escorted me was just a boy, younger than Maryel. An Ensign on his first tour of duty, no doubt."

"Ensign Stevenson is more of an age with me, I think," said Maryel. "They were both careful of our dignity."

"You must be thankful for that," I said.

"Oh yes," said Maryel.

Eliza nodded. "What will you tell Father?" she asked.

"I'm not sure," I said. "He must learn what happened, but I hate to add to his worries." Indeed, the Reverend Robert Addison had more than enough on his plate, what with the Salt Spring affair and Lieutenant-Governor Gore's political antipathy. Not to mention the prolonged delays in construction of the new church. "I won't lie to him, but perhaps we can break it to him gently."

"When do you expect him back?"

"Not until this evening. He's gone to meet with Mr. Dickson about the final arrangements for glazing the church windows."

As we helped Maryel into a fresh dress, I formulated a plan.

"I'll first tell him about your injured ankle, and then about your rescue by those kind young officers, from the drunken soldiers. I think I can ease his mind by emphasizing that they are subject to military justice. He'll be worried, of course, and may want to visit the fort to reassure himself that due punishment will be meted out, but I doubt he'll take it further." He won't want to stir up scandal in the town, I thought. That would do the entire family much more harm than good.

✴

Dinner that evening was an awkward affair.

Cousin Robert returned in high good humor after concluding tricky negotiations over the church windows. "Such good fortune the glazier is one of my congregation," he said, laying his round clerical hat on the hall table. He rubbed his hands together and beamed. "If he had been Presbyterian, now…"

"Come into the dining room, cousin," I said. "We have supper laid already."

He followed me and greeted his daughters absently, still focused on his afternoon's achievements.

"We have had an incident today," I told him. "Perhaps you should sit down while I explain."

His brows rose. "What? What happened?" He peered over his spectacles at us, slowly taking in his daughters' bruised faces and Maryel's bandaged leg propped on a chair. "What? How's this?" His smile was replaced by a frown, his eyebrows drawing together like two furry caterpillars going head-to-head.

"Be calm, cousin, and I will tell you." I recounted such details as I thought necessary, in an order that made less of his daughters' heedlessness and much more of their rescuers' timeliness. "So, the miscreants will be duly punished, and no lasting harm has come to your daughters. Some bruises, a sprained ankle. Those will heal long before the church dedication service."

"Well, well," he said at last. "'Tis a great pity such ruffians are let loose to harass innocent women. You are sure they have not been… harmed?" I nodded. He dropped his chin on his chest for a moment.

"I will have a word with the Fort Major to ensure it does not happen again. You are certain the men will be punished?"

"The young officers we spoke with were determined it should be so," I said. "How, I don't know, but I'm sure it will be severe." I paused. "I think it fortunate there were no other witnesses to the incident. We saw no one in the town as we returned."

"No, indeed. We must not become subjects of gossip." His face relaxed. "It seems to me all will be well. I will not look for more trouble unless it comes knocking on our door."

As the meal proceeded, Cousin Robert was most solicitous of his daughters, pouring them extra wine and telling us all about his after-noon to distract their thoughts. For an ordinarily distant, scholarly man, he was downright expansive. I was pleased he made these efforts to comfort them. He was a kind man, full of compassion for the unfortunate. I knew this well, having been the recipient of his kindness these many years. He had, after all, taken me into his household without question, during my time of trouble.

Later that evening, I helped Maryel upstairs to the bedroom she shared with Eliza. I sat with her a while, hoping she might talk more about her ordeal.

"Rebecca…" she said.

"Yes?" I waited again, thinking she might say more, but she remained silent so long I stood to leave.

"Don't go. I… that awful man."

I sat back down on her bed. "Are you truly uninjured?"

She stammered a few disjointed syllables, but finally continued. "He handled me roughly, but not what you mean. He put his fingers inside me. Nothing else."

My flesh crawled at the thought. "You're sure?"

She nodded. "But… his filthy hands… I don't know if I'll ever feel clean again."

"You will." I slipped my arm around her. "Nothing can make you that dirty. Good men touch women with respect."

"Can a good man's touch erase the memory?"

I shook my head. "I don't know."

Then we were both silent. Eliza came in, but she merely bade me goodnight, and I left them to console each other. Despite the age gap and much sisterly bickering, they were fond of each other. I was reassured to see—as I left the room—Eliza sat at Maryel's side, her arm around her sister's shoulders. They would do, at least for tonight.

How I envied my cousin Mary when first I entered their household… and yet here I was, living a part of the life that should have been hers. And trying my best to be a better parent to their daughters than mine were to me.

I slept fitfully, awaking nearly as exhausted as the night before, and even more uncomfortable. My skin prickled, and felt gritty. It took several rinses with the tepid water on my washstand, and a brisk toweling, to make my face and arms feel clean. A cool breeze off the lake helped a bit, but didn't dispel my uneasiness, punctuated by the distant howl of a wolf. How could I fend off all the dangers in this place? I felt small and weak.

Jack

"I want those bastards to get what they deserve," said Jack. They were due a flogging and deserved worse. Not that he wanted to mete out the punishment himself. The thought made him queasy. He had nearly disgraced himself by spewing his guts at his first sight of a flogged man's raw back. "Private soldiers can't be permitted to take liberties with respectable women. Surely there are camp followers or women of their own class in the town for such doings." Drunkenness was no excuse for attacking any stray female they encountered. He would ask for an example to be made. Extra time in the stocks both before and after the whipping, and the threat of hanging for a second offence—that ought to put fear into them. He stamped hard at the path. "I keep thinking…"

"What, Jack?" asked Dawson.

"I have two sisters. Suppose it had been them?" He swallowed hard as a vision of Miss Maryel Addison floated before his eyes. "What if those men had raped them?"

"They'd hang—but I take your meaning. Good thing we got there before serious damage was done."

"I'd have thought a clergyman's daughters would take more care for their safety."

"Isn't that harsh, Jack?"

"It's just… my sisters always have a maid in attendance, even in the better districts of the city."

Dawson frowned. "These colonial towns… they lack the advantages of civilization."

Jack barked a laugh. "Dublin—civilized? Some quarters maybe, but others… well. We'd better get accustomed to this God-forsaken outpost."

These thoughts persisted through an evening over drinks in the Fort George officers' mess. Jack had tied his dark hair back in a queue, but stray locks escaped to curl over his ears and partially obscure his still-sparse side-whiskers, and he habitually tucked them back again. Tonight, he cradled a fiddle in his left arm, and plucked at its strings. Drat, he thought, the tuning still wasn't right. He lifted a mug of ale in his right hand and tossed back half the contents. Ugh, bitter stuff. He wiped his mouth on his sleeve and resumed tuning his instrument.

"There, got it at last," he said. "What'll you have?"

"Play whatever you like, Jack," said Captain Sherrard. "We enjoy 'em all."

His fellow officers murmured in agreement. Music was a fine way to liven a dull evening. Upwards of twenty men lounged in chairs around the long table, some throwing dice and others writing letters or puffing on long-stemmed pipes. Tallow candles guttered in their pewter holders, building up towers of wax at their edges. Shutters stood open on this fine June night, letting in a welcome breeze that dissipated some of the fug.

Jack had barely started in on "The Dublin Cries," one of his father's tunes, when a young subaltern rushed in. "Have you heard?"

"Heard what?" was the chorus.

"The latest despatches from the Peninsular War—finally some good news. Wellesley's army has routed Marshal Soult's troops and pushed them out of Portugal into Spain. What I wouldn't give to be in the fight against Napoleon's armies!"

A ragged cheer went up around the room. Mugs clinked and the volume of chatter rose.

"Huzzah, I suppose," said Jack. "That news matters little to us, moldering in this backwater," He yawned ostentatiously, to cover up his excitement. Military zeal warred with anxiety over how he would respond when it came his turn to fight. Would he have the courage to stand fast with his men, or disgrace himself? Jack longed for promotion, but the expense of a purchase was far beyond his means. He'd have to achieve it through battle laurels. "A fight would be a great relief."

"You won't think so when you come under fire," said Sherrard. "Don't wish for our neighbors over at Fort Niagara to cannonade us. If war comes, it will be soon enough."

Jack shrugged and picked up his fiddle. He resumed his tune and followed it with others as the evening wore on. His listeners clamored for more, and he played until his fingers protested.

Only after he was lying on his straw pallet that night did his thoughts turn to his family. Devil the bit he cared for his father, selfish bugger that he was. It was the thought of his younger brother and sisters that caused him worry. In the years since their mother's death, he had done his best to compensate for their father's neglect, with limited success. Sir John, as he must now call him, Father being insufficient, was puffed up by his achievements as Vicar Choral to St. Patrick's Protestant Cathedral in Dublin. He was more interested in musical arrangements than he was in domestic harmony. Reminiscing brought a lump to his throat. He swallowed it as best he could, rolled over, punched at his pallet for a more-comfortable position, and sought relief in sleep.

Rebecca

I busied myself with mundane tasks the next day, leaving the sisters to their own devices. They were subdued but recovering. Turning out the kitchen tools might be a distraction from my aching head. If that wasn't sufficient, I could go over the linens.

So many of my family were gone, the most recent being Cousin Robert's wife, my cousin Mary. He said the dead are always with us. I didn't know whether he truly believed the dead became minor angels to guard the living, or simply thought we couldn't remove them from our memories, even should we wish to. I thought of my dead parents only with reluctance. Our differences were irreconcilable.

The kitchen cutlery clattered as I dumped it onto the table. Mostly pewter, it didn't need polishing, but the box generated a fine dust and must be cleaned lest our food be seasoned with wood particles. Ordinarily, I would assign the task to Hannah, but I needed to occupy myself with something practical.

My position, outwardly secure, felt less so now. I'd been content to mother my cousin's girls, and taken some pride in their becoming capable young ladies. It hadn't been easy. Eliza was steady, but I'd seen disturbing signs in Maryel of the same melancholia that had afflicted her mother. I hoped it was merely the vagaries of youth, but that remained to be seen. This attack would surely have had consequences on both girls beyond their minor injuries. They would need careful watching over the next weeks, maybe months.

I knew this from my own sad experience. I spent years patching the wound of losing Martin. And I carried the resentment over my parents' treatment of me in a deep inner knot. But I would not let myself revisit that now. Perhaps the knives needed sharpening. I stored the forks and spoons back in their box and assembled the knives and cleavers and the whetstone. The rasp of stone over metal settled my nerves.

Cousin Robert was an enigma. He remained unfailingly courteous, in fact, quite distant in his dealings with me. I supposed this to be typical of men of scholarly inclination, though I knew but a few. He preferred books to people, spending every spare moment in his library. Given the motley crowd of inhabitants he ministered to in this locale, I was not surprised. In all my years here, I had found few kindred souls. Perhaps that was why I still considered England home, though I might never see it again. My sister Sarah wrote that I should come to her, in London, but I doubted she would welcome an aging spinster to her household. Particularly one who harbored resentment over her good fortune. Still strange to think that she herself married one of Cousin Robert's brothers. How tightly our families were entwined, although I still felt an outsider. Would I ever truly belong?

Knives done. I mustn't wallow in self-doubt when there was so much requiring my attention. I needed to make sure the household ran smoothly. That was my role here, after all.

A few days after the distressing incident with the soldiers, we received a shipment from Cousin Robert's brother Thomas in

London. There were some packages, and one large crate, which turned out to be salt-evaporating pans. I received a letter and parcel from my sister Sarah. She inquired after our health and various endeavors I had mentioned, and provided her family news. My two nephews, who I had never laid eyes on, sounded like a handful.

Letters from England were scarce, and news always welcome, so I shared it with the family over tea, after our evening meal. Both Eliza and Maryel were sufficiently recovered to laugh over their cousins' antics. It looked as if the hurt to their spirits would mend rapidly. They retired early to bed, with one of my calming tisanes, wood betony and lemon balm, to aid their rest.

Having completed my day's labors, I took advantage of a rare free evening to compose a return letter.

25 June 1809

My dearest sister Sarah,

Please impart our thanks to Cousin Thomas for the salt pans. Cousin Robert still hopes the salt workings near the Fifteen Mile Creek may return to his care, but it appears less likely at every turn. Perhaps the acquisition of this necessary equipment will help his cause. On my behalf, I am grateful you could locate a copy of Culpeper's Herbal, a volume I have long desired. Cousin Robert's library is prodigious, but contains mostly sermons and other religious tomes.

This wretched colony becomes more trying with each day, and life seems more precarious. Bad enough that wild animals howl around our gates—bears, wolves, and the like, you would hardly credit it. But there are soldiers at the fort, and vagabonds as well, even in such a remote outpost as this. And constant rumors of war.

Yet I must not let complaints escape my lips. Marooned as I am in the colony, I have no recourse but to blend in as best I may. Such an assortment of creatures I never knew, even in London, and I refer merely to the humanity. But truly, I find more civilized behavior in our neighbors of the Six Nations than I do in the brash Americans, Loyalist or not.

Sarah, I miss you sorely. My friend Drusilla, who I mentioned…

At this point, the nib of my quill pen split. It would require mending before I could continue. The candle guttered and my eyes felt grainy. After a tremendous yawn, I set aside my letter and made my way upstairs.

JULY

Rebecca

"Do you suppose there will be war, Cousin?" asked Maryel from her seat by the parlor door. She still favored her ankle, though it had healed quickly. The color had returned to her face, and she no longer started at every loud noise.

"There are many who wish it," I said.

Maryel toyed with one of her carefully crimped locks, pulling it to its full length and examining its honey color critically against the sleeve of her blue Sunday dress.

"Mary Eleanor Rebecca Addison, stop fiddling with your hair. You'll tease those curls out before we leave the house."

She stopped fidgeting for the moment, and looked at me where I stood near the bottom of the staircase. "What will happen to us if war comes?" she asked.

"Time enough to worry when it happens. We'll have plenty of notice."

"But we're right on the border with the States, Cousin. Why, our town is within easy gunshot of Fort Niagara—we can see it from our front steps—directly across the river!"

"True, but remember. We've seen no untoward activity there. Or, for that matter, at Fort George. Be calm, my dear. Sufficient unto the day the troubles thereof." I stroked her hair and turned her around to face me fully. "Enough worry… and enough prinking, too, young lady. You should listen to your father's caution about vanity, else he'll have you in plain braids next Sunday. If you've no wish to attract young men, why must you fuss so about your appearance?"

Maryel pouted. "Just because Father is the rector… and why should I have to attract anyone? I shall never marry. Why won't you believe me?"

"Not now, Maryel. We'll be late for service." I called up the stairs. "Eliza! Make haste!"

Eliza, her fair curls pinned up in a net, came downstairs sedately. She was a pale copy of Maryel in both looks and demeanor, demurely dressed in dove-gray and carrying a knitted shawl despite the heat. I couldn't understand how she appeared so cool when I was wilting already.

"Your pardon, Cousin. I'm ready now," she said.

We walked along Prideaux Street, arm in arm, toward the Masonic Lodge, where morning service was to be held. The church was nearly complete, thank goodness. Subscriptions toward its building lagged, and craftsmen always demanded payment on the nose. I tried to make out the walls through the trees ahead, but they were in full leaf and too thick to see through.

Meanwhile, Church of England services were held alternately in the Masonic Lodge and the Courthouse. The congregation had stopped using Navy Hall except on rare occasions. It was a long walk across the Common in wet or wintry weather, and plagued by mosquitoes and deerflies in the heat of summer. Parishioners complained of the persistent smell of boiled cabbage from its use as the officer's mess. Drafts and clacking shutters competed with Cousin Robert's gently modulated speech. Perhaps the Lodge was not ideal either, used as a drinking establishment most of the week, but it was preferable to the Courthouse with its dark-paneled walls and general air of stuffiness and gloom. I admired its bright first floor hall, with windows open on all sides to catch whatever breeze came off the Niagara River.

Our neighbors seized avidly on every scrap of news presaging war. No matter how stale or contrived, persistent rumors had the power to raise a hubbub among the Niagara townspeople. The Americans had protested for years about the British Navy pressing American merchant sailors of British birth into virtual slavery on their ships. Complaints escalated with the British blockade of American shipments to Napoleon's France. We passed little knots of worried townsfolk deep in speculative discourse as we approached the Masonic Hall. Excited voices flowed over us as we entered and made our way toward the stairs. I nodded and smiled toward Mrs. Dickson, but could not speak with her then, owing to the noise of the crowd.

"I heard they're going to send an invading party over from Fort Niagara!"

"… just the commander… dine… Major at Fort George."

"The war against Napoleon… spill over here."

"President Madison favors the war-hawks."

"Indians… hemming in their expansion west… come north instead."

"American merchants want to trade with everyone."

"The British want to prevent… the French."

"If His Majesty's Navy presses… sailors, we'll feel the heat."

"… good thing they moved the Capital to York."

"Word from York… Lieutenant-Governor Gore… furor in the House."

"Will Gore be replaced?"

"You been talking to some of them radicals again."

"Thorpe and Willcocks have it right."

"… hear about Willcocks and old Russell's sister?"

"… Irishman… loud-mouthed libertine. Pay him no mind."

I shut the door of the upstairs hall behind them, and the sound of voices muted.

"Go on and take your places. I'll stay by the door."

Maryel and Eliza walked down the aisle, seated themselves on the bench closest to the front, on the right side of the room, and readied themselves for the services. While Eliza's head remained bowed in prayer, Maryel's gaze wandered.

Cousin Robert pored over the notes for his sermon. As far as I could tell, he had barely noticed our arrival. He certainly didn't acknowledge it. His left hand passed through his graying hair, settling briefly on a pesky bald spot, then fell back to the sheaf of papers in his right hand. With one forefinger, he traced a few lines. Voices rose outside the doors to the meeting hall, and footsteps shuffled up the stairs. He laid his notes on the desk that served as lectern, leaving them beside his hat. He adjusted his collar and gown and nodded for me to open the doors to the parishioners.

The heat was rising in the upstairs hall. Maryel surreptitiously brushed away drops of sweat from her forehead. I sympathized. My gown stuck to my back most uncomfortably, though I left off my stays in this hot weather, and permitted the girls to as well. There was no point dying of heat stroke for the sake of fashion. If only we needn't wear gloves and bonnets. But convention dictated a woman's head and hands be covered in church, and we could not flout it. I tapped her hand in warning, emphasizing it with a frown when she rolled her eyes.

When services were about to begin, Tom Strange slipped onto our bench. I tucked my skirts closer to make room for him. He was slim enough to not quite touch me, though the bench was crowded with a fourth person on it. I hadn't seen him in some weeks, and was happy he had finally shown up. Both girls peered round me with smiles for him. It wasn't so long since they were children together, out at Cousin Robert's farm, Lake Lodge. Though he had been apprenticed to the printer for the past three years, I still felt a proprietary interest in his welfare. Rescuing orphans will do that to you.

Cousin Robert's voice intoning the familiar passages of the service soothed his listeners as surely as a glass of warm milk. His gentle voice flowed over the sleepy Sunday morning like the balm of Gilead. Tiny snores and snorts erupted from the back benches. Church service provided a rare chance for many to relax. Colonial life comprised hardships and long days. Only Sunday broke the otherwise ceaseless toil. I glanced at my reddened wrists, showing above my gloves. Though vanity held no place in my life, I felt a little hard done by at times. I tried to focus on the service. Luckily, Cousin Robert didn't believe in lengthy sermons, especially on hot summer days. Before too long, we stood to sing Old Hundred, then followed him out of the hall and down to the lower reception rooms, where windows also stood open and it was cooler.

Cousin Robert greeted the emerging congregation, while Eliza, Tom and I waited patiently and Maryel fidgeted. At length, he joined us.

"Well, young Tom, are you joining us for dinner?" he asked. "We haven't seen much of you since you went to apprentice with Printer Jones." He turned to me. "You've invited this young fellow?"

I nodded.

"Good. He can provide my daughters with some youthful conversation. Since I requested the Major and his wife to join us, we will be seven to dine. I hope you asked Hannah to prepare a good spread."

I laughed. "I can't remember a Sunday when you didn't invite someone back to share our meal. Hannah is always prepared. It's too long since we entertained the Major. Do you anticipate talk of war?"

"It would be an odd day in this town if there were none. Ever since Governor Simcoe turned Fort Niagara over to the Americans, there have been Nervous Neds spreading rumors of imminent invasion. Someone is always ready to touch a spark to dry tinder. I would learn the Major's thoughts so we can be prepared for whatever comes."

✳

While I busied myself with household affairs, Cousin Robert spent most of his days at the church, inspecting the workmen's progress. There was still much to be done before the opening service, which he hoped to conduct before the end of August. Pews must be built and installed, and floorboards laid. He had already begun to make notes for his sermon. And his regular report for the Society back in England must be written. It would be a fraught time until the big day arrived.

I formed the habit of taking him a cup of tea when he retired to his office after breakfast. It gave him a brief respite before he went off to confront the workmen. One morning it took me a little longer than usual to do this and I discovered him slumped over a pile of papers and a half-written list. He looked up at me with bloodshot eyes.

"My goodness, Cousin, are you ill?"

He shook his head. "It's just… there are too many things demanding my attention. I'm weary."

I pressed the tea on him. "Come, drink this. It will restore you."

He sipped at it and nodded his thanks. "I would not burden you…"

"Is it the church? Or something else?"

"It is everything. The workmen need constant supervision. I must make arrangements for tenants to clear the required land on my parcels in the new counties." He patted a small pile of deeds. "The Society is pressing me to report on progress with the translation of the gospels into Mohawk, so I must find time to meet with John Norton, but I cannot leave town while the church is unfinished." His chin sunk onto his chest. "And I'm plagued by the chancy nature of my funds." In an undertone I'm sure I was not meant to hear, he continued, "if only the Society was as religious about paying its missionaries as it is in requiring our regular reports."

Money was a constant worry, but since I could do little to help, I merely nodded in sympathy.

He roused himself, straightening in his chair. "I thank you for listening to my litany of complaint." He stood, brushing down the wrinkles in his coat. "I must be off. Do not expect me before nightfall."

My days were filled to the brim, too. I needed to harvest each herb at the proper time, and that required tending them both at the town house and at Lake Lodge, Cousin Robert's farm a little over three miles from the town, near the mouth of the Four-Mile Creek. Vegetables and fruit required preservation, too, but I assigned most of the work to Eliza and Maryel. They were happy to remain close to home after their recent ordeal, and made no complaint.

I was so accustomed to work in the herb garden it left me plenty of time for thought. About families, about the past... but I shied away from my deep past. Cousin Robert, now, there was a safe subject. Or perhaps not. I cast my mind back to my arrival, a pathetic outcast on their Hampstead doorstep. My cousin Mary was well then, with a new daughter in arms and one clinging to her skirts. And Cousin Robert, her husband, welcomed me into their family with open arms. Nearly twenty years since.

I confess to a little hero-worship of him at the time. He was a pleasant appearing man, of middle height and build, with dark brown hair tied back in a queue, and clear hazel eyes. And more importantly, a kindly look about him. Kindness, I would come to know, was his defining feature. All too uncommon among men. Men like my father, who considered women chattels and bemoaned the fact that he only had daughters. But I avoided that line of thought.

Mary, though quite well at the time, was already a little faded. I still saw her early brightness in her daughters, and hoped her melancholic debility had not been passed to them. As her health declined, I had become a surrogate mother to both. Had they been my children, I could not have loved them more. And now Mary was dead, an ocean away.

Which meant Robert was free. I had not yet decided how I felt about it. Certainly, he had made no advances toward me since. Did I want him to? Would I willingly alter my state?

Willcocks

It was a fine July morning, sunny and warm, promising scorching temperatures later. Joseph Willcocks stretched and yawned on the steps of the red-brick house. He was grateful to his cousin William for permitting his tenancy there. William spent most of his time in York these days, so the house would have otherwise stood vacant. It was nicely private, slightly west of the town, but with everything still in easy reach. The adjoining lots held no structures, but one was planted with a young orchard. Peaches, he thought. Nearby, at the river mouth, there was a handsome stone-built lighthouse.

His trip over Lake Ontario from York was uneventful, clear sailing under a brisk wind. Clouds massing on the western shore at the lakehead dissipated before the sloop arrived at Niagara. His first impression on arrival was that Niagara was a pretty town, but menacingly overlooked by Fort Niagara, on the American shore. No wonder they moved the provincial capital across the lake to York.

He glanced behind him, through the open door to the hall. The newest volume of his journal lay on a small table. He retrieved it, glad it was sufficiently small to pocket, along with a pencil, so he could take notes and make sketches during his survey of the town. Which he must begin, if he were to do so before the heat of midday. Hat tipped to shade his eyes, he set off.

Niagara's streets were laid out on a grid, but houses were widely spaced, apart from the merchant's row on Queen Street and public buildings on Queen & King Streets. It was so quiet after York's bustle. Townsfolk nodded in greeting and he returned the courtesy. Best to begin on good terms with the neighbors. He walked at leisure, stopping frequently to jot notes.

6 Jul

Streets packed dirt. mostly level. Many frontages lined with boardwalk. Makes for easier walking after rain. Boardwalks and stone paths from street to many houses. Town must be prospering. if inhabitants have resources to spend on non-essential comforts. Most houses set in midst of gardens & orchards. Still some rough cabins. new sturdier houses built alongside old. Building materials local stone (v handsome). red brick. wood frame. Frame houses painted in white lead or earth tones. with colored shutters. One brave soul painted house sky-blue. shutters white. Unexpected frivolity—worth seeking acquaintance. Might be fellow free-thinker. Cuckoo among sparrows.

Town cannot contain over 500 souls. V numerous public buildings—must accommodate outlying farm district & garrison. Survey outlying areas another day.

Presbyterian church wooden with high steeple. white as angels' wings. Property contains an academy. Notice on door advertising spaces for boys to learn Latin & Greek. What good ancient languages will do even enterprising Scots in this raw colony escapes me. The mind boggles.

Church of England at opposite end of town. on hill overlooking river & Fort Niagara. Large burying ground. Structure incomplete—sturdy stone walls. roof on. no glass in windows. Carpenters busy with furnishings in yard outside. Must seek out rector to learn where services are held. Don't want to get on wrong side of established church. Besides. Presbyterians give me the colic. Rev. Addison seemed of like mind on several issues when we met during Parliament. Will hope he remains friendly.

Returned to Queen Street via King. Passed Masonic Hall: convivial noises issuing.

Frontages along Queen much smaller than on residential streets. Perhaps two dozen shops including printer & mercantile. Printer fully occupied: will return tomorrow. Six taverns, some mere alehouses, two larger post rooms to let. Must supply court house & jail regular stream of customers. No livery stable. Where to get a horse?

7 Jul

Belongings finally delivered. Pace of events here v sluggish since Capital removed to York. Ten years since—surely plenty of time for adjustment. Checked over to make sure nothing lost in transit.

Item – crate (1) containing shaving stand, chair, footstool, boot-jack, horse tack. Intact.

Item – trunks (2) clothing. All remained dry. Second-best hat slightly crushed.

Item – barrel (1) chinaware, glassware, cutlery. Intact save for two plates, chipped & one wine glass, shattered.

Nota – packing material reserved for use as tinder

Nota – hire or purchase sturdy horse

Willcocks surveyed his belongings with satisfaction, checking off the last item on his list. He sorely needed a change of linen. His gaze lit on a deed box, its corner peeking out from under a folded shirt. His brow furrowed as he remembered the last time he'd used it, back in April…

He'd known it might come to this since he had so openly denounced the Executive's policies, but to lose yet another position was hard to bear.

Lieutenant-Governor Gore sat behind his oak desk, thumbs tucked in his waistcoat pockets, smirking broadly at Willcocks. "You'll vacate your office at once. My clerk will accompany you, to see you don't take anything that isn't yours. If you don't want to bother to collect your things, I'll have them removed for you, and thrown in the street. Why," he pursed his lips, "you're damned lucky I don't brand you traitor."

Willcocks leaned across the desk toward Gore, fists clenched, itching to rearrange the position of the hooked nose on Gore's smug face. His dark eyes pierced his accuser. "You miserable excuse for a man. You may replace me as Sheriff, but I still have plenty of friends in the Home District. Your new man will do well to look to himself."

Gore recoiled, staring with alarm. "Guards!"

"Don't bother. I won't lower myself to touch you. I'll take myself off." Willcocks snatched his hat from the corner of the desk. "You'll regret this, I promise you."

He turned on his heel and stormed from the chamber, pushing his way past the weedy guards who had come at Gore's call. They, seeing his murderous scowl, thought better of trying to restrain him.

Gore's clerk, another wispy fellow, hurried behind him. Willcocks heard his footsteps and threw a thunderous glance over his shoulder.

The clerk cringed.

"Miserable worm that you are," Willcocks said, "I've no quarrel with you. I've no wish to see my belongings in the street. You can pack them for me."

Barely a quarter hour later, Willcocks emerged from his office, carrying a basket of papers, a deed-box tucked under one arm. His greatcoat hung askew on his shoulders and his gray muffler was thrown unevenly around his neck. He flushed a painful red at the stares of his former colleagues, his uncertain temper newly inflamed by their supposed scorn. All the way down the hall to the grand main staircase, he muttered a stream of oaths, vilifying Gore's anatomy in all its parts. "And damn all colonial officials."

And where was he to turn now? Where to begin? He shook his head and pushed out through the massive doors of the Parliament House.

An hour later, he met his friend and sympathizer, Judge Robert Thorpe, in Marlowe's Tavern, at the corner of Yonge and Newgate Streets, north and usually upwind of the tanyard. Thorpe had snagged a corner table with two high-backed armchairs, a little quieter than the long tables in the open area.

"Well, Jos, what news?" said Thorpe. He leaned back in his chair expectantly, pipe in hand. He took a puff and blew a ring toward Willcocks.

In return, Willcocks raised his mug of beer and blew off some of the foam in his friend's general direction. "Plenty, and all of it bad, boyo. The worshipful ass Gore claims me guilty of 'general and notorious bad conduct.'"

"What was it you called him again?"

"Tyrant…"

"Ah… Well, that's bound to get under a man's skin."

"… and head of a Scotch clique…"

"No wonder he gave you the air."

"So, there goes my position as Sheriff of the district." Willcocks gave a great sigh.

"Cashiered, by jingo!"

"True it is, and from his own dirty mouth I had it. The truth being my opinions differ from his. Especially on land laws, and his arbitrary use of power. Him and his cronies. Bah!" Willcocks leaned forward in his seat. "A decent man can hardly get a land grant with those graspers skimming off the cream for themselves."

"What will you do, then?" asked Thorpe.

"I haven't decided. The stench from Parliament House has

spoiled the atmosphere in York. Worse than the tanyard. Time for me to have a change of scene and a change of employment."

"I may be looking for a change myself."

"But you've just won a seat in the Legislature, and your judgeship is sound, is it not?"

"None who share our views are secure with Gore in charge. He'll never yield to any form of responsible government."

"Now, there's a true word. I'm anxious to put him and his clique at a distance."

"But you'll stay in the province?"

"Sure, I'll not be chased out of it by that great turd of a Scot. I'm thinking Niagara is a likely place." Willcocks stroked his chin. "Perhaps I'll run for the Legislature myself. Get into the midst of the law-makers. See if I can effect a change. Too many scions of privilege rake off the cream of the land and offices. Elected representatives should have more say. If you're out of the picture, small farmers and Loyalists and Irishmen like me will need a new champion."

"You're swimming upstream with those ideas, as I know too well, but I wish you success. I'm looking out for other opportunities, in case."

"In case…?"

"In case of war, Jos. Most are still loyal to the Crown, but some would sell us out to the Americans."

"Braggarts and hotheads. I don't take them seriously."

"I do. And maybe you should, too. I've heard the Americans think they can march in here whenever they choose, with little resistance. In fact, they seem to believe we'd welcome them with open arms. It'll be every man for himself, mark my words."

Willcocks's eyes re-focused on the deed box. He shoved it to one side and pulled out the shirt. He'd taken the first step and gotten elected to the Legislature. What he needed now was a clean sweep of his past, and a fresh shirt would make a good start.

Rebecca

I spent part of one Monday morning in the upper rooms of the Masonic Hall, clearing away dead flowers from Sunday's service and tidying the few hymnals and prayer books into a cupboard reserved for the church. Cousin Robert arrived as I completed these tasks. His face was reddened, but I put it down to climbing the stairs, which often winded him. He helped me move the benches and chairs to the sides of the room, leaving it ready for its next user.

"I hope to have only a few more weeks of services here," he said. "The carpenters have almost completed installing the pews, and the glazier has promised to come when they are done."

"How many promises does that make?" I asked.

"Far too many, but I think he was worried he might have the job to do over if he installed them while other workmen were still banging about."

"How much longer will it take?"

"With good weather, good fortune, the blessing of God and prompt workmen, we should be holding services in the new church by mid-August."

We descended the stairs and left the building. After the gloom inside, the sun dazzled my eyes. I could not see what made Cousin Robert gasp and halt in his tracks, but I stopped, too.

"Ah, Reverend Addison," came a baritone voice with an Irish lilt. "It's pleased I am to see you this fine day."

My vision regained; I saw a well-set-up man with a neatly trimmed beard approaching us. There was something familiar about him. He looked a little like my father, that was it, but with black hair rather than brown. He stopped in front of us and bowed.

"You will recall me from York, I believe. Joseph Willcocks, new Member for West York, 1st Lincoln, and Haldimand."

I glanced sideways, appalled at Cousin Robert's face, now a most peculiar shade of greenish white.

Willcocks stepped forward, reaching out his hand. "Sir, are you unwell?"

Cousin Robert recoiled as if from a snake and his face became suffused with blood, turning deep purple. I feared he might suffer an apoplexy, but he managed to speak.

"I am perfectly healthy, I assure you, Mr. Willcocks. Yes, I remember you. I'll thank you to leave me and my family alone. Sufficient damage has already resulted from our acquaintance. Good morning!" With which, he took my arm, turned his back on Willcocks, and walked me away down King Street.

I glanced back over my shoulder. Willcocks stood where we had left him, staring after us with a frown on his face. I turned to Cousin Robert. "Why did you cut him?" I asked. "It's not like you."

He compressed his lips tightly and said nothing, but quickened our pace. It was only when we reached the house that he muttered, "I'm sorry, but I cannot afford to be associated with such a man."

It seemed an insufficient response. "What has he done?"

"Made trouble, as always." He turned away and walked off toward the river. I stared after him, wondering at his odd behavior. I had never seen him so upset.

That evening before supper, he gathered us around the dining table. "I have received this from the Governor's office," he said, referring to a letter he held open before him. "Governor Gore has again allowed the York merchants and the Executive Council to bias him against me. My trouble over the Salt Spring has been hard to bear. And that was merely a dispute over the lease issued me by Governor Simcoe."

He paused and held up the paper.

"Now he believes I am in league with Thorpe and Willcocks, chief critics of his administration. A pair of cork-brained Irishmen—as if I would so demean myself and my position by associating with them. He is also convinced I sided with the Six Nations against William Claus, head of the Indian Department—when I only attended the meeting as liaison to the Mohawks. He judges me a dangerous radical, the more so because I can reach so many through the pulpit and my missionary work. When I have always been loyal to a fault, and made sure not to interfere in the business of the Legislature. He even calls my role as Chaplain into question.

"A radical, Father? And you the most tolerant and easy-going of men!" said Eliza.

He grimaced and sucked in a breath. "Worst of all, that man Willcocks… You may remember Mr. Thompson asking me to join with him in backing Willcocks as Sheriff of the Home District? I had heard Gore dismissed Willcocks from his post. I didn't realize until now that Gore believes I share Willcocks's political views and am a devoted supporter of the radical element in the Legislature. Nothing could be further from the truth." He shook his head in disbelief.

"But father," said Eliza, "hasn't Mr. Willcocks been elected to the Legislature?"

"Yes, and looks likely to be a thorn in Gore's side. Gore already thinks there is too much leeway given to the citizens of the colony, and fears a repetition of the American rebellion if the reformers' views are given credence." He shook his head again. "If only he were a moderate man, but he is so puffed up with privilege he believes any demand for reform is an attack on the Crown. As personified by himself, of course."

"You have often spoken of the need for more schools, Father," said Eliza. "And your arguments for universal education seemed sound to me. Why would he consider those sentiments radical?"

"Men such as Gore believe education breeds revolution, daughter. My proposal for schools would take place within the bounds of the system, and not through public discord." He sighed mightily. "And now Willcocks has relocated to Niagara and is bent on ingratiating himself with me. No doubt Gore will think that supports his views of our collaboration. I must distance myself from these scurrilous rumors—these unfounded suspicions. Or we all face ruin." He pulled out a crumpled handkerchief that showed signs of previous use, and mopped his forehead, leaving his hair on end.

"Surely you overstate the danger, Cousin," I said.

He shook his head glumly. "If Gore is determined to be rid of me, he will find a way."

It was difficult for me to feel as concerned as he did. Cousin Robert was one of the few establishment clergymen in the Canadas, and would be almost impossible to replace. Gore might continue to harass him, though. The girls looked horrified, so I was relieved when his mood lightened.

"Let us not be too downcast," he said. "We may hope Willcocks's antics will entertain the Governor sufficiently."

If our laughter was a bit strained, at least it dispelled the earlier gloom.

"I do beg your pardon, my dears," he said. "I am concerned for your future, should I be discredited and lose my position."

I tried to divert the subject. "Can we all not find ways to

contribute a little to our income?" I asked. "So, you will not feel so burdened by our care?"

"I'm sure I don't know how you may," he said. "Let it suffice for now that you assist me in the parish, as you already do." He smiled a little. "I am fortunate in my family, at least."

✳

Anxiety lingered over us for several weeks. Even the working bee carried out for the Church by Colonel Sheaffe's men failed to erase it. It was some satisfaction, though, to see the walls completed with limestone blocks brought down from the Queenston quarry, and the stacks of slates ready to finish the roof. Cousin Robert could report to the Society for the Propagation of the Gospel in Foreign Parts that

> … although the building advances slowly, the floors are laid, and the windows are ready for glazing. I do not wonder that it goes on no faster, as almost all the settlers about Niagara are Presbyterians, and subscriptions among them are few..

He stopped there and rubbed his eyes. "These spectacles are too weak for lengthy use."

"Can you obtain others?" I asked. "Is there not a lens grinder in York?"

"I fear I would need to send to Montreal at least, perhaps all the way to London. I will ask the Society for a Quarto Bible. Its large print would be easier to read from during services. We need more Prayer Books, too, and I hope they will consider that a reasonable request and directly related to my mission." He proceeded to read out the rest of his report, ending

"My mission is having mixed results as well, although I feel I am making progress in diverting many of the Six Nations Indians from their ruinous habit of drinking spirituous liquors, which they tolerate poorly."

I could use some of those liquors myself. I hated to see him fall into despond over matters beyond his control. My spirits did not fully revive until he returned from meetings with his supporters. Prosperous merchants from both Niagara and Montreal, and officers from the garrison at Fort George, all promised to intervene with Gore if need be. He had good friends in the different Regiments that stood garrison duty at Fort George over the years. Perhaps all would yet be well.

August

Tom

On a dreary Friday in August, Tom Strange was returning from delivering a parcel of leaflets to one of the local merchants. His thoughts weren't on work, but on Maryel. Lord, how he loved the fire in those blue eyes when she was vexed. The way she would absent-mindedly chew on the end of one honey-colored braid when thinking. The curve and sway of her body as she moved through her day. How she had a habit of smacking his face when she found his manners uppity, dating from the day Rebecca took him in. It was already a hot day, and these thoughts weren't making him any cooler. Nor were they making him any likelier to gain her attention.

He entered the print shop and found his master deep in conversation with a stranger, a stocky man with craggy features and black hair and beard.

"I'm glad you're back, Tom," said Mr. Jones. "Meet our newest customer, Mr. Joseph Willcocks."

Willcocks shook hands with Tom, giving him a piercing look. Tom turned to Jones.

"Mr. Willcocks is starting up a news sheet. First one here since the Tiffany brothers stopped printing the Constellation… or was it the Herald? Damned if I can recall. Never mind. Young Tom, I'm going to give you this job for your first assignment as journeyman."

Tom stammered his thanks.

Jones chuckled. "Aye, you're surprised at my announcing it like this. Well, no better time." He turned to Willcocks. "As I was telling you, I was just about to advance my apprentice here to journeyman status. He's fully up to his job and there would be no better person to work with you on the set-up of your sheet. You may put complete faith in him, as I do."

By this time, Tom had turned a fiery red. He ran a finger around his collar, which felt tighter than usual. "W-what w-was it you w-were looking for, Mr. W-w-willcocks?" he asked.

Willcocks grinned as he handed over a sketch. "I have in mind a large sheet that can be folded in half, giving four printing surfaces. See, with the fold on the left so the whole thing can be held for easy reading. I've plenty of material to fill it up, but I'll want you to figure out the look of the thing. Something to attract attention."

Tom nodded. Willcocks looked more approachable when he smiled. "Looks like other journals I've seen. You'll w-want a header on the first page, at least, and then smaller fonts for the body? We have a good supply of Caslon, in many sizes, from Brilliant right up to Inch. I ain't sure—"

"Ah, boyo! I don't require chapter and verse of how you'll do it. I can already tell you know your business. Now, what if I leave you with some draft copy, and you prepare some samples in a selection of type, as you see fit, at my expense, of course. We can review your work when I return and select the most advantageous. Shall we say… Wednesday week?"

"Yes, sir."

The two men shook hands on it, benevolently watched by Mr. Jones.

"Not many newspapers in the province as yet," said Jones. "The *Upper Canada Gazette* is the only other one right now. It used to be published here, too, until they moved it to York with the provincial capital. Back in '96 that was, as I recall. You should have a good market for your work. I'm flattered, Mr. Willcocks, that you chose my shop to do the printing."

"Wait until you see what reception it gets before you assume any favor, sir," said Willcocks. He tipped his beaver hat to them and left the shop.

"What did he mean by that?" asked Tom.

"No idea, my boy, no idea. Perhaps he's one of them radicals, pro-Yankee like poor old Silvester Tiffany. But from his conversation, Willcocks seems a fine, fair-minded gentleman. Gave me a good offer for the printing job, and that's the truth."

Jack

Jack stroked his chin with the end of his quill, pondering what to write in a letter home. He held no illusions that his father would have the slightest interest in his daily routines. What cared he for spit and polish, for marching and training and managing men? The only thing his father desired to manage was the arrangement of notes on the staff and the ordered procession of melody and harmony. His abiding memory of his father was one of a man puffed up by his achievements as Vicar Choral to St. Patrick's Cathedral in Dublin and his subsequent knighthood. After Jack's mother's death, his father had buried himself in his work and spent more time working on settings for Mr. Thomas Moore's lyrics, "The Last Rose of Summer" and others, and more time with Mr. Moore than with his family. He wasn't a cruel man, but indifferent to his children's needs.

They clashed over Jack's future. Sir John was dead set against his eldest son going into the Army, preferring him to take up a musical career. Only after much pleading did he agree to purchase Jack a cornetcy in a foot regiment.

"You won't like it, you know," his father said. "I know you think it an exciting occupation, but don't be surprised if it turns out otherwise."

Damn the old man for being right. There was certainly more drill than thrill about army life. Maybe he had also been right about other things, but Jack wasn't quite ready to admit that.

He missed his sisters and brother. They would be missing him, too. Olivia was the oldest, and his father had written that she asked for an account of his doings. He could easily dash off a few lines on his health and standing in the Regiment to Sir John. Then he could write with more genuine feeling to Olivia. He'd include stories for the babies, Anna and Joe. They'd like that.

He tipped back his chair, balancing one foot on the rough pine table, and stared at a spot high on the wall, watching an industrious spider spin its web. Thinking about the family constricted his throat and threatened tears, which would never do. He came back to the floor with a thump, refreshed his quill at the inkwell, and bent to his task.

After a quick missive to his father about their new posting and the scenery, he turned to the lighter task of answering his sister's request for stories about his Canadian adventures. These, he thought ruefully, were few. When he wasn't drilling his men, he was either on a hunting party or spending evenings with his fellow officers in the mess. He would have to fall back on stories of the local inhabitants, and the seasons, so much more extreme here than back home. Army life was tedious, unless you saw action. No matter how he dreaded battle, he'd be relieved to have his first one over.

Rebecca

When I awakened, before cock-crow as usual, my legs were tangled in sheets and the day already hot. My shift clung to me like a second skin, one I could willingly shed. I felt my way to the washstand in the pre-dawn gloom and shivered a little as I pulled the damp cloth over my face. Though the water in the jug was nearly as warm as the room, it gave me some relief when I sluiced it over my head and let it trickle over my body. Would I were still a child and could strip down outside and stick my head under the pump.

My friend Drusilla was supposed to arrive home from York today. I longed to hear her news and talk over my own worries. But first, I must ensure the household would not fall apart if I were to enjoy an afternoon in her company. She needed to stay close to her family, I knew, for her aged parents missed her sorely. If not for her sister's early and difficult confinement, she would have returned from York some days ago. I would have to visit her.

Cousin Robert's servant, Hannah, usually so reliable, turned up that morning with a raging toothache, and I sent her back to bed. Eliza, Maryel and I would have to absorb her duties for the day. I contained my frustration with Maryel's inept efforts in the kitchen as long as I could then sent her out to look after the garden and the chickens. It was nearly time for luncheon when everything was set to rights: floors scrubbed, steps sanded, livestock fed, a stew set to simmer on an open fire beside the summer kitchen. Too hot for a fire to be lit in the house.

Finally, Eliza handed me my bonnet and pushed me toward the door. "I can look after the rest Cousin. You must have your afternoon out."

I was thankful to escape for a few hours. The endless round of household tasks gave me too much time to mull over my worries. Thoughts going round in circles made my head ache. I needed to pour them out to a friend who might help me make some sense of everything.

The Bell house was on the landward side of town, away from both river and lake, and the heat increased with each step I took toward it. Barely two blocks in, at the corner of Gate and Queen Streets, I became embroiled in a three-way collision. A young boy barely escaped a cuff on the ear by a bearded man.

"Watch where you're going," he growled as the boy ran off.

Joseph Willcocks again. After what Cousin Robert had told me, he was the last person I wished to see. I drew my skirts back and attempted to move on, but he stood in my path. I moved to go around him and again he blocked my passage.

"Why won't you let me pass?"

"I want to know why Addison gave me the cut direct."

"I don't owe you any explanations. Ask him yourself." My head prickled with heat and perspiration trickled down my neck. I managed to dart around him and ran across the street, barely missing a careening wagon. I didn't look back. Blast the man. Why did he have to come here? I seethed as I approached William Street.

How dare he accost me so? He not only resembled—but acted

like—my father, with his high-handed ways. I breathed as deeply as I could while walking at speed. I needed to settle myself quickly if my afternoon with Drusilla weren't to be spoiled. I rounded the corner onto William Street, heading south. The Bell house was not far from the Presbyterian Church, whose white spire rose high above and beyond the occupied town lots.

Ah! Drusilla stood at her gate, waving. "Rebecca!"

I waved back and quickened my pace. "Drusilla, I'm so happy you're home."

"Come sit in the shade. There's cider. And a few ice chips, too. The last from the winter store."

Ice was a rare treat this late in the season. We had used up our blocks cut from the lake long since. "You're a godsend, my dear."

We relaxed under the oak in their front yard and exchanged our news. Her sister had delivered twins, an unusual and potentially dangerous situation. I was relieved to hear both mother and babes were thriving. In my turn, I laid out my fears for the girls, the household's solvency, and the outcome of the Salt Spring affair. "And now there's this horrid man Willcocks to worry about."

"Must you take on responsibility for every little thing in Reverend Addison's family?"

"Perhaps not everything." I wiped my brow and then my eyes. "But frankly, who else is there? Cousin Robert is preoccupied with his mission, the Church and his other official duties, Eliza is good at household affairs but ineffectual on important matters, and Maryel is too flighty. Without a firm hand, the whole house of cards might collapse."

"What of our plans to help women in need? Have you nothing to spare for them?"

My chest felt hollow, my heart thudded almost loud enough for her to hear. "I had hoped we could avoid discussion of that for a bit longer."

"I've had enough time to think and hoped you had too."

"It's too dangerous, Dru."

"But it's necessary. You know that. There are too many women afflicted with more children than they can support, and too many ruined by men of ill will. You have the knowledge and the means to help them." She stared at me, her expression grim. "After what my sister just went through…"

"You know I've helped prevent that situation for others. But no remedy works every time."

"That's why we need to do more."

I hung my head. "You mean ending a pregnancy already begun? Discovery of even the little I have done to prevent too-frequent pregnancies could prove disastrous. How can you bring this up now, when you know I'm struggling with so much else?" We met so seldom as it was. Why did she have to waste our time together rehearsing old arguments?

She put her hand on my shoulder. "I apologize. I should have waited," she said.

"I can't think about it now. Please, let us not quarrel, but delay our discussion until after the new church opening."

Tom

Tom hung his smock on a peg in his airless room above the print shop. He took down his summer coat, a rusty brown broadcloth, and brushed it down. It wasn't every day he had an invitation to dine, and with a customer at that. He clattered down the steps and burst out the door into a welcome evening breeze.

Willcocks's house was only a few blocks down Queen Street, but it was a world away from the print shop. A stone path led up from the gate to the wide steps and generous entrance of the two-story brick residence. Four-paned, double-hung windows graced either side of the door overhung with a porch roof promising cool shade on blistering days. Tom knocked firmly at the door and Willcocks himself opened it.

"Welcome, boyo, welcome!" Willcocks offered his hand to Tom, who grasped it.

"Thank you, sir."

"None of that, now. We're both men of business. You can call me Jos, Tom."

"Jos, then. Thank you. I've plenty to tell you about the

news sheet…"

Willcocks held up a hand. "I'm sure you do, but pleasure before business. We can wait until we've had our meal to talk about it. We should become better acquainted."

They sat down at the dining table, set for two, graced with a half-full decanter and sturdy tumblers.

"Tell me something of yourself."

"There's not a lot to tell, Jos." Tom scratched his eyebrow. "I was born hereabouts, and left in a basket on the doorstep of the Presbyterian church. The minister farmed me out to parishioners as a charity case. He browbeat them into offering me a home. I didn't get much care from any of them and was passed around from place to place. Miss Plummer rescued me from the last one, a harridan who thought the young did well under frequent beating."

"You look pretty well-grown for an orphan."

Tom laughed shortly. "No thanks to the Presbyterians. Miss Plummer," his voice softened, "fed me up and Reverend Addison hired me to work on his farm. He taught me my letters, too, and got me the apprenticeship to the printer. I owe them both my life and livelihood."

Willcocks clucked his tongue in sympathy. "So, you're not a Yankee."

"My parents might have been. I'll never know, I guess."

"There are many Yankees in this place. Former Yankees, I should say."

"Plenty of folks didn't care about politics, once the war for independence was over. More important to put food on the table. Harder than talk, too."

Willcocks nodded, "Sure, you've the right of it. Well, you've my sympathy—it's a hard life for an orphan." He poured a stiff measure of whiskey into one glass and pushed it toward Tom, then served himself.

Tom tossed back half his drink, choking a bit on the burning liquid. "Thanks. I don't dwell on those days."

Willcocks nodded in understanding.

The two men fell silent for a time. Then Willcocks replenished their drinks.

"Sounds like I owe you a tale. And mine isn't pretty either. See, I'm a bit of an exile, both from Ireland and from public office in York. Some suspected me of supporting the United Irishmen in my native land, though I never did, and here, the Tories in executive positions are sure Whigs are as bad. I'm tarred a radical wherever I go, never mind the truth of it. I've been booted from an office I held faithfully, because the Lieutenant-Governor doesn't like my brand of politics." He scowled. "He has too much power to dictate who is worthy of making an honest living."

Willcocks recounted his experiences in York, at length, embellishing his story freely with colorful oaths. "So, you see, we're up against it all around. But I'm no traitor even so. I'm all for working within the system, which is why I've gotten myself elected member of the Legislature. Sure, there are many in this region who chafe at the patronage system. Maybe we don't want American-style republicanism, but we do want our rights."

Tom nodded. It sounded reasonable to him. Although… he'd wager Willcocks and his friends would be happy to be on the receiving end of some patronage, and to have more power in colonial affairs. But he held his peace and tucked into his dinner. They ate in silence for a while.

Finally, Willcocks pushed the decanter toward Tom. "Do help yourself to more."

"Obliged," said Tom, and topped up both their glasses. They raised them in mutual toast. They'd reached the sipping stage of the evening, with the ruins of a round of hard cheese and a pork pie on the table between them.

"At least one of them, that old grasper Peter Russell, is due to pop his clogs any day now. My cousin sent word of his decline just last week. Can't happen too soon to suit me. I've not forgotten his slurs." Willcocks took a long pull at his drink.

Tom made a non-committal noise in his throat, to encourage Willcocks's discourse.

"Won't do me any good now, though. He poisoned his sister against me. Said I'm nothing but a fortune hunter. She'll never change her feelings. Says all men were born to be hanged and I'm at the head of the list. Women!"

"Aye, women," said Tom. "And don't you laugh at me, Jos, my youth is no barrier to discouragement at the hands of the ladies. I've twenty years under my thatch and a good trade to my name, but none of them will so much as look at me."

"Ah, I'm thinking there's one young lady in particular you'd be after," said Willcocks. "A daughter of the established Church, no less."

"And what if I am," said Tom. "Maybe my parentage is wanting, but I'm a decent man, ain't I? She could do worse."

"That she could, that she could. You'll need to keep a watch out for the competition then, what with all these young military sprigs around, them in their scarlet coats. Mark my words, there's many a lass gone for a waster in a uniform over the plain coat of an honest man."

Tom shrugged. "With or without the soldiery, she considers me a brother."

✳

The following morning, after a long night in which they drained that decanter and part of another, burned the candles down and fallen asleep in their chairs, Tom stood on Willcocks's front steps, watching the sunrise. He twisted his head from side to side, trying to ease the crick in his neck. The first rays of dawn back-lit the stone lighthouse on the Mississauga Point, across from the Willcocks house. His head was thick with Jos's stories, and he seemed to recall having promised to accompany him on a survey of the district. Printer Jones would surely not object, given the surety of more printing business. He rubbed the sleep out of his eyes, stretched, and headed off for work, rumpled clothes of yesterday notwithstanding.

Rebecca

The new church was a sight to behold on that morning. The women of the congregation, myself included, were called on to make it ready for this event. We had done so by decking the aisle and altar with choice blooms from our gardens. Flowers were a luxury, but townsfolk always kept a few rose bushes near their houses. Surely we had stripped all of them bare. The aroma saturated the air within and drifted out to greet the assembling congregation.

They gathered in a lot where most trees had been felled, leaving only saplings amidst the Loyalist graves in the churchyard. The crowd was a great deal larger than usual.

"Look, Cousin," said Maryel. "Why, the whole town must be here!"

I had to agree. "All the faiths must have turned out. Isn't that the Roman Catholic priest? And I'm sure the group over there are Methodists."

"Wonderfully strange to see," said Eliza. "They're not usually so cordial toward the Church of England."

"Maybe it's the novelty," said Maryel. "There's little happening.

But how gratifying for Father that so many should turn out for St. Mark's first service."

"Your father is known as a generous and sensitive man," I replied. "He knows the other clergy resent his official standing, and that they cannot legally marry or christen their followers, but he takes care not to ruffle their feathers or flaunt his power."

In fact, I thought, *he has more sense of humor in that regard than you understand.*

"He's respected by most and loved by his congregation. Yet he remains a modest man."

Of course, the townsfolk don't have to put up with his personal idio-syncrasies. I squashed that thought as we moved up the aisle.

"Look. There are the Hamiltons, and the Secords, from Queenston," said Eliza.

"And the Merritts, from the Twelve," said Maryel. "And some from further. They must have been up all night to get here so early."

I was pleased to see that Captain Norton, Cousin Robert's Mohawk translator, had graced us with his presence, along with some of his fellows currently resident at the Indian council house. In European dress, too, but for a few beads and feathers about their costume.

War was on everyone's mind, especially in summer when campaigning forces might live off the land they were invading. As always, people clustered around anyone who might have news. As far as I was aware, there was nothing imminent, but farmers from the outlying area tended to raise their concerns of a Sunday morning. It was often their only chance to speak with those outside their families.

I caught sight of Drusilla, seated with her parents in a pew opposite ours but a little way back. She smiled and nodded in my direction. Our recent conversation echoed in my mind. Determined not to let it ruin this day, I faced forward again and tried to concentrate on peaceful thoughts. Prayer was beyond my ability just then.

The heat rose as the church filled. I grew uncomfortably warm and brushed the perspiration from my brow surreptitiously. The press of people in the confined space smelled of seldom-washed humanity, old cheese, and best clothes laid too long in camphor. Along with the roses, it made me queasy. I began to wish none of the windows had been glazed.

Cousin Robert was fond of reminding us that his mission was mainly to the Six Nations of the Grand River, but he now took on his more familiar role to us, as rector of the parish. Always more comfortable reading aloud than speaking extemporaneously, he relied on closely written notes. He adjusted his spectacles and prepared to address the multitude. No doubt with some irony, he had chosen as text the Sermon on the Mount which he read out in its entirety. He then delivered a lengthier-than-usual discourse from his notes.

I'm ashamed to say I drowsed, and pinched my arm to remain alert.

Finally, he closed with another reading, this time from the Song of Ruth.

"All rise," he said.

We stood to sing Old Hundred then followed him out of the church and into a welcome breeze. But not the end of the tedium, as we joined him to greet the emerging congregation.

Eliza and I withstood this more patiently than Maryel did. She couldn't help fidgeting and watching the townsfolk milling around. When she stiffened against me, I turned to see a small cluster of red coats feigning an interest in the graveyard.

She tugged at my sleeve. "Look. There are the young officers who helped us. You know, when…"

"I see them. And they've seen you. They keep looking this way."

It was a good sign that she was showing an interest in young men, so short a time after her ordeal.

"If Father is inviting people for dinner, perhaps a few more?"

"We have a full table already. He has invited the Fort Major and his wife, and the Dicksons. Perhaps another time."

Her disappointment showed, so I laughed, and continued, "but I will introduce them to your father, should they come this way."

Jack

Jack joined a party of officers on their way to the church, his thoughts occupied by Maryel's blue eyes and creamy skin, and bent on furthering his acquaintance with her. Considering the manner of their first encounter, it would be proper to meet her again in her family's presence. He hoped she recalled him in an heroic light.

There was some excitement in the town, this being the first service to be held in St. Mark's Church, underway for nearly seven years. It was not entirely complete, but sufficiently so for services to commence.

The new church was a simple stone-built rectangle with no distinguished towers or cruciform design. Carved wooden doors in the western end of the outer stone wall opened onto a generous space with whitewashed plaster walls and plain, glazed windows. Box-pews had been installed but there was merely a table and rough lectern at the choir end. There were no screens of any kind, and no font for christening. A large china bowl sat on a small side table. English ware, Jack thought: it looked finer and more fragile than the local pottery he'd seen. No sign of anything musical. The building was light, airy and pleasant, and today, full of flowers. He gathered from the surrounding chatter that it had cost the small congregation nearly £1200 to construct it, an astronomical sum. Also, that most of the people crowded in were not part of the congregation, but members of other churches come to see the new building, and to congratulate the Reverend Mr. Addison on his successful project.

The building was packed. Jack stood near the door, separated from his brother officers, beside another young man, slightly taller than him and dressed in worn leathers. They bumped together in the press of people.

"Your pardon, sir," said Jack just as the man said "Beg pardon, Ensign." They laughed at their simultaneous excuses, and Jack offered him his hand. He shook it, and introduced himself.

"Tom Strange, journeyman printer."

"Jack Stevenson, 100th Foot. I haven't seen such a press of people since leaving the docks in Dublin. Even in Montreal there was more breathing room in the church."

"Then you've seen more than I, for I've lived my whole life here."

The general hubbub in the church settled, and they agreed to continue their conversation after services. Jack craned his neck to see if he could spot Maryel in the company, and after a few minutes he picked her out, sitting in the front-most pew, turning to speak with her sister. She wore a fetching bonnet in a blue that matched her dress. The splash of blue drew his eyes repeatedly as the service progressed. The Reverend Robert Addison's voice, pitched low but carrying through the room, formed a background for his thoughts which were definitely not on the Prayer Book.

Tom, standing next to him, fidgeted and mumbled unintelligibly when the congregation made their responses.

The service was completed within the hour, and Reverend Addison stood by the door, proudly greeting his parishioners and guests as they exited the building. This was a lengthy business, taking near as long as the service had, for everyone must stop and congratulate him, and exchange a few pleasantries. He beamed at everyone. Miss Plummer and his daughters attended him. Many chatted with them, too, before moving on.

Tom and Jack stood at the edge of the burial ground with some of the other officers until there was a gap in the crowd and they could approach the Addisons.

Maryel told her father that Ensign Stevenson had done her a service so the Reverend spoke to him with some warmth, as did Miss Plummer.

The two men moved off as the tide of people swelled behind them, neither speaking more than a few words to Maryel. Jack felt a stab of disappointment. It might not be so easy to get to know her.

He and Tom walked on through the burial ground, stopping to talk in a patch of shade.

"So, you're already acquainted with the Addison family?" asked Tom.

"Slightly," said Jack. "I… met the daughters a few weeks ago, out by the fort. Delightful young ladies, aren't they?"

"Yes," said Tom. "I've known them for many years. I was their hired boy when I was younger. In fact—"

Tom's story was interrupted by Ensign Dawson and Lieutenant Hingston.

Hingston called out to Jack. "Found a new friend?"

"Mr. Tom Strange—my friends and fellow officers—Ensign Irwin Dawson and Lieutenant Samuel Hingston."

"We've duty to attend to, Jack," said Sam. "Extra drill for malingerers."

"Even on a Sunday?" asked Tom.

"A soldier's life is bound by daily routine," said Jack. "We sometimes go weeks without leave."

"I'm glad to be a printer, then," said Tom. "At least some of my time is my own."

"We get off-duty time too. More now we're settled into our new post. What say we meet at McBride's Tavern one of these days? Quaff a pint or two, maybe roll the dice?"

"A good plan, friend."

Jack clapped him on the shoulder, and waved as he joined his fellows on the path back to Fort George.

Willcocks

Some days after the opening of St. Mark's, at which he'd been amused to spy the Catholic priest right next to the Presbyterian dominie, both strategically poised near the door for a quick exit, Willcocks collected Tom from the printer's shop and bore him off to survey the surroundings of the town.

"I've walked the streets from top to bottom," he said, "and dug out everyone who can help with my business. Now I want to see more of the environs."

"I've brought the map you wanted," said Tom, proffering a roll of paper tied up with string.

"Excellent," said Willcocks. "Let's start at the river's mouth."

They walked past the lighthouse to a point precisely opposite Fort Niagara where the waters of the Niagara River passed into Lake Ontario. The Upper Canadian shore was gently curved, while the American bank came to a sharp point where the fort was situated.

"What's the stone building directly across?" asked Willcocks.

"That's the old French fort," said Tom. "I think it's been there a hundred years or more."

"Looks formidable. And those guns. They can be trained directly on the town as well as at Fort George."

"Looks an odd place to found a town, doesn't it? But the British still held Fort Niagara then."

They walked southwards along the riverbank, past the town, and across the open common that separated it from Fort George. It was a grassy sward about a mile across. Tom pointed out the meager fortifications and the buildings within. Fort George itself comprised a few ramshackle blockhouses for enlisted men, a slightly sturdier building for officers, and a stone-built powder magazine, surrounded by a low perimeter of earthworks studded with a few bastions. As a defensive position, it inspired no confidence.

"I'd have expected better," said Willcocks, "given the American temperament and the superior fortress opposite. What was the Army thinking to let it get in such disrepair?"

"Not only that," said Tom. "See those heights upriver?" He pointed to the high ground from which the fort might easily be attacked.

"Damn me if I couldn't overrun this shambles with three cripples and a dog! Why, the… How many is it?"

"About two hundred soldiers, I think."

Willcocks pulled at his lower lip. "They'd have to give a good account of themselves to withstand any greater force." He fell silent, continuing to gaze at the shabby fortification in front of them, imagining such a scene. What might be his role in such an affair? He continued to look around him, with a hypothetical invasion in mind, trying to visualize how it might happen. "What are these other buildings?" he asked.

"Down there, right on the river, that's Navy Hall," said Tom, "built of local timbers during the Revolutionary War. Winter quarters for officers and seamen on Lake Ontario. There's a wharf and storehouses beyond. And back, on the lower banks, toward the town,

Loyalist barracks, and the Six Nations Council House."

"All within reach of a cannonade from Fort Niagara."

"Now you see why everyone in town is so anxious about the possibility of war."

They walked a little further along the west bank of the river. Once out of sight of the fort, Willcocks found a fallen log to sit on and unrolled his map, weighting it down at the corners with stones. With his left forefinger, he traced the major roads in the area. Along the west bank of the Niagara River there was a coach road running between Lake Ontario and Lake Erie, up past the Great Falls.

"If you want to follow the road, horseback would be best," said Tom. "Depending how far you want to go. It's a little over thirty miles to Lake Erie, at the other mouth of the river."

"A stiff day's march, then, or a couple of hours on horseback. There's an odd thing. A river with two mouths."

"You'll find plenty of settlement, too. Loyalist grants mostly. Not many settlers on the American side. Mainly bought up by speculators, I hear. Not much of a road along there either—more of a track. But there are settlements at intervals. Small ones."

They continued to examine the map. Tom pointed out more features, including the various creeks, named for how many miles from the Niagara River they entered Lake Ontario. He called particular attention to the great limestone escarpment and the large swamp that covered most of the area between it and the lake.

"You've given me plenty to think on," said Willcocks. "I must thank you for your help. Perhaps we may make another excursion like it, only further afield."

"It'd be my pleasure," said Tom.

Willcocks hardly knew why he was determined to know the terrain so intimately and was glad Tom did not quiz him on it.

Rebecca

I woke with a start. It was pitch dark and someone was pounding hard at the door. I shrugged on a wrap and hurried downstairs.

It was Ensign Stevenson. "Please, miss, you've got to come. It's Lieutenant Hingston's wife. She had a nasty fall and went into labor. He sent me rather than leave her."

I dressed and took up my midwifery kit, always packed and ready on the stillroom table. We hurried along Prideaux Street, then down Byron Street, which led across the common to the main gate of Fort George. Insects chirped while birds and small creatures rustled in the trees as dawn approached. It would be another stifling day. I remained silent, not wishing to waste my breath on unnecessary talk, while the young officer had evidently said all he cared to.

Ensign Stevenson ushered me past the guards, across the parade ground and into a long, low building. Officers' quarters were usually roomy enough to house their families. While some maintained lodgings in the nearby town, for others it was an unaffordable expense. The Hingstons were evidently among the latter. The ensign opened their door, then withdrew.

Lieutenant Hingston rose from his wife's side to greet me. "Thank goodness you came."

"It's fortunate we are in town." I moved to the bed where Mrs. Hingston lay, attended by a woman of middle years who I assumed to be a soldier's wife. "How long since she fell?"

"About an hour," he said. "Maybe more. She rose to use the commode and fell on returning to bed. She said she struck her stomach on something as she fell. Probably the table."

I turned to the woman who lay inert with her eyes closed. Too quiet. "Mrs. Hingston? Can you hear me?" I turned to Hingston. "What's her name?"

"Winifred."

"Winifred?" I repeated loudly, without receiving a reply.

The attending woman spoke. "She's been in and out of her head this past half-hour. I knows a bit, but this is beyond the likes of Jane Hawkins, miss."

Winifred's eyes opened, and she convulsed with another contraction. She groaned and rolled onto her side. I reached for her hands and clasped them firmly. "Someone, bring me warm water and clean cloths. And see if there's a birthing chair in the fort. If not, we'll use the commode chair. Winifred, can you hear me? How many months?"

"Seven," she groaned.

Much too soon. I swallowed hard. "Has it been lively?"

"Yes." The heaving renewed, and she groaned again, then cried out.

Hingston returned with a jug of water and a stack of flannels. He poured some of the water into the basin on the washstand and brought it to the bedside along with the cloths. "There's no birthing chair here."

"Close the door, then. Mrs. Hawkins can help me undress and wash her. You can make ready the commode. She'll manage better if we can get her up onto it."

As we bathed Winifred's body, I reviewed the list of remedies at my disposal. Angelica, bloodroot, blue cohosh, rue. So many of those useful in labor were also the ones Drusilla would have me recommend as preventatives to women who shouldn't have more children. For mostly the same reasons: they stimulated contractions and eased passage of the womb's contents out of the body.

Another, fiercer contraction. Each one left her weaker. There was no question, then. I would administer a mixture to hasten the proceedings, sparing the mother while risking the child. A seven-months child was unlikely to survive at the best of times, while this woman had other children who needed her. This was the hardest part of midwifery—making decisions for the family—but I had long since learned not to ask them to decide in cases such as this.

I roused Winifred sufficiently for her to drink the mixture, and its unpleasant taste kept her from sinking back into a stupor between contractions. We maneuvered her onto the commode chair, positioning her so the baby could drop easily into Jane's waiting hands. I checked its position. Thank all the powers that be, it was head down.

It took two more hours before the child was delivered. I sent Hingston out for hot water toward the end. Most men would have bolted much sooner, but he remained to give what comfort he could. I think it did help her somewhat, although it was hard to tell.

Poor mite. Her first cries were almost inaudible, and she had a worrying grayish-yellow cast to her skin. I washed the baby and tied the cord, wrapped, and placed her on her mother's breast. Jane massaged Winifred's stomach to get out the afterbirth, and it was finished.

I drew Hingston out to the corridor for a word. "You must ask Reverend Addison to baptize this child at once. The first day will tell, but you should be prepared."

His shoulders sagged. "She so wanted a daughter." Tears trickled down into his beard. He turned away from me and went back to his family.

I found Ensign Stevenson outside the officers' quarters, a young Hingston boy on either side. He offered to escort me home but I declined. His eyes spoke a question, and I shook my head. "Stay here, for your friend."

As I walked back to the town house, weary from assisting at Winifred's lengthy labor and distressed at the infant's weakness, everything that had built up for so long crashed in upon me. I might never take a complete breath again, or so I felt. The past weighed on me like a relentless tide, an undertow bent on drowning me in painful memories and an empty future. It was no good to imagine how life might have been, had I never met Martin, or if he had been able to save me from ignominy and ostracism. I had lost everything, and felt the more lost for assisting at the circle of a family not my own. If only a woman could be truly independent, and not have to rely on a man to define her worth. A woman alone was prey to all. There were too few occupations where she could achieve her own identity and manage her own affairs. I had sufficient skills, but not the means.

I arrived as Hannah was clearing the breakfast board. She cut me some bread and cheese, and made a fresh pot of tea. After a few bites, I laid my head on the table and wept.

Cousin Robert's entries in the register of St. Mark's told the sad tale:

> Baptism Aug 29. Jane Hingston. of Samuel and Winifred.
>
> Funeral Aug 31. Jane Hingston (infant. 100th Regt.).

September

Rebecca

Cousin Robert holed up in his study for several days, appearing only at mealtime and speaking little. When I confronted him about it, he admitted it was money again. That is, the family's lack thereof. I would have liked to relieve him of some of this burden, and proffered a few suggestions. My midwifery and herbal skills were generally sought but seldom paid for. Should I charge a small sum for my services?

"Your charity does you credit, Cousin," said Addison. "I cannot wish it otherwise, despite the earnings it might accrue. The health of the populace benefits us all."

"They often give me gifts of food."

"Let that suffice then."

Such other skills as we could muster were unmarketable because of the settlers' habit of general competence: wherever feasible, they made do with what they could make or grow and only traded surpluses for items otherwise unavailable. They might trade for an ax-head, but make the handle.

"If only the Society would pay my salary at York. It costs near twenty percent to transfer through from Quebec." He rubbed the bridge of his nose, marked from wearing spectacles too long. "Even so, we get some cash, though it never seems sufficient for our needs."

No, I thought, and as long as you have a passion for books, it never will be. "You received land grants, and have rents coming in, even if in kind. At least we're unlikely to starve."

I resolved to pursue my efforts to augment the family's income. There might be some less common remedy I could produce and sell. But there, my thoughts stopped short against the wall of my disagreement with Drusilla. For she was seized with the notion of selling a "woman's tonic" that might prevent a woman falling pregnant, based on my herbal recipes. And it was all my fault for telling her of the possibilities in the first place.

I shuddered to think of the consequences of such activity becoming known. Not only among the men—there were plenty of women who would be horrified at the thought. Never mind that I had quietly provided just such a remedy to some of the more downtrodden women in my care. To openly sell such a thing, no matter how innocently labeled, would be to court disaster.

While mild fall weather still held, Cousin Robert was off on his circuit, first heading west to the 40-Mile Creek & Head of the Lake, and later going upriver to Queenston and Chippawa. Eliza accompanied her father on the latter trip, visiting friends in both locations. I was happy to release her from household chores for a few days. We rarely had a chance to break the daily round, and she never complained, no matter how tedious the work.

After waving them off, Maryel approached me for a heart-to-heart. "I wanted to wait until we were alone to talk about my future," she said. "I'm sure Father wouldn't be sympathetic, and I doubt Eliza would either."

I smiled down at her earnest face. "You can count on a receptive audience in me. I may not agree with everything you have to say, but I'm ready to hear you say it."

"I rely on you for an honest opinion."

"Let's have it then. What's bothering you?"

Maryel took a deep breath then let it out without speaking. She tried again. "You know how I feel about marriage."

I couldn't suppress a snort. "You've told us all often enough. You don't want to marry."

"No, I don't. And nobody has asked me to, which is just as well for him… I mean…"

My eyebrows headed toward the ceiling. "Nobody in particular?"

She flushed. "That's beside the point. I want to be independent. We're always scraping for money and I want to contribute. Father's position seems so precarious. I've been trying to think what I could do. I had hoped to help with the Salt Spring operation, but…"

"You're right. We're cash poor. But then almost everybody is. Your father isn't too different from all but the richest merchants, or those with incomes from Britain."

"But there are other possible payments, or things that can be given in trade."

"Hiring oneself out for payment isn't an option for a well-bred young woman. I shouldn't need to remind you of the risks you would be taking. Besides, your father would never countenance it. He has the right in law to compel you to obey him."

Maryel giggled at this.

"I know, he's far too kind a man to resort to compulsion by force, but compulsion by love? Would you disobey if it truly pained him?"

"Why must his pain be my responsibility? Is a grown man not in charge of his emotions?"

I wished. "Grown men often have a child-like streak in them. We women are often the custodians of both our emotions and theirs."

Maryel rolled her eyes, earning a tap on the wrist. "I still want to find some way to contribute, beyond household chores."

"Have you anything to propose? Anything practical, that is."

"I had already ruled out domestic service before you spoke of it. My skills…"

"… are sadly lacking."

"I know. I have ten thumbs when it comes to making and mending clothes. So, dressmaking and millinery are out of the question."

"I would leave cookery alone as well."

Maryel bridled a little. "I haven't burned anything in years!"

"True, but your porridge is always too salt and your soup too peppery. You don't pay attention, and that's a fact."

"I can prepare herbs almost as well as you… Most of the time. But you're right, my indoor skills aren't up to much. I do better outside, gardening or churning or chopping wood. But everyone does their own." Her shoulders sagged and tears brimmed in her reddened eyes.

I leaned over and gave her a quick hug. My reward was a watery smile.

"I would rather work at something that would make use of my education. Something to do with books and letters, and figuring. I have several ideas, but nothing works out to the point I could advance it.

"My dear, you have some knowledge in that area, it's true, but nowhere near enough to convince a man to employ you. Even if you found someone willing, he would look for you to need almost no training. Men can rarely be persuaded to put in effort where they assume it will be futile."

"Then you think it's impossible?"

"Perhaps less so if you continue your studies a while longer. You need more practical knowledge and patience, Maryel. Give yourself more time. Do nothing in haste."

Her mouth drooped.

"You can always discuss your ideas with me, but until you have a realistic plan, it would be better not to bring it up again with your father. He was so grieved by his loss of the Salt Spring lease, and is likely to react sharply if you recall it to him. Even a fond father has his limits."

Tom

McBride's Tavern overflowed into its yard on market days, with townsfolk, farmers and soldiers from the garrison. Most of the shopkeepers ran longer hours, but the print shop closed at midday and Tom was free to join the carousers.

He headed for McBride's, a few doors down. He pushed his way through to the bar where he bought a pint of hard cider to wet his whistle. Taking it out of the crowded tavern, he found a likely spot and sat down on the ground, his back propped up by the oak tree that shaded him. He took a long draft of the cool drink and hummed with satisfaction. Using his broad-brimmed hat as a fan, he kept off the flies as best he could.

A party of officers approached the tavern. Tom spotted Jack among them and waved him over. "Get yourself a drink and join me. It's like a pot of stew in there."

Jack nodded and disappeared into the tavern, emerging in a few minutes with his own drink, or rather, drinks. He held a pint of ale in one hand and a glass of whiskey in the other. He sat down beside Tom, sharing the backrest of the oak tree.

"Good thing your kit's strapped on, or you'd never be able to manage both of those," said Tom, laughing.

"Rough morning on the battlements," said Jack. He tipped up the whiskey and downed half of it, following it hard with a large swallow of ale. "Ah, that's more like it." He wiped his mouth on his jacket cuff. "Bad enough if we were repairing a properly built wall, but these earthworks aren't worth what we're putting into them."

"Listen, Jack. I'm no rebel, but there are plenty around here. You'd best keep a lid on that subject."

"Fine. Fine, but I'm telling you, a more useless lot of men…"

Tom interrupted him. "You said you wanted to hear my story."

"That's right. You were going to tell me when we met at church. So?"

Tom told of being a foundling, and his early life. "It wasn't much of a life until Miss Rebecca—Miss Plummer—rescued me from the Reverend Addison's neighbor. I was always hungry, and beaten for stealing food that went missing. Rebecca found the real thief and then took me to live with them. Reverend Addison needed a hired boy out at his farm at the Four-Mile Creek, or so he said. They gave me a home and something to hope for. And now I'm an independent journeyman, making my own way."

Jack pursed his lips. "Quite a story… In a way, I envy you."

"You can't be serious."

"But I am. My father has too many notions about who I should be and what I should do. He's a church musician and wanted me to follow him. I love music, but not as a profession. And he's ambitious for his children—he was knighted for his talents and wants us all to marry into the gentry or even the nobility. Raise our social standing. Not my kind of thing at all. Maybe if there was money—but there isn't."

Tom murmured sympathetically as Jack shook his head.

"He finally agreed to buy me a commission in the Army. Probably thinks I'll gain some connections and discipline and come home willing to do his bidding."

"Nobody ever expected anything of me—but me."

"You don't know how appealing that sounds."

"No fun, I assure you—having nothing and nobody. I can't imagine the pressure you describe, either. I thought having family should be a support, not a burden."

"Maybe we were both changelings—born into the wrong places."

They were laughing over this notion when a party of other officers joined them, well-equipped with a sweating pewter pitcher of ale. Tom nodded to Ensign Dawson, one of the party, and Jack introduced him to the rest. The ale was passed around freely. One jug followed another over the course of the afternoon, and they became increasingly merry.

Jack had just given a shout of laughter over a lewd joke told by one of his fellows, when Maryel walked by. He nudged Tom, who was drooping over his drink. Maryel's back was ramrod stiff; her posture radiated disapproval. She kept her gaze fixed forward and clutched her basket. The men watched, admiring her trim figure, as she disappeared around the corner.

"What is it about women?" said Jack.

"What is what?" said Tom.

"They take such offence at a fellow having a good time."

Tom shook his head. "Dunno. Maybe they're jealous-sh."

"No… that's not right. More like they despise us."

"Not all the time. S-seems to me they like us, more often than not."

"Unless we're in our cups, I guess." Jack giggled. "How about another cup?"

Tom shook his head again, then held onto it with both hands. "Better not, thash not good." He leaned back on the tree, eyes shut, and took a deep breath, still holding his head.

"Say, Tom" said Jack, "you know we were talking about names? Maryel is an odd name. Sounds almost French, but the family is English."

"No myshtery there. She got shaddled… s-saddled with a bunch of names at her christening, and the whole boiling s-settled out to Maryel," said Tom. He hiccoughed.

"Oh. Hmph." Jack lay back on the grass under the oak tree and stared at the sky.

Tom opened his eyes. The sky swam above him as if it were an ocean. It was blue, like Maryel's dress. And her eyes. He closed his again and began to snore.

Rebecca

Eliza and I were busy with the mending when Maryel stomped into the parlor, a flurry of fallen leaves in her wake.

"MEN!" she said. Then she slumped onto the settle, shoulders drooping, mouth twisting, and sniffed.

"Let me guess," said Eliza. "Public drunkenness on market day? Why so surprised?" She paled. "You weren't… insulted… again, were you?"

"I'm not surprised," said Maryel. "I'm disgusted. Maybe it's all right for farmers and laborers, but educated men?"

"Ah," I said. "I begin to see clearly. People of your acquaintance, Maryel?"

"Tom. And Ensign Stevenson. And a whole group of other officers, who should know better! How can they make such a spectacle of themselves?"

"It's a common vice, my dear," I said. "I agree, not a pretty sight, but, what would you? There are few entertainments at this time of year, with so much to be done before winter sets in. Men work hard and they want some relief. Liquor gives them that, if only for a while."

"Do they all do it, Rebecca?" asked Eliza. She was still pale, I supposed, from the memory of drunken hands on her body.

"Most, I'm afraid, at some time. Some with more moderation than others. Your Father, for instance, is fond of a glass of wine. As am I, you know. I've seen you both drink a glass with pleasure, too."

"This was nothing like a glass of wine with a meal," said Maryel. "They were… quaffing ale. By the pitcher! In public, too. All sprawled on the ground or weaving when they tried to walk. It was horrible." She scowled. And shuddered. Both girls still carried some disturbing memories. I mustn't forget.

"You think it the more horrible because it was Tom and the Ensign, don't you," said Eliza.

Maryel blushed. "What if I do? Why should I pursue the acquaintance of wastrels and drunkards?" Her eyes sparked. "Gentlemen should behave better. Father is always speaking against it from the pulpit, too."

A few home truths were in order. "I recall your saying Tom could have no pretensions to being a gentleman. You may well end up having few men who wish to pursue your acquaintance if that is the set of your mind. Remember that occasional indulgence doesn't make a man a drunkard. Any more than going to church makes one good, or education makes one wise. Or having money makes a man a gentleman, for that matter. Take care not to become priggish, Maryel. Nobody likes a kill-joy."

She dropped her eyes, pouting.

"Come now, my girl. Let's have no sulks. You're not too old for a switching if you act like a child."

After a moment, in which I could almost see the thoughts swirling round her head, she sighed. "Why do you always have to be so… so right? It's all very reasonable to preach tolerance to men's foibles, but how could they…"

I laughed a little, not unkindly, I hoped. "How could they what? How could they have fun without you?" I shook my head. "Long time since you understood this is a world made for men. Even the best among them takes their pleasure as they please, not as it pleases women, no matter how closely related to them. And respectable women are excluded from much that is pleasurable."

The conversation with Drusilla that I dreaded was not long in coming. One rainy morning in late September, I was tying up herbs in my stillroom when she arrived for a visit, calling out as she entered by the kitchen door. I brushed debris from my apron and went to greet her.

"Leave your cloak on the hook by the door to dry," I said.

"It's still too warm for it, but I don't care to sit around in a wet dress, either."

I ushered her into the parlor and closed the door. Hannah was busy in the kitchen, and I had no desire to be overheard. "You wish to resume our discussion?"

"We have dithered over it endlessly. I need to be sure you will help. In case my sister falls pregnant again."

We had gone over the details so many times. Could I bear one more? I was content to provide herbs to married women that could prevent—or at least delay—conception, though the notion it was possible would horrify most men. I was much less sanguine when it came to inducing miscarriage in the unfortunate ones who fell pregnant unwillingly. Not only was it considered anathema by the Church, men had recently passed laws to punish those who sought or practiced it. From a personal standpoint, I resented the fact that men ruled over women's lives to such a degree, but I was all too aware of the risks of poisoning from the herbs necessary to achieve such a revolt within a woman's body.

"It's one thing to help a woman space out her children so she can regain her strength and provide each sufficient succor. Quite another to put her life at risk by attempting to disrupt a pregnancy already established."

"But what of unmarried women, preyed upon by men?" asked Drusilla. "What of your cousin's daughters, in such a case?"

That was harder to answer. "I don't know. I pray I may never face that decision." Bile rose in my throat and I swallowed against it. "I've had to consider it all too recently. Perhaps… But abortifacients are mostly poison—or ineffective at lesser doses. And I would never try a physical disruption. It could damage a woman so badly she might never conceive again. Even kill her." I hesitated. "And… you may think me a coward… I fear many women who might seek to miscarry may prove untrustworthy at a later time, when they regret doing so. They can excuse avoidance of conception to their consciences, but not deliberate abortion."

Drusilla nodded. "I understand your fears. And if I were the one to pass along the means, you would naturally be suspected as my close friend."

"I'm not ready to take that step. I don't know if I ever will be."

Tom

The tavern was full to bursting with both townsfolk and travelers. Tom had a hard time pushing through the market-day crowd to reach the table where Willcocks sat. The few tallow dips on the tables did little to light his way through the dim interior. Willcocks took his hat off the chair he'd saved for Tom who sank down with a sigh.

Their neighbors at the table greeted Tom boisterously, slapping him on the back as if they were close friends. He didn't recognize any of them, but privately labeled them as they spoke.

"Well, gentlemen, another round?" asked the publican. "You'll be down from York, will you?"

"That's right, landlord. More drinks all around," said one traveler, a smithy, by his scarred hands.

"Aye, from York, right enough," said another, a bag of carpenter's tools slung over his chair.

The publican bustled off to draw more beer from the barrel.

Willcocks said, "I'll stand this round, friends."

Carpenter clapped him on the shoulder. "I knew you were a right one, friend."

"It's all friends together. And damn all traitors," said the third traveler, with a loud belch.

This got a laugh around the table.

"Traitors? Surely there are none in these parts," said Willcocks.

"Ah," said Smith, "you'd not want to wager on that, friend. It's a long time since the late war, and not many of them Loyalist fellers left."

"Aye, aye," said Carpenter, his voice slurred.

"Even their families have moved on. At least, some of them," said Smith. "The old Governor, Simcoe, he encouraged more Americans to come in. 'Late' Loyalists, they call 'em."

"Aye, aye," said Carpenter, his head drooping.

"Nearly half the people round here are newcomers from the States. Come here to avoid the tax collector or militia service, I hear tell," said Belcher.

Carpenter's head drooped further and further toward the table until it rested on it.

"Can't hold his drink, that one," said Smith, and they all laughed.

"Just because they're newcomers doesn't make them traitors," said Willcocks.

"Nay, it doesn't," said Belcher, "but it doesn't make 'em loyal, either. And if they were shirkers at home, stands to reason they'll be shirkers here too."

"Hmm," said Willcocks. "Could be."

The publican returned with their drinks and Willcocks put down his coins in payment. Tom raised his glass in a toast to the company.

In the temporary silence around the table, as they drank, voices rose in another part of the tap-room, where nine or ten men were gathered. Their conversation had turned to the attack upon the Chesapeake, surely stale news after two years.

One man, obviously in his cups, read in slurred tones from a grubby broadsheet: "If Congress will only send us a flag and a proclamation declaring that whoever is found in arms against the United States shall forfeit his lands, we will fight ourselves free without any expense to them."

His comrades hushed him, and one of them drew him outside to cool his hot head.

"See what I mean?" said Belcher. "Lots like him around. Mouthing anti-British slogans. Damned Republicans!"

Tom's brow furrowed, but he remembered Willcocks's advice and remained silent. Willcocks nodded to him, and raised his mug in salute.

November–December

Jack

Life at Fort George was an endless sequence of drill upon drill, with an occasional working party to shore up the battlements. Jack found time to play both fiddle and flute, and thought himself none too badly off. He must send his father a note of appreciation for the latest batch of musical scores. He had rounded up the regimental bugler, fifer and drummer and chivied them into an ensemble of sorts. His fiddle taking the lead, they became a regular feature in the fort.

As winter set in, many entertainments sprang up in the town, with music in demand, so Jack and his ensemble were invited everywhere. This was greatly to his liking, but something of an impediment to his pursuit of Maryel. It was only in the lull between dance sets, or at an interval for supper, that he could converse with her.

"I'd like to dance with you, Miss Maryel," he said to her, as they met over the punch bowl.

"Can your fellows play a set without you?"

"They might. If not tonight, we could prepare one for another time."

"I'd like that."

"Would you take supper with me?"

"Why don't you join our family table? My sister and cousin are here, too."

"That'd be delightful."

Jack could hardly wait to consult the other musicians. He needn't have worried. The bugler and fifer were keen to take a greater role and felt prepared to do so at once.

The food was plentiful. Jack piled his plate high with pigeon pie, cold ham and pickled beans before joining Miss Plummer and the Misses Addison at supper. There was a wide range of game available here to supplement farmed livestock, both animals and birds. Vast flocks of pigeons flew low over the fort in spring and autumn, and could be brought down merely by throwing sticks into the multitude. Some were salted down for winter fare, and pigeon pie was one of his favorite dishes—an agreeable change from the soups and stews that made up so many army meals, and even a welcome change from roasts.

"I don't think I've ever eaten so well," he said, after swallowing a large bite of pie.

Miss Plummer's eyes twinkled. "I see it's true an army marches on its stomach."

That drew a laugh from her juniors.

"True," said Jack, "but our army cooks don't make pies as good as this. It's better fare than we got at home, too."

"Was your cook not a good one?" asked Maryel.

"My mother was a good cook," said Jack, "but after she died, the cook my father hired wasn't up to much. She boiled everything: beef, potatoes, puddings. She'd have made a better laundress."

Maryel giggled. "Poor you." She tilted her head to one side. "Did you speak to the other musicians?"

"I have the set after supper free," said Jack. "May I engage you to dance it with me?"

"You may."

Under the smiles of her sister and cousin, Jack led Maryel onto the dance floor, his heart pounding.

Rebecca

Cousin Robert had said Captain Norton was due soon, to go over his latest translations of the gospels into the Mohawk language. The adopted son of Thayendanegea Joseph Brant, being half-Scot and half-Indian, he was uniquely placed to straddle the difficult boundary between Indian and British societies. I opened the door at his knock and beckoned him to enter quickly, out of the biting wind.

"Good afternoon, Miss Plummer," he said, "the Reverend is expecting me."

Norton was a striking figure, taller than most, with dark hair and flashing dark eyes, almost always in Indian dress. His appearance in any room provoked a frisson of female admiration, and I was no exception to the effect. He spoke all the languages and was a respected warrior, hand-picked by Brant as his successor. If he felt any frustration with his role, he was stoic enough not to show it. I envied him that. When I felt discouraged, as I had for many days, I drooped, at least on the inside. I kept going, as I must, lest the household grind to a halt, but was worn out by day's end and often weary when I awoke.

I knew the two men would spend the greater part of the afternoon poring over correspondence and church business, and with a free hour ahead of me, removed to the stillroom. They did not lower their voices which rose and fell naturally, snippets reaching my ears at intervals.

"I have news of Catherine Brant, Thayendanegea's widow," said Norton. "She plans to remove from Burlington to Brant's Ford."

"I'm not surprised," said Cousin Robert. "She was always dedicated to Mohawk traditions and less interested in British ways."

"If all goes well, she will be a supportive voice for me in our councils. There are still some who question Thayendanegea's wisdom in making me war chief. And we cannot rely on Governor Gore. His favor waxes and wanes with his need for our support."

Cousin Robert harrumphed. "You're right, of course. He and his cronies resent the special treatment of your people by the Crown."

I wondered if that was partly why Gore held such a distaste for Cousin Robert. His close association with the Six Nations might be one more factor adding to Gore's general annoyance.

"I've brought you my latest efforts on the Gospel of St. Matthew…"

My preparation of horehound and rose hip lozenges was well under way. I boiled up a cup of each in some water, strained the liquid, and added honey to the mixed extracts. While it was simmering, I took up quill and paper to write to my sister.

12 November 1809

My dearest Sarah,

You are unlikely to receive this letter before spring, but my heart bids me write you now. I am sorry to unburden myself to you, but there is none other I can tell of my feelings. Don't despair of me, but grant me the mercy of your patience.

But what could I say? I could fill the page with trivial matters, describe the bloody mess of hog slaughter and meat preserving, speak of the girls' activities… but could I get to the meat of my issues? Could I finally admit to my envy of her prosperous London family, my resentment that our parents had treated her better than they had me, that my poor judgment had led to my life's history since? Would doing that finally cut my last family tie? And what impact might there be on Cousin Robert's brother Thomas, married to my sister, and their relationship? As usual, I could not disentangle my personal troubles from the welfare of others. Must everyone have rights to a piece of me? Was I never to belong wholly to myself?

I attempted a few more lines.

> My position here grows more tenuous as Cousin Mary's daughters mature. Once they have married, I have no assurance of a place. I have nobody, Sarah. I feel so alone. The girls are kind, and Cousin Robert generous, but I long for a home of my own.

I couldn't keep on like this. Paper might be at a premium, but I tore up the page and fed the pieces to my brazier. As I watched it burn, its acrid smoke irritating my nostrils, my attention shifted back to the men's conversation.

"… and my difficulties have increased since Chief Brant's death," said Norton. "Even though he adopted me as nephew, there are some among the tribes who question my worth."

"Your worth is not in question here, my friend," said Cousin Robert. "Your work translating the Gospel of Saint John into Mohawk was masterly. And your latest efforts bid fair to match the former."

"I'm honored to receive such praise from a noted scholar."

If the conversation were at the mutual admiration phase, they would want refreshments soon. Removing my unfinished lozenge mixture from the brazier, I retired to the kitchen to chivy Hannah into making tea and setting out slices of fruit cake.

Tom

Tom did not put the newspaper into circulation until November. Willcocks approved his four-column design and the Caslon fonts, and he prepared a further sample page in a forme and pressed a run of fifty copies for Willcocks to use in marketing his concept to potential subscribers, advertisers and distributors.

In the meantime, Willcocks was full of talk of his parliamentary concerns, as representative of the riding of West York, 1st Lincoln, and Haldimand. This riding was large, and populated by many recent immigrants, both from Britain and the States.

"My first essay will deal with Gore's new land policies," said Willcocks. "My constituents are sorely vexed by the increase in fees, and his rule changes, too. It's getting so men can't buy or sell property without him sticking his nose in. For no reason but to enrich himself and his cronies."

"Is this likely to affect your conveyancing business?"

"To be sure, it is. New land transfer fees, taxes on this and that… It never ends. Interfering with a man trying to make an honest living while speculators run wild. It's a damned shame."

"What's the temper of the Legislature? Are there sufficient members with your views?"

"Perhaps too few to set fire to Gore's new britches, but enough to make a noise. Sometimes that's almost as good."

"How so, Jos?"

"Once like-minded people hear there is outrage over the plight of the small farmer or businessman, they'll add their voices to ours. Members of the Agricultural and Commercial Society, for instance. I'm sure there are others. It's all about privilege and preferment, boyo. There's many a man with a grudge."

Yes, thought Tom, and you're one of them.

Willcocks continued, "Mark my words, we'll create such a ruckus, Gore's nuts will sport a heat-rash."

Tom was already busy typesetting the first edition of the new *Upper Canada Guardian; or, Freeman's Journal.* A pretentious title, he thought, but it was what Jos wanted. He had left space for the essay on the front page.

Willcocks had indeed brought in another printing press, one he bought second-hand in New York. Tom couldn't figure out how he had negotiated for it to be shipped, New York being almost as far distant as London, by sea, and the difficulties of moving it overland not to be thought of. The expense must have been something awful. But it had arrived and was set up to run. Tom thought Mr. Jones might decide to go into partnership with Willcocks, or sell his business outright. But then, Willcocks was no printer.

Willcocks was an ambitious man, and a well-connected one, too. Tom didn't doubt that. The first issue of the paper listed over two dozen distributors ranging throughout the Niagara District and the rest of Upper Canada, and in New York State, too, as far as New York City. Tom was doubtful about the American connections, but Willcocks reminded him how many residents of Upper Canada still had friends and relatives in the States.

"There's a deal of trading done, too," he said. "We'd not get such a variety of goods if we relied on everything coming from England. Besides, see how thinly our Province is populated. We could use more immigration, more farmers to improve the land. Every reason to encourage our neighbors to think of us as a suitable location to settle."

"Provided they can accept a change of allegiance to the British Crown," said Tom.

"To be sure. That must go without saying," said Willcocks. He frowned. "As all who come here do."

Tom hastened to change the subject. "You're a devoted advocate of Reform."

"Indeed, I am. Natural justice and freedom must prevail. Where they're suppressed, it's the duty of every citizen to remark upon them and seek to remedy the situation."

"Suppressed?"

"There are powerful men, friend Tom, who would usurp the Royal prerogative to themselves and their kin, and deny natural justice to their fellow men. Such rogues and scoundrels would keep all the best of lands and positions for their cronies, and withhold them from newcomers or those they think less worthy."

"I suppose you refer to some of your fellow legislators, then?" asked Tom.

"Yes, among others. There are many men of privilege who aren't elected but receive favors from the Administration, not by the will of the people."

"You mean land speculators?"

"And office-holders. And appointed representatives of the Crown, who take too much on themselves and don't listen to the elected body." Willcocks leaned forward and spoke more earnestly. "It's both the sacred right and sworn duty of a responsible man to voice his disagreement to laws and practices he finds unjust. The people must be made aware of inequities and their opinions must be heard. Only thus will a just society be formed."

"I can see you take this seriously, sir. You've given me many things to think on."

"I hope others will think on these ideas too. I've said so in my opening essay."

Which you've just quoted at length to me, thought Tom.

Rebecca

I was not happy to hear Tom spout Willcocks's words. We were sat down to Sunday dinner when he did so. His time and place were ill chosen indeed.

"Governor Gore should listen more to his legislators and confer fewer favors on un-elected men of privilege or views matching his own," he said, somewhat pompously. "And he should heed the concerns of the general population when it comes to handing out land grants and official positions."

"You'll do yourself no good by taking part in radicalism, young Tom," said Cousin Robert, whose opinion clearly matched mine. He harrumphed and drew his chin inwards, frowning. "Nor in parroting the words of Joseph Willcocks. There are many among the powerful ready to label such views as seditious, even treasonous. Why, some claim that I, the representative of the Church of England, sympathize with sedition."

"That ain't possible," said Tom. He flushed at Maryel's lifted eyebrow. "I mean, isn't."

"Governor Gore has not the flexibility of mind his predecessors did. He sees revolutionaries, chiefly American ones, behind every bush, threatening his authority. There are too many sycophants in York who bolster his views, to satisfy their lust for wealth and power. Truly, the European wars have so infiltrated the minds of the powerful, they can no longer see any path but that of tradition and privilege. I fear moderate men are espousing more conservative views." He shook his head. "Reason goes out the window when revolutions threaten the powerful."

"But isn't that exactly what Mr. Willcocks is saying?" asked Eliza. "It sounds reasonable to me."

Her father glared at her. "He goes too far," he said shortly. "I caution you, Tom, if you have such thoughts, keep them to yourself. Your association with him in the way of business suffices to color you the same in some men's eyes. Do not openly espouse his views if you desire to advance in any occupation in this Province." He cast his eyes around the table where we listened attentively. "We should all moderate the expression of our views in public. This Province is not a comfortable climate for radicals of any stripe, whether men or women."

Here he looked pointedly at me. I was not amused.

"I understand your point, Cousin," I said, "but I will not forego thinking new thoughts on the chance my neighbors might dislike them if they knew of them."

There was a moment of tension around the table, but all relaxed again when Cousin Robert smiled.

"I would not have you lessen your intellectual pursuits, Cousin. Only take care to moderate their expression in the marketplace. Keep the notions of Mrs. Godwin within our household, if you please."

"Do you disapprove of my sharing them with your daughters?"

"No, although there are many other volumes in my library that might be more improving. But... No. You may share any of your readings and thoughts freely. As long as my daughters…" He peered over his spectacles at Maryel and Eliza. "… take care to heed my caution. I would not have them censured for forward behavior or speech." He uttered a bark of laughter. "Despite their radical views on individual rights and democracy, our immigrants from the American states are notorious for their traditional position on the role of women. We mustn't shock their sensibilities, my dears." He removed his spectacles and polished them on the edge of his cravat. "This parish is full of prudish Dissenters, and we depend on their goodwill for our standing."

"Who is Mrs. Godwin that her views are so scandalous?" asked Tom.

"She was one Mary Wollstonecraft, who married a Mr. Godwin, who promoted her writings," I said. "She expressed progressive views on women's education and advocated a greater role for our sex in society at large. I brought a copy of her essays on the Rights of Women when we came from England and have read them to Eliza and Maryel—as part of their education."

"You never read anything like that when I lived here."

"Well… no, I didn't, Tom. But that was more because you were all much younger. Some may find Mrs. Godwin's ideas… confusing… or difficult. They're more the food of an educated mind than a treat to entice a young one to learning."

Tom grimaced. "It sounds like tough going to me."

I laughed at this. "Don't worry, Tom. Mr. Addison plans to read to us from the writings of Mr. Swift."

"Gulliver's Travels? Excellent!" said Tom. Maryel and Eliza also smiled. Their father so often read sermons, which they found tedious.

Cousin Robert took up the book, turned to the first chapter, and began to read. He read the tale of Gulliver among the Lilliputians, making it come so alive in my mind, I imagined I could see tiny figures scurrying around my toes. He was indeed a gifted reader. A charming way to spend a quiet evening. It soothed my worries, if only temporarily. At length, he closed the book and we said our goodnights, Tom making his way back to his billet with some of my maple sugar biscuits tucked inside his jacket.

As Advent drew to a close, Maryel and Eliza determined to make the house look festive for Christmas, which I thought a splendid opportunity for an outing, so I invited Drusilla to come along. We gathered branches of the native yew bushes that, with their dark needles and red berries, acted as a replacement for holly. Nearly three inches of snow had fallen the night before, and a few flakes drifted down as we worked. We shook each branch to remove most of the snow and then laid it in a cloth-lined basket. The girls looked for mistletoe, too, but found none.

"Oh well," said Eliza. "No doubt it's for the best. Father wouldn't like a lot of strangers kissing his daughters."

"Come on, these baskets are full, and I'm freezing. Let's race back!" said Maryel.

We skittered around in the snow-covered grass. Maryel put down her basket and bent to gather some snow.

Eliza, seeing what she was about, did the same.

"No. Ugh!" A snowball hit me full in the face, its melt trickling into my collar. "Brrr, that's cold!" I wasn't going to stand for being a mere target so followed suit, lobbing snowballs at both Eliza and Maryel. Drusilla joined the fray at my side.

Before long, we were all out of breath from dodging and laughing, and looked more like snow-women than respectable townsfolk.

"Whatever possessed you?" I asked Maryel.

Her eyes sparkled. "It seemed like a good idea. Why not have a little fun?"

"Fun, is it?" asked Eliza, coming up behind her, and pushing snow down her neck.

Maryel shrieked and laughed harder.

We talked a deal of nonsense on the way home. I'm sure we looked like a lot of unruly children, but what odds? It lightened our hearts.

As we arranged the greenery around the house, Maryel asked questions about her mother, which I was happy to answer. I worried that the girls seldom talked about her. It didn't feel right.

"Wasn't Mother born in Whittlesey too? I know you were," said Maryel.

"Yes, that's right, her father was curate of the two Whittlesey churches, St. Mary and St. Andrew. Did you know your father held those same offices after your grandfather died?"

"No, I didn't."

"I remember Whittlesey a little," said Eliza. "I remember taking a boat on the lake, and a flock of ducks taking off in front of it. They splashed us!" She grinned.

"That's Whittlesey Mere, a big lake southwest of the town. You would think it nothing now, of course, after these great inland seas we call Lake Ontario and Lake Erie, but to us, it was an enormous lake."

"Did you and Mother play as children?" asked Maryel.

"No, your mother was eight years older. Our families were close, though, and she used to visit. We would gather of an evening to sing."

"What did you sing?"

"In church we sang psalms, but at home we sang ballads like 'Barbara Ellen' or 'Captain Kidd,' and even some of the Methodist hymns. Your father sang a good bass line in the hymns."

"Perhaps we should sing some carols," said Drusilla.

"Could we?" asked Eliza. "I remember some of the tunes. Maybe not the words, though."

My voice was nothing special, but it didn't matter. I could at least carry the melody. We sang *"Adeste Fidelis,"* "While Shepherds Watched" and "Good Christian Men Rejoice." Drusilla managed a creditable harmony. Our voices drew Cousin Robert out of his office to add his bass to the mix. A delightful day.

1810

"Women are systematically degraded by receiving the trivial attentions which men think it manly to pay to the sex, when, in fact, men are insultingly supporting their own superiority."
—Mary Wollstonecraft

"If women be educated for dependence; that is, to act according to the will of another fallible being, and submit, right or wrong, to power, where are we to stop?"—Mary Wollstonecraft

January–March

Rebecca

We capped the round of celebrations through Advent and Christmas with a smaller gathering of family and close friends on Twelfth Night. Tom came, and Drusilla, too, with her parents. A few neighbors without nearby kin also attended, so the house on Front Street was nigh to bursting with company.

Hannah and I had (though I say it myself) outdone ourselves with the Twelfth-cake. Having no almonds, we made do with local hazelnuts, which served very well. We made sure to include a dried bean and pea in the cake, the finding of which would decide the King and Queen of our party. Hannah fairly staggered as she carried it out to the already groaning table laden with meat pies, sausages, a whole roast goose, a squash pudding, cornmeal and wheatmeal breads, preserves and all manner of crispy biscuits, some flavored with maple sugar and some with dried fruit.

Cousin Robert had his hands full concocting the wassail, made from apples grown at Lake Lodge and seasoned with cinnamon bark, nutmegs and a healthy dollop of Jamaica rum. Enough to warm our insides thoroughly without producing any inconvenient effects like drunkenness. There were no fresh lemons to be had, but he produced a dried lemon from some secret store, that gave a welcome tang to the punch.

When we had stuffed ourselves to the utmost, and needed time for our digestions to settle, Cousin Robert pulled out his latest report to the Society, drafted that afternoon. He made a habit of reading it out to us before he sealed it for delivery.

"… We have so far finished the Church at Niagara that Divine Service has been constantly performed there since last August. It's the best Church in the Province, & we hope to compleat it next spring if our funds do not fail. It's a beautiful place, set in a clearing between the town and the Fort, of pale gray stone quarried locally. The glazier has done his work well, if slowly, and the building was finally enclosed by the end of August last. Since then, there have been a good number of pews sold, which will help defray the costs of finishing the interior. The pews are handsome, & sold for more than £300 [freehold, conditional upon an annual rental payable to the Wardens]. I have hopes of obtaining a chamber organ to provide some music while we amass the huge amount required to install a pipe organ. The churchyard is already well populated with graves, having been in use since the original Loyalist days of the 1780s…"

He usually included some details that saved his report from unrelieved dullness, and his pride in the new church was clear in this edition. He had tried to educate his superiors about the extent of his parish, but they refused to comprehend that its area was over half the size of Middlesex County, and far greater than the City of London, with few roads over rough country. And they wouldn't even provide him an allowance for keeping a horse!

"Really, Father, you should include a map showing the scale of things," said Eliza. "Would they not be interested?"

"I doubt it," he said. "Remote colonies, no matter their size, are of little importance to their operation. They see only names on pages. They don't know, and don't want to know, how huge an area I serve."

It must be difficult to serve both as missionary to the Mohawks, his official role, and pastor to an ever-increasing congregation of immigrants to the region, most of them not members of the Church of England. Dissenters, and American ones, at that.

Our thoughts must have run along similar signs, for he chuckled a bit. "If only the population of this town was as peaceful as the sleeping congregation in the churchyard. You will not repeat this, but I appreciate their calm repose. They are less quarrelsome than those still above ground."

The company joined in his laughter. It was good to see him in a whimsical mood. Too often, he was weighed down by care, and too often ill.

"I could wish my Niagara parishioners to be as assiduous in their devotions as the Indians at Brant's Ford. Why, there are now more communicants there than I have in St. Mark's and the outlying chapels combined. But that owes much to my dear departed friend, Joseph Brant." His gaze fell for a moment, but then he brightened again. "At least we have accomplished something there, with the Prayer Book and part of the Gospels now translated into Mohawk."

"Is Captain Norton still working on the translations?" I asked.

"Yes, although there are always more demands on his time than he can fulfill. So, the work goes slowly. If only..." He paused. "If only I could be with them more often. Twice yearly visits are not enough, I know. But... with the roads so bad, and the trip by water so long."

"You mustn't chastise yourself, Father," said Eliza. "We know how voyages on the water affect your innards. You will do what you are able, and perhaps the Society will send someone to assist you one day."

The enormous meal having settled somewhat, our gathering

broke up into smaller groups for games or gossip. The youngest got up a game of marbles, and I shooed them into the woodshed so they could make all the noise they pleased. The elders chatted quietly or dozed by the fire, and the rest played at Consequences, laughing more than the children over the silly stories resulting from their random choices of names and actions.

Drusilla pulled me into a corner for a chat. "I've heard from my sister in York," she said. "She's increasing… again."

"So soon? And… after the last time? Surely not." This was terrible news. If she carried it to term, that would give her three babes under two years old, and she so poorly after the twins.

"Her husband is exceedingly devoted."

"Yes, to his own pleasure, I'll warrant." It would be worse, I supposed, if he used a doxy and brought home disease, but really— men could be so selfish, considering their urges over their wives' needs.

"I wondered whether you could… perhaps… whether I might…?"

"Dru, why must it always come to this subject between us? I cannot and will not discuss it again. Certainly not at a party."

Drusilla looked down at her hands, twisted together in her lap. "I'm sorry"

We sat in silence for a few minutes. Then I took her hand and squeezed it. "Come, let us talk of other things. Did you know Miss Kendall is being courted?"

"By whom?"

"Isaiah Morris."

"But wasn't he courting Miss Susannah Watson?"

"Yes, and she's out for Miss Kendall's blood, I hear."

And our conversation passed into common channels, relieving me no end.

✳

It seemed strange to me, but winter was my favorite season in this country. Back in England, it was too often dreary, with incessant rain and clinging mud. Here, everything sparkled—not only the snow—in sun or moonlight. We had so many more events to occupy us, with the harvest taken in and all the preparations for winter made. In the dead of winter, there was some relief from the constant work demanded during the brief summer months. The snows piled high and the lake froze out as far as one could see. The roads froze, too, and that meant easier travel by land for everyone in our region. People traveled many miles to visit family and sometimes stayed for weeks on end. I accompanied the girls to social events and enjoyed myself as chaperone.

Even though the Capital of the Province had moved to York, Niagara was still a center of commerce and transport. We counted some wealthy merchants and professional men among our residents, and there were always the officers at Fort George, many of them unmarried. I tended to consider myself past all that, but I supposed it wasn't beyond the scope of reason. However, I did not dwell on it.

Drusilla was often my companion, and we did not always talk of herbology. She shared many of my ideas on women's rights. I knew that well, but, despite our friendly relationship of several years and our discussion of women's health in general terms, we had never delved deep into personal matters. That was a benefit of a new land: one could leave painful subjects unremarked. But Drusilla was some years younger than me and we were well enough acquainted for me to probe a little one afternoon over the teacups.

"If you'll forgive me for asking, why have you not married?"

She tilted her head on one side. "Mainly because of my parents, I suppose. But even if that were not so, I've never seriously considered marriage."

"You've had prospects, though?"

"I encouraged no one. My sister married too young and look at her now. A year younger, but looks twice my age, worn out with child-bearing before she's thirty." Drusilla sighed. "I've envied the men for a long time. They can go where they please and do as they wish, not be tied to endless rounds of making and mending and child-rearing."

"Did you not wish for children?"

"No. Oh, I like them well enough, but the thought of enduring pregnancy and childbirth…" She shook her head vehemently. "Maybe it's why I feel so strongly about helping women who can't face the ordeal any longer." She shot me a piercing look. "And you? Surely you might have married?"

Of course, I had opened myself by probing her past. "I so nearly did." I paused, collecting my thoughts. "My intended was pressed into the Navy. We had been… indiscreet, and I was increasing. We should have had time to marry—the banns had been called—but he was seized and taken away."

It was harder than I had thought to speak of that time. I swallowed back the bile that had risen, and continued.

"I couldn't call on Martin's family, and my parents… I sought out a herb-wife who dosed me with pennyroyal. I lost the babe, and was ill for weeks. Now I know more about herbs and physick, I wonder I survived. My father said he wished I had died, that I was no daughter of his, and threw me out of his house. My mother did not attempt to stop him. If not for the kindness of my cousins Mary and Robert, I know not what would have become of me."

Drusilla reached out to hold my hand. "Did you lose all contact with your family?"

I rose and moved to the window, where I stood with eyes unfocused on the snow-covered fields and the gray river beyond. "My parents are both dead. I correspond with my sister. She married

Cousin Robert's brother Thomas. They have two boys." I bit my lip. "It's easier not to resent her happiness at this distance."

I turned back to Drusilla. "Let us not speak of this again. The past is past."

Jack

Jack arrived late to the assembly after a lengthy duty shift on the battlements. His fellow musicians had gone ahead and had things well in hand. He vowed to get to the next party earlier, even if he spent most of his time playing the fiddle. He had some trouble composing his face.

It was nearly the end of the evening before he got a chance to dance with Maryel. Jack took a deep breath as he crossed the floor toward her. He waited impatiently, chatting to fellow officers gathered near the punch bowl, tapping his foot to the music, and glowering as Maryel stood up with other lucky fellows.

Maryel gave him a questioning look as they took their position for the waltz. "Is anything wrong, Ensign?" she asked.

"Not now, Miss Maryel," he said, "and I wish you will call me Jack."

"Have I known you long enough?" She laughed. "I suppose I must call you Jack, then. And I suppose you may drop the 'Miss.'"

"I wouldn't want to be too forward, but I notice more of the younger set here use each other's Christian names. It's less formal than at home."

"Home being Dublin?"

"Is the accent so strong, then?"

"Not at all." She colored faintly. "I heard most of the 100th was raised in Ireland, and many of the officers from Dublin." She looked up at him. "Besides, it's a pleasant accent, more attractive to my ear than the Yankee drawl."

"Kind of you to say." He twirled her in place. Her feet followed his as if attached to them. It felt wonderful, like dancing on a cloud. He took a chance. "So, Maryel, now we're on a first name footing, may we go one step further?" His heart pounded heavily. Was he too forward?

"In which direction, Jack?"

It was to be a game, then. "Why, toward courtship, of course."

She smiled up at him. It was a mischievous smile, her eyes peeping blue through her lashes. Oh, but she was enticing. All he could do was to keep his composure and maintain his steps in the correct pattern. "I'm not sure. Could we not just be better friends?"

"If that's what you wish. But know I wish for more. A great deal more." Her color grew deeper and his groin tightened.

The music drew to a close, and their conversation with it. Jack led Maryel back to the company of her cousin, with due correctness, heart still pounding at how much he had dared and revealed. He bowed to them, then joined his fellows, in need of a drink to calm his nerves. As he downed his second glass of punch, Tom approached the bowl. He filled a glass, then turned to Jack.

"Waltzing with the lovely Maryel, I see," he said.

"Yes."

"A pleasure, isn't it?" Tom's smile was a bit lopsided.

Jack's teeth clenched, and he had to force out the words. "A great pleasure." He stared at Tom, trying to gauge his intentions.

Tom grinned. "She'll never look at me, you know."

Sam Hingston tapped Jack on the arm. "Time to be going, Jack. Early rota tomorrow."

After one last look at Tom, Jack turned away and left in a crowd of his fellows, joining in their inconsequential chatter as best he could. He hoped Tom was right about Maryel's preferences. He'd rather have him as a friend than a rival.

Rebecca

Dances, dinners, sleigh rides… The entertainments were many and enchanting, and I probably allowed the girls too loose a rein. Cousin Robert delivered an occasional homily on the dangers of dissipation and vanity, but he was pleased to see his daughters received so kindly by the community. Provided we were dutiful and assisted in the household and parish as needed, he encouraged our social endeavors.

Eliza was also sought after as a dancing partner. She was still of an age to be swept up in the round of social activity. By London standards, she was a little past her prime, but age mattered less in our frontier town, so she could well enter into the spirit of the season, and encouraged the attentions of a traveling merchant. Of more concern to me was her inclination to dance too often with Joseph Willcocks, but it would soon be the parliamentary season and he would move to York for the session. Better she not pursue that acquaintance.

Maryel's head was turned by all the attention she received from the local swains. Her progress around the dance floor with other men was followed closely by Ensign Stevenson, and she was all too well aware of it. I also noticed that Tom kept a watch on her, though she was oblivious to his regard. Though nearly twenty, she was in no hurry to express a preference, and bent on enjoying herself. Only Eliza and I could spot the truth. Eliza teased her mercilessly, but I refrained from comment until one afternoon I caught her mooning over the carrots she was supposed to be peeling for a stew.

"You need to pay attention to what you're doing, Maryel. I want vegetables for this dish, not bits of finger." I looked at her closely. "I hope you're not leading that young man on."

She jerked upright and the knife and cutting board flew off the table. "What?"

"Oh, my dear. You mustn't spend all your time in the clouds. What were you dreaming of this time? Or should I say, whom?"

"Am I such an open book, Cousin?"

"To me you are." I bent to pick up her dropped utensils. "And it's clear he's smitten with you, too."

She smiled shyly. "I do find him attractive. He charms me with his musical skill. And he wants to court me, but I'm still not sure about marriage."

"Plenty of time still to think about it, my dear. I'm glad to see you fully recovered from last summer's incident." I patted her hand. "But please, try to concentrate on your task. Your father will return from York this evening, and I would have a meal ready when he arrives."

She returned to the carrots, and no doubt her dreams.

It was not dreams I heard the two girls discussing later in the week. While bringing a pile of linens upstairs to sort for mending, I saw the door of their room was ajar. I made no secret of my approach, but they continued talking.

"I don't know what you see in him," said Maryel. "Why, he's quite old, and too political for my liking."

"Wait until you're my age," said Eliza. "You may find an entirely different set of attributes attractive. I find him distinguished, and his political ideas sensible."

"But Father despises him. And considers him dangerous, too."

"Father doesn't care for your swain, either. He thinks him vain and too Irish."

"Mr. Willcocks is Irish, too. At least Father doesn't think Lieutenant Stevenson a potential traitor."

"No? Then he's being hypocritical. Mr. Willcocks and Father hold opinions in common."

"Like what?"

"Education for all, for one thing. And they both despise Governor Gore."

"But isn't Father's problem that Gore's lumped him with the radicals?"

"The problem is that anything deviating from Gore's narrow outlook is automatically called 'radical.'"

Oh dear. Should I intervene, or would it make things worse? I continued into my room, resolving to think more on the matter before dropping a careful word or two in Eliza's ear. Their voices continued for some time, but I could no longer hear their words.

In February, we all traveled to York for the Parliamentary session, so Cousin Robert could fulfill his role as Chaplain to the Legislature. He did his utmost to stay in the background and avoid being identified with any issues, especially those promoted by Willcocks. Doing so went against the grain, for he dearly loved the notion of universal education.

With the girls caught up in the social whirl of the political season, I bore the brunt of his grumbling.

"It galls me that such a notorious radical should mouth the words I would prefer to myself."

"But… the Church supports education."

"Yes. For some. Education for the entire population is another matter. The Church wants to begin with higher levels and select training for professional men."

"Nothing for ordinary people and their children? Nothing for women?"

"Those ideas are considered too radical." He frowned. "I wish you will contain yourself on the subject of women's education. It will be difficult to attain a universal basic education for boys. To include girls at this stage might well undermine the enterprise entirely."

This was a hard pill to swallow, but I wasn't surprised. But to silence my voice? I found that the hardest thing.

"Is there any way for girls to become educated, then? Even in England they may attend dame schools, and more learn to read and write and figure, at least. Surely men can see the advantage of having a wife and daughters with these skills?"

"I'm sure, once the colony grows a bit more, establishments for girls may become more common. You know there are one or two already."

"Yes, for the upper-class girls to attain the social graces. That's not what I mean by education."

He shook his head. "I cannot even back the current proposal by the radicals. You will have to be patient."

"But…"

"No, Cousin, press me no further. I will work in the background for now. I have no vote in the Legislature. I am merely Chaplain. But I have influence and, as more clergy enter the Province, I will work with them toward a more enlightened system. Be you content with that." His posture was stiff and unrelenting.

Be content. Be subservient, more like. Be placid, docile…

Inwardly fuming, but outwardly calm, I nodded my acquiescence. Really, I was too annoyed to speak. And in any case, there was nothing I could do now. Would the time ever be right?

Social life in York was more political in alignment than in Niagara. There were no regular dancing assemblies, but occasionally a ball was held in a private house. Attendees were divided along partisan lines here, too, distinguishing Tory and Whig circles. No Whigs or persons inclined to reform views were invited to the Governor's ball. This was something of a relief to me since I needn't make a special effort to dissuade Eliza from consorting with Willcocks. Equally, no appointed office-holders or colonial government sympathizers were welcome among the reformers. There were but few fence-sitters, and they avoided large assemblies altogether, being of the poorer sort.

Because of Cousin Robert's appointments, the family received mainly Tory invitations, and duly accepted them. It did not do to offend those in power lest they withdraw their patronage and decrease the family's income. I attended as chaperone for Eliza and Maryel, and enjoyed the company of other political families. Such a relief to see unfamiliar faces and hear fresh stories. Though single, my place among the political matrons was secure owing to my expertise in midwifery. Most of our talk dealt with the exigencies of keeping a household and raising children on the edge of the wilderness. But I could also keep a weather ear out for gossip about Parliamentary goings-on that might relate to Cousin Robert's position, his friends and adversaries.

Tom

"Can't you calm down a bit, Jos?" Tom asked Willcocks. He looked over the pint pots at his mentor and friend. They had stopped at the first tavern on York's outskirts after the trip from Niagara over the frozen winter trail. The ale was pissy, but the room was warm.

"How can I, boyo? When that great dunderhead of a Governor continues his underhanded business? He and his cronies siphon off all the prime land for themselves. He gathers more of the same type by outright bribery. And they have the gall to treat everyone who doesn't suck at the colonial administration's teat as if they are traitorous fiends." He spat on the floor as if to get the taste of Gore's iniquity out of his mouth. Or possibly the sourness of the ale.

"Are you sure about the bribes?"

"I had it from some fellows I used to work with, right inside the Governor's offices. You can't get any nearer the horse's mouth."

Tom shook his head. "Are they looking to make this a little England, then?"

"They want to establish the Church of England, set up a patronage system, and make sure the best land is reserved for a few. You tell me." Willcocks's head sunk on his chest for a moment. Then he raised it, eyes flashing, and thumped the table. "We won't let them, though. We'll keep up the pressure in Parliament and in my news sheet." He fished in his pocket and held up a pamphlet. "This will help."

Tom took it from him. "A View of the Political Situation of the Province of Upper Canada by John Mills Jackson."

Willcocks leaned across the table. "A good friend of Judge Thorpe's and a proponent of more equitable treatment of Loyalist settlers. And of other incomers, too. He makes a rational case against Gore and his predecessor, Hunter, in their high-handed treatment of land claims, favoring their cronies and disadvantaging everyone else. The Executive Council is nothing but a damned clique, doling out bribes and favors where they will."

This was dangerous—even libelous—talk and Tom looked around at the others in the tavern. Most were already in their cups, or focused on a game of dice. Nothing to worry about here, where the tavern keeper was half-seas-under.

Not so in the following days, as Willcocks made his opinions known in York's muddy streets, often at the top of his voice, as he made his way around the town. And he didn't stop there. Articles accusing the high and mighty appeared in the *Guardian*, which was read by all, even if they despised its content. Tom became more concerned for his friend with each passing day, and worried he himself might suffer from guilt by association.

Willcocks

1 Feb

Opening session of the Legislature. Usual crowd of bootlickers and sycophants. Few of us reformers with no hope of passing forward-looking legislation. Exec. Council would likely veto even if we could do so. Rumblings in corridors about Jackson's pamphlet. Heard some talk about my articles. No direct confrontation as yet. Tom Strange standing ready with more material for next edition—this time giving names and quantity of land bribed with. These scoundrels then voted against their constituents' interests. Appalling! I must remain here to represent my constituents but he can return to Niagara to put out the news sheet.

15 Feb

One boring speech after another. Enough to make a grown man weep. Saving grace—today Strange brought new edition of Guardian to York. This ought to make the jackasses sit up and bray louder.

20 Feb

Gadzooks! I'd never have believed my words would have this effect. I can hear them still—Guilty. Guilty. Guilty. Only a few loyal associates abstained. and that to prevent their own fall. Nobody dared vote against. So. Gore has his revenge. I'm guilty (according to the legislators in his pocket) of contempt and libel against them all. Of breach of privilege. They read me out a Speaker's Warrant. impeaching me from my elected office! Worse yet. I'm sitting in the infernal Common Gaol at their pleasure. Thanks to Strange I have my journal for company. at least. He promises to bring books and wine.

Rebecca

A political scandal erupted a few weeks after we arrived in York. It was with some relish people spread the news of Joseph Willcocks's latest antics in the Legislature. This time he had not stopped at being a gadfly proposing anti-establishment reforms, but had been impeached and ejected from the Legislature and thrown into the York Gaol.

"It's naught but what I expected," said Cousin Robert, "since he was determined to harass Gore and made such wild accusations about him. Here," he brandished a copy of the *Guardian* "have a look at his latest article."

I read it with increasing astonishment.

Willcocks had learned, from acquaintances in the colonial administration, that certain land grants had been issued to members of the Legislature, that did not appear to relate to any legitimate claim or warrant. Perhaps coincidentally, these same members were devoted supporters of Gore. However tenuous the information, it prompted Willcocks to write several articles alleging bribery by the Governor, consisting of a grant of twelve hundred acres of land each, to vote against the interests of the electorate in their constituencies. He accused them—individually and severally—and in this latest version he accused Gore specifically. No wonder he had been accused of contempt and libel.

"I only wonder they stopped at locking him up," I said. "Could Governor Gore not have banished him from the colony?"

"That is a measure rarely used. I cannot recall the last time I heard of it."

"Wouldn't he be happier in the States? He shares so many of their views."

"I have thought so, too. But he has sworn loyalty, and apart from uttering libel, has done nothing illegal. So, here he stays." He pursed his lips. "There's another thing, Cousin."

"To do with Willcocks?"

"Yes, unfortunately. I have noticed Eliza has lately argued in favor of reforms such as he proposes."

"Is she not merely supporting those issues you favor?"

"It seemed to me she was adopting a more extreme position." He paused. "But then, perhaps I am over-sensitive to anything associated with that man."

He was right. It had been wishful thinking on my part that our stay in York might pass without incident. The Willcocks affair echoed into our household. More than that, I worried about the effect Willcocks might have on Tom, who was like a son to me. That he might be endangered by Willcocks was intolerable.

Eliza was vocal in his support and threatened to take her opinions abroad. That would never do so I made our excuses and we shortened our stay in York because of it. Cousin Robert was livid, and vowed she must either mend her ways or be sent away from Willcocks's influence. He remained in York while we retired to Niagara. I made no bones about my opinion to Eliza, at some length, since she had made so free with hers.

"How could you be so indiscreet?" I asked at the end of my homily.

Eliza was unrepentant. "I'm a woman grown and can consort with whom I wish. And voice my opinions, too."

"Not while you live under your father's roof, you can't," I said. "Your behavior reflects on the whole family. Do you really wish your father to be cast out of his positions, and for your sister to suffer censure as well?"

She hunched a shoulder and turned away.

Maryel had listened to my diatribe with an open mouth, which I advised her to close lest something nasty took up residence there. I had little patience left for any perceived fault from either girl. Girl! I must stop calling them so. If they demanded to be treated as women, I would do so, holding back nothing of the world's realities from them. They were, so they claimed, past the need for sheltering. We would see about that.

Willcocks

28 Feb

Adding a new cause to my list. Conditions in this dungeon like to be the death of me. Squared logs with gaps admit the winter gale and the dirt floor no doubt crawls with insects when it's warmer. Naught but a small brazier and thin blanket for warmth. I can barely keep the ink unfrozen. Am I to die of rheumaticks. and me not 40 yet? Even murderers should be treated better. I suppose they only stay long enough for someone to string up a noose. Surprised not to be fined and released on parole. What's their intent?

13 Mar

Parliament prorogued yesterday. Gaoler came today with the key to release me. Clear they wanted me contained while Parliament still in session. Still surprised not to be fined. Blankets at Jordon's much better quality than gaol. Strange ordered private parlor. good meal. hot rum punch. Finally warm both inside and out.

Tom

Tom checked in on Jos the next day, finding him ensconced in a comfortable chair.

"You don't look the worse for wear, I'm glad to see," he said.

"It's an experience I've no wish to repeat, you may be sure," said Willcocks, feet up on the grate. "But they haven't seen the last of me yet. I'll never forget their perfidy."

"Surely you'll retrench a bit? Ease up a little on the articles?" asked Tom.

"I may do, I may." Willcocks pulled at his lower lip. "But I'm going to stand for election again. As soon as there's an opportunity. I'll win, too, you'll see. The farmers in my district want a voice, and they know I'll give it to them."

"But until then?"

"Until then, I won't be silent, either. I might not put it in writing for a while. But damn me if I'm going to keep my mouth shut. I don't mind goading them with my words, and I'm happy to voice my opinions to anyone who will listen."

"You don't think yourself in danger?"

"These lazy bastards won't stir from York for a few outspoken words in the hinterland. And they've already cashiered me from public office. I'm a man of my own means and not subject to their whims. If my accusations are false, let them prove me wrong." He chuckled. "That's how I know I'm right, boyo, they have no defense against my complaints. If they did, they'd have published it long since."

April–May

Rebecca

We didn't fuss over anniversaries, but Cousin Robert's sister had sent a parcel of books for him in which she enclosed a birthday gift for Maryel, her goddaughter. I placed the package by her place at the dining table so she would see them at breakfast.

"For me?" she asked. "Why, what's this?" She carefully loosened the ribbon and the wrappings fell open to display two slim volumes. Picking up each book in turn, she read out the titles. "*Lyrical Ballads* by Mr. Coleridge and Mr. Wordsworth. *Songs of Innocence and Experience* by Mr. Blake." Her eyes shone. "These are wonderful!"

"I think it was clever of her to ask Uncle Thomas to conceal them among Father's religious books," said Eliza. "For you have never shown the slightest interest in those."

Cousin Robert was amused by this. "Truly, Maryel is in no danger of becoming overly religious." He assumed a mock frown, drawing his brows together, but winking at her underneath them. "A clergyman has much to bear from his recalcitrant daughters."

"Father, you're funning. You know you are," said Maryel.

"If not religious, at least the tone of these is unexceptionable," he said, picking up the Blake. "Poetry is somewhat fanciful for my taste, but I'm sure you will take great pleasure in them."

"It's a little thing after such a treat," I said, "but here's a small token from me." I handed Maryel a pair of gloves I had purchased while in York.

"Perfect," she said. "My old ones are beyond mending."

✳

Cousin Robert brought home a guest one day in mid-April, and introduced him to the family.

"Mr. Josiah Burton," he said. "Newly arrived in Niagara, apothecary by profession. And a member of our church, I am pleased to say."

He waved at us.

"These are my daughters, Miss Eliza and Miss Maryel, and our cousin, Miss Plummer."

Mr. Burton, a man of moderate height and pleasant appearance, perhaps in his thirties, so a little younger than I was, made an awkward bow. "I thank you for the introduction, sir. Ladies, it's my pleasure to make your acquaintance." He turned to me. "Miss Plummer, I hear you have some skill with herbs, and preparing various types of physick. I anticipate conversing with you on the subject."

The conversation turned to general topics, and I did not try to return to herbology.

When it transpired he was a bachelor, I could not refrain from speculation on what kind of husband he would make. Not that I seriously considered a relationship on so slight an acquaintance, but any single female in as precarious a position as I, should not ignore any opportunities that came her way.

So far, I had been content with my position as housekeeper to Cousin Robert and chaperone to his daughters. My sad story of loss reconciled me somewhat to my subordinate position in life, but never completely. I could never be sure of my future, with his daughters now of marriageable age. He might die or choose to alter his living arrangements once they had their own homes. If my parents could do me no further harm, they could do me no good either. My sister had her burgeoning family back in London. My probable welcome would still be as an extra—subordinate—female.

I must look to my own resources to assure my future in this world ruled by and for men. So I resolved to engage in a friendly association with Mr. Burton and see what came of it.

✳

We waved Cousin Robert off on his circuit to the Forty-Mile Creek on a fine May morning. This gave me an excellent opportunity to review the preparation of herbal medications with the girls. He disliked my filling the house with odd smells, so his absence was a blessing. We could also do some of the dirtier preparation steps outdoors, weather permitting.

I demonstrated the proper technique for infusing herbal teas to give the required strength of the ingredients. Eliza could repeat the process to my satisfaction, but Maryel's attention wandered and she could not reproduce the solution reliably.

"I don't know where your mind is fixed, Maryel, but it's definitely not on preparing remedies. I had thought to give you a less arduous task than weeding the herbs, but either you have less aptitude for this work than I imagined, or you have lost the ability to focus your thoughts. It's too bad. We all have need of medicines at times, and it's convenient to be able to make your own. I had thought you would continue to apply yourself to this study."

"But Rebecca, the apothecary…"

"Is still a new feature here and may not always have a good supply of what you need. But I suppose with the enlargement of the town, it will become less essential to know these things. It was already tending that way back in England when we left, and why should it be different here? Perhaps one day we'll buy all our bread, and butter, and other perishables from a special shop."

Maryel giggled at the notion. "Surely that can never be! Why, it would all be stale, or melted, or spoiled, before it ever arrived home."

"I'm sure our mothers believed there was no alternative to an open fire for cooking and heating, but see how the invention of the closed stove is changing things. They say it's both safer and more convenient than bending over open flames. We may be able to afford one ourselves before too long. You should keep an open mind, Maryel. The world is full of possibilities."

I had been dreaming of home so the commotion that woke me one May morning at Lake Lodge struck me first as London traffic, on a day when beasts were driven to Smithfield market. It only took a moment for my fuzzy head to resolve this into the cries of sheep in the paddock.

I shrugged on a wrapper and ran down the stairs. From the doorway, all I could see was a cloud of dust in the pen beside the barn, with a suggestion of moving shapes within. Then, one of them resolved into a large, dark shape with something limp in its mouth. A deep growl made my skin prickle and the hair on my arms stand to attention. A black bear! We heard they sometimes approached settlements, but I had never seen one close, and didn't want to now.

I swallowed hard. The hired men were nowhere in sight, probably plowing a distant field. It was up to me. I seized the musket and cartridge box we kept at the ready for such emergencies, and ran out the door, barefoot.

The bear had, by now, disposed of one lamb and looked likely to devour another, if I did not act quickly.

Heart pounding, I pulled out a cartridge, loaded and primed the musket and raised it to my shoulder, mindful of my single chance to kill, wound, or scare the creature off. I could never reload in time. One deep breath… exhale… squeeze the trigger. The noise of the shot was deafening, and my shoulder near dislocated by the gun's kick.

The bear gave another great roar, then lumbered away toward the creek. I had not hit it, of course, but perhaps it had encountered guns before and was wary, or maybe its hunger was dulled by a small meal. I sank to the ground, breathless and aching.

By now, Hannah and my cousins were awake. They joined me in the yard and helped me up.

"I'll be fine in a moment," I said. "For pity's sake, look to the flock. I think the creature broke down part of the paddock fence. All we need now is to chase escaped sheep around the countryside."

Maryel and Eliza looked after the frightened sheep while Hannah helped me inside. It turned out we had lost two lambs, one eaten and another shaken to death. The rest of the sheep remained huddled together, giving the girls time to prop the broken fence in place and brace it until more secure repairs could be made.

It took me the better part of the day to get over the shock. It would take us longer to get over the loss of two lambs. We could at least salvage the meat from the second, but our efforts to expand the flock were stymied for this year. Especially since both had been female. A male might have graced our table, providing a single fleece, but ewes could be counted on for years of wool, milk and new generations of lambs. Every loss counted enormously, living on the edge of survival as we did. Some years, it felt like we took two steps forward only to fall three back.

After the incident with the bear, we moved back into town for a while, leaving hired help to manage the farm. It was fortunate for us there were always men searching for work, unable to buy or lease land of their own. Most moved on after a season or two, but there were always more newly come into the district that we could call upon for heavy labor.

Over the next few weeks, I formed the habit of stepping into the apothecary shop mid-morning for a brief chat with Mr. Burton. I brought him samples of some of my herbal preparations, which he examined and found suitable for addition to his wares, offering me a fair price for them. In fact, he could sell my products for more than I could myself. Useless for me to bemoan his advantages. The simple fact was that as a man, his word, deed, and merchandise were considered more valuable than mine. However, he did not presume upon this advantage in his dealings with me, and rose in my estimation thereby. We exchanged our experience on common ailments and their treatments. His knowledge of the symptoms of unusual conditions exceeded my experience, while I outstripped him in midwifery and other female complaints.

We were soon on easy terms with each other and explored our respective backgrounds. His family came from King's Lynn, not thirty miles from Whittlesey, both East Anglian towns. Something else we had in common. It turned out he knew my hometown well, having traveled through it when visiting cousins in Peterborough.

"How long have you been in Upper Canada?" I asked.

"Only a year, which I spent mostly in Kingston," he said. "The five years before that I spent in Halifax, where I came as a journeyman. My master was seeking new opportunities. I had no ties to England, so was happy he agreed to pay my way in return for my services for two more years. I might be there still if it were not for notices offering large new territories to serve in this province."

"Did you like Halifax then? I've never seen it."

"It feels much like an English town, despite the populace now being about half American. Although I suppose the Loyalists still consider themselves Englishmen, even after generations in the New World. I was pleased with life there, but never put down roots." He gave me an arch glance. "Perhaps I may do so here."

Not to encourage him too quickly, I lowered my gaze. "How does Niagara compare?"

"To Halifax? Smaller, and less sophisticated. To Kingston? Similar. Both are garrison towns so have rough edges, but there are some fine houses and streets, and many prosperous farms surrounding both. But what of you, Miss Plummer? How do you come to be here?"

"My cousin Mary was Reverend Addison's wife. I've lived with the family since their daughters were small, and brought them out to him when she stayed behind in England with their young son. They both died there."

His face grew serious. "Ah. A great pity, but a common sorrow." He brightened. "Let us not dwell on tragedy, Miss Plummer. I wanted to ask you… do your household duties allow you some time for frivolity? If they do, I would like to request your company on a trip to Queenston one day next week."

I was astonished, and said so. Some might question the propriety of such a trip, but Queenston was a mere seven miles distant, and in an open carriage…

"It will be a combination of pleasure and business. I expect a shipment of ginger and quinine coming up through the States. I would be glad of your company, and there may be some other herbs and spices that would interest you." He rubbed absently at a small blemish on his lower lip. "I have hired a horse and cart for the purpose."

Surely no one could object to such an excursion. "I will need to arrange affairs with the household so they can spare me, but it should be possible. It's early enough in the season that we're still making use of last year's supplies and have few new crops to harvest and store."

He smiled broadly, reminding me painfully of Martin who always had a ready grin. "I will hope for fine weather and speak to you on Sunday after church."

✳

The following Tuesday dawned fine. Mr. Burton brought a cart and horse to our gate. The May morning was still cool and I donned a shawl. I wore sensible boots in case we were required to walk any distance. Mr. Burton handled the reins competently and the drive along the river road was accomplished in a little over an hour, in no way taxing the horse. We spent a little time going over merchandise in Mr. Clark's store. I made a few small purchases while Mr. Burton loaded his boxes into the cart. Our business completed, we strolled along the pretty street of houses by the river.

"A sparkling day, Miss Plummer."

"Indeed, it is, Mr. Burton."

"Need we be so formal? At least in private? My name is Josiah, and I'd be honored if you would use it. I believe yours is Rebecca. May I have the privilege?"

I nodded. "I don't object, as long as propriety is maintained." As much as I might dislike it, it was a man's world in which women must adhere to their standards.

We walked on for some moments in silence, then by mutual agreement, turned for the carriage, and returned to Niagara. Our conversation continued on many topics, with just that added note of warmth to increase my pleasure in his company.

✳

Drusilla was all agog to hear how it had gone. I assured her Josiah had behaved as he ought.

"He's well-set-up," she said. "And I love curly hair on a man."

I laughed at that. "As if it mattered. He could be bald as an egg for all I care." I arched a brow. "Don't I have enough curls of my own?"

She pouted. "Surely you wouldn't want to walk out with an ugly man?"

"Perhaps not. But a kind man, with expressive eyes and a comfortable manner? I wouldn't care about his looks."

"Kindness is important, I agree," said Drusilla. "Perhaps that's why I've never found a man to suit me."

Given her sister's troubled marriage, and her views on the subjugation of women by men, this was understandable. At least she knew where she was with her parents who were not demanding and did not constrain her activities or interfere with her friendships.

"Mr. Burton seems kind. But only further acquaintance will confirm or refute that impression," I said.

June–August

Jack

Jack completed his day's duty, training with the artillery officers. He now had a fair notion of how to organize the gun teams in the field, should it become needful during a battle.

It had been a long, scorching afternoon and he was glad to strip off his heavy woolen tunic and roll up his shirt sleeves. A welcome breeze through the open window in his quarters soon dried the sweat from his neck and arms, though his black curls and side-whiskers remained damp. The acrid stench of gunpowder still filled his nostrils and made him sneeze. With a mug of ale at his elbow, he reviewed the latest missive from his sister, and prepared a quill to compose a reply.

To Mrs. Edward Tuite Dalton, Dublin, Ireland

7 June 1810

My dear sister Olivia,

You may imagine with what surprise I received the notice of your recent marriage. My warmest felicitations to you and your new husband. I remember him well, from when we were choirboys together. He is a lucky dog!

I can't help but think you are young to be married. Forgive me. I suppose having attained fifteen years you consider yourself a woman grown. It's hard for me to picture my baby sister heading up a household, but I am sure you will make Edward an excellent wife. You assure me it's not a device of Father's to ensure a connection with a promising musician, but that your affections are engaged. I hope for both your sakes it's a true match and will be blessed with healthy children.

Nothing much has changed here since my last. We're into our second year of posting to Fort George. I have made many acquaintances in the town, in particular the family of the rector, Reverend Addison. I confess to a growing admiration for his daughter, Maryel. We're of an age, and our tastes are compatible. I have danced with her at assemblies, and accompanied her on walking parties. However, her Father does not favor either soldiers or Irishmen. She has other admirers, but so far expresses no preference. Besides which, the Regiment's frequent rotation between locations makes it difficult to court in earnest. There is still great uncertainty about the intent of the Americans. For now, though, the border is quiet.

Please give my love to Father, Anna and Joe, and my wish they remain in good health. Tell Father I will write him soon.

Yr affectionate brother,

Jack

But what would he write to Father? In recent months, he had realized he must have been a sore trial to him, but was he ready to admit this? He felt the need to prove himself and to justify his choices. If only some opportunity would arise for him to show his mettle. Perhaps a brief note, in a more-cordial tone than usual, would suffice for now. Let Father think he was changing, but not that he had become compliant to his wishes. He bent over his papers again, considering what to write, but failed to find the right words and set all aside, draining his mug and going in search of another.

Rebecca

With Gore still in power, Cousin Robert faced the cruel reality that he might have to sacrifice some of the lands he had received, in lieu of cash payment, to settle his debts. He felt himself ill used as a victim of guilt-by-association in the Governor's mind, and told me so, repeatedly, in no uncertain terms. Often over the dinner table.

"It's a constant worry, Cousin," he said on one occasion, to which all I could do was nod. "There are so many small appointments I might obtain, were it not for the Governor's blocking them."

"Are the family coffers in such dire straits?"

"It is in Gore's purview to award small stipends for clerical duties I could perform easily. His patronage is essential for one in my position." He shrugged. "I suppose I became used to Governor Simcoe's generosity, and under his tenure the capital was here in Niagara, too. I may have assumed from his behavior that I might continue to get preferment for such posts. But it's as hard to receive preferment here as it was at home." He rubbed his forehead. "And when I see the Irish preferred…"

"Why have you such a dislike of the Irish? Surely, they're no worse than any other people?"

"There are too many of them in opposition to the colonial administration, and I find myself tarred with the same brush in the Governor's eyes. My loyalty should be unquestioned. Besides which, all I have seen of them shows their lack of restraint, their proclivity for strong drink, and their general lack of decorum."

After one such diatribe over an otherwise pleasant meal of spit-roasted lamb and new peas, Maryel spoke up. "I'm sorry you have such a dislike for the Irish, Father," she said. "Some of them are quite affable, you know."

"You mean Ensign Stevenson and other officers in his Regiment, I suppose."

"Yes, for they aren't your enemies, are they?"

"Perhaps not, but I am hounded at every step by Governor Gore who links me with their fellow countrymen residing in this Province."

"Is there nothing you can do about it?"

"I fear not. I have already written to my acquaintances in England who might assist me. They have been silent so far. The distance is so great that any efforts made on their part could well backfire, with the Governor so set against me." He sighed. "I confess, I am discouraged."

"What shall you do, then?" I asked.

"I still have many friends in this district and their help is likely to be more useful."

"You do, and some very good ones, like Mr. Dickson and Mr. Nichol. I would think they could influence their fellow merchants, at least," Maryel said.

He nodded. "It helps a little that the Governor is fixed at York. He rarely ventures from there. The only time I must be within his direct notice is during my duty as Chaplain to the Legislature, and that is infrequent." He cast his eyes upwards. "I am more concerned to retain the goodwill of the garrison commander. Though he could not help when Macdonell and Moore challenged my rights to the Salt Spring. That affair turned out so poorly… But do try to be at ease, my dear. We have not reached the end of our resources yet."

"As long as you don't extend your objections to the Regiment, Father. For they are decent and loyal men."

He still looked skeptical, but said no more. I reassured Maryel, who favored a certain Irish ensign, her father would not forbid him the house.

Tom

Sweat ran down Tom's back in waves as he labored over the press on a stifling July day. Wouldn't you know Jones would give him a big assignment at the last moment. Darkening clouds loomed over the buildings visible through the print-shop window, and he felt the odd prickliness in his nostrils that foretold a storm. When rain began to fall in earnest, he was about to close the front door against it when he was bowled over by a woman rushing inside. Her hat was clutched to her head against rain and blustering wind.

He had no chance to avoid her. She ran full into him and he fell against the frame he had been filling with type. Tiny bits of metal scattered everywhere, and the wooden edges of the forme fell from their clamps and clattered to the floor. He toppled into the press and nearly knocked himself out on the forestay. The frisket and tympan, raised above the stone so it could receive the new forme, collapsed on him. He lay, momentarily stunned, in a welter of type and chunks of wood, sheets of paper fluttering down over the whole.

It took a few moments for his head to clear enough to see the ruin of the afternoon's work. And the woman who stood laughing at him. It was Maryel. He was entirely mortified she should see him in such a state. Never mind that she had caused it. So, he ignored her, pushed aside some of the debris and crawled out from under the press, examining its state. If it were badly damaged, his head would surely roll. He inspected it carefully and folded back the frisket and tympan. To his great relief, there were only a few chips out of the wooden frames. He rounded on Maryel.

"Don't you ever look where you're going? How could—" But he could not go on. Maryel shrieked with laughter, holding her sides as if they pained her. He rubbed his head, gazing at the mess. And chuckled. It was a mistake to look over at Maryel whose spasms of laughter continued. Finally, too weak to speak, she sank to a bench near the door, and Tom leaned against the wall, sliding to the floor.

It took them a few minutes to recover. "That's two hours' work gone," he said, suppressing a random chuckle. "And it was almost done, too. I was just checking it over when you exploded into the room."

Maryel viewed him sternly, but couldn't hold her expression, which relaxed into a grin. "I don't explode," she said. "I make an entrance." She rose and swept him a curtsy.

"Don't, you'll set me going again."

"I'm sorry I spoiled your work, though," she said. "It really is a terrible mess. I suppose I'd better help you clear it up. Where should I start?"

"Let me make sure the press won't fall on us." Tom rolled the carriage under the platen so the moving parts of the press were contained. "This will make it easier to get at the type." He looked at Maryel's skirts. "I think I'd better do the picking up part, so you don't end up with ink all over your dress. You can sort the type back into the case. And then I can begin the composition over again." He sighed. "No early leaving today."

"Oh no, Tom! You must be done today?"

"It's an order for a letter bill. Being picked up tomorrow."

"I feel terrible to have made you all this extra work."

"Well… if you can stay longer after we clean up, and read me each word, I can set the type faster. I've marked the font size at the beginning of each group of text. If you give me that first, I can focus on the right section of the case."

"I hardly know where to begin."

"They don't have fresh ink on them yet," said Tom. "You should be able to keep your clothes and hands clean."

Maryel perched on a stool in front of the text cases, while Tom knelt by the scattered heaps of small metal letters.

"How will I know the right size when I'm sorting?"

"You should see the size marked on the stem of the type. If you can't find it, set it aside and we'll match it later to others in the case. I only used four sizes for this piece, one wooden for the big capitals and three metal for the rest. You shouldn't find it hard to figure out."

"So, capitals go…?"

"In the upper part of the case," he pointed, "and lower case in…"

"The lower part of the case. Now I know why they're called upper and lower case."

Tom picked up a tin bowl from the window ledge and wiped it with a rag. There was no need to take on the extra work of cleaning the fonts until it became absolutely necessary. There might be some letters that had picked up grit from the floor, but they could be set aside for cleaning later. He scooped type into the bowl and poured it out on the work-table in front of Maryel. "Here's a start."

He picked his way around the floor, gathering all the easily visible pieces of type into the bowl. Some of them had fallen into cracks in the plank floor, and would need to be carefully pried out. The thin stick he used for this purpose was up on the work-table.

Relieved to stand and stretch, he took a moment to watch Maryel as she sorted the type. She had flung her honey-colored braids over her shoulders, but escaped tendrils of hair hung round her face and she blew them out of her eyes. Reaching up to push them behind her ear, she left an inky smudge along one cheekbone. Tom was charmed. When she turned to see why he wasn't making any noise, he dropped his eyes and retrieved his tool. He could feel her eyes follow him as he bent to his work, then she resumed hers.

"Handling type isn't so hard. It certainly doesn't take a lot of strength," said Maryel. "Do printers ever hire women?"

"I've never heard of any," said Tom. "Are you looking for employment?"

"I was just curious."

"You'd have to ask Printer Jones. I'm not master here."

The rain drummed down without ceasing as they worked. When Tom thought he had found most of the type, he joined Maryel at the sorting, first checking the pieces she had set aside. Within less than an hour, they could start the composition, and it took about the same to complete it. Tom locked the forme and placed it on the stone, ready to ink.

Maryel peered out the window. By now it was dark. She was probably overdue at home. But the rain continued as heavy as before. She turned back to him. "How many sheets do you need to print? Will it take long?"

"The order is for fifty. It will take some time." Her brow wrinkled, and she pouted. "Don't fret, Maryel, I'll see you home and come back. I would have taken a dinner break before running the press, anyway." He hauled out an umbrella and pulled on his jacket. "Come, it will only take a few minutes." He crooked his elbow, offering her his arm.

She hesitated a little, but accepted.

He placed his other hand on hers and smiled. "I'll see you safe home," he said, and she smiled back. Heat rose all along his arm and flowed up into his face. He felt something else rising too, and hastened to open the door to conceal his embarrassment. She didn't notice, he saw with relief—she was still smiling. He opened Jones's umbrella and they left the shop under its protection.

Rebecca

Cousin Robert sent off his report to the Society in early July. It was more optimistic in tone than usual, for which I was glad. He had good progress to report both among the Indians and the settlers in the Niagara countryside. Two small "convenient" chapels had been built in settlements ten or twelve miles from town, and he had baptized some members of all the tribes on the Grand River, including a few from the least approachable tribe.

He returned from posting it with welcome news.

"There is a new commander for His Majesty's forces in Upper Canada—Brigadier-General Isaac Brock. He's said to be an able man."

"Isn't he the one they say is forever applying for a post in Europe?" Military gossip was rife with such rumors, and they circulated freely in the town.

"I hear he thinks his talents would be better used to fight Napoleon. No doubt better rewarded, too. But we have need of talented men, though Upper Canada is a backwater among backwaters. Everything I hear describes him as a man who knows his duty, which is to fortify our Province against invasion from the United States. I'm eager to meet him."

Within the week, Brock arrived in Niagara to review the border defenses. The whole town was excited, and more rumors flew. Brock was to defend not only against the Americans, but against a possible French-Canadian rising on behalf of Napoleon's France. Cousin Robert pooh-poohed this.

"What nonsense. What loyalty should they feel to France when she abandoned her colony outright? My friend Dr. Mountain writes me from Montreal that the Quebec French consider themselves treated generously by the British on religion and land rights. They're much more worried about an American invasion. They remember the occupation of Montreal and the attack on Quebec City during the American revolution."

I hoped he was right. We didn't need to feel ourselves surrounded and beset upon from all fronts.

The day after Brock arrived, Chief Norton came to collect Cousin Robert for a meeting at the Fort. Both possessed a vast knowledge of the region and many years of continuous residence. We were agog to hear what transpired, and the hours of waiting were tedious.

Finally, in the lengthening afternoon shadows, he returned, full of news. He joined us in the parlor before we set out the tea service.

"What can you tell us, Father?" asked Maryel, bouncing on her toes.

He laughed. "I declare, it would be too bad if I told you nothing at all." He winked at Eliza, who was biting her lip to control her excitement. I felt as keen to hear his report as they.

"How fortunate that I can relate almost all of what was said," he said, eyes twinkling. "For I think you would surely burst if I could not. Well now, where to start…"

"Oh Father, do go on. What did they say?" asked Eliza.

"Brock," he said, "was just returned from a meeting with the Shawnee chief, Tecumseh, at the Thames Valley settlement. He wished to consult with Norton about the Six Nations warrior strength, and with me about the general temper of the region."

"Very flattering," said Eliza.

Cousin Robert nodded. "I thought so. He has either not heard of Gore's opinions, or gives them no credence. Most satisfactory." He paused, collecting his thoughts. "He plans to meet with local dignitaries and men of business throughout the Province, to determine what strength of militia could be raised, and where to best dispose his forces, should the Americans invade."

"His understanding is sound, then," I said.

"He was already well aware of the value of local insight, more so when it comes to dealing with our Indian neighbors. I gave him my best appreciation of the population and forbore to mention my personal grievances. It was neither time nor place. He must know there is considerable discontent among the recent American incomers, and that some might defect to their former country in the event of war. I mentioned that most of the new settlers are scattered throughout the countryside, rather than in town. I also gave him a list of those who he would find it useful to consult about local defenses apart from the Fort."

"And what of the disaffected?" I asked.

"He was already aware of some of the more prominent radicals, like Willcocks." He snorted. "Hard not to know of him, when his scurrilous journal is so widely distributed. I mentioned a few additional names he had not heard, but only those who have professed their views in public. I would not slander a man without proof." He paused. "I'm parched. Have Hannah bring some tea, or at least water. I feel as if I have preached ten sermons this afternoon."

After a drink of water, he was able to continue.

"I felt privileged to be there for the exchange between the

General and John Norton. I learned more about some aspects of Mohawk society than I have in all these years of working with them. Brock needs both their warriors and their tribal networks to successfully defend the Province. They will be invaluable as trackers and spies on both sides of the border. It's well known that connections remain between separated tribes, and they consider tribal custom and loyalty above that to King or State. Perhaps not all will take part, but there is hope that enough will."

"What was it you didn't understand, Father?" asked Maryel.

"Their society is founded on principles so different from our own we often talk at cross-purposes." He glanced in my direction. "I know you admire their system of matrilineal descent, Cousin. I will try to give their discussion verbatim, since Norton explained it so clearly."

"I have heard of your abilities as warrior, interpreter and negotiator," said Brock to Norton. "And your record as an Army officer, naturally. You carry on the legacy of your uncle, Joseph Brant…"

"Thayendanegea, in our tongue," said Norton. "As I am Teyoninhokarawen."

"… just so… he was a man of many parts, and a good friend to the King. His support during the war of rebellion was invaluable. Your position as his designated heir is secure?"

"I stand in place of his sister's son who died ten years since. According to his wishes, I was made war chief to the Mohawks, but there are some among us who question my worth."

"I wasn't aware of your difficulty," said Brock. "Who are the dissenters?"

"The peace chiefs, in particular, and some of the clan mothers as well."

"I'm new to your system of government, and the involvement of women in it. Can you elucidate?"

Norton stroked his chin. "On the men's side of the longhouse, the war chiefs conduct military operations, while the peace chiefs are more like the provincial Legislature, to draw analogies with the British system."

"But the women?"

"The mothers are in charge of the land and have a powerful voice in our councils because of it. It means our culture rests on a three-legged stool. Each has their role to play."

"Most intriguing. I gather some legs are less firm on some issues?"

"Many of the peace chiefs and clan mothers disagreed with Thayendenagea's decision to move the tribes here as Loyalists. Some of them stayed behind, splitting our people so that half our hearts lie on each side of the border. But more came here, and continue to sow dissent among us." He grinned sardonically, teeth flashing in his weather-beaten face. "If it comes to war with the Americans, we shall see which of us can pull the warriors of all the tribes together. God willing, I will earn their trust then, if not before."

Our conversation continued as Hannah called us to supper. We continued to question him about the details. Though he was tiring, we begged him for more, long into the evening.

"There was a deal more about raising militias, and what the General calls our 'porous border.' He is gravely concerned about the exposure along the Lakes, but believes our own Niagara River poses the greatest challenge to defend. With the Indian tribes in support to the west and south, he hopes to concentrate his forces here and on the upper St. Lawrence River, and leave the lakeshores to the Navy as much as possible."

"I know the General must focus on war," I said, "but to me the role of Mohawk women is fascinating, and most enviable. More sensible than our approach. What might we not do if such things could be adopted into our society?"

I lay awake a long time that night. Too many questions still unanswered for my comfort. Such as, what preparations need we make, and how long might they take? And how close were we to needing them? And… we had been told much. What was being withheld ? I didn't know what might come next. A chill ran down my spine at the thought of the proximity of the danger. Women were not cannon-fodder as men were, but were equally at risk during a battle, and in its wake.

My few encounters with Josiah over the summer were snatched during my trips into town to exchange produce for goods, or after church on Sundays. I must be content for our friendship to proceed at a sedate pace. We continued to find enjoyable topics of conversation; I found his attentions pleasing. It reignited my youth to have my company desired by an eligible bachelor. I longed to discuss this with Drusilla, but at this season, she seldom made the Sunday trip to town from their farm near St. Davids, also on the Four-Mile Creek, but four miles inland, under the limestone ridge.

I found time to write to my sister—a poor substitute for conversation, but an outlet for my turbulent thoughts.

> *… We're deep in the fruit harvest now, and my pantry shelves are filling up with jars of jewel-colored jams and whole fruit in heavy syrup. I cannot keep sufficient sugar in the house, and often resort to honey. The bees have been good to us this year, so there is plenty of that. I feel a sense of achievement, even when fatigued. Thankfully, Eliza and Maryel have taken over much of the cheese-making.*
>
> *I am always lonely. And yet I am in the midst of family. I know I have*

said this many times, probably too many. But now I feel it more keenly, because there is some prospect of easing it. Since meeting Josiah Burton, a spark of hope has emerged where I had carefully damped it down after losing Martin and the subsequent crisis. I dare not assume too much, but I hope for a great deal. It would be grand to partner with someone who shares my views. Well, at least some of them. Like all men, he would never consider a woman a true equal, but he appears to value my mind and my abilities, which is more than most men do. He has a well-set-up figure, a pleasant face, an agreeable speaking voice, and a well-informed mind. We have become friends. How can I resist dreaming a little?

It seems I must always crave your forgiveness for some megrim or other that afflicts me. You will probably throw this missive across the room in disgust and exhort me to keep a journal instead of writing my feelings to you. I hope, though, you may understand and wish me better times to come...

✳

Summer days, apart from Sunday, were filled with work from cock-crow to past sundown. Although Cousin Robert hired men to plow and plant field crops and care for most of the livestock, a large share of the farm work fell to us women. Ours the care of fowl and kitchen garden, processing milk into butter and cheese, and preserving fruit for winter storage. Ours, too, the making and mending of everyday garments, preparation of daily meals, and maintenance of the household.

Necessary work like candle-making or corn-husking was better done in a group, with products shared at the end of the task. So when Drusilla sent a message one August day that she and her neighbors were holding a quilting party, Eliza and Maryel declared it was time I had a day out. I gladly left my regular chores to them and walked the four miles to the Bells' farm.

The road along the Four-Mile Creek was flat most of the way, with farms at intervals. The only troublesome part was where it crossed the Black Swamp, but this was already in the process of being drained into ditches along the roadside, and summer's heat discouraged all but the most persistent midges. Blue cornflowers dotted yellow fields of wheat and barley, and the sweet odor of ripening stone fruit in the orchards assailed my nose, making my mouth water for a taste.

I arrived mid-morning, in good time to help Drusilla set up the quilting frames: lengths of wood we lashed into rectangles and propped on chair-backs, to stretch the fabric over while working.

"You have almost everything ready," I said as we embraced at her door. "It looks lovely, too." I admired the spread of food Drusilla prepared to sustain us during the day's work. She laid it out on the veranda, under a thin muslin covering to ward off the bugs. I added my fresh cottage loaf to her dishes of sliced meats and green salad. "We certainly won't go hungry."

"There's plenty of space left for whatever they bring," she said. "I'm so glad it's a fine day. We can have the doors and windows open and take our breaks outside."

She patted the edge of one frame then turned to face me. "The rest will be here soon. But I wanted some time to talk with you before they arrive." She hesitated, frowning.

Surely, I thought, we could have one meeting without her bringing up—

"It's about Mrs. Ferris."

For once, it wasn't what I thought. "Does her husband still beat her?"

She nodded. "Their farm doesn't prosper as it should. He drinks up the earnings and comes home to take out his improvidence on her. She denies it, but I've seen the wounds and bruises. And she walks with a terrible limp."

"I haven't seen her since I delivered her last child. A son, I think?"

"A sickly boy. Their oldest is barely fourteen, and between them, he and his mother have a hard time keeping food on the table."

"What can I do to help?"

"I'm not sure, but I thought if we both tried we could think of something."

"Are they church members? I don't recall seeing her there."

"I believe not. Perhaps Methodists."

"If they were members of our church, I could have a word with Cousin Robert. He might wield some influence over the man, especially if it involves drunkenness. If not, there's little I can do. Unless… They have circuit riders, don't they? And the Methodists frown on strong drink, I know."

She brightened. "Perhaps I could learn more of their traveling preacher and he might intervene."

"He might, I suppose. Or he might take the man's part as they so often do. We women are mere chattel in their hands. If he thinks she complained about him, it could well make things worse." Men. So often indifferent to their impact on women. "Do you expect her here today?"

"She finds it hard to walk this far. Their farm is up on the escarpment, and the path down is steep. But her neighbors are sure to be here and we may inquire discreetly of them." She smiled. "Here come some now."

I stood by her as she greeted her guests. There were women I recognized from Queenston and Niagara, but also from communities as far away as Chippawa, beyond the Great Cataract, and Shipman's Corners on the Twelve-Mile Creek. It was too bad Mrs. Ferris couldn't come. It would have done her good.

Everyone brought something to contribute to the lunch, and we had six coverlets to quilt, and materials to make at least five others. It was as well we were a large group. The quilting had priority, with materials traded amongst us for later cutting and piecing at home.

I took charge of the lunch table. It would be a feast of noble proportions. Cold chicken and ham, roasted corn on the cob, cucumber salad, breads and biscuits, fresh plums and grapes, and all manner of pickles and preserves. Drusilla had prepared a large jug of cool-steeped tea with mint leaves floating in it, and rolled a small barrel of cider onto the porch where glasses could be filled from its spigot. My mouth watered at the sight. But we must put in some work first.

After a little jockeying for position, everyone wishing to sit beside the host, we gathered around the three quilt frames and began our work. Drusilla hummed a familiar tune and soon, other voices joined her. Quilting didn't require rhythm, but it was still pleasant to have accompanying music. We sang as we worked, ballads and hymns we all knew. I felt quite hoarse by the time we finished the three quilts, and glad to wet my whistle with a glass of cool mint tea. No more soothing herb than mint, and no drink more refreshing than tea.

"Shall we reward ourselves with lunch, or continue our work?" Drusilla asked.

Most were in favor of having a brief respite, perhaps a biscuit or slice of bread, and continuing on, so we rested for perhaps fifteen minutes and resumed our work. We had sung ourselves out and were ready for a good gossip. One woman from Queenston told a funny story about a man chasing a pig. The one from Chippawa told of a near-tragedy from a fire. This was something we all feared, but the story was exciting. It was a relief to hear of the daring rescue of her neighbor's children from a burning barn, and how the fire had been extinguished before all was lost. Each told some tale or other, often poking fun at the foibles of our menfolk, with gales of laughter as the result. Eventually, our storytelling lapsed into more subdued conversation around each quilt frame. My group was mostly silent so I clearly overheard a woman at the next frame mention Cousin Robert's name.

"Did you see that newcomer, Mrs. Herbert, after church last Sunday?" This was obviously a rhetorical question, as she continued, "Wasn't she making a dreadful fuss over the Reverend Mr. Addison? I thought he seemed flattered by her attentions. She's a widow, I believe."

This was news to me. I remained in the church after the service, tidying away the prayer books, while Cousin Robert greeted the congregation outside.

"Flustered, more like," said another. "If he even noticed her. You were probably imagining things."

Our conversation picked up again, so I heard no more about it. But I learned from Mrs. Secord that the Methodist preacher was due to arrive within the week. I made a mental note of this for Drusilla to act on. We worked faster, probably because we were all getting hungry, and soon attacked the groaning board. I confess, I stuffed myself shamelessly. So did we all. Afterwards, we spent an hour in trading materials, and people began to take their leave.

I buttonholed Drusilla as I prepared to walk home. She was packaging up some of the leftover food. "For Mrs. Ferris?"

"Yes, I'll run it up to her this evening."

I told her about the preacher, then addressed the subject uppermost in my mind. "Do you know a Mrs. Herbert?"

She shook her head. "I haven't been to town since July. Perhaps she has arrived more recently."

I walked home with that on my mind. Why would a newcomer single out Cousin Robert? And what if he encouraged her?

September

Tom

Tom settled himself at a table in a quiet corner of McBride's tavern, with a pint of cider, a sausage and a chunk of bread, intent on making a good lunch. He cut open the bread and piled it with slices of sausage. There was a pot of mustard on the table, and he put a huge dollop over the whole, mashing the bread down with his ink-stained fingers until he achieved a thickness he thought might fit in his mouth. He propped his book—Tom Jones—open with one elbow and supported the sandwich in the other hand. Just as he was about to take his first bite, a shadow fell over the table. He looked up to see who blocked his reading light. It was John Norton, whom he knew from his visits to the Addison family.

"Greetings, my young friend," said Norton. "May I sit with you?"

"Yes, of course," said Tom.

Norton placed his pint on the table between them and waved Tom to continue eating. "I have a proposition to put to you, and it would be best if it appeared to be a casual conversation over a drink. Can you make it so?"

Tom nodded and took a bite. As he chewed, he listened in

growing astonishment to Norton's proposal.

"You know General Brock is now in charge of the British forces in this Province?"

Tom nodded again, mouth still full.

"He wants to locate and train some men whose occupations and interests put them in a position of assisting his defense of the Province, should it become necessary. Because of my position as an ally, at arm's length from his command, he thinks me well-situated to locate such men. To train them in the woodcraft of my people, and to lead them in covert activities."

Tom nodded his understanding, and Norton continued.

"Brock wants to learn the most he can of potential disaffection among the local population, of potential traitors, and of the flow of money and information across the border. He is ideally situated to recommend positions for likely people. I've listed several occupations that would be most useful to a covert agent of the Crown. He handed Tom a paper. "In your case, setting up as an independent printer's agent would be a plausible change. Especially since as journeyman you've been… well… journeying already."

Tom chuckled at this, and Norton quirked an eyebrow at him, sharing the mild jest.

"You would still be in the printing trade. You could enter into contracts with many customers, and have a wider territory to cover on legitimate business. Moreover, you would have a ready-made reason to be inquisitive and always in search of news." He grinned at Tom. "You may be curious why I'm being so open with you. After all, you could take this information and work against us. Well, you have been recommended by people I trust. So, young Tom Strange, I have chosen to trust you."

"Th-thank you," said Tom, his color rising. "I hope I'm worthy of your trust."

"So, with no further thought, you accept?" Norton laughed,

shortly. "I think you had better at least sleep on it. This is no light matter I ask of you. You may have to betray former friends. Have you considered that?"

Tom felt his Adam's apple leap in his throat. "I'm no fool, sir. You mean Joseph Willcocks, don't you?"

"I do. He has such a volatile nature, there is no telling what he might do. At the moment, he is fairly quiet. Brock has cultivated his acquaintance and hopes to retain his loyalty. But who knows what the future may bring? Your primary task, for now, will be to monitor his activities. Is it something you think you could do?"

Was it? He admired Willcocks, to be sure, but for his drive and some of his principles. "If there is a question of loyalty, you may be sure of me. If anyone I know turns traitor, I wouldn't hesitate to inform on them." He hesitated. "I don't know what the future may bring. I know Willcocks is loyal now. But... he's a man who holds a grudge. He already thinks himself hard-done-by."

"Would you be willing to watch him? In case of a change?"

"I think I can do that." It wouldn't be a comfortable position, he knew.

"Those are fine words. But be careful. I think you will find these matters aren't as clear-cut as you think. Be aware there could be others—no matter how unlikely you think them—who might turn traitor. We know not the pressures that may be brought to bear in war-time. Anyone could be affected. Anyone. Do you understand?"

"Sir, that may be. I don't think it will be easy but I can try. And your suggestion of taking up as an independent printer attracts me greatly. I'm happy in my trade, but have longed to see more of the world. But... I don't have many resources. You know I'm an orphan. How may I set myself up in business?"

"We would not do it all at once, to avert suspicion. When we do, there are some small funds available to me. I can support you in the purchase of a horse, its tack and accoutrements, saddle bags, riding gear and boots, and travel kit, including a musket. I trust you can ride?"

Tom nodded.

"You should be able to design and print up a prospectus and list of fees for different services. You'll need a base—lodgings you can use here in the town. That I leave to you. When traveling, there are inns—or you can seek lodging with local residents. I may… accidentally… join you on some of your trips." He paused. "I can't help asking… did you enjoy that?"

"What?" Tom's gaze followed Norton's, down to his plate, where only crumbs remained. He laughed ruefully. "I didn't even taste it."

"Never mind, there will be many other meals. He rose. "I'll be in touch soon."

Tom leaned back in his chair, ostensibly reading his book, his thoughts in turmoil. If only he could talk it all over with Jos. But, of course, he could not.

Rebecca

"Your Tom will be useful to us as a close associate of Willcocks." Norton barked a short laugh. "Brock doesn't trust many people, you know." He gazed around at us: Cousin Robert, Tom, and me. "You should consider yourselves privileged."

"I have no doubt that's due in part to your support, my friend," said Cousin Robert.

"Brock needs people like you," Norton continued. "A network of agents that can provide rapid and safe communication in the event of war. He has entrusted me with setting it up. But in addition, he wishes to establish safe houses where his agents may seek refuge, in case of invasion."

"Ah," I said, "you wish this farm to be one such."

"Exactly," said Norton. "You are ideally positioned and trustworthy." He smiled, something I rarely saw. It gentled his face extraordinarily. "You are near to, but not in the town, have legitimate reasons to travel back and forth, are accessible by land and water, and are respected by ally and antagonist alike. How could Brock not include you in his strategy?"

"How are we to accomplish what he desires?" I asked.

Robert had an answer for that. "I think we could excavate a second cellar, to be accessed by hidden points within and outside the house. I have considered several possibilities. On balance, the best location for a hidden room would be beneath the pantry, at the west side of the house."

"If I recall rightly," I said, "that part of the foundation required us to dig down deeply and sink long posts to reach a secure footing. It's better supported than the other side."

"I also thought to enlist Tom's help in digging it out."

Tom nodded, eyes bright. "As I can get time away from my duties."

Norton grinned, this time with a wolfish look. "General Brock is looking to the future, in a somewhat Machiavellian manner. 'Pay more attention to your enemies than your friends' is his dictum, though he doesn't neglect his friends either." Norton's expression grew more serious. "But you must tell me if there's anything about his plan you can't manage. He's asking a great deal of you."

Cousin Robert turned to me. "I think Miss Plummer must be the judge of that. She is the most likely to be affected by the modifications required at Lake Lodge. And she could well find herself alone when agents need refuge. Whether or not war comes."

"I think we can count on war coming, soon or late," said Norton.

"I will do what I can," I said. "My concern is how we'll keep it secret from your daughters. Their lack of knowledge will be an important part of the disguise. We must have some excuse to keep them away from the farm while we're building the hidden room."

"We will need to plan carefully, to be sure," said Cousin Robert. "I don't see how it can be achieved before winter. The ground will then be too hard to work until next spring."

Tom stayed silent while we discussed Brock's proposal. He did not look surprised when Norton laid out the basic plans, and he did not ask questions then, but let the information sink in. Finally, when the rest of us had run down our discussion, he spoke up.

"How are we to be identified amongst ourselves and our fellow agents?"

"Good question," said Norton. "To keep our communications secret, there are various codes you'll become acquainted with later, but each agent is given a code name, for protection. We've settled on names of birds. When I did similar work for my mentor, Thayende-nagea, I was known as 'Snipe.' Can you think of one that would suit you?"

Tom mused for a moment. "How about 'Thrush'? They're inquisitive birds, always poking around the underbrush."

We all laughed, and Tom's face colored.

"Excellent choice, Thrush," said Norton. "Well done."

"Indeed," I said. "I have no idea what to choose."

"Nor I," said Cousin Robert. "Tell me, Captain, what will Tom's duties be?"

"For now," said Norton, "he'll have a roaming remit, and simply keep his eyes and ears open in the marketplace and workplace. It helps that he's a quiet young man. People are used to his comings and goings for Printer Jones. He fits into almost any background, and nobody thinks anything of his being wherever he is. Ideal for information gathering."

"Won't Willcocks suspect?" I asked.

Tom shook his head firmly. "He sees me as a useful muttonhead. He's always preaching to me about politics, and I know he thinks my questions are stupid."

"Your advantage is that Willcocks doesn't know you as well as he might," said Norton. "If he thinks you're dull of wit, he won't watch his tongue around you. But there's danger in that too, don't forget. You'll need to be on your guard."

Jack

"Assemblies and dancing are all very well, but give me a good card-party for real fun," said Jack.

"I don't see how you continue to enjoy cards and dice, Jack, when you so rarely win," said Dawson. He laid down the ten of trumps, beating Jack's nine by a whisker.

Jack grumbled. "Maybe I'll give up whist after all." He tilted his chair back and reached behind him for his flute that lay on the bunk. He had polished it until the wood gleamed. "But I won't give up whistling," he said with a wink, and played a jig.

Dawson groaned at this sally. "If you're going to make terrible jokes, I need something stronger to wash them down with." He reached into an inner pocket and drew forth a flask. "I don't know if you deserve a share of this, but to show we're still friends." He took a small swig and handed the flask to Jack, who did likewise.

"Ah, brandy! I didn't know you had any left."

"There's a little more—but well concealed, so don't you go hunting for it."

"Not enough here to get more than slightly elated. Oh well, I'll have to go back to ale. I have my doubts about the latest batch, though."

"I hear they had to shoot the horse," said Dawson.

"Go on. I knew there had to be a reason for that sour taste."

Despite the poor quality of the ale, they were well into their cups by the time they decided, yawning, that bed was the best plan for the rest of the night. Dawson climbed into his upper bunk and Jack into his lower, and both were soon snoring.

Jack's dreams were not of cards, nor dice, nor brandy. He dreamed he was whirling around an endless ballroom, with Maryel in his arms. He smiled in his sleep.

The next morning, far too early for the state of Jack's head, he and his fellow officers were rousted out of bed and called to a special meeting with the Fort Major. They dressed hastily, checking each other's uniforms to make sure all was correct. If it was a surprise inspection, no man wanted to have a button or collar point out of place. About twenty of the officers of the 100th gathered in their mess to await orders.

To their great surprise, General Brock himself came to address them. He took up an easy stance in front of the group. Jack was impressed by his height and air of authority. Here was someone worth following.

"At ease, men. This is no inspection. Although you've turned yourselves out well. I like that. I need three volunteers to assemble a squad for remote detachment."

A hubbub arose at this announcement. Finally, something to do besides drill.

Brock signaled for silence. "Given the quarrels between the western Indian tribes and the American settlers, we need better communications links to Fort St. Joseph. Fort Amherstburg will be the pivot point. Three officers will form a message transfer rota, giving me rapid intelligence. You'll have one soldier-servant each, and since the garrison there has been pestering me, I've assigned them a new cook."

"How will this unit relate to the remote forts?" asked Jack, his headache forgotten.

"You'll report to their commanders in the normal way," said Brock, "but they're aware of your mission and will not assign duties to conflict with it. Whichever of you is on duty at Fort Amherstburg will be in charge of local scouting parties. All reports are addressed to my attention. Anything marked 'urgent' will be brought to me at once."

"How would you define urgent, sir?" asked Dawson.

"Unusual activity on the American side. An increase in messengers or supplies coming to their encampments. Or word from our Indian friends of troop movements in their interior where we cannot observe them." He looked intently at each member of the group. "I have good reason to trust the tribes of the Grand River and the western territories. If any of you feel unable to work with them, you may be dismissed." He waited a moment, but none of the officers stirred. "Good. We must be prepared to make use of all the resources at our disposal." He straightened to his full height. "Now, which of you is interested in this assignment?"

Every officer present volunteered. Brock barked a laugh. "Garrison duty palls on you? I've been there myself. I expected this outcome so I will accept you all on rotation. The first three will depart tomorrow, for a posting of three months." He consulted his list of names. "Ensigns Stevenson, Dawson, Rea."

"Sir, a request," said Jack. "We have friends in the town. May we take our leave of them?"

"Since your duties for this evening consist of packing, I see no reason to deny you leave to visit your friends. Granted. But," he raised a hand in warning, "be careful to tell them only that you are going on detachment. There are many of dubious loyalties in the town, and I see no reason to alert potential or real enemies to our intentions."

Jack and Dawson were happy to be in the first rotation. Rea grumbled a little but came around in the end, when they pointed out to him that their duties at this stage would be light, and it would be better to be on detachment in late summer and fall than during the winter.

"Have you talked to any of the men who've been up at Fort St. Joseph? When we exchanged with the 41st, they told horror stories about snow higher than the palisade, and weeks on end where they had to hole up indoors. And the cold! I saw what frostbite looks like—one poor fellow lost two fingers to it. A thousand times worse than chilblains, I assure you. No, we're better off going now." Jack was firm on that point. He'd rather be in Niagara over the winter and see Maryel more often. In summer, her family spent most of their time out at Lake Lodge, at the Four-Mile Creek, and he couldn't often get leave to visit there.

October–November

Rebecca

I jerked upright in bed. That noise—metal on stone or wood? Nothing to see in the light from the harvest moon. Tom was here overnight, bedded down in the barn to watch over a sick ewe. Might he be unable to sleep in the barn and be wandering around? Or was it some wild animal? Surely I had closed all the doors and downstairs windows?

Another scraping sound, then a thump, coming from downstairs. Drawers pulled open and slammed shut. In all my forty-two years, whether in England or Upper Canada, I'd never heard of an animal that would open and close drawers. This must be a two-legged animal, and it couldn't be Tom. He could find his way around the house blindfolded. I shuddered.

More soldiers had been posted to Fort George, and strangers passing through the town were viewed askance. Either soldier or stranger could be in the house right now. If their intent was rape, I vowed I wouldn't let them. But I mustn't let my imagination run wild.

I was alone in the house, for once. The town was four miles away; our closest neighbor a mile off. Cousin Robert and his daughters were spending a few days in town, where Eliza and Maryel were readying the leased house for our winter occupation. Drusilla had been visiting, but returned home that morning. Tom was out of earshot and probably asleep. I had only myself to rely on. But perhaps the intruder might believe the house was empty.

Scrape. Scra-ape. Thump. Clatter. Squee-eak. That must be my medicine cabinet.

Heavy footsteps moved toward the stairwell.

I reached for the candlestick. Something, anything, to defend myself.

The footsteps sounded hesitant, dragging. The third step creaked when trodden upon.

I swung my feet over the side of the bed, shivering as they hit the icy floorboards. I pulled a shawl over my nightgown. No time for slippers.

Slowly, excruciatingly slowly, my bedroom door opened. The hinges creaked in protest. I must oil them tomorrow, if tomorrow came.

A shaggy-haired man loomed in my doorway, a pistol in his left hand and a musket slung over his left shoulder. I clutched my shawl tighter. The man grimaced as he entered my room. Only then did I see a dark patch on his right sleeve. It didn't look like water.

"Oh. You— You're injured." My voice quavered. I must hold on to my nerve.

"Aye, that's so." He barked what I took for a laugh. "Smart woman."

"What do you want?"

"How about you tend to my arm?

"What makes you think I can help you?"

He laughed again. The sound made my flesh crawl.

"Can't you? Fair enough." The hand holding the pistol dropped. He staggered across the room and collapsed into a ladder-back armchair by the fireplace. "Only I'd heard there was a healer-woman hereabouts, name of Plummer. 'Zat you? Maybe you got some water?"

At the banked fire, I pulled a straw from a jar and held it to the coals. Once I raised a tongue of flame, I used it to light the candle, hands shaking. The flickering flame showed the intruder's face more clearly.

He looked young: dark brown hair with no hint of gray. American, by his accent. But his face was pale, cheeks drawn in. Poor boy!

I must focus on his wound. I poured water from the jug on the wash-stand into a tumbler and held it to his lips.

He drank a little, then pushed it away. He tried to rise when I picked up the musket, then sank back as I propped it against the wall.

"I'm Miss Plummer. Gunshot wound?"

"Yes."

No need to rush. He wasn't going anywhere. Keep him talking. "Where were you hit?"

"My arm. High up."

"Can you move it?" He shook his head. "I'll have to cut your sleeve off, then. My shears are downstairs."

He grabbed my arm with his good hand as I turned to go, digging deep into the muscle. I winced. "No, stay right here. Take the knife from my belt. Slit the stitching with that."

I pressed my lips together. A slim chance to escape, gone, but replaced by another? I pulled the knife from its sheath, hefting it in my hand. The blade caught the candlelight and I blinked at the sudden flash. Could I possibly…? But no, I could not.

My patient coughed. "You'll not kill me, missus. Too tender-hearted you'll be. Or too soft-headed."

I tossed my head, throwing my nightcap askew. "I'm a healer, not a killer." I bent to my task, picking at the stitches. The bleeding appeared to have stopped, or at least slowed. Finally, the sleeve fell away from the shoulder of his coat, revealing the wound. A ball had penetrated his upper arm, near the shoulder, but as far as I could tell, had missed the bone. The wound's edges were ragged and ugly. Removing the sleeve caused it to ooze slightly, but I could see the bullet had passed through the muscle. At least I wouldn't have to dig out a ball but simply clean it and bind it up. After that, the outcome would be up to his constitution and his fortune. If he needed prayers to support him, he could provide those himself.

I bathed the wound with the remaining water and bound it with cloth torn from the huck toweling I kept on the washstand. It would hold firm and absorb whatever bleeding persisted. He had lost a great deal of blood already. He might yet die from that, or from infection if the wound turned putrid. I tied off the bandage and used his musket strap as a makeshift sling.

"You'll need to keep it raised or the bleeding will start again." I sat back on the bed, gazing at my patient. He was still drawn, but appeared more comfortable now. "You owe me your name, at least."

"My name's Sam. You don't need more." He gave me a gap-toothed grin. The grin faded, his chin dropped toward his chest, and his eyelids drooped.

Slowly, I stood, and inched toward the door. Just when I thought I might escape, his eyes opened again. I jerked backwards. He reached down with his good arm and drew the pistol from his belt.

"No need to worry, missus. I'll sit here, quiet-like, and rest a bit. But I'll be watching so's you don't get out and raise the alarm." He coughed and spat. "Don't you go thinking I won't shoot you. 'Cause I will, sure as death."

If I were any judge of the amount of blood he'd lost, he was going to need more water soon, or weaken and grow faint again. Best to string him along and wait for another chance to move. "Well, Sam, who shot you?"

Sam gazed over my left shoulder, eyes unfocused. He adjusted his arm, grimacing.

"I can get you something to ease the pain, but I need to get to my medicine cabinet."

"No, I'll manage." He hesitated. "Not rightly sure what to say. I suppose you can tell I'm not from these parts."

I nodded. "You're American, aren't you?"

"Yes, missus, that I am. Born and bred. Never figured on making it this far from home, and that's a fact. But when duty calls…"

"I see. So… you're a spy."

"Clever, ain't you? I suppose it's no big surprise, what with all the unfriendly goings-on between our countries, is it?"

"No. If all the gossip was true, there would be a spy behind every bush. I never thought I'd find one in my bedroom, though."

That drew a weak grunt. "Don't suppose you did, now. And I'm not a proper spy anyhow."

"What are you then, Sam?"

He spun an unlikely tale of being a surveyor sent to scout landing places around Lake Ontario and the Niagara River. Would he need to skulk around the shore at night to do it? Surely he could find out more by day, raising less suspicion. What did ring true was his description of a well-concealed landing place nearby, where he had an altercation with a band of armed men. I knew the spot he meant: the creek mouth. The lagoon behind the headland where two creeks joined would be ideal for smuggling or other illicit activity.

Sam's words came fainter now. "Not sure if it was smugglers or soldiers. Sure was a gang of angry men. Lucky to come away with a single shot to my arm. Don't know how I made it this…" His voice trailed off and his head slumped to one side. The pistol dropped from his fingers; the thud of it hitting the floor failed to rouse him.

I waited a moment to be sure he was unconscious, then picked up both pistol and musket. He didn't stir. Now what? I'd have to hide the guns quickly, somewhere out of reach. Even a weakened man would be hard for me to handle alone. The barn! I would rouse Tom. The moon was sinking now, nearly below the trees; dawn couldn't be far off.

The yard between house and barn was beaten down by traffic, but littered with corn husks. As I ran barefoot with my awkward burden, one foot skidded on the husks and the other caught the fringe of my shawl. I sprawled, momentarily stunned, midway to the barn, crying out as my ankle twisted. Then I cried out, "Tom! Tom! Help!"

Pain shot through my foot, hampering my other senses. When it dulled a little, I could hear rustling in the barn. I shivered in the damp autumn air, thankful I lay on relatively dry packed earth. It smelled of horses and corn husks and fallen leaves, familiar things I would usually have found comforting. But now they only emphasized the danger I was in—immobile and helpless.

I could hear but not see clearly. A few more minutes of waiting stretched painfully, and my heart beat in time to the throbbing of my ankle, rapid and insistent.

Someone knelt beside me. Thank God, it was Tom. I sat up, pulling the shawl around me. "I've twisted my ankle."

"Can you walk?"

"I'll try, if you help me stand. Listen. I've got an intruder in the house. A wounded man. I need you to check on him."

Tom stared, jaw agape.

"You won't believe the night I've had."

"Stay here. I won't be but a moment."

"No, wait. Did you see any others? Sam… the intruder… he said he was attacked by a gang of men."

"I didn't, no. But I don't want to chance it. I'll be right back."

My worry grew as the minutes passed. Had something gone wrong? What if I had sent Tom into an ambush? In the pre-dawn gloom, I still couldn't see well, and my breath quickened at the renewed sound of footsteps.

It was Tom, returning. "All quiet. I didn't see or hear others. They must have run off. Let's get you into the house."

He put an arm around me for support as I rose on my good foot. I tested the other and found that as long as I leaned on him, I could limp without too much pain. I hadn't noticed before that he was taller than me. He had changed so from the scruffy orphan I had adopted. I felt old beside him.

Tom settled me at the kitchen table, my injured foot propped on a chair, medicine chest in reach.

"You go upstairs. Check on Sam while I bandage my ankle."

Tom took the stairs two at a time as was his habit, but came rushing down faster. "He's gone!"

"What?"

"There's nobody there. I mean, I can see there was, from the muddy footprints and the bloody rags on the floor, but your intruder has gone."

"He was unconscious when I left him. And he'd lost a lot of blood… I have a bad feeling about this. Can you help me out to the back? My foot should bear me enough for that."

We went through the house and out toward the lake. Cautiously, in the pre-dawn glow, we approached the bank, about fifteen feet above the lake at this point. A motionless form slumped at its edge.

"Is he dead?"

I felt under Sam's chin for a pulse. "Not yet." I knelt beside him in the dewy grass. "Get me some water, quickly!"

Sam's eyes opened. He groaned. I felt his forehead. Cold. Too cold.

He tried to speak, but only managed a whisper. "Didn't want to hang."

"You'll not hang, Sam, but you'll not live either."

He lay still, breath rattling. "Thought you'd gone for soldiers."

"Do you have family? Someone I can contact for you?"

His voice came so softly I had to bend close to hear. "Mother. Bertha Jenkins. Albany."

Tom arrived with the water, too late to do Sam any good.

"Not much older than you, was he?" I said.

"Guess not. What do we do now?"

That could so easily have been Tom… or me. Tom joggled my elbow. "Oh… best ask at the next farm to borrow their wagon. Then you can take him into town." My knees buckled under me as the tension from the long night released. I sank to the ground. Tom hovered over me. Tom, who had just enlisted to spy for the Army. Might he meet the same fate as Sam?

"Will you be all right?"

"No. But go anyway." I sat, gazing out at the lake. Its surface was calm in the early morning, barely a ripple showing. My pulse continued rapid, and I shivered even as the day warmed.

Would I ever feel safe again?

Early in November, we removed back to town, to the house Cousin Robert used to own, but now hired for the winter months only. I wished it could have been sooner. I remained unsettled by my encounter with the American agent. I felt insecure everywhere now.

We would only visit the farm when in need of supplies, perhaps once or twice a month. I thought to resume more regular contact with Josiah, but found him laid low by a variety of ailments, suffering from sick headaches and bouts of the grippe. Unsurprising in our harsh climate, but frustrating to me. I could not presume to nurse him, a single man, so was obliged to wait for his recovery.

I observed for myself the obsequious attentions paid by Mrs.

Herbert to Cousin Robert. Really, the woman made herself ridiculous, fawning over him like that. He seemed oblivious, though she was exceedingly persistent.

In the meantime, Ensign Stevenson being away on detachment from the garrison, I had my hands full with Maryel. She showed a distressing tendency to flirt with other officers, and even with Tom.

"You mustn't tease him, my dear," I said. "He knows you only do it because Jack is away."

She pouted. "Why should I not dance with respectable men at assemblies? Including Tom. Why, I've known him forever."

"You know he cares for you, and he knows you don't return his feelings. It's plain cruel."

She flounced her skirts. "I shall enjoy whatever company I find myself in at public assemblies. I won't let anyone assume my affections are engaged by them, or take liberties, either."

With that, I had to be content. There was no surer way to make her flout convention than to protest too much. But I watched her behavior with uneasiness.

✳

Drusilla spent many hours with me in the stillroom. She wanted to further her knowledge of remedies for women's ailments, and not merely those to prevent or end conception. I found it easier to reconcile my conscience when guiding her in preparing less-extreme mixtures for lesser complaints.

"So, for a woman breast-feeding a child, who may develop cracked and aching nipples, I find it best to use goose fat, rendered down to remove impurities," I told her. "It keeps well in a stone crock, in a cool place, and can be used as a base for many salves."

"Do you not add herbs?"

"Not in that case, for they might be transmitted to the babe."

"And what is best for belly cramps?" she asked.

"Culpeper suggests bayberry, but I prefer a mixture of St. John's wort and raspberry leaves, in equal proportions, infused into a strong tea." I opened the jar containing the yellow flowering tops of St. John's wort and reached for the box that held dried raspberry leaf. "I find it best to crush these together just before making the infusion."

"Isn't it bitter?"

"You can add peppermint leaves to ease the flavor, and a little honey, too."

"We grow both mint and raspberries in the garden."

"Sometimes raspberry leaf will suffice if the cramps aren't too severe. And they make a good digestive tonic, too. But…"

"But what?" she asked.

"All the herbs efficacious in lesser ills of the womb may also be used in the stronger preparations. I have already told you of yarrow and angelica, and rue. And pennyroyal, which I advise you to avoid altogether. An excess of raspberry leaf tea may also bring on a miscarriage." I weighed my next words carefully. "So, it's wise to determine whether a woman may be increasing, or wish to have a child, before advising on which herbs to offer, and in what strength."

"You're cautioning me that all remedies carry a risk."

I nodded emphatically. "Exactly. No remedy is certain, and all may be chancy, depending on the patient. I find it best to start with small amounts and gauge the response of each person. Unless it's an extreme case where I might save a life. Such as the administration of an emetic to a child who has swallowed poison berries."

"Or a case where a woman should not bear another child."

Must she continually harp on this? Did she not recognize the hazard of being overheard? "I may do, after due consideration. But the need must be extreme, and I must be certain of her discretion."

"I wonder you can remember all the different plants, how to

gather and store them, and their medicinal properties."

"After so many years handling them, I suppose it's ingrained in me. But you flatter my knowledge." I reached up and hauled Culpeper's *Herbal* off its shelf. "I still need to check to make sure of myself. It wouldn't do to accidentally poison a neighbor."

DECEMBER

Tom

"Have you been avoiding us?" Maryel asked Tom as he twirled her in a waltz. "I haven't seen you at church for weeks, or about town either."

"Not at all," said Tom. "My duties for both Printer Jones and Mr. Willcocks have been more arduous of late. I think Jones may be feeling his age, and looking toward retirement."

"Has he spoken about it?"

"Not yet, but it's a possibility. He's having me do a lot more. And putting out each edition of the *Guardian* takes more time than I thought it would." He executed a complex turn. "I have to seek advertisers to help cover the cost of materials and circulation, as well as setting and printing the sheet. We could use an apprentice."

"Really? Would Mr. Jones consider hiring a woman?"

Tom stared at her. "Why on earth would he do that?"

Maryel pouted. "I just thought... handling type isn't heavy labor. I saw that when I helped you with the page last summer."

The music ended and they walked to the side of the room, making way for couples setting up in lines for a country dance.

Maryel continued. "I don't know if I could operate the press."

"I very much doubt it. It takes a grown man's strength to turn the screw."

"But everything else—sorting, setting and cleaning type, preparing ink—there are many tasks within a woman's scope."

Tom shrugged. "While there are plenty of young men looking for a trade, why would Jones look at a woman? More specifically, why would he look at you? Because that's what you mean, isn't it?"

"And why not?"

"You've had this bee in your bonnet for ages now. I'm tired of hearing about it. Printing is a man's job, like all the others you've talked about. Nothing is going to change that."

People were looking their way. "There's no good reason, is there," she said in a lower tone. "It's just the way men have set up the world for themselves."

"Women have their own sphere. You should stay there."

"Humph!"

He stared after her as she flounced away to join a group of young women. All of their cheeks were flushed, no doubt from the exertion of dancing. Except for Maryel's, which he knew reflected her anger. He had put his foot in it, for sure. But what rational man would encourage such outrageous notions? Not him.

Rebecca

With Josiah having continued in poor health for some weeks, my first proper opportunity to meet with him came on Christmas Day, after the church services. Cousin Robert desired there to be a grand feast for his congregation and engaged the upper rooms in the Masonic Hall for the purpose.

We ladies of the church prepared furiously for the event. The tables groaned with roasts, game pies, preserves of all sorts, breads, cakes, and confections hardly seen in these parts. Wine, beer and cider flowed freely and the congregation mingled and made merry.

Once sated, I took a seat along one wall, and soon Josiah came to join me.

"I trust you're feeling better now," I said.

"Much, thank you," he said. "I fear I may have to alter my coat, however." He held up one arm where the sleeve hung loosely from his wrist. "I appear to have shrunk."

I smiled at this gentle humor. "The grippe can do that to you."

"It has kept me from your side and delayed a conversation I desired." He paused, and my throat constricted. "Miss Plummer…

Rebecca… may I have your permission to pay my addresses to you formally?"

I had been anticipating, even hoping, for such a question. "You may."

His smile became a grin, and his eyes shone. "That's the best Christmas gift I could receive."

"And I."

He took my gloved hand and kissed it. In front of the entire congregation. Heat flooded my breast and face. However, the only glances I saw were congratulatory ones. If any disapproved, they concealed it. I was encouraged our courtship might flow smoothly. The one fly in the ointment was Cousin Robert's lack of enthusiasm. And yet, he had made no overtures himself. Surely he couldn't consider Josiah a rival? Though I had to admit Cousin Robert was not without admirers of his own. That Mrs. Herbert, for instance. I had met her a few times after church. Overdressed for our community, I thought, and such ugly moles. But then I felt sorry for my unchristian thoughts, so unsuitable for this season. She might have a good heart.

I was less sanguine about Maryel and her swains. Jack Stevenson had returned shortly before Christmas and I was near the door when he arrived at the feast.

"It's good to see you back in town, Ensign," I said warmly.

"Why, thank you, ma'am. We were lucky to return from our posting before there was too much ice in the river. I don't envy the next men their posting." He looked around. "Is Miss Maryel here?"

"Yes. With such a crowd, I'm not surprised you can't pick her out at once."

"I could pick her out of any crowd." He flushed. Such a handsome boy.

"Yes, well… she's with the group by the fireplace."

He bowed and headed toward her. Perhaps he wasn't a paragon

of all the virtues, showing the casual intemperance of youth, but Maryel was fond of him and it wouldn't hurt to give them some encouragement. While I sympathized with her views on marriage, it was the most practical life for a young woman. Even for an older woman, I thought, looking down at and rubbing the back of my glove where Josiah had placed his lips.

When I raised my head, it was to find myself under scrutiny from Cousin Robert. There was no other word for it. He caught my eyes for a moment, then turned away.

1811

"Virtue can only flourish among equals."—Mary Wollstonecraft

"Friendship is a serious affection; the most sublime of all
affections, because it is founded on principle and
cemented by time."—Mary Wollstonecraft

January–February

Rebecca

The round of entertainments continued in the new year. When I could attend, I enjoyed Josiah's attentions. He was an excellent dancer. I did my best not to tread on his feet. It felt good to be on the dance floor. I had spent far too long on the sidelines.

"You are animated this evening, my dear," he said.

"I love to dance," I said. "It's so exhilarating."

He laughed. "Your candor is becoming. I believe you always speak your mind."

"Indeed, I do. What, should I speak someone else's words and try to pass them off as my own?"

"No, indeed." His eyes twinkled. "I hope you never do."

Both of us in high good humor, we turned our attention to the steps of the country dance, weaving in and out of the ladies' and gentlemen's lines as directed by the caller. There was little opportunity for further conversation in this set. My mood was light and I desired no weighty discussions. I was perfectly happy to enjoy some frivolity.

Josiah was an attentive suitor. He bestowed small gifts of candied fruit, sugared nuts, and potpourri (blended by his own hands) upon me.

I was quite smitten. A small inner voice whispered that I must not grow too accustomed to such trifles, but I shushed it and enjoyed the moment.

∗

Toward the end of the month, Cousin Robert was laid low again with his common winter complaint, aggravated no doubt by a trip to visit the Indians. He fretted for months about the state of the roads preventing him from visiting them in the autumn. I tried to dissuade him, but he was adamant. Now, his coughing echoed through the house.

I searched through my supplies for a tincture or tisane that might calm it. So far it resisted treatment with horehound or slippery elm, and my supply of laudanum was depleted. I would need to visit Josiah's shop to get more. Meanwhile, I sent Eliza and Maryel off to a party with Mrs. Dickson, while I stayed at home to nurse their father.

Seated on the chair beside his bed where he lay propped on a stack of pillows, I applied a hot compress to his chest.

"You are far too good to me, Cousin," he said between coughing spells.

"Nonsense," I said. "you've given me a home and a purpose in life. I cannot repay you."

"Now it is you who is nonsensical. There must be no talk of debts between us."

"As you wish." I felt his forehead. Still too hot for my liking. I moistened a cloth with cool water and applied it. He seemed to get some relief.

"Cousin… Rebecca…" He sat forward and stuttered a few syllables, then fell to coughing again.

"Shh, now, don't try to talk. It can wait until you are recovered."

He tried to speak again, then fell back on the pillows and closed his eyes. I sat by him until the cough eased enough for him to fall into a doze.

Jack

Lieutenant Sam Hingston sat mulling over his records in the officers' mess when Jack found him. He motioned Jack to sit.

"I find it easier to reconcile them here than in my quarters with the children underfoot."

"I can help, if you wish," said Jack.

"I would be obliged if you would," said Hingston. "I could use a few quiet hours to myself." He showed Jack the borrowed registers from St. Mark's. "I wanted to finish the transcription this afternoon. Promised Reverend Addison I would return them as soon as possible. The poor man acted as if I was kidnapping a child when I asked to borrow them. If you could take them over…"

"I'd be happy to," said Jack.

Hingston chuckled. "I thought you might."

Jack flushed. It was no secret, and the subject of rude gibes, how much he fancied Maryel.

After Hingston left, Jack glanced over the register.

Four weddings, numerous births, and only six deaths. He transcribed the former categories, then paused for a moment over the deaths. One of those six had been Hingston's infant daughter. No wonder he'd been eager to delegate the task, and taken it away from his own fireside. It would have been cruel to have that document lying around for his wife to see.

He shook his head. They were concerned primarily with deaths in the Regiment. It meant ruling out the Wrath infant as well. He would simply annotate their birth records. So, only four losses to the line. He carefully transcribed them into the Regimental register.

> In 1809. Oct. 5. Thomas Arangey. Sergt.
>
> In 1810. Feb. 7. James Walsh. 100th Regt
>
> Aug 31. The Master Tailor of 100th Regt. (killed by lightning)
>
> Mar. 11 Capt. J. Andrews. late Fort Amherstburg garrison

Damn, what was the Tailor's name again? He shouldn't forget something like that. Why on earth would Reverend Addison have given the cause of death and then not put the man's name down? He'd have to check with the Sergeant-Major—he kept track of all the lower ranks. On further consideration, the man might actually have been named Taylor, but the record must be accurate. And then there was poor Captain Andrews. Such a sad case, leaving a wife and three children nearly destitute, with squabbling in the mess over who would purchase his captaincy. Jack knew it wouldn't be him, even if he were eligible. He was stony broke, as always. Too much carousing and gambling, he supposed. But damn-it-all, a fellow couldn't live like a monk.

Hingston had left a few other documents on his desk. Jack couldn't resist having a squint at them. One was the list of detachments, including the new one at the Forty-Mile Creek, toward Burlington Bay, at the head of Lake Ontario. If they needed to fall back from the border in a hurry, that one would be in the right direction. All purely hypothetical, before war began.

Jack was also happy to see his own report from his stint on the far western detachment duly annotated. That belied the common belief among junior officers that their reports were mostly ignored. In fact, he felt downright welcome on his return. His fellows urged him to bring out his fiddle and flute. He had countered that his fingers would need to thaw properly, but was glad to have been missed. He'd had only his voice to make music with while on detachment.

At the bottom of the pile was a report marked "urgent," giving observations of Indian scouts that told of parties of two or three militia-men arriving every few days. It looked as if the Americans were fortifying Fort Detroit for an attack on the least populous part of the Province. No doubt the General had already been apprised. Hingston would have seen to it.

Army life was full of dichotomies. On the one hand, boredom, and on the other, battle. Jack was all too familiar with the first, but the latter was still on his horizon. How would he respond under fire? But he mustn't fret unduly. How could he possibly know what it would be like until it happened?

Rebecca

I trailed a little behind the girls as we walked home from church one winter Sunday. Their voices carried back clearly over the crusted snow.

"Did you see? Lester Vansickle is in the stocks again," said Eliza.

"Brrr… a terrible day to be out there. He must be freezing," said Maryel, tucking her hands more securely in her muff. "What do you think it is this time?"

"I suppose it's either drunkenness or failure to pay his debts. Maybe both? Why do so many men drink to excess or gamble away their money?"

"I have no idea. Father says some men are born to vice, but poor Lester is such a meek man. It's hard to think of him as vicious in any sense. Even if Father only meant it as a kind of flaw in his character." She twisted her curls and looked sidelong at Eliza. "Sister…"

Eliza turned her head. "What?"

"Cousin Rebecca says not all drinking leads to drunkenness. So, drunkenness is the vice, not the drinking itself."

"Yes, and…?"

"Well… I was wondering about gambling. Whether the same thing applies."

"Any particular reason? You don't wish to take up playing cards or dice for money, do you?" Her voice carried a teasing note.

"Silly! As if I would. How boring. And if I wanted to, I have no money to speak of. No… it's just… Ensign… Jack Stevenson, that is… he told me the other evening, at the Dickson's party…" She lowered her voice till I could scarce hear her. "Eliza! This is in the greatest confidence."

Eliza nodded. I kept my distance, but strained to hear.

"He said his father had stopped sending him an allowance and he was without funds—'stony broke' he called it—until the Army's back-pay came in. He says it never comes on time. But when I asked him what he spent it all on, he said, 'Oh, tobacco, whiskey and dice,' as if it was no great issue."

Eliza shook her head, clicking her teeth in disapproval. "That's no great recommendation of character, is it?"

I agreed, although he was surely too young to be deeply steeped in vice.

"But then he said, 'Ah, Miss Maryel, those are all things I could give up, if only…' And then I strongly suspect he was going to profess his feelings, but we were interrupted by someone else asking me to dance, and he left the party before we spoke again."

"I confess, I cannot like the idea of overindulgence in any of those things. At least he was frank about his faults. That's uncommon among men."

"You have had more experience than I, sister."

"Maybe, but it hasn't done me much good, has it?" She looked back toward the stocks. "Would the magistrate object if we took poor Lester a blanket? Whatever he's done, he doesn't deserve to freeze to death."

I judged this a good time to catch up with them and endorsed their plan to relieve the miscreant of some of his misery.

✳

Maryel attended as many of the winter's entertainments as she could, with my blessing. Cousin Robert was indulgent, too, and did not object to her taste for frivolity. I was pleased to see Eliza was also keen to attend, especially when there was conversation to be had, as well as dancing. We were treated to performances by visiting elocutionists, a troupe of traveling players, and regular musical evenings.

Musical evenings always included dancing, in which every able person took part. Only the aged or infirm sat on the sidelines. There were enough officers added to the townsfolk to ensure no young lady wanted for a partner. While I danced mostly with Josiah, I kept an eye on Maryel and Eliza to see they did not bestow their favor too often on any partner. The rules were not as rigid as I had heard they were in high society, but it was considered best for a young lady to dance with a variety of partners unless an engagement had been announced.

Maryel often danced with Jack, but she chose other partners over half the time, so there was no point in spoiling her pleasure with criticism. With Jack's return, she had ceased her pursuit of Tom, who appeared resigned to relinquish hope of her favors. Eliza had plenty of partners, too. She divided her attentions among some of the older men, leaving the callow youths to Maryel. I was more than a little disturbed to see her frequently in Joseph Willcocks's company, both in the dances and the conversation around the refreshment table.

"Have a care, my dear," I said one evening, when we sought refreshment at the same time. "You know how your father feels about Mr. Willcocks."

Eliza scoffed at my concern. "I enjoy his society, that's all. You shouldn't fuss so much, Cousin."

I wasn't so sure. Willcocks attracted a crowd everywhere and liked to declaim his radical opinions at large. She hung on his every word when she was part of the group, and had taken to repeating some of the more inflammatory gems at the dinner table. On several occasions, I had to direct the conversation away from a potential conflict.

Cousin Robert was unusually forbearing, but finally approached me. "I need you to have a word with Eliza. As soon as possible. I do not wish to myself, although if it comes to it, I will."

"About Willcocks, I assume."

"Yes." He hesitated. "The situation is grave, or I would not interfere. There is an uproar over his newspaper articles, and renewed accusations of libel from the Lieutenant-Governor's office."

"After last year, I wonder he takes the risk."

"Perhaps he won't be imprisoned this time, but it's impossible to tell whether he can moderate his speeches in the Legislature. I fear he will link me again with his seditious views."

"Why is he so resentful and rebellious? He has done well for himself here."

Cousin Robert shook his head. "I cannot understand it myself. Unless it's simply part of the Irish temperament. But Irish or not, he persists in criticism of the government. That must eventually bring him to ruin."

"I will need to tread lightly," I said. "The mood Eliza is in, criticism of Willcocks could drive her closer to him. She's inexperienced in matters of the heart."

"I hope she is not so insensible of the situation as that." He rubbed his creased forehead. "I don't wish to have to send her away."

"Our best hope is she will find another interest."

After Willcocks left town for the Parliamentary season, Eliza had a brief flirtation with an artist who had traveled to see the marvel of the great Falls some miles upriver from Niagara town. He divided his time between sketching the frozen landscape and warming himself in the heat of her regard. He was an amiable man of five-and-thirty, with a ready smile and a flattering tongue. His brush strokes were sure and, she confided to me, his compliments smooth. He read her love poetry, quite turning her head.

I was happy to see her enjoying herself, apparently unmoved by Willcocks's absence. So many of the young men ran after Maryel, overlooking Eliza. She basked in the artist's admiration… for a while.

Her pleasure was soured somewhat when she came upon him reading a letter from his wife back in England, but, as she said, it was pleasant to dally and flirt, and no permanent harm done. If she wept a little in their chamber for a few nights, nobody except Maryel was the wiser. Her face was a little paler for a few days, but she looked fully recovered after that. I hoped this experience gave her more insight into the danger posed by Willcocks.

Willcocks

Willcocks was gravely concerned about his reception in the Legislature.

After the first day back, he turned to his journal, his constant companion and confidant, to summarize his impressions.

1 Feb

Resumed seat in Legislature. thanks to my constituents. Still under a cloud here. Members have long memories. Allegations of libel and last year's imprisonment not forgotten. Gore and cronies in a swivet over Jackson pamphlet and Guardian articles. They confuse sedition with legitimate dissent. No chance of rational discourse there. Will continue to publish articles in the Guardian. but trim sails on action in the Assembly. With Thorpe gone. our colleagues look to me for leadership. Agreed we must press for Common Schooling for the population. Sense Addison tends to agree but won't take a stand. blast him. Impatient for results. Thorpe's parting advice—more might be gained through moderation— hard to follow. but after last year's fiasco. treading lightly.

Damn, he'd snapped the nib on his quill. Too late to mend it now. He'd write more later.

*

"I'm surprised at you, Jos," said Benejah Mallory, member for Oxford and Middlesex. "I was sure you'd want to hear Jackson's pamphlet read out to the house." He snorted. "Or read it out yourself."

"If I'm going to be charged with libel, I'd sooner it be for my own words than his. Besides, it's more important for me to continue with our efforts on fiscal review and education. I don't mind suspending my words for the duration of the session."

"So, you'll vote against?"

"Yes. Don't think my opinions altered, Ben. I'll be blunt in the articles I print after Parliament retires."

18 Feb

Fiscal questions remain unanswered. review denied. Poor accounting of militia funds. including fines for non-reporting to annual muster. With funds gone missing and militia in shambles. Americans could walk in with little resistance. Does nobody care?

March–April

Willcocks

1 Mar

Sycophants continue to lick Gore's boots. Education bill quashed. Traditionalists fear an educated population. perhaps rightly for their interests. Nothing smacks so much of republicanism and revolutionary tendencies as universal education. So they say. Winter drags on. Sometimes wish I was back in Dublin. Situation there no better though. Still ruled by English patronage system.

Willcocks and Mallory attended a gathering of their fellow members towards the end of the session. Since Willcocks had moderated his approach to reform, he had attracted more of the fence-sitters to his cause, strengthening their numbers and opposing voices in the Legislature. How delightful it was to see Gore fuming impotently. Even if the reforms they so fervently desired took longer because of it.

15 Mar

House of Assembly prorogued. Uncertain season—ice breaking up. Not clear enough to permit cross-lake travel. Must brave long trip by partly frozen road back to Niagara. or wait here a few more weeks. Ambivalent. More political connections in York. but need to get next issue of Guardian in press. Drafting report on Parliamentary session. Could send to Strange by messenger. Will decide tomorrow.

In the end, he took his copy back home with him. A message from Tom about the state of the press, apparently on its last legs, made sending it futile.

24 Mar

Back in Niagara. Problems with press. Quandary whether to repair or purchase new. Guardian not making money. More profit in conveyancing—respectable fees available for assisting with land transfer. Enough to maintain my comfort and prop up the news sheet. For now. Warmer weather brings spring mud. Travel by road becoming harder.

Rebecca

One morning in late March, I attended the lying-in of a member of the Presbyterian congregation and was returning after a successful birth. I did not expect to see Josiah exiting Emily Wilson's cabin. I might not have noticed him but for the fact that he hesitated in the doorway and lifted his hand in farewell. I froze in place, shocked. Josiah walked on. He didn't see me where I stood near a clump of dogwood bushes. Thank God for that.

Even a small town like ours is home to unfortunate women who have no other resources but their persons, and insufficient skills to earn a living other than providing bodily comforts to men. Emily was one such, a woman of middle years who took in gentlemen's laundry and helped during the harvest. This meager income gained her the lease of a tiny cabin at the end of Johnson Street, near the creek. But a woman must eat, and clothe herself, and for those purposes, she entertained men who had the means to pay. It was a side of life I deplored, and I pitied her most sincerely. Despite Church teachings and society's strictures, I could not find it in me to condemn her. How close to such a fate was I, or any other single woman left to her own resources?

I am a mature woman and know the ways of men. What shocked me was less that Josiah visited a prostitute, but that I saw on the palm of his raised hand a telltale brown rash. Previously unremarked observations came together in my mind and forced an unwelcome conclusion. Surely all of his symptoms added up to but one thing: the secret disease, scourge of our time—syphilis. Pimples on the lips, headaches, weight loss, episodes of grippe—by themselves quite innocent, but taken together with a distinctive brown rash on the palm… There was no other cause I knew of. And no cure.

For once, I was glad to have complied with the proprieties. We never so much as kissed. I had wondered why he hadn't made more attempt at a physical relationship, but now… I was struck by a pang of grief for Josiah; he faced an ugly death.

And yet, even after seeing the evidence, I questioned my conclusions. Could I have been deceived by shadows? Or might his hand have been stained during the preparation of medicaments in his shop? For more than a week, I turned the problem over. I slept poorly and drooped over my daily tasks. I left the house only to attend church. Josiah was absent that Sunday, a small mercy, but a welcome one. However, I did pass Emily Wilson in the street, and was sorry to see signs of the affliction in her as well: sores on her lips, bloodshot eyes and brown spots on her gloveless palms.

What on earth could I do? Nothing without more conclusive evidence. I finally resolved to confront him with my suspicions.

On Monday, I attempted to meet him but there was a notice pinned to his shop door. He had business in York and would not be back for several days. I wrote a brief note and pushed it under the door.

Dear Mr. Burton,

I must meet with you at your earliest convenience, on a matter of some urgency.

Please convey a message to me as soon as you return.

Respectfully,
Miss R Plummer

If my suspicions were verified, I could not possibly marry this man. In fact, I must find a way to sever our association, and one that would not harm Reverend Addison's family. If there were to be any scandal, it must rest solely on me. I waited for Josiah's reply, sinking further into anxiety with each passing day.

Maryel complained of the extra work required of her due to my lethargy, finally reaching proportions that penetrated Cousin Robert's scholarly fog and he remonstrated with her.

"Don't be too cross with Maryel," I said. "I've not been myself lately."

"Are you ill, Cousin?" he asked.

"Not ill, merely fatigued. I'm sure it will pass."

But it did not pass. I grew more perturbed by the day until finally, my distraction from mundane concerns led to a near disaster.

We usually saw some days warm enough in March to send a man up on the roof with brushes to sweep the chimney. But by mid-April, snow and ice still covered the shingles, making the surface too slippery to attempt. I put it out of mind entirely.

I was preparing a salve for chilblains, savoring the odor of crushed wintergreen I used to counter the musky pungency of henbane, when Hannah shrieked from the winter kitchen.

I dropped the mortar and hastened to her side.

Black smoke issued from the chimney and burning cinders were scattered on the floor. A large one fell into the soup kettle, splashing her with boiling water and fat.

I ran outside to fetch snow to treat her burns and saw the same oily smoke billowing from above, with sparks scattering everywhere.

My first bucket of snow doused the kitchen fire, my second, I gave to Hannah for her face and hands, calling for Maryel to help.

"See to Hannah. I must get the chimney."

I didn't wait to see if she complied, but ran to the shed and dragged out the ladder, a shallow reed basket and a coil of rope. Ice or not, I must put out the fire I knew was raging inside the chimney, in the soot and tar built up over the long winter.

I scooped up more snow onto the basket and tied the rope to its handles, so they came together with—I hoped—enough snow inside for me to drag up to the roof.

Skirts were nothing but a nuisance at such times. I kilted them up around my knees and mounted the ladder, hauling the snow behind me. I lifted the basket and settled it, somewhat precariously, a little way above the eaves, and untied the rope.

A steep slope of icy shingles lay between me and the chimney. I needed another ladder, but there was none to be had.

I shivered, understanding I must risk a fall if the house was not to catch fire, either from within or from the rain of sparks from the chimney.

Maryel appeared below me. "How can I help?"

"Bring hot water," I said. "Or soup. Whatever there is. And some rags."

There were patches where the ice looked thinner. I would try to melt them enough to give me purchase on the shingles.

I saw Cousin Robert had joined her and called down to him. "I need more rope and another container."

"Should you not let me attend to it?" he asked.

"I'm already up here. I may as well continue."

He nodded his acceptance and fetched the items from the shed.

"Do be careful, Cousin," he said, lips pursed and brow wrinkled.

They attached the new rope to the end of mine that I lowered.

Cautiously, I raised the half-full bucket and bundle of rags. Soaking a rag in the hot liquid—it was the soup, deemed no longer fit for food—I thawed the ice in a path toward the chimney, creeping upwards as I went.

I dragged the basket of snow along, keeping it on the side away from the heat, hoping hard it wouldn't slip. The soup ran out when I was nearly at the top, close enough to haul myself onto the ridge. Once there, I dumped the snow down the chimney, and heard a great sizzle greet it. Was it sufficient?

Maryel darted inside and came back out immediately, grinning. "There's a lot of steam, but some snow made it down. I think the fire's out."

I thought so, too. The sparks and black smoke had stopped, with only a thin gray trickle remaining. I slumped over, heart still pounding, exhausted.

"Are you all right, Cousin?" His voice quavered slightly.

"Yes," I said, it being all I could manage. Going down wasn't going to be easy either, but after a few deep breaths, I inched my way down the slope, doing my best not to slide. After a few anxious moments, my feet found the ladder, held steady by my two supporters. Such a relief to land on solid ground. Maryel took one arm and Cousin Robert the other, and they helped me get back inside, my feet unsteady and stumbling.

"Thank God in His mercy for sparing you," said Cousin Robert.

No more was said then, but later in the day, he called me into his study and asked if he could assist me in any way. I could not let the opportunity pass.

"If I might speak with you…"

"Please do," he said. "What troubles you, Cousin? Is something amiss in the household? Or is it some spiritual matter?"

"It's more of a personal nature," I said. Such a delicate matter, and one not usually spoken of between women and men. "It concerns Mr. Burton. You know we have been courting."

"Yes, and I have been concerned about how we would manage without you." He made a show of cleaning his spectacles. "I feared we might lose you today, with your escapade on the roof."

"It appears unlikely you will need to do without me after all." I explained matters as baldly as I could, my face increasingly flushed. One does not discuss the pox every day. "You see the quandary I'm in? Although, to be fair, he has not yet requested my hand, but if he were to do so, I could not accept."

His chin rested on his chest, and his eyes were shut, though I could see them moving under the lids. Was he praying? I hoped not. Rational thought was the requirement in this case.

"Is there a possibility you could be mistaken?" he asked.

"Perhaps. I intend to verify my suspicions as best I can."

"I agree. You cannot marry a man with a loathsome disease."

"But... the possibility of scandal... I would be mortified if I caused further grief to you."

"You have never caused me grief, Cousin. Quite the opposite."

"But what shall I do?"

He did not reply at once, and I grew apprehensive. Then his eyes opened, and he sat forward in his chair. "I may have a solution, if you will entertain it."

"I will welcome any suggestion, for I have mulled it over endlessly and found none myself."

He took my hand. "Marry me instead."

I stared at him, stunned.

"You must know I have always admired you." He held my gaze until mine dropped.

Marry Cousin Robert... Reverend Addison? My jaw surely dropped a foot. Could he be serious?

"Don't answer until you have had time to think. Sleep on it, at least."

I nodded, not trusting myself to speak. Not only would I have to deliberate, I must make some attempt to resolve the issue on my own, rather than accepting his offer at once. His attempt at knight-errantry was heart-warming but I was accustomed to relying on my own judgment in most things. I would do so now.

Thoughts raced around my head the rest of the day and long into the night.

It was years since I had speculated on what kind of husband Cousin Robert might make. And that never seriously. Even had Cousin Mary not still lived, he seemed so distant, unapproachable, disinterested. So apart from reality, if I were honest with myself.

But he had plenty of virtues, as I knew from my long residence with his family. Gracious, it was now over twenty years! But for most of that, he had been a married man. I had briefly wondered if he might make overtures after Cousin Mary died, but he never showed the slightest inclination to do so. The possibility of marriage to him had completely receded from my thoughts. We were friendly with each other, but there had been no spark between us. I felt more his daughters' contemporary, most of the time. He was sixteen years my senior; I was about midway between him and Eliza. Disconcerting to look at the family from such a different angle.

What would they think? Their mother had been dead these two years, and they had not seen her for over ten years before that. Could we continue our family affairs as usual, or would there be new friction? On the whole, I was optimistic they would accept the change. But one never knew.

And what of the congregation? I suffered slurs as an unmarried woman keeping house for the rector, and resentment over church duties some felt me not entitled to perform. How would marriage to him affect my social standing, and how might it impact the family? Mrs. Herbert had been pursuing him assiduously. How would she react?

Most puzzling of all were my feelings about Cousin Robert, and his about me.

Tom & Jack

"Halloo!" came a voice at the door of the print shop.

Tom started, nearly dropping the row of type he was setting. "Jack Stevenson. What brings you here?"

Jack brushed some imaginary dust off his tunic. "Why, looking for your company, of course." He grinned. "And also, on an errand for the Fort Major. He has some proclamation or other he wants posted around the district, and also some blank invitations he can use for formal dinners." He handed Tom a folded sheet. "Here are the specifications."

Tom glanced at the list. "You know," he said, "I've just got hold of a portable press. It's the right size to do these invitation cards."

"Really?" asked Jack. "Can you actually carry around a press?"

Tom nodded. "If you only care to print such things as calling cards, invitations, letter bills, short notices. A lot of merchants and farmers want those. You'd be surprised how many requests we get."

He motioned Jack to come to the back of the shop.

"See?" He displayed the small contraption with some pride.

"Looks like a waffle iron to me," said Jack, examining the hinged device.

Tom laughed. "You know, it's not unlike one at that. But you can't eat the product, worse luck."

Jack picked it up with a grunt. "Doesn't feel portable to me. Weighs almost as much as a private soldier's pack."

"I wouldn't be carrying it myself. At least, I hope not for any distance. There's a special pack to carry it by horse. And one for toting it short distances on my back. I'll have to carry fonts, too."

Jack's eyebrows rose. "Are you planning long trips, then?"

"Not now, no, but Printer Jones isn't getting any younger. I have to look to my future." Tom sighed. "I can't take over his shop. Too rich for my purse. No, I'll have to take to the road to earn my living when that day comes."

They returned to discussing the terms of the order Tom promised to have ready the following Monday.

Their business concluded, and Tom's afternoon's work done, they repaired to McBride's for ale and conversation. With Tom having quit the field for Maryel, in Jack's favor, they had become good friends.

Rebecca

Nearly two weeks passed before I could confront Josiah, during which I avoided contact with Cousin Robert as much as I could. For his part, he did not press me for my decision.

I met Josiah after church and we walked through the graveyard surrounding St. Mark's. It was an unexceptionable activity, and we could talk privately.

Josiah forestalled my attempt to open the conversation by saying, "You are distressed. I can see. Perhaps I know the reason." He stripped the glove from his left hand and presented it to me, palm up. The brown rash—like a speckled bird's egg—was unmistakable. I raised my eyes to his, stricken to see the proof.

"How… how long?" I couldn't keep the emotion from my voice.

"I'm not sure. It could have been as long ago as Halifax, or England. The spots have only appeared recently. Until then, I had thought myself merely to have some recurring fever." His gaze dropped to the ground, and he tugged the glove back over his disfigured hand. "Since you recognize the symptoms, you may also know they can take years to appear, or disappear for a time before reappearing."

I nodded. "I saw many cases of the disease in England, but fewer here."

"You know there is no cure."

"Yes. Although some have tried mercury pills, have they not?"

"Indeed, but I know of no successes." We walked on a few paces in silence. "And so… you wish to discontinue our courtship."

He was making it easy for me. "Yes." That sounded too bald, so I searched for something more to say. "I regret the necessity…" That felt worse, but he cut me off.

"How do you wish to handle this? In a small community where everyone knows we were courting, it's hard for either of us to break things off without blame being cast on one or both of us."

This was a good time to break my news. "I've been made another offer. One that, if I accept it, would put our courtship out of people's minds."

He quirked an eyebrow.

"My cousin, Reverend Addison, has offered me marriage." Josiah exclaimed, but I pressed on. "He knows, Josiah. He knows. But he will say nothing."

"I see. Does he know what I know?"

"What do you think you know?" And how?

"One of your Plummer cousins was a tradesman in King's Lynn. He was indiscreet, in his cups. Told a story of a girl cousin disowned. He spoke of scandal."

"What if he did? So many years ago—a different country— untraceable to me."

"Even rumor has its effect."

"I don't believe you would be so cruel, Josiah. Nor stoop to blackmail to guarantee my silence. I believe you to be unfortunate, not malicious or irresponsible."

"Thank you for that, at least."

I had to say it, though it was hard. "You will do what you can to avoid further contagion?"

"I suppose you would feel obliged to inform against me, should I do otherwise?" He took a deep breath. "And what if I should then circulate what I know of your past?"

The blood rushed from my face. "You wouldn't!" We stared at each other for long moments.

Finally, he shook his head. "You needn't worry. I won't reveal your secret. Nor will I pass this scourge to others. Enough I must suffer it." His fists clenched. "I regret any I may have afflicted in the past."

Though it felt insufficient, there was nothing more for us to say. We continued to walk until we had circled the church a second time, then parted ways. Whether my state of mind showed on my face, I cared not.

One problem settled, with equal parts of pain and relief. I would put Josiah from my mind as best I could. If only he would continue to keep my secret, as well as his own.

The other problem… should I or shouldn't I? I was still undecided. One day, it seemed the ideal solution. The next, impossible. What would the consequences be if I refused Cousin Robert's offer? Would everything change, or nothing? How did I truly feel about him? I had contemplated giving up my independence, limited as it was, for Josiah. I had felt a physical attraction to him. Similar enough to what I had felt for Martin to rejuvenate my desires. What demands would Cousin Robert place on me, and could I welcome them? I knew him to be a kind man but was he still a virile one? Sharing a bed would be a novel experience after so many years alone.

But… a woman became her husband's chattel upon marriage. Could I reconcile that with my beliefs regarding women's rights? My stomach sank at the thought that our friendly relationship, the product of so many years living in the same house, might suffer if he exerted his authority. Could I rely on him to behave much as usual, or would marriage to me change him, too?

One moment, I reveled in thoughts of finally gaining my own family; the next, I descended into the abyss of despair. For every benefit I considered, there was a potential negative outcome. The longer I thought about it, the harder my head ached.

I lay awake for hours with my restless thoughts that Sunday. My carefully constructed world was turned upside down. My inner calm shattered. I wished I could speak to Sarah—or even Drusilla—but the one was an ocean away and the other at odds with me.

Toward dawn, I dozed fitfully and woke to a decision.

Robert, as I must call him now, positively glowed when I told him I would accept his offer. He took my hand in his and raised it to his lips, embarrassing me no end. I never suspected a romantic soul lay under his formal shell.

"It's now two years since your cousin, my wife, left this world." He paused. "In truth, she was dead to me for longer than that." He gripped my fingers tightly, and I winced. "Rebecca, you have been a friend to me these many years. More than a friend. I could not show it—my position here is so precarious—I feared to lose all."

"I never thought… I… Mrs. Herbert?"

He waved at me for silence. "She is merely a parishioner, and an irritating one. Your position here has been a delicate one. I know some of the women, including Mrs. Herbert, resent your standing in connection with the established Church and have hypocritically censured you as a single woman caring for a married man. You have remained so far above their niggling complaints. I am not so oblivious as to misconstrue their jealousy."

"Can they not censure you further if you marry me?"

"Nonsense. Who would hear them and not know their pettiness?"

Plenty of people, ones ill-disposed to him for other reasons. "What of your daughters?"

"They will no doubt find homes of their own. Why should we not make a home together?"

Why not, I thought, as he drew me to him and kissed me, first on the cheek and then on the lips. His were warm and firm, promising more than an alliance of convenience. I returned his embrace with some enthusiasm. Friendship and compatibility might prove a good foundation for this marriage.

The banns were read in church the next Sunday. Members of the congregation gathered around us, offering congratulations so my worries on that score had been groundless. Eliza and Maryel, too, both expressed pleasure at our decision, having worried about how their father would manage in my absence. They hinted there was more romance to be discovered, embarrassing me greatly. All was for the best. Except, of course, for Josiah. And in some ways, for me.

When next I saw him, he looked dejected and my heart ached anew.

"So," he said, "I must felicitate you on your coming nuptials. I had hoped for a different outcome."

"As had I." I hesitated. "I hear you plan to sell up and move to York."

"I feel I must."

I extended my gloved hand. "Goodbye, Josiah."

"Goodbye, Rebecca."

And that was that.

May-June

Jack

The Adjutant of the 100th Regiment ordered a meeting of all officers one Tuesday evening in May. There was much speculation about the cause, but none came close. He stood before them, holding a document that bore a large red seal.

"Men, you know our scheduled rotation is coming up this year."

Jack and his fellow officers mumbled their assent. Some grumbled that Bermuda was too far, and insalubrious to boot.

"Silence! Now, if I have your attention—"

More mumbling.

"—new orders have been cut." He waved the document. "We're not bound for Halifax and Bermuda after all. Events are building faster toward war than most of us had thought. General Prevost has ordered us back to Lower Canada."

Much rumbling and muted cheers among the officers.

Jack shouted, "Hurrah!" and suffered his fellows' laughter at his naive enthusiasm.

"Enough! Listen. We're to be headquartered at Three Rivers with detachments quartered at Fort William Henry in Sorel and Fort

Chambly on the Richelieu. The garrison at Montreal is being reinforced with new recruits—we'll be getting some of those, too—but they want experienced troops on the Lake Champlain corridor. It's the most likely invasion route toward either Montreal or Quebec. I expect we'll call in our remote detachment from Fort Saint Joseph soon. General Brock believes our allied Indian tribes can take care of any outposts so far north and west."

"Captain Sherrard will surely welcome relief from that command," said Dawson.

Laughter all around. Jack joined in, counting himself lucky to have remained in the lower Great Lakes as liaison for his usual company. "When can we expect to move to our new quarters?" he asked the Adjutant.

"We'll make the usual summer progress," said Hingston. "While we can still travel by schooner, we should make good speed. I fear, once war comes, we'll be restricted to travel by land."

Many groans greeted this remark, in recollection of the hard slogging it took to travel overland, using bateaux and canoes to cross the rivers and carry the baggage, while hugging the lakeshore.

Jack shuddered at the thought of the portages, where even junior officers took part in shouldering the loads.

"General Brock says the Americans are of two minds when it comes to war. He hopes to have enough time to strengthen all our fortifications before they make a declaration. And the negotiations continue—there could yet be peace."

"Come now, Hingston, you don't really think so. Surely there must be war," said Jack.

"If it's promotion you're after, Stevenson, perhaps you should save your pay rather than gamble it away, and you could purchase a captaincy in, say, fifty years."

"Exactly so, which is why I spend my money now. If my father relented—which he won't—I could have had it sooner, but he said he could spring for an ensign's commission only and I would have to earn the rest."

"I thought your father was knighted," said Dawson.

"For his music, yes," said Jack. "He's not as flush as he'd wish, for all the honor. Sir John he may be, and a celebrated tune-smith, but he still earns his bread as a church organist and choirmaster. The old man disapproves of the military, you know. He wanted me—his eldest son—to follow him as a professional musician, but no thank you. He claimed I got in with a pack of rowdies who led me astray."

"No!" said Dawson, with mock surprise.

Jack nudged him with one booted foot. "I may have pulled a few pranks, but nothing so bad. He was embarrassed, though. Finally, he let me join up. Give him his due, though I grudge it, he went to some expense over the matter. I don't know where he came up with the money."

"If he's as skint as you say, he'd have found it hard to scrape together… What is it now? A cornetcy was three hundred and fifty pounds when I bought mine," said Hingston.

"Four hundred for an Ensign of Foot," said Jack. "It was all he could afford. Not that I wanted the cavalry, anyway. But if I'd had some mathematical skill, I'd have joined the Artillery, or the Engineers. The pay is better, and they count seniority toward promotion."

"Yes, but the Artillery make such grand targets for the enemy." Hingston quirked an eyebrow. "Be content with where you are."

Rebecca

I thought things might settle down a bit, now Robert and I were betrothed, and the wedding date set. We were to travel to York so we could be married by his colleague, Reverend Stuart, and make of the entire event a family holiday.

I hadn't reckoned with Eliza who, despite her usual compliance, chose this time of all times to create a ruction. It had been long a-building, and I should have foreseen a crisis. That it should come now, when my mind was all in turmoil over the wedding, seemed the last straw.

It began one morning at breakfast. This was usually a silent meal, since none of the family was at their best in the early hours. We served ourselves eggs and toast and preserves and passed salt and butter without fuss, and I poured out the tea.

On this day, Eliza was determined to converse even if she got no response. Her topic, an ill choice at any time, was politics and the need for reform of the province's land tenure laws. She held forth at some length, while the rest of us ate. And then came the explosive moment.

"For," she said, "so many have been encouraged to come into the province with little hope of land either by grant or purchase, and must resort to becoming tenant farmers. It's as if the Governor were bent on establishing a new feudal system here. Mr. Willcocks says the American incomers won't stand for it."

I held my breath. Willcocks was a perennial sore spot with Robert.

"What did you say?" he asked softly.

"Why I said that Mr. Willcocks—"

He raised his voice. "You will not utter his name at my table, daughter. And I do not wish to hear you parrot the speeches of that man."

"But Father—"

He overrode her in a louder voice. "You will obey me in this, Eliza." His stern look softened a little, and so did his tone. "Come, I have not been unreasonable. You have accepted him as a dance partner and socialized with him at assemblies, and I have not protested. But I cannot countenance a daughter of mine expressing sentiments that border on the seditious."

"Do you agree with all the Governor's policies then?" she asked.

"Whether or not I do, I keep my opinions to myself. Governor Gore's policies are subject to debate in the Legislature, not in the marketplace. Nor at my table."

Eliza pouted. I was tempted to tell her she looked like a petulant child, but that would fuel her temper.

Maryel added her pence to the pot. "I think Mr. Willcocks is a prosy old bore. He's always complaining about something."

Eliza's cheeks reddened. "That's not true! He's an educated and cultured man."

"Enough," I said. "If you have finished your meal, you may go about your separate ways until your tempers cool."

Eliza flounced away from the table and ran upstairs, while Maryel stared. She stood and made to follow her, then turned and left the room. Her receding footsteps were followed by a slammed kitchen door.

"Well," I said, "we have a problem, don't we?"

Robert rubbed his forehead. "I had thought Eliza to be past the difficult stage. She should be more circumspect. And she knows how I feel about that scoundrel, Willcocks."

"She's an intelligent and educated woman with few matrimonial prospects in this town. Willcocks can be charming and a persuasive conversationalist. I think she has felt flattered by his attentions. And you know, Robert, you yourself have concurred with many of his opinions."

"Perhaps so, my dear, but in a more moderate fashion, I hope you will agree."

"Yes, Robert."

Their opinions were more closely aligned than Robert would admit, but he was not the firebrand that Willcocks was.

He rubbed his forehead again, as if his fingers might iron out his worries. "So, you think the situation with Eliza is serious? She might encourage him?"

"She hasn't enough wealth to tempt him. But she could become indiscreet. Trying to put her against him will make things worse."

"Then perhaps it's time she had a change of scene." He dug a letter out of the inside pocket of his coat. "I've recently heard from my old friend and colleague, Jehosaphat Mountain, rector of Christ Church in Montreal. We were at Cambridge at the same time, you know."

"You've mentioned him a few times. Is he in good health?"

"He is, but his wife has been poorly, and his youngest child also. It strikes me they might welcome a guest who could help with the household."

"You would send Eliza away?"

"It seems the best solution. Eliza would be exposed to a whole new social circle and taken out of that man's sphere at the same time. It could be described as something of an adventure, and also a Christian duty to aid her fellows. You will know best how to put it to her."

Naturally, it would be up to me. Well, it was a reasonable idea.

"We'll need to find someone who is traveling that way, who can escort her."

"We need make no undue haste, I think. For one thing, there is no immediate danger of more contact. I believe Willcocks is spending some weeks in York."

I wasn't eager to have this conversation with Eliza too soon. I also wondered about the impact of separation on the sisters. Would Maryel demand to accompany Eliza, or would she welcome her absence? I would miss Eliza myself, but less so if she was bent on this divisive behavior.

"You're frowning, my dear," said Robert. "Come, sit by me and be comfortable. We will set aside our worries about our daughters for a while, and plan for our future."

As the sloop rounded the swampy peninsula protecting York harbor, we could see the town's defenses, from the western battery at the harbor mouth up to the Don blockhouse in the eastern crook of the bay. The town had grown, but there was still only a modest scattering of buildings between them. Most were concentrated along the eastern shore by the blockhouse, near Parliament House.

It wasn't long before the sloop drew up to Allan's Wharf at the base of Frederick Street. There, a few porters with handcarts awaited our arrival.

I chivied the porters, impatient for them to collect our boxes. I was keen to get to Mrs. Johnson's boarding house, where we had booked rooms. Finally, all was loaded and settled to my satisfaction. Robert offered his arm, and I accepted it gladly. Eliza and Maryel followed.

Our path took us one block up Frederick Street and three more to the east on King Street. We women kilted up our skirts to avoid the inevitable mud. June had been unusually rainy, and the streets were deeply rutted by wagon wheels. Horses passing at a trot threw up clods of dirt and mud in all directions. King Street, at least, had plank walks fronting the shops, so we could avoid the worst.

"I hope Mrs. Johnson has a sturdy boot-scraper. She won't be pleased to have her guests track in bushels of mud." Robert examined his boots and trouser cuffs ruefully. "We will appear like ragamuffins."

I laughed. "There's a reason they call this 'Muddy York.'"

The boarding house lay on the north side of King Street; opposite Jordon's Hotel on the south, and was slightly the smaller building. Both had two stories and could house about two dozen guests. Jordon's catered mainly to the military and other itinerants, while Mrs. Johnson tended the more genteel traveler. We had arranged for two bedchambers, one for Robert, and the other for myself and the girls. We would only need to share a bed three ways for a night or two, until the wedding. I was prepared to withstand the crowding—I might have worried myself into an apoplexy if I had been alone.

Tuesday, 25 June, 1811, dawned clear and fresh after an overnight rain.

"Cousin Rebecca, you'll be a lucky bride with the sun shining," said Maryel, smiling.

"To think of myself as a bride!" I laughed. "At such an advanced age, it's a wonder I survived to become one. I'll not see forty again. But your father and I have been friends these twenty years and more. In fact, long ago I had a fancy that, had he not met my cousin Mary

Atkinson first, we might have made a match of it. I was young and foolish then. But so life goes."

"A secret romance? Cousin, you never said!"

"Don't tease her, Maryel," said Eliza. "She speaks of friendship, not love."

I frowned at this. "Eliza, Maryel, you should know that romantic love does not always make a good marriage. Your poor mother, bless her memory, would tell you, were she here. It's better to have compatible views and interests, and a kindly friendship, if you wish to have a comfortable life. But there," I smiled at them, "you are still young. Who knows—you may find both love and friendship yet."

"I am surely on the shelf, Cousin, but Maryel can still hope," said Eliza.

"This is a new land, Eliza, and things are different here. Your father and I will hope to see you both well-settled in your own homes before we leave this world."

"What gloomy talk for such a day," said Maryel. "Here, Cousin, your veil. It will frame your face softly and protect against mosquitoes, too." She arranged the soft netting around my face and stepped back to view her handiwork. "There. You don't look a day over twenty! Does she, Eliza?"

A knock came at the door and Robert stood outside. He took my hand and bowed over it. "You look delightful, my dear," he said. "I had not thought to have such a lovely bride, and me an old man."

"Nonsense!" I said, blushing. "You aren't in your dotage yet. And you look so distinguished in that suit of clothes. It's so unusual to see you heading for church in something other than your clerical robes."

"Well, well," he said, "it's nearly time for us to leave. I have hired a carriage to take us the few blocks to St. James' Church. We mustn't keep Reverend Stuart waiting. And Mrs. Johnson promises a sumptuous wedding breakfast to follow."

We were both flattered and embarrassed to find the church

packed with well-wishers. And Drusilla was there, too. I had not thought to see her, but she greeted me at the church door with a spray of delphiniums, their clear blue a perfect match for my dress. I hoped this meant our differences were at an end. I wanted nothing to spoil this day.

Our vows exchanged in the dim interior, it was a relief to emerge once more into the brilliant sun to be congratulated by all and sundry. So many of those in the Legislature—or indeed in other official positions—had lived in Niagara before the Capital was moved to York, and knew us well. It was gratifying to see and hear so many voicing such warm regards to us.

Mrs. Johnson was as good as her word. We arrived back at the boarding house to find such a spread. I thought she must have employed three bakers to achieve it, but doubted the town held so many. No, she had obviously been apprised of our event some time ago, for the number of pies, cakes and other delicacies was immense, and must have taken days to prepare. When I exclaimed at such a feast, Eliza noted in a wry tone, that we must expect the congregation to have prepared something similar when we return home. We would all end up as fat as force-fed geese.

Mrs. Johnson's parlor was barely sufficient to contain the crowd. We were joined by many who had been at the church. The mix included our small family, Robert's Parliamentary colleagues, some few of our acquaintance who had traveled from Niagara, and Drusilla, who drew me aside for a brief conversation in which we agreed our quarrels had been pointless and renewed our friendship. I could look forward to seeing her more regularly again as her sister's husband was taking up a post in Halifax, too far distant for her to call on Drusilla as dogsbody.

I had to endure some teasing from those assembled, since I

needed prompting to recognize myself as "Mrs. Addison."

"After so long as Miss Plummer," I said to Maryel, "surely it is no wonder. And I wish you and Eliza will call me Rebecca. I will not consider it disrespectful, and for you to call me Stepmother is unthinkable."

Both Eliza and Maryel thought this a good joke. "Since you won't answer to Mrs. Addison, what choice have we?" asked Eliza, eyes a-twinkle.

True to form, Robert capped the event with a remark that he must write his report to the Society the following day. But later, he pulled me to him, in one of our landlady's comfortable beds, and we drew the bed-curtains on our wedding day.

Jack

Jack stood in the yard of Jordon's Hotel, across the street from the boarding house, early the next day when Maryel emerged carrying a shopping basket. She halted when he called her name.

"Maryel! This is an unexpected pleasure!"

"Why, Jack… I had thought your Regiment long since on the road to Lower Canada."

"I'm here as rear-guard, to rally any stragglers and bring up the sick and the last of the baggage. It's a pleasure to see you. I hope nothing untoward brings you to York?"

"We have just been seeing my father and my cousin married. It's a happy occasion."

"My felicitations to them, then. May I escort you wherever you're bound? Carry your basket?"

They chatted amiably as they ambled down King Street toward the market.

"I trust your family are all well?" asked Jack.

"They're in good health, at least. Father has been troubled lately by more false allegations made against him by those close to

Lieutenant-Governor Gore. Father's loyalty to the Crown is known to all, but his courtesy toward people such as Thorpe and Willcocks caused a suspicion in Governor Gore's mind that has never dissipated. Now, with Willcocks provoking American sympathizers in his news sheet, old suspicions have been renewed."

"You're well-informed on the subject."

"It would be impossible not to be, living right on the border. Little else is talked of these days. But tell me… Are your family also well? Do you hear from them in Dublin?"

"All well, and my young siblings probably grown out of all recognition. Indeed, my sister Olivia writes me of her first child, born this spring. Strange to think I'm uncle to a boy I may never see. My father sounds much the same. He doesn't write often, and says little when he does."

They continued to exchange family trivia as they browsed the stalls at the market. Jack was careful to keep things on a neutral plane. Still unsure of her feelings, he didn't want to frighten her off.

Maryel made several small purchases and placed some larger orders for later shipment to Niagara. She took great care over it. "It's the first time Rebecca has let me do this on my own," she confided.

After her errands, they went back to a trader in small household items where she purchased a hand mirror. The craftsman had mounted it in native maple, carving and polishing it to show off the grain. She ran her hand over the wood's well-oiled surface with obvious pleasure.

Jack was amused, but impressed, too. "Your cousin will be pleased with your efficiency. Perhaps not so much with your personal purchase."

Maryel laughed. "I know it smacks of vanity, but I will share it with my sister. And… my cousin… my stepmother now, I suppose. She wishes us to call her Rebecca. She's more mother to me than my own ever was."

"My mother died when I was twelve. My recollections of her grow fainter. You're fortunate to have had someone as amiable as Miss Plummer—Mrs. Addison, I mean."

"Yes, and I must get back to them now. We're bound out on the afternoon sloop and I have not yet finished packing."

They turned back, heading east along King Street toward the hotels.

Jack grew more serious. "Since our time is short, will you permit me to correspond with you? Your letters while I was on remote posting were so reassuring. If war comes, it may not always be easy to exchange letters, but it would mean a great deal to me to hear from you."

She hesitated a moment, dropping her gaze. He twisted at the braid on his uniform and cleared his throat as if to speak again, and she looked up. "Yes, you may."

An enormous smile lit his face. "But Jack… Please don't take too much from this. I'm not ready…"

"I understand."

July–August

Rebecca

I never found it easy to delve into my feelings. There were too many dark corners I did not wish to probe. But when Robert went off on a circuit round the neighboring settlements, I indulged in that very thing.

Thinking was easier when my hands were occupied so I set myself the task of preparing an inventory of the contents of my stillroom. This was a necessary task I could perform with a minimum of concentration so long as I was careful to handle one item at a time. Each container required emptying, cleaning, and disposing of any decayed materials, with a note of the stock level of each item as I refilled the containers. I would also note items to be replenished.

The last few weeks were a revelation. I didn't know, when I married, I would become both emotionally and physically altered so much. My relations with Martin were so far in the past as to be a dim recollection, so Robert's attentions in that regard came as something of a surprise. He was gentle with me, and not overly demanding, but still more virile than I had supposed. It was pleasant to find I had not lost my ability to respond to his advances. I had come late to the comforts of a lusty conjugal relationship, but enjoyed them none-theless.

And I held Robert in great affection, too. Perhaps it was not the love I felt for Martin as a young woman, nor the romantic feelings I held for such a short time for Josiah, but I felt our friendship, already of long standing, expanding to a level richer and more rewarding than those. For Robert was, above all else, a kind man. True, he was not always thoughtful, and his tendencies to worry overmuch about trivial matters, or to become lost in a book, could be exasperating, but these were slight irritations to which I was already well accustomed.

My reverie was rudely interrupted by Eliza who burst into my sanctuary in a fit of temper.

"You should have told me!" were her first words. Her face was scarlet and her eyes bulged most unbecomingly. "But no, I had to hear it from Maryel, who overheard you and Father discussing it. I'm to be exiled to Montreal? For what? For having my own opinions and the gumption to air them? For meeting a respectable man in a public place? For being eldest and unmarried and in the way of my sister's prospects?"

"Calm down, Eliza, you'll have an apoplexy. I meant to tell you first, but…" I drew up a chair for her to sit by me. "Please, you must calm yourself. Let me make you some chamomile tea. You know how settling it is."

She sat, but refused the tea. "I thought you would take my part with Father. But now I see how it is. You have caught him and now you would separate us from him."

Now I was getting angry. "Caught him? Eliza, do you know how ridiculous that sounds? When I have lived with your family all these years. I might have expected this from the church ladies but you should know better." I stared her full in the eyes. "You do know better."

Her eyes wavered under my gaze, but her jaw remained set and her expression mutinous.

"Is this to be my life then? Can I not have a beau, or even a friend?"

"If you're referring to Joseph Willcocks, he's such a persistent flirt, I wonder you would consider him your beau. You know, he casts his eyes over every presentable female in his vicinity."

"People are jealous of his charms."

I shook my head. "Eliza, the reason your father wants you to go to Montreal is to broaden your sphere and meet a new circle of friends."

She raised her eyebrows at that.

"Yes, and remove you from Willcocks's company. It's true. But think, my dear, this is an opportunity, not a punishment."

Her eyes dropped and her shoulders drooped.

"Surely you have not formed an attachment to him?" Or gone any further than a few kisses, I hoped.

Her gaze rose and was steady, with no telltale blush. "Not really. I have enjoyed his attentions, of course. And I value his opinions, which I think sensible on most issues. And… I find him attractive, but I know how unlikely a match it would be. I would not pursue him to spite Father."

"No, I didn't think you would."

Her face relaxed, temper spent. "I wish it needn't be so far away, if I must go."

"Your father wants you to enjoy the company of his friends, the Mountains. He speaks most fondly of them. In fact," I grinned, "it sounds like he and Reverend Mountain were a couple of regular rips in their Cambridge days. Can you picture it?"

"No, I can't." She sniffed, not yet mollified.

"Neither can I. You will have to report back any stories he tells, so I can tease your father with them."

"I suppose I had better start packing." A deep sigh. "Father said I would need to hasten if I were to have a suitable escort. He thinks to ship me off in the Army's baggage train."

"Which regiment?"

"The 100th. He made the arrangements when we were in York for your wedding."

Canny Robert. "At least you will be familiar with the officers in charge of the voyage."

"Yes, Maryel said that Ensign Stevenson is one of them."

"Then she will be envious of you, I guess."

Eliza looked brighter when she finally left me, but my thoughts were all in turmoil. Only a few weeks married and I felt more responsible toward Robert's daughters—now my daughters—than ever before.

Jack

Three Rivers, L.C., 10 August, 1811
My dear sister Olivia,

My fondest felicitations on the news of your son's birth. I hope you are fully returned to health by now. I appreciate the honor you do me by making me a godfather, although I trust you have also nominated another who lives locally. My only contribution to his welfare is to advise you to call him by George rather than Gustavus, unless you wish to make his schooldays a nightmare.

You will see from the address that the Regiment has completed the move of our Headquarters from Niagara to Lower Canada. We had hoped to be stationed in Montreal, where there is more commercial bustle and diverse activities, and many former acquaintances. We stopped there several days to recover from the arduous journey through the Cascades. Montreal reminds me somewhat of home. But our final destination was Three Rivers, midway between Montreal and Quebec on the St. Lawrence River. It's a distinct change from the congenial society of our last posting. I find it odd, and slightly jarring, to hear French spoken everywhere, after two years away from it. I confess, my limited facility with the language is sadly rusty. Perhaps it will return with practice.

I was particularly distressed to leave Niagara, since I wished to further my acquaintance with Maryel Addison. She has agreed to exchange letters, which must suffice for now. I hope some other lucky fellow does not engage her affections in the meantime. Her sister, Miss Eliza, traveled with the Regiment's baggage train as far as Montreal, to stay with friends of the family. Would it had been Maryel.

My duties have increased lately, to assist with the drilling of the local militia. I expect to go on detachment at some stage, but am not yet sure where. We have been stepping up our border patrols, so somewhere south of here is sure. We're positioned to guard the approaches through the Champlain valley. You may consult Father's atlas to see our general position. The latest despatches from Europe are not encouraging. With so many of our forces arrayed against Napoleon's armies we have little hope here of reinforcement, should we need it. Prevailing opinion is the Americans will, soon or late, take advantage of this.

I would not have you think all is gloomy here. My fellow officers are always ready for some entertainment and I find myself called upon for music. I am sure Father will be pleased to hear this encourages me to maintain my proficiency.

With fondest affection,

Jack

Rebecca

We had not been back from York three weeks when Robert brought Captain Norton out to Lake Lodge. I was turning out the pantry when they arrived, and was not a little discomposed.

"But how can I meet with him in all my dirt?"

"Never mind that," said Robert. "We have much to discuss." He raised his brows. "Besides, your appearance is satisfactory."

Men. I removed my apron and tucked the loose strands of hair behind my ears. At least I wore a clean dress.

Norton was seated at the dining table, a satchel of papers at hand, and one long leg stretched to the side. He rose to greet me. How he towered over us! I always found him intimidating by presence alone. His powerful physique must be truly formidable in battle. I was quick to seat myself, to ease the atmosphere.

"What's so urgent?" I asked.

"General Brock is becoming concerned about the advancement of our network of agents," said Norton. "He has asked about the safe room here, and I promised to inquire."

"We have begun, although somewhat later than planned," I said.

"We did survey it last spring, but some pressing issues prevented progress. Tom started digging just last week. He will complete it, you may be sure."

Robert chimed in. "He will not fail us. I would trust him with my life." A wave of love for him rose in my breast. I had not thought him to value Tom as I did.

Norton nodded. "We're agreed on that. He may yet have a greater role to play."

My heart sank back further than its normal position. "That sounds ominous. But you are right to place your faith in him."

We continued to discuss what Brock required of Crown agents like us. Our chosen code names, Partridge for Robert, and Moorhen for me, were approved by Norton. He gave us a list of words for recognition and demonstrated a few necessary signals. It all sounded so complicated. Was war nothing but a game? A game with horrific consequences.

Our principal business over, Robert and Norton relaxed, leaning back in their chairs. I brought us cool water Hannah had dipped from the well and some of her small oatcakes, with a pot of straw-berry jam. The conversation turned to family and church matters.

"I've had another letter from my sister," said Robert. "She is well, but writes that Father is in poor health. I don't wonder at it—with eighty-nine years in his dish, he has far exceeded his biblical allotment."

"Indeed," said Norton. "Few among our elders reach such an age."

"I never thought to be gone so long," said Robert. "The Society proposed a mission term of five to six years. I hoped I would be recalled for a position in England. Perhaps a curacy… but it was not to be." He sighed. "I tried at one time for a position in Nova Scotia, but it never came about. I might have braved the Atlantic again from there, I suppose."

"Surely not, Robert," I said. "Why, you become seasick on Lake Ontario!"

He huffed a little. "The storms on these lakes are no laughing matter. I have seen you become queasy, too." He sighed again. "Though you are likely correct in your assessment. I have no love for the sea. And the Atlantic crossing is terrible. I barely survived it the first time."

He turned to Norton. "And you, John, have you accomplished any more of your translations of the Gospels?"

"I regret to say not, Reverend sir. I have too many hats vying for a seat on my head. Besides my work with General Brock as Captain Norton and 'Snipe,' I've been occupied with tribal affairs, as Teyoninhokarawen, although I know that's a poor excuse for the lapses of John Norton the translator."

We laughed together at this.

"But I've lately been pondering whether these translations will benefit my people in the ways they need most. It's good to preserve our language, and to have books available in it, but the world is changing. I have come to believe we need to be literate in the languages of Europe to plead our causes in your Parliaments and courts. English and French should be the languages my people learn to read, as well as and perhaps even before our own."

Robert's eyebrows rose. Norton had been one of his staunchest allies in the translation project Joseph Brant originally sponsored. "How did you come by these notions?" he asked.

"It comes out of my association with some evangelical members of the Church of England, while I was in England arguing at the British Court for the restitution of my people's lands. It's a strange duality, for they deepened my conviction in the need for translation, as I saw that their methods of persuasion could never be conducted in our native tongues. I also saw why I had been sent to the Court by Thayendenagea. It was my command of English and French and our languages. I could spot the nuances in negotiations that I could not without that proficiency."

"And you would see more of your people share this ability? Well, I cannot argue with that. Although I still think it a useful project to continue, at least with the Gospels, and have them printed in both Mohawk and English, to smooth the transition, perhaps?"

Norton smiled warmly at his friend. "You see at once what it has taken me time and struggle to learn. I hope you will not be too disappointed if I delegate the next set of translations to other men. I have much else to contend with now, and could not devote the required attention."

"Of course, my dear fellow, you must follow your own path. I will be pleased to work with whoever you send me."

I cleared away the cups and plates as the men continued their conversation. In the kitchen, I checked on the progress of the evening's meal, a stew of duck and dried apples, as it simmered in an iron kettle at one side of the open fire. I turned the kettle around and stirred the pot so it wouldn't scorch.

Our evening meal was a subdued one, so much so Maryel remarked on our silence. How on earth could we keep our secret roles as Crown agents from her?

October–December

Rebecca

"Rebecca, where are you?" called Robert as he ran up the path to the town house. I watched in amazement out a window as he mounted the steps two at a time, as if he were half his age.

"What on earth is it?" I asked as he burst through the door.

He gasped for breath, then choked out "Gore is gone!" before collapsing on the settle by the door.

Great news indeed. No wonder he was excited.

Still wheezing a little, he found his voice. "Gore put on leave, gone back to England. Not fit for position during war-time. Brock named President of Executive Council. Military governor."

"Slow down, Robert, you'll choke," I said. "I'll get you some water." I had never heard him speak in other than complete sentences. Often lengthy and convoluted ones.

After a few moments rest, he was more himself. "General Brock is now in charge of the administration of the Province. In effect, it is military rule, although the House of Assembly will continue to sit. Brock will report to General Prevost, who is named Governor-in-Chief for the whole of British North America."

"I'm sorry for the reason—nobody sensible wants war—but glad of the result. Brock values your contributions, while Gore did not. He has made us all miserable long enough. Good riddance to him."

"I hope to demonstrate my loyalty to the military administration so thoroughly it can never be questioned again. Brock and Prevost are both good friends to the Church of England, which fortifies my hope."

✳

For the past several weeks, whenever he could get leave, Tom had come out to Lake Lodge to work on the secret cellar. Sometimes I thought he might sport black fingernails until his dying day, but at least it was honest work.

"It won't be remarked by anyone else. The shop dirt helps conceal the grime I get digging, too. Nobody looks twice at me in town," he said.

"I should hope not. Hannah spends hours heating water so you can bathe before you return."

"And I appreciate it, all the more for easing my sore muscles after all that digging. I've often wished there were three of me."

"How much do you have left? It won't be long before we have ground frost."

"The main chamber is roughed out and I've shored the tunnel at the lakeside bush end, where I started. I'm still working on the main part of the tunnel, and the connection to the root cellar. Don't think I can finish before hard frost."

"Will you put down any flooring? It's going to get cold down there, and no possibility of a fire, or even a brazier."

"I had thought to put wood but beaten earth will better muffle sound. A cot with blankets will have to suffice for warmth. The most important thing now is to secure the connecting door behind the shelving in the root cellar. I should be able to keep working on that over the winter and finish up the tunnel when the ground thaws."

The entrance in the bush was not likely to be found. But the entrance in the house—I didn't care to think of the result of an enemy discovering it. Summary execution would be the least of it.

"I hope we don't have to house anyone longer than a day or two."

"If you do, I hope it isn't me," said Tom.

He did his best to choose times when Maryel might be off on some errand or other, but one day she arrived home just as he ascended from the cellar.

"Why are you covered in mud? What's going on?" she asked.

"I suppose you'd have to know, sometime," I said. "But you must swear secrecy." I told her about our involvement in Brock's plans.

Her eyes grew wider until I thought they might pop from her head. "How exciting!"

"More dangerous than exciting," said Tom. "Especially when I fear the tunnel may collapse on me as I dig."

Maryel turned to me. "You should have told me right away. Now I know why you kept sending me to town, or the neighbors, on those endless errands."

"Your father wanted to protect you. The fewer who know about this, the better."

Willcocks

Biggest grasper in the Province has sailed home. Won't be missed. Now to see if Brock improves on Gore. Generally deplore military rule. but Brock seems a sensible man. Anything better than what we've had. Must sound him out if opportunity presents. Meantime reform articles continue. Sales of Guardian reduced of late. Can't continue to run at a loss. Conveyancing brings in as many contacts and more income. Land transactions slow in winter. Guardian can continue for now. Decide which to focus on by spring. Morning frost showing on the Common. Autumn leaves falling fast.

"Is the press still holding together?" Willcocks stood at the door of the print shop, watching as Tom worked setting a page of type.

"Barely," said Tom, eyes fixed on his task.

"It may not need to all that longer. This will be the last issue this year. I won't put a new one together until sometime next spring, unless there's enough advertising to pay for it, or some big change in the politics. Let's see what happens in the next session of the Legislature. With my prime target gone home with his tail between his legs, we may get a respite from his policies."

Tom finished up, and wiped his hands. "Are you thinking of closing the paper?"

"Not yet, boyo, not yet. As long as there's life in this old girl." He patted the uprights of the printer.

"Careful there," said Tom. "The uprights are still sound, but I'm worried about the moving parts. Some have got woodworm real bad."

"Take measurements of the worst ones then. We must be able to get replacements made locally, at least well enough to grind out a few more editions."

Tom shook his head. "I hope you're right."

Rebecca

Winds must have set fair on Lake Ontario and the portage through the St. Lawrence rapids been faster than usual, given the frequency of correspondence between Maryel and Jack. She still read them out to us, though I suspected a few omissions, particularly in the salutations which she did not read out.

In mid-November, she received a reply to her October letter. Jack confirmed some news we had already heard, then went on about himself.

"I have but little French myself and find it difficult communicating with the locals. We all persevere, since it would be the worst of things if they were to turn on us for want of a little application in learning their language. Not everyone in the Army thinks this way, but I find my Irish brethren to be most sensitive to local feelings."

Robert scoffed at this, muttering something uncomplimentary about Irish sensitivity, but I shushed him.

Maryel continued.

"The Regiment is headquartered in Three Rivers, but I am on remote detachment on the Richelieu River which flows north from

Lake Champlain toward the Saint Lawrence. Life on detachment is the same as ever. We drill, we have target practice (but not too much because powder and ball are expensive) and we await orders. Mostly, it seems, we wait."

"It sounds extremely tedious," said Robert. "No wonder so many soldiers find themselves in trouble. Idle hands, you know."

"I hardly think them idle, Father. The officers work hard to keep the men in fighting trim."

"Humph," he grunted. "Better an honest farmer than a soldier."

"Oh Father, you know you like Jack. Even if he is Irish."

Robert harrumphed again, but we could both see the twinkle in his eye. Maryel giggled and went off to find paper to compose a reply.

"Waste of paper and ink," he grumbled, but I could tell he didn't mean it.

✳

To Ens. J.A. Stevenson, 100th Ft. on Detachment
20 November 1811

My dear friend,

There is little enough news to share with you, but I will give what I can.

Father was pleased to hear on November 18th of his appointment as assistant Chaplain to the 2nd Battalion of the Royal Canadian Volunteers. The Bishop had promised to send them a Chaplain but had not found it possible to locate a suitable candidate. Since Father performs most of these duties anyway, owing to his being available to the Fort, it's only right he should receive some credit and remuneration. I am sorry to speak so frankly of money, but it's of increasing concern here in the Province, with everything so dear. I suppose if war comes it *will only be worse. But I try not to think of that overmuch.*

Your previous letter encourages me to return to my studies, when Rebecca can release me from other chores. Father has often spoken of his friends in Montreal, the Mountains, where Eliza is now visiting, and if I was ever to go there it could be advantageous to speak some French. I will advise you of any progress I make, although I fear it will be small. Eliza writes that Montreal society is entertaining, but I suppose you see none of that while on detachment.

I hope to hear more of your news. My life is even duller than yours.

With best wishes
Your friend
Maryel Addison

✳

Robert brought home an invitation for us to dine on the 28th in the officers' mess, as part of General Brock's official visit to Fort George. He was flattered by the attentions of the General. While there was much of the political in such occasions, I was convinced there was a genuine esteem between them. I found Brock's manner most congenial and open. He had to keep truly important things secret, but he had the knack of saying just enough to reassure anxious listeners. Besides softening us up with an excellent dinner, of course.

I was especially happy to attend this social gathering, since Drusilla had been occupied of late in tending to her ailing parents. Despite our reconciliation, I saw less and less of her. I had hoped we would have more opportunities to meet, with the winter coming on, but she remained at their St. David's farm most of the time. Too great a distance was growing between us, to my regret. Despite my new standing as Robert's wife, I had no other close women friends.

With few exceptions, women were too busy with family concerns to spend much time cultivating each other's company.

The General was most expansive regarding his assessment of the populace. He had spent several days in the community, holding meetings both public and private. He shared his thoughts with us over dinner.

"I believe the majority will prove faithful."

There was murmuring around the table at this pronouncement, but all fell silent when he raised his hand.

"I have good reason to think this. First, those to whom I spoke professed their determination to defend their property and support the government. I heard this not only from the principal inhabitants, but in casual conversations and remarks made in the marketplace. Since my installation to head the government, people's confidence in our ability to defend the Province has increased. They welcome our aid."

I thought that had more to do with the general dislike and distrust of Gore than confidence in Brock. But there were nods and smiles around the table, so I supposed the statement was not hubris on the General's part.

"But what of the others, those who would rebel?" asked the Fort Major. "We know there are many disaffected people in this region. Not all of them recent incomers from the States."

"I'm perfectly aware of these improper characters," said Brock. "You're right. There are many whose principles foster insubordination, detrimental to military administration. Many, but not most. But it's my view we must act with the utmost liberality, as if no mistrust exists. This has the potential to spike the guns of all but the most radical. Without the faithful aid of the greater part of the inhabitants…" He rose in emphasis, leaning on his hands at the head of the board. "… it will be utterly impossible to preserve the Province. We simply don't have enough men."

He sat down again, surveying his audience. We were rendered speechless. Not from surprise, but from his vehemence. The silence lasted only a moment as a buzz of discussion rose around the table. Some were skeptical or discouraged, but I felt a tiny surge of hope, a small easing of tension. His pronouncements rang true in my ears, for they reflected my views on human nature: if you expect the best from people, you will often receive it, while if you expect the worst, you will surely get it. With such a leader, we might overcome the odds.

As we prepared to depart after a most-interesting evening, the General pulled Robert aside for a word.

"I must tell you frankly, I'm under no illusion as to the defensibility of this vast, underpopulated territory. My mandate—even with the goodwill of the people—is all but impossible. I say this so you may understand that I will exert every means in my power to defend it nonetheless. I depend on you—and others—to support my efforts, as I will support yours."

Robert gripped Brock's hand. "You may so depend, my dear sir. And you may count upon my blessing, besides."

25 December 1811

My dear Sarah,

Our Christmas festivities being complete, I am remaining awake a little longer to write to you, at the end of a most surprising year. I have settled comfortably into my new estate, and finally feel a genuine part of this family. You may chide me I have been for many years, but it's not how I felt. The girls are most generous with their affections, and Robert is all I could wish for in a husband. He is neither demanding nor neglectful and respects my opinions almost as his own. The years have not been easy for him either, and I think we find each other a welcome refuge. I am satisfied.

My erstwhile suitor, Josiah Burton, has meanwhile found Niagara no longer to his liking. He departed for York some weeks ago, but was generous enough to offer to replenish my supplies against such time as another apothecary bases himself here. Naturally, I accepted his offer, and he discounted his prices outrageously, for which I was grateful. I confess to relief he has left town. It was awkward to encounter him so frequently. I suppose he must have felt the same.

Maryel feels the loss of the 100th Regiment on their rotation most keenly. She was on the way to forming an attachment to one of their officers, and is corresponding with him. At least she shows no signs of melancholy.

We're missing Eliza greatly, although she writes from Montreal that she is content to be with Reverend Mountain's family and has made many new acquaintances. She was always a prop and stay to me in the household, and Maryel has neither the skills nor the inclination to compensate fully. However, I believe we did the right thing in sending Eliza away from Mr. Willcocks's influence, and there the matter must rest.

There are many more entertainments than usual this year, and their gaiety approaches the feverish. I suppose this is only to be expected when war is imminent. It cannot come before spring, however, more likely summer.

I wish, as always, for your family's continued health and prosperity.

Your loving sister,

Rebecca

Jack

To Miss M. E. Addison, Lake Lodge, Niagara, U.C.
28 December 1811

My dear Maryel,

I take this opportunity to write that I have attended at church services delivered by the Reverend Mountain, and was privileged to receive an invitation to dinner thereafter. There I conversed with your sister and was happy to hear she has been in regular correspondence with you and that your family enjoys good health.

Here in Montreal, we have snow as high as ground floor window-sills, and most everyone travels by sleigh. The Regiment maintains winter quarters here and rotates officers on detachment back to headquarters at intervals. The change is welcome, since remote postings can be exceedingly severe even in good weather. I am fortunate to have a few weeks respite before returning to that duty.

Our quarters here are snug and well-provisioned. Our dinners are accompanied by mulled ale and punch, both welcome for their warmth. Anything that can be done to keep out the cold is seized upon with gratitude. There is much merriment here at this season, and the dishes prepared by "les habitants" are rich and filling. Huge, fat-laden pork pies called tourtières and equally grand maple sugar pies are pressed on us at every turn. I find it an assault on my digestion, but will doubtless have an extra layer of fat to keep me warm when I go back on detachment.

You may imagine my head turned by Montreal society, but I assure you that none of the young ladies I have met and partnered with on the dance floor can compare with you. I wish I had my father's flair for composition, so I could write an air or song to commemorate my admiration for you. But perhaps at our next meeting, whenever that may be, I will play some of his compositions for your enjoyment.

With fond regards,
Jack Stevenson

That would have to do, thought Jack, laying his pen down and rubbing his eyes. Writing by candlelight tired them.

"How about those new recruits?" asked Dawson from the doorway.

"A lot of Johnny Raws, that's what," said Jack. "Probably take us months to whip them into shape."

"I thought you were against whipping?"

"You know I meant drilling." Jack hunched a shoulder. "Flogging may be needed for miscreants, but it's no way to train soldiers. I've seen no good come of it."

Dawson shrugged. "Possibly, but I've already noticed a few troublemakers who are bound to come under the lash, soon or late. A few of the lads from the rougher part of Dublin. They were acting up at the Christmas feast."

"They had only just arrived then. See if they do the same thing tomorrow."

"Lucky sods to get extra rations twice, so soon."

"You're a pessimist, Dawson. They're not such bad fellows. They'll soon blend into the companies like old hands."

"And you're an incurable optimist. But we'll see." Dawson grinned mischievously. "Care for a wager on it?"

Jack turned out his pockets, which were empty, as usual. "With what?"

"Take over my night duties for a week if you lose?"

"Too steep. Make it two days and you're on."

They shook hands on it, and Dawson left. Jack settled back in his chair, reading over his letter, and dreaming of Maryel. But as he did so, he found himself disturbed by the thought that, in Niagara, she was right on the border.

PART 2
Perilous Times

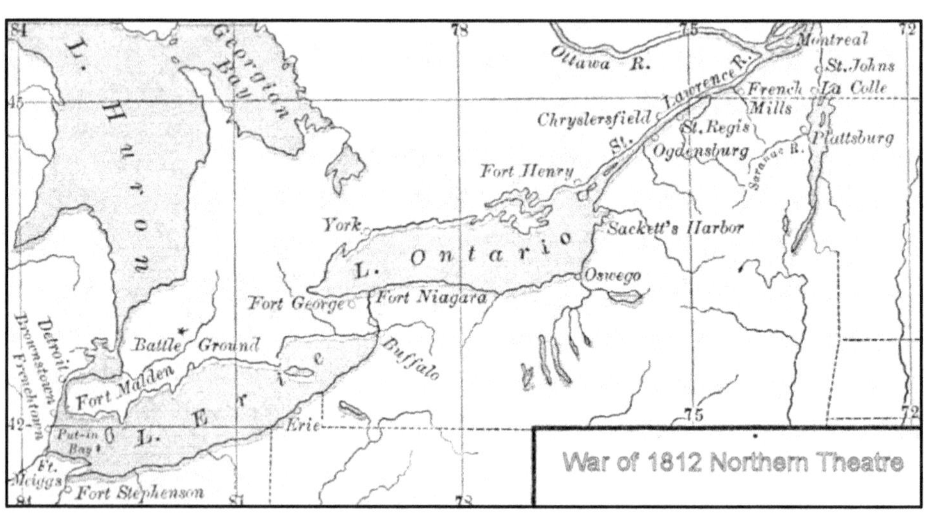

84
78
75
72
L. Huron
Georgian Bay
Ottawa R.
Montreal
St. Johns
St. Lawrence R.
French
La Colle
Mills
Chryslersfield
St. Regis
Plattsburg
45
Fort Henry
St.
Ogdensburg
Saranac R.
York
L. Ontario
Sackett's Harbor
Fort George
Fort Niagara
Oswego
Detroit
Brownstown
Frenchtown
Battle Ground
Buffalo
Fort Malden
L. Erie
42
Put-in Bay
L.
Erie
75
72
Ft. Meiggs
Fort Stephenson
81
81
78
War of 1812 Northern Theatre

1812

"In fact, it's a farce to call any being virtuous whose virtues do not result from the exercise of its own reason."—Mary Wollstonecraft

"Simplicity and sincerity generally go hand in hand, as both proceed from a love of truth."—Mary Wollstonecraft

January–March

Rebecca

The year's turning brought new anxiety. Robert was laid low with an extremely severe attack of the grippe, and I was at his bedside for the better part of two weeks. I feared I might lose him in one of these attacks, and near wore through the pages of Culpeper in search of better remedies. Winters grew harder on him with each passing year.

Maryel and Hannah worked together to run the household while I concocted poultices and tisanes to ease Robert's troubled breathing. The house reeked of horehound, mustard and onion. He required assiduous nursing to prevent an inflammation of the lungs.

At length, his cough eased enough for him to fall asleep. I pulled the covers close around him, tiptoed out of the room, and descended the stairs.

Maryel hustled me into a chair by the fire, plied me with hot bone broth and tea, and wrapped me in a shawl.

I found this most amusing, and said so.

She shook a finger at me. "What would we do if you fell ill? You mustn't lose your own health in tending to Father."

"That's unlikely, but thank you for your concern. It's a shame Eliza was not here to keep you company."

"I've been trying to improve my cooking and other household skills. It's not right to leave it all to you."

I sipped the broth. "If this is of your making, you have made good progress."

"Hannah stood by while I roasted the bones and helped me adjust the kettle so the broth wouldn't scorch." She wrinkled her forehead. "It's not too salt, I hope?"

"No, indeed I couldn't have done better myself."

She beamed.

I realized Maryel had been rather in Eliza's domestic shadow. Perhaps I had not encouraged her enough. She was making up for lost time now.

"I've not had time to reply to Jack's latest letter," she said. "If you are comfortable, I'll do so now."

"You will have scant news for him, I fear."

"There's always something to say. I can tell him Father was ill but is recovering, and the rest of us are well."

"And there's always the matter of our over-stretched nerves."

"That's not exactly news." She bit her lip. "Some days I feel my head must shatter with worry. It's a good day when I don't think about the coming war at all."

"Life goes on," I said. "I try to concentrate on the task at hand and not drift into worry."

"That's a trick I'd like to learn."

"Give it time, my dear." And don't count on finding it easy. I didn't.

✳

Robert was teasing Maryel about another letter from Jack. I was pleased to see it, since it showed the improvement in his health.

Maryel took it in good part, sharing tidbits of his news.

"Jack sounds like he's having a hard winter," she said about his latest, over tea one afternoon. "Listen to this."

"The winter drags on here in Lower Canada, a snowbound land. We entertain ourselves, and practice our marksmanship, too, in hunting deer, which are abundant in the surrounding woods. Venison makes an agreeable change from Army rations. By this time in the winter, the biscuit has weevils. Most unpleasant."

"Not very lover-like," I said.

She blushed. "I don't mind. I'm happy for him to be a friend."

Robert raised both of his eyebrows and I quirked one of mine at that. She ignored our skepticism.

"We cope with the intense boredom of the forts, relieved when we exchange one for another much like it. The best posting in this area is St. John, but I have been spending most of my time at Fort Chambly or Ile-aux-Noix. The latter, despite its name, is barren of nut trees and I hesitate to give any other construction to its name. Bedlam might suit it better."

"It sounds bleak, doesn't it?" she said, folding the letter and laying it on the table beside her.

"It's not an easy country," said Robert. "If I had known…"

"Well," I said briskly as I rose to clear the teacups, "we're here, and managing pretty well. We'd be no better off in England. Perhaps worse."

"You're right, my dear," he said.

"It's not so bad, is it?" asked Maryel. "I like it here."

I carried the cups into the pantry and set them down. Clutching my thick woolen shawl tightly around me, I stared out the window at the drifting snow and frozen lake.

Willcocks

Willcocks shook the snow off his greatcoat and stamped his feet on the mat before entering his York lodgings. He examined one boot ruefully, noting the thin leather sole was nearly detached from its upper. Bugger these Canadian winters! A pair of boots that would have lasted him several years in Dublin was useless here. Damned if he'd resort to the clumsy boots the clodhoppers wore. There must be a boot-maker in this town. Sure, he'd found none in Niagara. He'd best get these to a cobbler, or take a chill from wet feet. This thought brought on a shivering fit, in memory of his time in the York Gaol. Someday, he'd pay back those bastards for their treatment of him.

4 Feb

General Brock seated as President of Executive Council at opening of Legislative session. Time to see what he has to offer. Still not sure military Governor is right for the Province. Better than Gore? Might turn out more arbitrary. Might be amenable to reason. Chilly wind off Lake Ontario bringing snow squalls. Old boots too thin for winter weather.

8 Feb

Dined with Brock yesterday. He sets a good table. A choice round of beef done on the spit. Best wine I've had in many months. Maybe best since Dublin. Very persuasive man. Seems to favor some reforms. Might convince him on public education petition. Warrants cautious support.

12 Feb

Heckled in Legislature for supporting Brock. So far his proposals reasonable. Sensible amendments to Militia Act. specifying young bachelors eligible for call-up. Limits on terms of service. Cannot expect farmers or family men to serve lengthy terms. Even-handed: no substitutions permitted. That will gall the privileged classes. Winds still bitter. Mercury dropping.

Damn, there was Markle again. Willcocks ducked into a nearby doorway to avoid his colleague. He'd been at the head of the hecklers. Could the man not understand there were nuances to reform? It was galling to be the butt of ridicule from men who claimed to be his allies when he was attempting fresh tactics with a new Governor. Sometimes it felt like everyone was against him. Including those who claimed to be his friends.

24 Feb

First setback under Brock. He moved to suspend the writ of habeas corpus. Would have permitted detention without justification. Not at war yet: not warranted. Motion soundly defeated. Heckled again by Crown sycophants for voting against Brock. Still in good charity with him. Sound views on many subjects. Each motion considered on merits. Not surprised to encounter some disagreement. Overcast skies but warmer. Brief thaw makes for muddy streets.

"Well now, Tom, what brings you to York?"

"Problems with the press again. Begged a spare part from the *Gazette*. I don't know how much longer I can keep it together."

Willcocks poured them both a generous measure of gin. "If you can get me two more editions, I'll be well pleased."

Tom nodded and tossed back the liquor. "Should be possible." He turned the glass around in his hand, but waved off Willcocks's offer of more. "Early sailing tomorrow. Don't want a sore head."

5 Mar

Supper last night with young Strange. Seems uneasy about new militia requirements. Has no exemption on religious grounds. Certainly no Quaker. Bachelor of 24. eligible for the draft. Discussion skirted loyalty issue. He must decide. Brock has my personal loyalty. For the time being. Still free to disagree.

Rebecca

Robert went alone to attend the Legislature this year, while we continued our preparations for war. With the war-hawks in the ascendancy in the States, this now seemed inevitable. He returned in mid-March with a mixed bag of news he didn't discuss with me until we were readying ourselves for bed.

"Willcocks has been charmed by the General's winning ways," he told me. "You would have stared to see him so conciliatory. I thought his behavior contrived." He loosened his cravat and grunted. "That was too tight."

"Are the skies falling?" I turned for him to unfasten my dress. He fumbled over the buttons.

"Not completely. He voted against martial law, as did many. Most members feel it a premature request on Brock's part. But those same ones voted for the changes to militia requirements. Everyone can see what the lack of men means."

A coughing fit seized him. I tested his forehead with the back of my hand. It was cool.

"Is it that different?"

"Only in the formation of units that can be better trained, gathered from the unmarried youth. Bachelors aged eighteen to twenty-five."

My heart sank. Tom was squarely in the eligible group. Already enlisted as a spy, what would this new provision mean for him?

Robert pulled off his shirt and folded it carefully, placing it over a chair-back, then sat on the bed to remove his shoes and stockings. "I know Brock is worried there are so few trained men. Even if he calls up the full muster—all aged eighteen to sixty—there are few who would be of any use. And he will have to rely on them, with so few regular soldiers available." He rubbed his feet before drawing on his slippers.

By now I was down to my shift, and ready for my night-dress. Woolen, necessary for winter, but scratchy. "It's a grim situation."

"I can't make it sound any better than it is. Some locals may decide to equip and train semi-permanent militias—and I do not doubt they will—but the number of soldiers will be hundreds when we need thousands. A few hundred Indian warriors will surely help. But… that doesn't allow for the disaffected, who probably won't turn out at all, or might help the invaders."

"This supposes the Americans invade in force." I removed the warming pan and got into bed.

"I think we must assume that, my dear." He climbed into the bed beside me and we pulled up the covers. "I wish it were otherwise."

"Well, I believe I used your absence well. We're as ready as we can be. I still hope war may be avoided. No sense in borrowing trouble. It's sure to arrive in its own time."

My words may have been philosophical, but my thoughts were far from it. I lay awake long after Robert's breathing turned into a gentle rumble, listening to the wind howling off the lake.

May–June

Jack

Jack dumped his forage cap and musket on the lower bunk, and sank down beside them in relief.

"Finally, back at headquarters. I'm sick to death of going on detachment. Especially in winter when there's nothing happening. Throw another log on the fire, throw another round of dice. It's all the same thing."

"You shouldn't complain of boredom," said Hingston. "At least you have your fiddle, or your flute."

"A lot of good they are when my fingers are frozen and the strings, too." He made a business of filling his pipe from his tobacco pouch, lit it, and leaned back with satisfaction. "But they'll thaw out soon now spring is finally here. Did you ever know of such a place for snow? My sisters don't believe me when I write home about it."

"That reminds me, they've bestowed a new title on the Regiment."

"What, are we no longer the 100th?"

"We're still that, but now styled the 100th Prince Regent's County of Dublin Regiment of Foot. Probably in lieu of more pay."

"Typical. Well, well, a fancy title. Does it go down with an extra tot of grog?"

"Yes, but you'll have to wait until it's announced in the mess. There's a proclamation to be read, and then we get to toast the Regent's health."

"I'll toast anyone who stands me a tot of grog. And anyone who makes something happen—anything!"

"Haven't heard from your young lady then, is that your problem, Jack?"

"Damn you, Hingston, you know too much. An old married man like you, too, it's a rotten shame. No, not since early April."

"Don't be too discouraged, Jack. Give her time. It's hard to woo a woman from a distance. She needs you there in person."

"Yes, and when will that ever be possible with these everlasting postings and rotations and detachments? We might just as well be on the Moon!"

"If General Headquarters is right, and they have a nose for these things, it's all going to come to a head this summer. You could be in the way of seeing her again sooner than you think."

Rebecca

I took a mid-morning cup of tea into Robert's study at Lake Lodge where we were spending a few days to direct the spring planting. He hunched over his desk, quill in hand.

"A shame, on such a bright morning, to shut yourself in here, my dear." I set down the cup and looked over his shoulder at the page.

To the Society…

… It gives me pain to mention that the draft for my Allowance for the last half Year came back protested. altho' I have never failed to write whenever I draw. I have been very ill…

The querulous note in Robert's report was quite understandable. To me, at least, though I knew it would be unlikely to move the Society to make more concessions or increase his pay. They appeared entirely unable to comprehend the scope of his mission. Such pettiness from a group supposedly dedicated to Christian charity.

"Can that not wait?" I asked. "At least join me on the veranda for a short while. The spring air will do you good."

He shrugged and bent further over his missive. "I must get this done. Perhaps later."

It was no use protesting any more. I took my own advice and went outside, using the door nearest Robert's study, that faced inland. I stood there briefly, surveying the garden and farm buildings. The fruit trees lining the lane—cherry, apple, and peach—were in simultaneous bloom in shades from white to deep rose and their sweet scent flavored the light breeze off the lake.

Someone appeared the end of the lane—a visitor speeding toward the house. The dress looked familiar… Drusilla. My, but she was in a hurry. Dust scudded around her hem, her bonnet hung askew and wild locks of fair hair fluttered from her makeshift bun.

"Drusilla," I called to her. "Welcome."

"Rebecca." She came up to me, almost at a run, and embraced me. Her entire body trembled, so hard that I shook with her. It took a few moments for her to catch her breath.

"I need your help. Right now."

"Calm down, my dear. What's so urgent? Can I bring you a cool drink?"

"I have need of your medicines and skills. You know. The special ones."

Not again, I thought. Please, not again.

"Drusilla, you know I can't. How can you ask again?"

"I was going to make the decoction myself, like you showed me. But I'm afraid I might do it wrong, and poison her." She gulped. "I think it'll kill her this time."

"Who?"

"Amanda Ferris." Her eyes welled with tears. "I can't just stand by, Rebecca. Even if she's only a neighbor."

I stared at her, my stomach roiling. She had pressed me for the knowledge, and now she was afraid to use it. So much for shared responsibility.

"Please, Dru, you must let this go. It's too risky for all of us." I ached for Mrs. Ferris, but must put my family first.

"But why? Why are you so adamant against it now? You used not to be."

I looked over my shoulder at the open window of Robert's study and lowered my voice. "You know why." Any indiscretion now wouldn't only affect me. It would reflect on Robert and might jeopardize both his position and my life.

"There's more to it than that. I'm positive." Her voice rose to a point where I feared Robert might notice and overhear something I was desperate to keep from him. I took her arm and drew her away from the house, out of earshot, I hoped. I held a fist to my stomach, willing it to settle. Bitterness filled my mouth regardless.

"No, there isn't." Did she suspect something more? Had I been indiscreet and let slip something about our role as Crown agents?

"That's your last word?"

"Yes."

"Then I will bid you good day. I won't bother to seek you out again, *Mistress Addison*, and I don't care for you to contact me, either."

"But Dru…"

"You are a cruel and heartless woman." She kept her voice low, but full of venom. "You don't care about anybody but your family. She'll die and it will be your fault."

It was too late. She turned away and walked up the lane as swiftly as she had come.

"What's this commotion?" asked Robert from the doorway.

"Nothing important," I said, pushing past him. He caught my arm.

"It sounded like something," he said, regarding me over his spectacles. "You've quarreled with Drusilla?"

"It's nothing," I repeated, and pulled away. He let me go.

The bright morning spoiled, I kept to the house where I busied myself in my stillroom, preparing harmless remedies for trivial ills.

✳

I descended the cellar stairs carefully, the tray balanced in one hand. Tom would not thank me if his lunch landed on the steps, or worse, his back.

Not for the first time, I thanked God for Robert's foresight in providing internal access to our cellar. That we did not need to brave wintry conditions to get at our food stores was not only convenient, it was crucial to our preparation of the secret room to conceal extra supplies and harbor Brock's spies if need be.

"Tom. It's rabbit stew." I addressed his backside, facing toward me as he worked at the cellar wall. "Your favorite."

He turned toward me, face smudged and grinning. Was it really ten years since I had adopted a scrawny, ill-treated waif? My heart flooded with warmth as he rose to his full height, some few inches above my own. Ah, Tom, the son I might have borne, had my life gone otherwise. Tender emotions embarrassed him, so I carefully kept a neutral expression.

"That smells wonderful," he said, reaching for the tray. "I knew before you said." He perched on a flour keg and balanced the tray on his knees. At the rate the stew was vanishing down his throat, he'd be done before it had a chance to cool."

"Don't choke on it."

He rolled his eyes, waggled his eyebrows, and tossed his ginger curls flirtatiously.

I had to laugh. "You'll be the death of me, you scamp. You'd put the most shameless coquette to shame."

"I hope not. Who'd make me my favorite dish?" He wolfed down the rest of the stew and washed it down with cider. "That hit the spot."

"How much longer can you stay?"

His eyes clouded. "I need to get back soon. I don't know when I can come again."

We depended on his regular trips to visit us going unremarked by the master printer. Or worse, Joseph Willcocks. It would wreck Brock's plans if our activities became known. We would all be in some personal danger, too.

"I've an edition of the *Guardian* to set and print." He handed me the tray and rose again. "I'll get rid of this dirt and sluice off in the lake."

He followed me back up the stairs, hauling two heavy baskets of earth.

Tom

“Ho, there!”

Tom straightened up from the page he was setting. “Yes?”

“I have the editorial for you.”

“It’s taken you long enough.”

“Cranky, you are today. Fly up your arse?”

Tom growled a muffled response as he bent over the forme again, carefully placing more small chunks of metal type into the current row.

“Never mind,” said Willcocks, “just listen to this.” He flourished a sheet of paper. “Your correspondent is proud to assert that he is a constant adherent to the interests of the Country. However, he remains an enemy of the measures of the King’s Servants in this colony.” He set the paper down on top of Tom’s unfinished work. “How do you like that?”

Tom looked up, one eyebrow raised. “You looking to get locked up again?”

“It’d be worth it.” Willcocks rubbed his hands together and

grinned. "But I don't think Brock will bother me. Besides, I want to go out on a firm note."

"This is the final issue of the paper, then?"

"Yes, it is."

"Good," said Tom. "This broken-down old beast has limped through enough years. I'm sick of trying to keep it together."

"You'll appreciate the joke when I tell you I've found a buyer."

"Some fool, then. Why, it's little better than a pile of firewood."

"The fool, one Robert Hatt, has bought the lot. I confess, I almost choked at his offer."

"How much?"

"Sixteen hundred dollars. In cash, no less."

"Cash? I didn't think there was so much in the entire colony." Tom's eyebrows threatened to rise all the way up his forehead. "What was he thinking?"

"I don't know, and I don't care." Willcocks rubbed his forehead. "But keep it to yourself, boyo, or I'll have every man in the district claiming me as a friend." He grimaced. "In truth, I don't know how I'll keep such an astronomical sum safe."

"I suppose you'll spend most of your time with the conveyancing, then?"

"It certainly pays better than the *Guardian* ever did."

"That won't matter now, will it?"

"Ah, but a man must do something. People need help with land transfer negotiations. Most of the poor sods can barely sign their names, much less deal with official correspondence. What of you, Tom? Has Jones enough business to support you both?"

"It seems so. He's taken on a new apprentice and not given me my notice." Tom shrugged. "That could change, I suppose. I won't borrow trouble though. Things are fine now."

✳

Later in the month, the United States declared war on Great Britain. Too bad Jos couldn't have put out one more issue of his paper. Missed it by little more than a week, by gum!

The news was met with a great outcry by the citizens of Niagara, but with no immediate action by the Americans, their lamentations soon died down. Fear lurked in the background, for now.

Rebecca

Robert considered it necessary to travel to the Grand River Indian settlements to firm up his contacts before an invasion made it impossible. While his mission had been initiated by the Mohawks, he must take care to show them no undue preference over the other members of the Six Nations Confederacy. Each tribe had its sense of pride and would provide individual informants, and he needed to acquaint himself with their nominees. I wished I could have gone with him, so I would recognize them, too, but he felt it might look suspicious if I did so. He had always traveled to visit them alone.

I found it harder than usual to pass the time of his absence. I worried about the weather—it rained non-stop for over a week—about his inevitable seasickness on the boat across Lake Erie, from Fort Erie to the mouth of the Grand River, about so many small ills I could not protect him from. No amount of busyness around the house and farm could prevent my imagining the worst. My relief was tremendous when he returned a fortnight later, unscathed.

"Do stop fussing, Rebecca," he finally said after I had pressed food and drink and other comforts on him. "You would think I was a babe in arms, or had never traveled before."

I had to admit I had cossetted him enough for one day. "Now war is declared by the Americans," I said, "every day is full of anxiety. You mustn't blame me for worrying over you."

"I had little to concern me. John Norton sent one of his sons as escort and porter. I was thankful he was along to carry my bags." He chuckled. "Perhaps I should not have taken so many books."

I shook my head at him. "You and your books… But you didn't find the boat trip difficult?"

"No, the lake was like glass. Barely any wind to carry us along. Thank God for that." He smiled up at me. "And thank God for John Norton. He is a staunch friend to me."

✳

Some days later, I awaited Robert's return from a hastily arranged dinner at Fort George, with great anticipation. He had gone to take part in a council of war, as one of the few non-combatants requested. After all he had told me of his recent trip up the Grand River, I knew his contribution would be a valuable one as Brock developed his plans.

Nearly a year since we married. I could scarce credit it. With all the bustle around preparations for war, it felt mere weeks ago. All the long years of loneliness had resolved into a life with loving companionship. It would seem a miracle, if I believed in those. Even the women parishioners had thawed toward me, or so I believed. I was sure there were still one or two who felt me undeserving, or envied my fortune, and there would always be some with whom I could never get along.

But just when I felt secure, new threats loomed on the horizon. How would we cope with an invasion? Would I be able to help Robert survive it? He was not a young man, nor yet a middle-aged one. I must simply support him as best I could and contain my fears within. I had plenty of practice doing that.

Robert bustled in as I was about to head for my bed.

"My dear," he said, "such a paradox you've never seen. Why, one week the officers of the two garrisons are dining together, and the next they're preparing to shoot at each other. It was all I could do to keep up with the military talk. I ate and drank and listened."

"I'm sure you dined well, but did you learn anything of use?"

"I learned that being a General is no sinecure. Such a cacophony of opinions! Some would have the Army take the initiative without a formal declaration of war on our part. Others would undertake clandestine raids. Still others would set up and arm outposts at every landing spot that could be used for invasion. Why, Brock would need ten times the men he has for the latter. And then there is the dual question of the Indians and the militia. And in the militia—do you know there is talk of forming a colored company?"

"If they will fight for the Crown, why not?"

"I agree, but some of the other settlers aren't keen."

"Stuff and nonsense. If Brock has such need of men, whoever is willing should be allowed to fight. From what you say, he will need the militia, Six Nations warriors, and men of all colors if he is to fend off invaders."

"Brock is determined to invoke martial law. There's a deal of opposition over that, too, but otherwise he can't compel the militia to fight. He needs the force of law behind him." He shook his head. "It's a complicated business, this waging of war."

July–September

Jack

No sooner did the United States declare war than skirmishes erupted along the far west Upper Canadian border. News arrived of an action at Fort St. Joseph where, on July 17th, a detachment of the 41st Regiment captured Fort Michilimackinac.

This was greeted with both relief and regret by the men of the 100th, still in Lower Canada, especially Captain Sherrard's company.

"An opportunity for promotion lost," said Jack.

"Hey there, what do you mean? You were lounging around on the lower Lakes while we were freezing our balls off up there," said his Captain. He sucked hard at his long-stemmed pipe and exhaled a cloud of smoke. "Even if we hadn't been recalled last November, you'd not have been there at all." He pointed the stem of his pipe at his subaltern in mock-seriousness, poking it forward for emphasis. "What's more, if you had been with us, I'd have assigned you to the baggage train, and lucky you'd have been to find the way frozen solid."

"Why," Jack asked of the room at large, "do fellows coming off detachment always exaggerate their tribulations?"

"Perhaps," said Sherrard, "it's not an exaggeration at all. If you'd had to traverse those trackless forests and sucking swamps, you might not scoff."

"Yes," said another, "not to mention mosquitoes the size of cart horses."

"Bigger than the ones around here?" asked Jack.

"At least twice the size," said Sherrard. "Right, men? Thank the powers-that-be for a winter return trip. At least the ground held firm. I fear we'd not have survived a summer trip again." He puffed at his again. "We couldn't have traveled by water, that's sure, not now war has come."

Jack continued to lament, but privately. He longed for action, not only for promotion, but for the adventure of the thing. The smoke of musket fire on the practice-ground was no longer enough.

"Come, fellows. A round of dice?"

Jack turned eagerly to Dawson's suggestion. "Anything to relieve this dragging routine. I have little to wager, though."

"Never mind, Jack. We all know how you're fixed. Let's play for European principalities. Maybe we can oust the little French corporal—in our imaginations, at least."

They laughed, and Dawson pulled a pair of dice from his pocket. All thoughts of duty were banished for a while.

Rebecca

News of the actions along the border arrived in Niagara almost daily in late June and early July. By the end of July, Robert was so worried, he determined to consult with General Brock, then at Fort George and consumed with his duties as Lieutenant-Governor.

Brock made no bones about the dire situation on the border, nor his advice to Robert to send his womenfolk as far away as possible. York would not be far enough. Montreal or Quebec would be better. From there, they might take ship to England as a last resort.

"The General spoke of the Lakes as a porous border between us and the Americans," Robert told me. "He compared it to cheesecloth."

An amusing comparison, perhaps, but this was no time for levity. "And so…?"

"I will send Maryel to join Eliza in Montreal. Brock says it would be comparatively safe there, although somewhat vulnerable from the Richelieu River. At least from Lower Canada they can take ship to England, if the worst happens."

Montreal might as well be all the way back to England for the difficulty in travel between us.

"The Mountains would take her as well?"

"I have no doubt of that." He eyed me sidelong. "And you, my dear? Won't you accompany her?"

I could not read his expression. "No, certainly not," I said. "You mustn't try to convince me, either. I'm sure there will be others leaving the area to whom we may entrust her."

"We will speak more of this later," he said. "For, despite Brock's advice, I am not sure what might be the best course of action." His face brightened. "I nearly forgot. There's some good news on this dark occasion. I have been confirmed in the appointment as Chaplain of Fort George. It will bring in a salary of £25 per annum and a subaltern's allowance. This puts me on the same footing as Dr. Strachan in York."

Robert was well aware of Dr. Strachan's privileged position as rector in the capital. It was a source of some grievance with him, Strachan having begun as a Presbyterian schoolteacher and having obtained elevated standing in the Church of England. This rankled with Robert who resented Strachan's arrogance in his dealings with other clergy in the province. I was pleased on his behalf, and for the added resources.

"Most welcome news. With the added income, we'll be better able to supply the secret room."

Willcocks

27^Jul Post-haste to York for emergency session of Legislature. Can't let Brock declare martial law without opposition. Once military takes hold of the Province, might as well abandon hope of any reform.

5 Aug

Stalemate. Legislators argued strongly against martial law. Even Tories don't favor seizing person and property without proper warrant. Brock frustrated—thinks necessary for his conduct of war. Ended with his proroguing session, in effect imposing martial law even if no actual law exists.

Whole affair with military control limits my activities sorely. Brock's intentions good. Many of his fellows less so. He could be transferred or killed. If Brock were not leading, we might fall under control of tyrants. Risk I'm unwilling to take. Still have lines of communication into New York. Must keep options open. Holding back for now.

Damn all soldiers. Damn all tyrants. Damn all obstacles in my path!

Rebecca

In late July, Robert was called to a special session of Parliament. He returned with stunning news. After the invasion at Amherstburg, in the far southwest of the Province, in early July, Brock had made a defiant counter-proclamation, then called upon Parliament one last time. The session lasted for little over a week. He attempted once more to get habeas corpus suspended, but Willcocks and his associates blocked him again. Though the province was now at war, Brock failed to implement martial law. Stymied, he prorogued the session to carry on with his preparations for combat.

Before Robert returned to Niagara, he attended a meeting where Brock confided his intentions to a few trusted colleagues. He had hatched a daring plan to bluff General Hull out of Fort Detroit.

"I fear for his safety," said Robert, "for if he is lost… But that is unthinkable."

I squeezed his hand, unable to find words of reassurance. We knew how few regular soldiers Brock could detach from Niagara, and how risky it could be to rely on the militia.

By August 8th, the expedition to the southwest corner of the

Province was ready to go. We were among those waving off the troops. A few days later, we learned General Prevost had sent Brock word he should sit tight and exercise caution. By that time, Brock was well on his way.

Norton brought the news of the stunning victory.

"We had only a small striking force," he said. "We embarked from Long Point with about three hundred men, only about fifty regulars, and the rest untried militia."

"But surely this would be like hitting an anvil with a feather," said Robert.

Norton shook his head. "I was convinced the whole affair was madness, and said so. But the General was determined. So, we sailed along Lake Erie and landed opposite Fort Detroit." He laughed. "I was one of the few who knew what we'd find there."

"And what was that?" I asked.

"The Shawnee chief, Tecumseh, with six hundred warriors and about four hundred militia from the southwest of the province. I had to laugh at the faces of our local militia who thought they were on some kind of forlorn hope. You may imagine their relief."

"I suppose it was kept secret so no word could get to the Americans?" asked Robert.

"That was Brock's plan. A good one."

"What happened next?" I asked. I sat so close to the edge of my chair I was in danger of falling off.

"Brock had intelligence from our brethren on the American shore that General Hull had over two thousand men inside Fort Detroit, with about another five hundred protecting his supply lines. He was well-equipped with cannon and ammunition. We were the lesser force and yet had the greater strategists." He paused for a drink of cool cider I had brought up from the cellar.

"In spite of our smaller force, Brock crossed the river to make a frontal assault on the fort, backed by artillery firing from our shore.

Meanwhile, Tecumseh's warriors, in full warpaint, marched round and round, yelling and screaming at full volume, confusing the Americans as to their numbers and, as we later discovered, demoralizing them entirely. Hull believed us to be the stronger force and surrendered. We gained thirty-five artillery pieces and a great deal of powder, shot, and other much-needed supplies."

"But I don't understand," I said. "How could the Americans be so deceived?"

He grinned. "That was the greatest joke. Tecumseh paraded his six hundred warriors around the fort, coming out of the woods and circling back around to repeat the maneuver, making Hull think there were many more warriors than was the case. The Americans have a great fear of our people, and failed to recognize the same faces passing by them again and again."

"The Americans won't forget such a humiliation," said Robert.

"No, but it was worth it," said Norton. "Brock took counsel with Tecumseh and the other Indian leaders and applauded the mutual confidence and regard established between them. He said, 'It's the Indian warriors who will make all the difference in this war.' He confided to me he knew his superiors would credit the battle to his leadership, but he was aware that help from the Six Nations would make it possible to defend the Niagara River. He places great faith in our people, and I will do my best to ensure we support him."

"I am pleased he recognizes your worth, John," said Robert.

"I'm not so naive as to think the British are any better at keeping their promises than the Americans, but my people live here now, and we must defend our land."

"So now we wait," said Robert, "for the Americans to attack."

I shuddered at the thought.

✳

After due consideration of Brock's unwelcome advice, Robert

decided to send Maryel to Montreal. He broke the news to her one evening in early August.

"Father, how could you? Just when things are getting exciting!" cried Maryel.

"Hush, Maryel, you must go," I said.

She continued to mutter, only subsiding when I glared at her.

"But Robert, I will not leave your side."

"But, my dear…"

"No, I won't. We already went over all this. Don't try to persuade me, or order me either. You'll need my care if you're to be exposed to the upheavals of war. The very idea, trying to send me away." My cheeks grew hot, and I shook my head. "I won't go!"

"You know the dangers are real?" he said. "I was shocked myself when Brock made such a definite recommendation, but have thought on the possible consequences for days now. I have come to agree with him. I would not have you face injury or death. Or suffer starvation, which is likely, if war drags on."

"My mind is made up."

He sighed. "I hoped to convince you to go, but I knew you would not, and so I told Brock."

"But what about me?" Maryel asked, refusing to be cowed by parental disapproval. "Must I go so far away? Is Montreal so much safer than here?"

"If war comes here, there are few refuges," he said. "If war comes to Montreal, you may yet evacuate back to Britain, where our family would welcome you."

"Do you think it could become necessary?" I asked. Such an extreme step was hard to contemplate.

Robert closed his eyes for a moment, taking a deep breath. "Brock has convinced me. We must prepare for the worst outcomes. He is despondent about our situation all along the Lakes. His Majesty's forces are hard-pressed against Napoleon, and can send no reinforcements. Our militia is weak, and few. Those who fought as Loyalists against the Republicans are now old men. Many of the newer settlers have no great love for the Crown. You can judge for yourselves how serious our situation is. Only by good fortune—and God's aid—will our Province survive an invasion. My mind is made up. You must go."

He looked at our open-mouthed faces. "Maryel, you may find yourself some occupation, as you have longed to do. I will send a letter to Dr. Mountain and perhaps he can assist you." He put his arm around her, a rare gesture. "We will all be turning our hands to unfamiliar tasks, to aid the war effort."

Packing occupied every spare moment for the next week. Maryel needed to leave before the end of August to be sure of reaching Montreal before the fall rains began in earnest. Eliza had taken some of our Atlantic crossing trunks earlier, but some remained. Maryel packed her clothes in the two sturdiest, leaving behind only the most battered to store seldom-used household linens and utensils. I made sure she had sufficient warm clothing for the harsher Montreal winter Eliza and Jack had written about.

Tom

Tom met Willcocks at Dickson's South Landing Inn in Queenston where Willcocks had engaged a private parlor so they would not be overheard. Tom placed his hat on the table and leaned on his elbows.

"I keep thinking about your last editorial, Jos. You condemned General Brock's tactics in the House of Assembly yet consider yourself a patriot. Aren't those opposing views?"

"Not at all, Tom, not at all. I consider it my sacred duty to protest against the Crown's officials when they act against the best interests of the population. That's true democracy for you, boyo. Consider it well. The *Guardian* only published articles encouraging the people to seek their rights under a lawfully elected Parliament—the ones they should enjoy by natural law."

Tom took this in. "Well… I don't suppose you asked me here to talk politics. You have a job for me?"

"Indeed, I do. It's of the greatest importance and urgency," said Willcocks, rubbing his hands together. "I'm asked to contact those of the Six Nations whose lands are within my former constituency, to verify their support for the Crown in the coming conflict. The request is made by none other than General Brock!" His eyes glowed with pride. "So, you can see he has no questions about my loyalty, whether or not if you and others do. Gore described me and all Whigs as rank traitors, but it's the damned Tories who are lining their pockets with the people's and the Crown's money... Well, well, enough of that. I'm talking with a friend, not stumping for the Legislature. If Brock thinks I can assist my country, then I am bound to try."

"What's my role to be?"

"Let me show you. It's easier if you can see the routes."

Willcocks unrolled two identical maps of the Niagara region, showing all the roads and rivers, settlements, forests and swamps. He had marked and numbered several places along the Grand River and at Burlington with red ink. He proposed to split the communities with Tom, and noted a list of names on the back of each map, linked to the numbers. There was no telling when the Americans would invade, so the time to accomplish their task was short.

"These are the most receptive of the leaders of each of the Six Nations. Spend only three days with each group. We meet back here no later than two weeks from tomorrow with the information which I will convey to the General. Can you help?"

"My list of clients takes me along the Lake Erie shore so I can speak with the ones nearest the mouth of the Grand River." Tom examined the lists. "You know... I've met some of these men already, when I was living at Addison's. They would visit him when he couldn't come to them. I was only a boy, of course, but it may help ease the introduction."

"Splendid. Between us, we can deliver Brock's message to our Indian associates. I'm sure they will follow him and support the Crown. They've no love for the Americans who seized their Mohawk Valley homelands."

Despite ill health owing to spoiled food, probably the meal at Dickson's Inn, Willcocks was enthusiastic about his task, and departed a day or two later. Brock's audacious actions had convinced him he was a leader worth following—one with the people's interests at heart.

Tom followed him soon after. He continued to wonder at Brock's apparent trust of Willcocks, and at Willcocks's apparent adulation of Brock. Neither seemed characteristic of either man. He found his own ambivalence on the matter disturbing. Why was he watching Jos at all, if he was in league with the colonial establishment? Where had Jos's suspicions of military rule gone? And what was Brock's true motivation? All Tom could do was watch and report, as ordered.

Rebecca

With Maryel safely away, Robert insisted on moving our valuables, and most of our household goods, to Lake Lodge as soon as practicable. Though we would still lease the town-house, for now. So, we had the additional task of packing up almost all our possessions and household effects. And the books. Thousands of books. He insisted his entire library must be conveyed to the farm. Not only that, he would take the silver plate and chalice and china christening bowl from the Church.

"I can use them for services in the long room over the lakeside veranda. How fortunate we enclosed that space. It can serve as a chapel if the need arises."

I shook my head. "When I think of all the dirt to be tracked in… But at least it can be reached by the outer stair. We must have the loose step repaired, though." I lifted a book and wiped it clean. "I suppose I should be happy to dislodge twenty years' worth of dust from some of these volumes, but there are so many!"

Robert peered over his spectacles at me, frowning. "My dear, those are the tools of my mission. A bastion of learning in this wild land. No, I cannot do without them." He had no sense of humor when it came to his books.

"That may be, husband, but if I had known how many boxes we would need to move them, I don't know if I would have agreed," I said. "Mr. Dickson's lad has been hammering away all week at crates for us. As he gets more done, we fill them. And where do you suppose we're going to put them all once they're moved?" I wrapped a shawl around the christening bowl, perhaps sufficient to cushion its passage over the rutted road, if held on my lap.

"Now, Rebecca, I brought them all safely over the Atlantic Ocean. I am sure we can transport them the four miles to our farm. I will feel more comfortable when they are there, where surely they can be maintained more safely than in town. Our lodgings here are only leased. Who knows what might happen if the Fort was invaded, or the town? We will take them out in easy stages. Maybe we could have some ferried out by water, although I hesitate to risk it. The ocean voyage was bad enough. I was so worried I almost forgot my seasickness."

"You and your books!" I shook my head at him. "I'm sure you could have had worse vices, but certainly none heavier to bear."

He cracked a rare laugh at that. I was pleased to have taken his mind off his worries, if only for a moment.

But he sobered almost immediately. "I thought our efforts to move the books would provide some cover for the transport of stores for the secret room. We are acquiring so much. Some can be explained away as gifts for poor parishioners in outlying homesteads, but not all. Whereas my weakness for books is well known, and the subject of some little ridicule amongst the uneducated. A few boxes, more or less, will not look strange to them."

I was impressed. "I never suspected you had a talent for intrigue, my dear. I had wondered a little at the number of crates, even considering the size of your library."

"Perhaps you might make your displeasure known to some of the more… sociable… ladies in the parish?"

"You mean the inveterate gossips? To be sure, I will." Several names leaped to mind at once. Nothing like church ladies to put the word around.

"We will have some extra supplies of our own, although probably nowhere near enough, if the war drags on. We must hope for a good harvest this year. If battles are fought on our territory, we could go longer than one year with poorer harvests."

I agreed. "Especially if most of the men are off in the militia during planting and harvest seasons. And what of the armies themselves? We must suppose they will raid the land for their sustenance."

"I fear you are right." He shook his head. "There is little we can do about it, though. We must expect both sides to live off the land. I have taken my ideas on the relief of those who suffer wartime damages, to Brock and the York merchants. I hope they will take heed of them and do some planning for compensation."

That meant his stamina would be taxed further, both during and after any conflict. My worry for his health increased at every turn.

✴

Toward the end of the month, General Brock himself rode out to consult with Robert. He spent some time inspecting our progress with the secret room. I proudly showed off Tom's work. Brock exclaimed over the cunning concealment of the entrance to the room, and the tunnel connecting the cellar to an exit hidden by bushes on the lakeshore.

"It isn't quite finished, I'm afraid," I said. "You can't walk the entire length yet. He has connected both ends, but still has to crawl in the middle."

"But this is marvelous," said Brock. "I doubt anyone who didn't know of it could find it."

"Which is the whole point," said Robert. "The shelving that makes the doorway is a nice touch, isn't it?"

"Ingenious," said Brock. He drew himself up to his full height, the top of his head brushing the room's low ceiling. "I hope I don't have to use this."

We laughed, but my heart sank at the thought.

"We must hope it doesn't come to that," said Robert.

The two men mounted the stairs while I replaced the camou-flaging stores onto the door-shelves. I arranged bags and boxes so they could be removed rapidly. To a casual observer, that wall of the cellar presented an unbroken set of shelving. Tom had shown an unexpected talent for joinery.

When I returned upstairs, the men were bent over a map Brock had unrolled on our dining table. I peered around them to see. It charted the full length of the Niagara River, from Fort Erie at the south to Niagara-town at the north. The different fortifications were sketched in side panels. Brock pointed out the positions he thought most vulnerable to attack.

"I expect an invasion sometime this autumn."

I was aghast, but Robert merely nodded. "You think it likely the town will be assaulted first?"

"It might be, but with our forces concentrated at Fort George, I think somewhere upriver more likely. Somewhere above the falls, or perhaps at the landing place at Queenston. Our fortifications are lighter there than at either major fort, and it would take time for troops from here or Fort Erie to offer support. Invaders might gain a foothold before we could arrive."

"Can we not rely on our Indian allies?" Robert asked.

"That's a ray of light, to be sure," said Brock.

"I gather Willcocks proved useful there?"

"To a certain degree, yes. But Norton prepared the way. As did you." Brock raised an eyebrow. "I thought it well to enable Willcocks to see himself as our benefactor. He can be led by his vanity." He returned his attention to the map, pointing once more at Queenston on the Niagara River below the limestone ridge. "It will be here. Norton concurs."

But when? Waiting was almost worse than an attack might be.

✳

We received a letter from Maryel in late September, which I read to Robert as he was eating supper on his return from a few days' visiting outlying communities.

"'I have been in Montreal for a few days now & am recovered sufficiently to write a little of my trip. After the long journey, I was fatigued, but I am in good health. I must commend Miss Bell for her kind chaperonage during the trip. She and her family have removed to Quebec, where they may remain or take ship for England. Or perhaps travel to Halifax and settle there, near kin.

"'I hardly remembered our previous journey, so the route felt rough and long. Eliza assures me the trip was both faster & more comfortable now. I can hardly credit it. The sloop to Kingston was the only comfortable part. After that, it took a full twelve days to pass through the countryside with its various swamps & rapids. I never want to see another canoe, bateaux are as bad, & the roads! Montreal streets are cobblestone, a little smoother. I arrived safely in the end, so no more of that.

"'I am determined to find some useful activity here, or at least pursue the study of French so I may assist with the marketing and communicate with the servants. Eliza has already gained enough proficiency in the language to put me to shame.

"'Dr. & Mrs. Mountain bid fair to spoil us with their kind attentions. We're sensible of the favor the Mountains do us and wish to perform every service we can for them.

"'There have been no battles nearby as yet, but Dr. Mountain says an attacking force might come up from Lake Champlain or somewhere along the St. Lawrence River.

"'I pray the war will be over quickly.

"'Eliza sends her love and promises to write soon.'"

Robert pushed himself back from his emptied plate as I finished reading. "She sounds well enough. Are you content?"

"I miss both of them," I said. "But it's reassuring to have them somewhere less hazardous than here."

"Would you had gone, too."

"Now, Robert, you know you can't get along without me."

"Too true." He smiled. "We'll muddle through together, then."

I folded the letter and handed it to him. "We will. And it would please me if you would not refer to me leaving again. I haven't the slightest intention of doing so."

He smiled more broadly. "It would serve me right if you did."

October

Jack

The 100th Foot's Montreal headquarters lay in a nondescript stone building on a side street. The only indicator of their presence was a soldier posted outside the door.

Jack leaned out an upper window, facing a dreary cobblestone street lined with equally drab buildings. Two weeks of incessant rain made him long for the wooded surrounds of the riverside forts. Maybe going on detachment wasn't so bad after all. He watched the passers-by with scant interest.

A tall, elderly man in a clerical hat, accompanied by a woman wrapped in a hooded cloak, stopped at the door and queried the duty guard.

"Is this the headquarters of the 100th Foot?" he asked.

"Yes, sir. The Adjutant is in his office, sir." They entered the building.

Ho-hum. Probably some mendicant body seeking donations. They'd find slim pickings here.

A loud voice interrupted his thoughts. "Stevenson! Jack Stevenson! Plague take it! Where is the man?" It was Hingston. He must be on desk duty. "Stevenson, at once! You have guests!"

But who would call for him?

"On my way!" he shouted. The way things echoed in this place, Hingston was sure to hear him.

Jack buttoned his tunic and made sure everything was straight before heading downstairs. It wasn't every day a man had visitors. He was thunderstruck to see Maryel's face under the hood. Behind her stood the clerical gentleman.

"Maryel!" He caught her hands in his. "I never thought… Your letters stopped… What are you doing here?"

He might have embraced her, but for the audience.

She giggled at his confusion. "Father sent me to join Eliza. He was worried about my safety on the border. My letter must have gone astray. The post has become so unreliable. It's such a surprise to find you here. I thought you were on detachment." She blushed. "I wrote you a note, thinking it could be passed on."

"We rotate to headquarters occasionally. I'm glad we do." As Hingston frowned at him, he continued, "I'm on duty now, but I will hope to pay a call on you later."

"We're staying with Dr. Mountain's family." She looked over her shoulder at the clergyman, who spoke up.

"You will be welcome to call on Mrs. Mountain, and my young guests will doubtless find it agreeable as well." He turned to Maryel. "Come, my dear, we must return home."

Maryel took a folded paper out of her pocket and handed it to Jack. He bent over her hand and pressed his lips to her glove. They parted after an exchange of bows all around.

Jack visited the Mountain residence whenever he could wangle a few hours of leave. Dr. Mountain was an affable man who didn't mind Jack's repeated presence in his house. The family was musical and welcomed his violin.

October in Montreal varied from mild sunny days to bitter frost and sometimes snow. On the better days, Jack and Maryel took long walks, Eliza trailing behind. They found plenty to discuss in their surroundings and discovered a convergence of viewpoints. Both were taken by the handsome stone buildings of the town, and the bustle of *Les Habitants*. There was a great deal to admire, and little to deplore. Jack whistled a brisk tune as he returned to quarters.

On the colder, wetter days, when they were forced indoors, they made do with conversation over the teacups. Eliza occupied herself with rolling bandages for the hospital and other mundane tasks, and only rarely interrupted his conversation with Maryel. Maryel often had some stitchery or other in her lap. Most of the time, they talked of the town, how different it was to hear French spoken all around, how beautiful the autumn colors were, and other innocuous topics. Jack mentioned some new compositions sent from his father last year that Maryel expressed an interest in hearing. He hesitated to act too lover-like and bent his efforts on establishing a firm friendship.

Inevitably, the day came when he must return to his remote posting. When Eliza stepped out of the room on some errand, he summoned up the courage to renew his addresses.

"We have become good friends, have we not?" he asked in a low voice.

"Indeed, we have," said Maryel, smiling.

"Would you… Might you… Can I hope for more?"

She bent her head over her needlework and was silent.

He swallowed back a lump. "Please tell me if there is any hope."

She raised her head, eyes shining. "Yes, you may hope," she said.

Jack grasped her hand and raised it to his lips.

"But we must wait," she said, "until the war is over. And it's just begun. Who knows what may come?"

Jack, torn between delight and frustration, bent over her hand again, kissing it fervently. His brow furrowed as he looked up at her again. "I had hoped… but no. You're right to hesitate."

"I'm of age and can make my own decisions, but I would wish to involve my family. I could not make final plans until I see them again." She chuckled. "And I require some courting, sir."

Jack grinned. "Happy to oblige, miss. I'm afraid letters will have to do for now."

Eliza came back into the room. She clucked at their intimate pose. "I suppose I must wish you happy?"

"Early days for that, sister," said Maryel, "but we're agreed on a period of courting."

"Good for you," said Eliza, "I always liked him best of your swains." She returned to her bandage-rolling.

Maryel and Jack stared at each other for a moment, then burst into helpless laughter. Trust Eliza to turn romance into prose.

Rebecca

We grew accustomed to hearing desultory gunfire from posts on both banks of the Niagara River. Robert, who had traveled its thirty-odd miles' length in recent weeks, said it was the same from Niagara to Fort Erie. Shots originated mostly from the American side, since there were more targets on our well-settled bank. Few found a mark.

Brock made it clear to Robert that the British Army spared little thought for the troubles in their far-flung colonies, nor could they, with Napoleon running rampant through Europe. Ingenuity, not superior numbers, would save the day. He had little time to spare for this, relying on other officers to fill in the gaps, including both regulars and the local militia.

"If you were trying to reassure me, you have failed," I said over my knitting, after one such conversation. Drat, I had dropped a stitch.

"I don't suppose it's as bad as that, my dear," said Robert. "Brock was most complimentary about the troops quartered in this district. Although he expressed some doubts about the militia. But he was amazed there had been no losses to illness, and almost no desertions."

"Quite astonishing, in fact." I could not keep the sarcasm from my tone.

"Now, Rebecca." Robert gave me a reproving look. "I have seen for myself that the harvest is mostly in, and our country well-prepared to stave off an attack. If only the border wasn't so long, and the troops were greater in number."

"And if only we weren't situated squarely on the border," I added. And there was another stitch gone.

I could understand Brock's misgivings about the militia. The recent American origins of many men gave the Army regulars much concern. So-called "Late" Loyalists were an unknown quantity, suspected of harboring republican sentiments. In my visits to the sick, I frequently heard rumblings of discontent from the unwary.

Our uneasiness over the fragile truce between Forts George and Niagara was heightened on the evening of the 12th of October, when Tom arrived at our door, breathless, with news that the flag of truce at Queenston had been fired upon.

"Men were massing on the American side of the river. There is no doubt they will attack, and soon." He wouldn't stop, even for water. "I must carry the message to others." And he was off before I could press him for more.

What sleep I got was unsettled, disturbed as it was by the inter-mittent gunfire. I may have been accustomed to it, but that did not mean it failed to wake me. An hour over my herbs failed to comfort me, but I persisted in preparing such medicaments as would be of use in the field. I made up small packets of willow bark and gol-denseal root powders to be distributed to the soldiers. More potent remedies would only be available as needed, since most of them must be prepared fresh. The most potent, laudanum, kept well but was in short supply. I locked it away with the salt and tea against future need. I had requested—and was fortunate to get—an additional supply, which I transported to the farm and stored in the secret room.

✳

The next morning, before dawn, I hastened to the fort with my packets for the troops. Even at that early hour, preparations were well underway for a battle. Men moved in all directions in some organized pattern I couldn't discern, that kicked up a lot of dust. As I turned for home, a messenger arrived, his horse laboring under him, and shouted to all, "The enemy is at Queenston!"

His words were all but drowned out by a barrage from Fort Niagara. The first balls fell short of Fort George but sparked more activity within. I wanted no part of that and ran as fast as I could across the common ground between fort and town. I turned for a last look back. Troops marched forth from the fort's gates toward Queenston. I hoped—even prayed—they might be in time to repulse the enemy. We would have to wait it out, along with the remaining defenders of the fort.

As we learned over the course of the day from runners to the fort, General Brock had taken a large force to the defense of Queenston, leaving General Sheaffe to guard against invasion from Fort Niagara. Fort George had been under bombardment the entire day. Many of our neighbors did not have the fortitude to remain in town, but scurried away to nearby farms to stay with family or friends. Naturally, Robert felt the need to set an example to others by remaining, and so must I. But the Americans seemed satisfied with their bombardment, and didn't invade our town after all. There was a scare in Fort George when fire broke out within, threatening the powder magazine. Our soldiers kept up their counter-barrage of

Fort Niagara despite having to put it out.

During breaks in the two forts' exchange of fire, we could hear the echo of cannon fire from Queenston, at a distance of seven miles. Then, late in the morning, General Sheaffe also set out for the battle with a large contingent, so we knew the fight must be serious. How serious would only become clear later that evening.

Willcocks

Willcocks did not consider himself a sentimental man, but he shed some tears on that October day. Only a few were because of the pain of a dislocated shoulder. More were for the General.

"Damn him for a foolhardy hero," he muttered as he wrote in his journal with his good hand clutching a stub of pencil.

Queenston, 13 Oct 1812

Hard march out of Fort George this morning, alongside Genl. Brock's force. Several others from town came along. Heard soldiers call us "gentlemen volunteers". Evidently not a compliment. Helter-skelter of battle unforeseen. Main force from Lewiston climbed hill to attack battery. Rough limestone cliffs, sparse trees, not much cover. Our small force atop hill pushed back by attackers. Battery in enemy hands. Brock attacked uphill. Disastrous move. Red coat too good a target. He fell, many others with him. Too great a loss to comprehend. Fighting continued. Reinforcements under Sheaffe came mid-afternoon. Surprised Americans on hill. Norton & Indian warriors, full war paint. Terrified Americans jumped from cliffs, died on rocks, drowned in river. Took a tumble myself.

injured shoulder. Victory at terrible price. Without Brock, whither Upper Canada?

He repeated this last thought to Tom, who came to check on his comfort in a Queenston billet. "What think you?" he asked, propping himself on his uninjured arm.

"We beat them off in the end."

"But Brock—such a leader—such a loss."

"I don't know." Tom rubbed his chin. "I'm no strategist, but didn't Sheaffe show better generalship than Brock on this day? What was he thinking? And what use is he to us dead?"

"Who's to say what Sheaffe would have done without the warriors? I'll reserve judgment until I see more of him. At least I knew Brock wouldn't let the high command interfere with his judgment on the ground. He'd act first and ask forgiveness later."

"Yes, and see where that got him." Tom turned for the door. "I'm off to Niagara. I'll return later."

Willcocks lay back on his pallet, easing himself into a more comfortable position. Little he could do about anything right now.

Rebecca

Tom choked out the news of Brock's death to us, his worn face streaked with sweat tracking down his dust-encrusted cheeks. He clung to me like a child seeking refuge, shuddering with fatigue. Behind me, Robert fell to coughing. I had to turn from Tom to settle him. Truth to tell, I was surprised we hadn't collapsed together onto the floor. Brock's personality had been so potent, he had seemed invincible.

When we were calmer, Tom sketched out the day's events as he knew them: the invaders' ascent of Queenston Heights, the fight for the battery, Brock's fatal charge up the slope, his death along with his second-in-command, Sheaffe's approach from the interior, and the charge of Norton's Indian contingent. The Indians saved the day, all were agreed on that, he reported. The militia proved useful, too, better than expected.

Finishing his tale, Tom broke down, lowering his head to my shoulder and sobbing freely. I could do little but replace his soggy handkerchief with my dry one, my own tears falling unheeded down my dress. Finally, he was cried out and hiccoughing. I got him a glass of water and a cloth to wipe his face and hands.

"I can't stop longer," he said to Robert. "I'm sure an official messenger will bring word soon, but I thought you should know at once. General Sheaffe has given orders for a lavish funeral to properly honor Brock's heroism. Captain Glegg will bring the body and manage the arrangements. You are to conduct the service. I must take my leave. I'm wanted back at Queenston."

"You're not wounded?" I asked.

"No, but I'm helping the field surgeon. He gave me a chit to pick some more laudanum at the fort." He paused. "Mr. Willcocks is among the wounded."

"Willcocks!" Robert exclaimed.

"He was devoted to Brock," I said. "But I confess I'm amazed to hear of his participation."

"He acquitted himself well."

"I suppose wonders will never cease," I said. "Return when you can, Tom."

He nodded, gave me a hug, then strode out.

Robert sat quietly, slumped slightly in his chair, head bowed. He didn't raise it for many minutes.

"Such brave young men." He pulled a handkerchief from his coat pocket and wiped his eyes. "I can hardly comprehend our loss."

Brave? Or foolhardy. I wondered if there was a difference when all was said and done. What good could Brock's self-sacrifice do our poor province? He was an experienced soldier. Surely, he had not been carried away by a sense of heroism? But it was done, and we would have to bear the consequences. This was but one battle, only the beginning of the fight for the colony's survival. Our future looked grim.

St. Mark's Church now became an emergency hospital, with

wounded brought in from Queenston to its sheltering walls. I learned more details of the battle from the pain-wracked men under my care, including the pivotal role of Captain Norton and the Indian warriors. Regular soldiers were in awe of the raw courage they showed in battle, and welcomed the impact of war paint and battle cries on the American militias. They lamented the fall of their General, but were loud in praise of General Sheaffe, who had rallied them and won the day.

Brock's funeral cortege was the most impressive sight seen in Niagara since its days as the capital of the Province, under Simcoe. From my position outside the gate of the fort, I had an excellent view.

Precisely at 10:00 a.m., a slow march began from Government House, with the Fort Major leading regulars and militia in black arm-bands, followed by a military band, its drums muffled in black cloth, playing a dirge. Then Brock's horse, draped in black, was led out, followed by the General's servants and the Army surgeons. Next came Robert in his clerical garb, followed by the caskets of Brock and his aide McDonald mounted on caissons and attended by pall-bearers and mourners. This official party was followed by Provincial officials, Brock's civilian friends, and the townsfolk. The procession made its way along a route lined by regulars, militia, and Indian war-riors, to Fort George, to the sound of minute guns firing. The two comrades were buried in a single grave in the north-east bastion of the Fort, nearest to Fort Niagara. Robert, as garrison Chaplain, read the service. He wept openly as a twenty-one-gun salute was fired over the General and his fellow officer.

At sunset that evening, another salute was fired by the Americans at Fort Niagara. I sat by the fire with a cup of tea, listening, while Robert busied himself over the church register.

"Even our enemies respected the good General," said Robert.

"Their respect doesn't comfort me, my dear," I said. "I fear what may become of us without him."

He didn't answer but dipped a fresh quill pen in his inkstand, and made an entry in the register. I leaned over to see what he had written.

Oct. 16. General Sir Isaac Brock. Colonel John McDonald. They fell together at Queenston and they were buried together in the N.E. Bastion of Fort George.

He put down his pen and bowed his head in prayer. I hoped that might ease his mind after such a long and painful day. I could find no such solace myself, and no respite either, for tomorrow my duties with the wounded would resume.

Robert had long been abed before I felt sufficiently forward with my household tasks to follow him. When I finally retired for the night, I could not settle to sleep. I indulged a rare fancy that from their position in the bastion, Brock and his aide-de-camp might still guard the border. But that was mystical nonsense. I shook off my foolishness, turned over, and sleep finally overtook me.

Tom

As the funeral drew to a close, Tom saw Norton on the edge of the crowd and hurried to meet him. They walked to the command post. Norton showed a token to a lone guard, who admitted them. He led the way to the commander's office, where they sat down to wait for General Sheaffe. The sad remnants of Brock's last meal were still on a side table, and his coat and hat were draped over a chest, the coat pierced near the second buttonhole. The shot had gone directly to the heart. It was a sobering sight.

Norton took one of the straight-backed chairs beside the desk and motioned Tom to the other. They must wait while the general spoke with local dignitaries and his other commanders. Norton closed his eyes and appeared to be napping.

Tom was restless. He reached for a book that sat on the corner of the desk. It was a copy of Sterne's *Tristram Shandy*. To think that on the eve of battle Brock chose a light work. And yet… it was consistent with what Tom knew of the man. He had a grand sense of the ridiculous and was quick to depress pretension. No doubt he found his cares lessened by the humorous situations drawn by

Sterne. As Tom riffled through the pages, looking for a favorite passage, his head drooped and the book dropped from his hands, splaying open on the floor.

By the time Sheaffe arrived, Norton was alert, and gave Tom a poke. "Smarten up, Thrush."

Tom picked up the fallen book and replaced it where it had lain earlier. They faced Sheaffe across the desk.

He was sorting through Brock's recent correspondence, and held up a list of names.

"It's fortunate our late commander saw fit to share his covert activities with me," he said. "He chose a rare flock of birds. And I must say, Snipe," here he addressed Norton, "your band of spies has provided invaluable intelligence about the enemy. Brock could never have held the province up to now without it. But," he raised his hand, "we're on a different footing now we're fully engaged. We need to get behind enemy lines. For this, I can think of none better than the Indian warriors you have enlisted." He snorted. "The Americans are mostly an unobservant lot. They tend not to differentiate one Indian from another and are accustomed to solitary hunters. They fear large groups, but ignore one man passing through. But we also need a different sort of agent." He turned to Tom. "You're in the confidence of Joseph Willcocks?"

Tom nodded.

"I have grave concerns about him. He had a personal loyalty to Brock, but I don't know if he'll work with me. I don't have Brock's easy ways with fools, and Willcocks is as big a fool as I've ever met."

Tom interjected at this point. "I believe he's truly devastated by Brock's death. You're right that he found Brock a man in authority he was willing to follow."

Norton nodded his approval of Tom's analysis. "I agree. Moreover, I suspect he's now like a rudderless boat, liable to drift with the prevailing wind."

Sheaffe rubbed at his chin, making a rasping noise as his rough fingers passed over a two-day growth of beard. "Well now, Thrush, if you think you can handle it, I've got a new assignment for you. Or rather, I would like to double your current one. We need to get inside the American command and we can't do it with Norton's warriors—or with women. Of the remaining men on the list, you're the best candidate. We want you to—"

"To turn double-agent?"

Norton laughed. "I told you he was quick!"

Sheaffe smiled and continued. "This could well be the most dangerous assignment of the war." He leaned over the desk, resting on his forearms. "Your position as associate and confidante of Joseph Willcocks will be the base of the project. I'll feed you pieces of information we're fairly sure the Americans have already found out or will soon. You'll gain credibility by being able to confirm them. As well, we'll learn if Willcocks is already passing information. Meanwhile, he'll feel more confident to share secrets with you. It's my opinion he'll eventually turn traitor, and see you as a potential agent behind our lines. If he jumps ship, he'll want you with him. If you need to, you can communicate through Norton's warriors who can move most freely."

"So I'm to take on the appearance of a traitor to my friends?"

"Yes. Your double game will be invisible to all but the people on a very short list, who are all equally at risk. I know I'm asking a lot. You may be shunned or arrested. If you're charged with treason to the Crown, we'll make sure the evidence is insufficient and you'll be released, but we can't lift the cloud of suspicion until the war is over. And there's no way we can guarantee your treatment should the Americans get wind of your true role. The risks are real. To your good name and your life. Are you prepared to hazard them?"

It was a weighty decision. Not to be undertaken without sufficient thought. "Are the Addisons on the list?" he finally asked.

Sheaffe looked down at his papers while Norton placed a hand on Tom's shoulder.

"Not yet," said Sheaffe. "The fewer who know, the better."

"How can I possibly keep it from them? They're already involved!" Tom's tone grew shrill as he thought of the implications. To risk the loss of trust of those he loved. Perhaps to die with them convinced he was a traitor. Could he do it? Could he not do it and keep his self-respect? His head sunk onto his chest. Could he keep this from Rebecca?

Sheaffe and Norton were silent, waiting. Finally, Tom raised his head. Pale, voice wavering a bit, he said, "I'll try." His audience relaxed, and both men moved to shake his hand.

"This is a great thing you do," said Sheaffe, "whether or not you ever get credit for it."

"Those of my people who know of this will make stories of you, when the time is right," said Norton.

Tom was silent. Great things and stories were one thing. How he could deceive everyone he knew was another.

November–December

Rebecca

I watched as Tom emerged, dragging a basket of earth from the lake entrance of the secret room. He dumped it onto my kitchen garden, then returned to the house.

"That was the very last one," he said.

"Don't you come near me until you've washed," I said, trying to sound cross.

Tom wiped his hands on his grubby shirt and caught both of mine in them. "Done, at last," he said. "Can't I at least get a huzzah?"

"Huzzah, I'm sure." I pinched his cheek. "There's a bath prepared in the scullery, you rascal, and clean clothes laid out. Go to it."

By the time he was done and came into the kitchen rubbing his curly head with a towel, I had prepared a substantial meal of bread and ham and mustard pickles. He accepted it gratefully and tucked in with a will.

"Good," he said, wiping crumbs from his mouth.

"The end of last year's ham. We've yet to slaughter the pigs this year."

"I'm honored. And so's the pig. That was good ham." He washed down the last of the pickles with cider. "That's the new batch of cider, though, am I right?"

"Yes, fresh from the press. I kept back some juice, but the rest is fermenting in the barn loft."

He leaned back, replete, balancing the chair on two legs. "So, do you want a tour?"

"Not if I'm going to get as filthy as you were."

"I've tamped down the floor and shored the sides. If you hold your skirts close, you should stay fairly clean. But you'll need to watch your head. I didn't dig it full height. There wasn't time."

I took a lantern off the shelf and lit the candle inside it. "Come on then."

We went down to the cellar and entered the tunnel. The air inside it was noticeably cooler than in the cellar, and smelled of damp earth. The candle burned steadily.

"Did you put vents in?"

"Yes, a few. We must be able to breathe and keep a candle burning without suffocating. Someone might be forced to remain here for hours at a time."

"Well thought of," I said. "It might not be safe for a man to enter or leave."

The first part of the tunnel was nearly as wide as the cellar it abutted, and fully framed with wood to support its area. This was the room in which agents might hide. Along one side was a wide bench that could hold a sleeping pallet. A small folding table and chair leaned against the wall beside it. An empty brazier and lantern stood on a box containing a few candles and a hempen bag of charcoal.

"It's going to be cold here in winter, but the brazier is for emergencies only," he said. "Smoke rising from it would surely betray the location. And the smell of the fire, too."

I shivered at the thought of spending more than a few hours in such conditions. "And the tunnel?"

"It's fully shored where I struck sand, but otherwise the clay is so compacted it needed only some light framing."

I followed him along the length of the tunnel which ran about a dozen yards toward the lake, stopping just short of the high bank down to the shore.

Tom used a stout hooked stick that lay at the end of the tunnel to push up the trap door exit. We climbed a ladder, then stood in a thicket of shrubs through whose branches we could barely make out the house in the evening gloom. He showed me how he had fitted the branches of a small prostrate shrub to the door so it would appear to be part of the underbrush.

"Best we return the way we came." He hooked the trap door down behind us, and we returned to the house.

I made a pot of mint tea to warm us after our chilly expedition.

Tom fidgeted with his cup. "I should get back to Printer Jones's tonight."

I gave him a sharp look. "What's wrong?"

"Nothing."

"Tom…"

He shuffled his feet under the table.

"What are you keeping from me?"

He shook his head. "Nothing." He rose abruptly. "Look, I have to go."

"But…"

But he was gone, the door swinging shut behind him.

The aroma of mint, usually so soothing, failed me on that occasion.

Jack

"Stop champing at the bit, Jack." Sam Hingston laughed at the junior officer who had been pacing around the Fort Lennox blockhouse floor for most of the morning. "We're not leaving until tomorrow, so you may as well save your energy for then."

"It's a damned shame," said Jack. "We won't make it back to Montreal until Christmas Eve, if we're lucky."

"I'm sure there will be plenty of food whenever we get there," said Dawson. "Which interests me most. While I'm eager to get off detachment, too, I don't have a sweetheart waiting for me there."

Jack grinned at him, but continued to pace. "Her last letter…" He pulled a bedraggled scrap of paper from his breast pocket.

"You've damn near worn it through, folding and unfolding it. Haven't you memorized it yet?"

"I have. Touching the paper makes her feel closer."

"You won't miss her so much when we go into battle," said Hingston, sagely. "Wait and see." He let Jack wander a bit more. "For pity's sake, man, go and pack. Or re-pack. Just get out of here."

Jack scrambled up the rough stairs to his quarters above. There wasn't a lot to pack, but no room to pace either. He stuffed his clothes into his pack and then flung himself down on the pallet. His dreams, waking or sleeping, divided themselves between battle and Maryel. Maryel and battle. He might go mad if he didn't get one or the other.

✳

When they finally reached Montreal, Jack found a message inviting him to join the Mountain household for dinner on the day after Christmas, the family having church commitments on the day itself. He counted himself fortunate since he would enjoy sumptuous seasonal feasts two days in a row, and one of them in company with Maryel. It would almost make up for the long weeks of boredom and uninspiring rations on detachment.

Christmas Day was marked by the roasting of an enormous round of beef, escorted into the officers' mess by their servants, flanked by a great bowl of rum punch and another of mulled cider. It was accompanied by assorted breads and sauces, plum pudding and plates of gingerbread and Scotch cakes. Everyone attacked it with gusto. Many toasts were raised to everyone from His Majesty King George III down to the spit boy who turned the roast.

"That's it," said Jack, pushing his chair back from the table. "I can't eat another scrap." He belched out a cloud of cider fumes.

"And you've got another of these, tomorrow," said Dawson. "You'd better miss all the meals between now and then."

"I may sleep until noon. I've got leave both tomorrow and the next day."

"You'll be all the busier the day after that, then," said Hingston. "I've been working on the duty roster, so I know."

"I'm glad we're in Montreal for New Year's Day, too," said Dawson. "The locals know how to throw a party. I can just taste the tourtière and sugar pie."

"I hope the surgeon has plenty of stomach remedies on hand," said Jack. "A week of rich food and we'll all be needing them."

His appetite was not diminished the next day despite his previous excess. He tucked in to the excellent meal provided by the Mountains with a good will, accepting second and third helpings of roast turkey.

"I don't know where you put it," said Maryel, laughing.

"My mother used to say I had two hollow legs and she couldn't fill up either of them." But he did balk at another serving of his second plum pudding in as many days. "I'm as stuffed as the turkey was."

The family moved to the parlor where they played at charades until everyone ran out of riddles and rhyming answers to them. Jack drew Maryel into a corner while the Mountains dozed near the fire and Eliza read a book. He held her ungloved hand and ventured to drop a kiss onto it.

"Sir!" she whispered in mock horror.

He could tell she was joking by the gleam in her eye, and risked a light kiss on her cheek, at which she colored prettily, but shook her head. In company, he dared no more.

He whistled merrily as he returned to headquarters, happy his suit was progressing.

Rebecca

How I missed the girls. The house felt so empty without their voices. I missed Drusilla, too, though we had parted on unresolved terms. I determined to write her a conciliatory letter, hoping she would respond in kind. Good friends were hard to come by. Maryel had mentioned her kindness on the trip to Montreal. I could thank her for that and go on from there.

But letter-writing would have to wait. I had all the extra work to do that Eliza and Maryel would have helped with. I could only put so much on Hannah, so every waking moment was now occupied with some necessary task. Robert commented that he only saw me stop at mealtimes.

Then he fell ill earlier in winter than usual. I nursed him to sufficient health for him to conduct Christmas services, but afterwards he retired to our bedchamber with a severe cough that threatened to shake him to pieces and the room along with him. Or so it seemed to me, as I added carrying his meal trays upstairs to my routine.

If there was one advantage in all this, it was the dearth of winter festivities. There were no assemblies and few large gatherings of any sort, outside of church and market. At least I need not add preparation for those to my duties. I felt a measure of guilt at that, though. People must have an outlet. Especially we women, who were already beset with extra worry for our families, having had our baptism of fire in caring for the wounded after Queenston. The men could frequent the taverns, but we had no such release.

What might the next year bring?

1813

"Every political good carried to the extreme must be productive of evil."—Mary Wollstonecraft

"No man chooses evil because it's evil; he only mistakes it for happiness, the good he seeks."—Mary Wollstonecraft

January–April

Rebecca

As winter advanced through 1812 and into 1813, I noticed how stiff Robert was of a morning, and taxed him with it.

"These bones have taken to reminding me of my age," he joked.

"Now, Robert, you're as spry as ever." I looked him over. "Once those old bones warm up, that is."

"And you are a wonderful wife to look after me so well, but when I think of the good General at his last rest, at only forty-two, I feel as old as Methuselah."

"I think there are a few good years left in you, God willing. Why, you're not yet sixty."

He colored slightly and changed the subject. "Do you wish to accompany me to the auction of Brock's belongings?"

"Indeed, I do, after seeing the inventory. Fifteen pages of it. He was a wealthy man."

"Most of the items are beyond my means, especially in these hard times. I would like to see what books he has, though."

"Ah, the ruling passion. Now, Robert, you must be prudent… in these hard times."

Robert's love of books had emptied his pockets on too many past occasions, and doubtless would in future. It was fortunate his parishioners still paid in kind for his services. They would always spare some produce for his table or wood for his fire, should our own fall short.

"I think we should try to get some of the General's books for the Niagara Library," he said.

"Now there, I can agree wholeheartedly."

Our efforts to rally library subscribers for that purpose were rewarded. About fifty of Brock's books were added to the Niagara Library. Such titles as Maria Edgeworth's *Tales of Fashionable Life*, Gifford's *Life of Pitt*, Mrs. Burney's *Camilla*, Scott's *Lady of the Lake*, and Sterne's *Tristram Shandy* were added to the shelves. As well as novels and biographies, there were numerous magazines and histories, and Park's *Rudiments of Chemistry*. Brock's interests had been broad, and it benefited the library. Thankfully, none of the volumes was added to Robert's overcrowded bookcases.

The auction had been a welcome diversion. I was nervous living in town, lest some chance cause Fort Niagara to fire their cannon. But Robert would not forsake his duty, though he shared my fears. He pointed out they were trained on Fort George and not our house, but that didn't help.

After the actions at Fort Amherstburg and Queenston Heights, the border was quiet. The American militia went in terror of the Six Nations warriors, and everyone retreated to winter quarters to lick his wounds and contemplate the future. We were glad of a respite.

It had been a hot summer followed by a good harvest, so there were no privations as yet. The few gatherings were marred, to my mind, by the number of men in uniform. Militia uniforms had been cobbled together out of such clothes as the men already had, mostly homespun and rough woolens. Not much uniformity about them, but jackets had been dyed a dingy green and they made do with that. Men walked with an extra degree of pride when wearing them, I noticed, although women weren't as buoyed by their appearance.

For myself, I thanked whatever powers might be that Robert would not be a combatant. Bad enough that our house could come under fire at any time. We shared worries over our daughters, too. The enemy might well reach Montreal, and Robert fretted he should have sent them back to England. Of course, that was not guaranteed safe either, with naval ships skirmishing in the Atlantic as well as on the Great Lakes, not to mention the ongoing war with France.

A letter from Maryel was thus a welcome event. Robert read it to me as I occupied myself with my knitting—a warm vest for Tom.

Montreal, 25 December, 1812

Dear Father and Rebecca,

We have just finished a sumptuous Christmas repast, and most of the household is dozing as a result, but I am wakeful and so am penning this to you in hopes it will reach you before too long.

We're concerned for your safety. You must take the best of care. Would we could be there to support you.

Soldiers from several Army regiments and militia units are quartered here. The movement of troops stirs up local interest. Eliza cautions me against too much excitement.

The 100th is still headquartered here, and I have seen Ensign Stevenson several times, although he is most often on detachment. Eliza says we're too close to the front lines to become complacent, but you know what a pessimist she can be. I prefer to hope our troops will be able to safely defend us and the Americans will never reach Montreal. We're on an island here. That should provide some extra defense.

We helped Mrs. Mountain sort through her linens this past week. She plans to send worn sheeting to the nuns for bandages. We tore the worst ones into strips, but will send some intact for them to use as they see fit. Both of us continue to attend at the convent to learn nursing skills, and have graduated to the care of small wounds suffered by soldiers in garrison duty. I am proud of my new ability to set a broken finger. It's difficult to witness pain and suffering, but we must all do what we can.

We're in good health and hope the same for you.

Love,

Maryel

A mixed blessing of a letter, for Eliza had the right of it. We must hope and pray their position as members of the Mountain household would keep them secure.

The letter upset me more than I realized at first. My daily routine was disrupted and I needed something to restore my composure. Thinking some physical activity might help, I wrapped up well and went outside.

There, I busied myself chopping wood. The effort took my mind off my worries. I actually enjoyed myself. The cold bit into me like a host of tiny thorns. Quite exhilarating. I amassed a healthy pile of kindling and split some medium-sized pieces for the cook-fire. My breath made an ice ring around my hood and a frosty cloud as I exhaled. I needed to stop every few minutes to tuck my gloved hands into my fur muff. My fingers felt like the icicles that hung from the eaves of our house, and I chaffed my hands together inside the muff, trying to warm them. I could hear the roll of drums and faint fife notes playing "Lilliburlero." It wasn't clear whether the sound reached me from our fort or theirs. Some troops, somewhere, were drilling to music. I hummed along with the familiar tune and was sorry when it stopped. If they were drilling, they weren't shooting. I shivered. I had chopped enough wood to last us for the next few days.

Tom

York Gazette, 31 January, 1813.

"Be it known that His Majesty's Government is from this day in a state of War with the United States of America. Any of His Majesty's Subjects found to be consorting with or aiding the Enemy will be considered Traitors and will be Punished accordingly."

Tom snorted as he smoothed out the proof of the new edition. The Americans had declared war the previous June, and fighting had begun even earlier. His Majesty's Government was only now getting around to acknowledging the fact? He would never understand politics if he lived a hundred years.

He must make his excuses to his landlady and wind up this brief contract in York. General Sheaffe had told him to be ready to move out when he got word from Norton. This morning, a brief message had come. He was to join the Six Nations for a powwow at the landing place below Brant's Ford. Then there was Willcocks. The Legislature would be in session soon, even if there was a war on. He must keep tabs on everything if he was to handle the job of agenting for both sides.

Tom chewed the inside of one cheek while he mulled over his options. Willcocks had not yet spoken treason openly and appeared to favor Sheaffe's approach. But how long would that last? His disillusionment with the British was obvious, and his dislike of martial law ingrained. Which way would he swing? As for himself, he must maintain a neutral stance for now lest he arouse suspicion in either side. This role of double-agent was like balancing on the ridgepole of a barn roof. One wrong step…

He finished his printing job and headed through the snowy streets for a nearby tavern where he procured bread and cheese and a mug of mulled ale. The bread was stale and the ale sour but what odds? They warmed his belly on this frigid night. He sat over the crumbs at a corner table when the door burst open, letting in flurries and a snow-covered man. Willcocks, at last.

"Tom, how goes it?" Willcocks unwound his muffler and shoved his hands in his pockets.

"Well enough, Jos." He looked Willcocks over. "You're frozen. Sit, and I'll get you some mulled ale. Or wine, if they have any."

"Ale will do, thanks." Willcocks seated himself with his back facing the tavern's fireplace. He accepted the warm mug from Tom, cupped his hands around it and inhaled the spicy aroma.

"So, what news?"

Willcocks shook his head. "Naught but uneasiness everywhere. Both sides appear reluctant to act. Perhaps it's the season. The cold has gotten into their heads, I swear."

"Winter warfare is chancy."

"Near impossible to live off the land."

Tom chose his words carefully. "Are you confident in Sheaffe's abilities?"

"Do I think he's an able administrator? Do I think he can inspire confidence in men like Brock did? Do I think he can defend the province? Yes, no, and maybe."

Tom pressed on. "You think the province may fall?"

"If the Americans make a better showing than they did at Queenston, it's possible. But if Norton's warriors continue to inspire such fear in them, it's not likely."

"What if they did, though? Have you thought on what you'd do?"

Willcocks eyed him seriously. "Having doubts, are you?"

Tom nodded. "I've been considering things from all angles. It'd be foolish not to."

"Well then, boyo, you've more sense than most. It's prudent to assess the situation, and a man must review all his options. I've thought along those lines myself."

"And…?"

"And the matter is still open. It'll depend on what happens when hostilities resume, as I suppose they will soon." He sat back in his chair and drained his tankard. "Time for another. And some food." He made his way to the bar.

Tom worried at a piece of chapped skin on his lip. It came away, his lip bleeding a little. He grimaced at the metallic taste.

Willcocks returned, two tankards in one hand and the other balancing a large dish of stew covered with a slab of bread. "I got two spoons. We can share." He sat and tucked into the food.

Tom took a few bites and then concentrated on his ale.

Willcocks finally wiped the dish with a piece of bread and pushed it away, belching. "I wish the York militia showed the promise the Niagara ones did. We must wait and see. See here, Tom, I can't settle your doubts for you. God knows I wish I could, and my own, too."

Willcocks

The Legislature opened later than usual that winter. It was nearly the end of February before they got down to business. On the whole, thought Willcocks, that was as well. Sheaffe was in charge of the provincial executive now. There was little activity by peacetime administrators apart from some handwringing over how to deal with military depredations on civilian property. As if there had been any of that yet.

25 Feb

Wartime session of Legislature not expected to last long. Military in firm control now. Little to be done in way of reform until war concludes. Sheaffe replaces Brock as President of Executive Council. De facto Lt-Gov. Sheaffe is no Brock. but still a worthy commander. Have no personal love for the man. but acceptable as temporary leader. Hard to see how his appointment might advantage my position. Restraints of martial law hard to bear.

26 Feb

Fellow legislator Markle and his friend Mallory press me to do something. Unclear what they would have me do. I put forward what reforms I can. protest unjust legislation. Within the system. there's little else available. Not ready to step outside the system. Not yet.

"Will you leave me be, Ben?"

"But Jos, we can't just lie down and let the Army have its way with us."

"Can't we?" Willcocks quirked an eyebrow at his choleric colleague's bulging eyes. "I see no point in harrying those in charge. We're at war—like it or not—and they're in control."

"What can we do then?"

"Wait and see, Ben. And do keep Mallory from doing something foolish, if you can. This is no time for personal vendettas."

10 Mar

Near interminable session of Parliament. Only a few days left. Little accomplished. Martial law chafes at my sensibilities. A pox on all Generals. If only I could see my way clear.

13 Mar

Only real achievement this session was alteration of militia laws. Former arrangements haphazard at best. Temporary conscripts unwilling to leave families and farms. Short duration of militia term led to desertion. New incorporated militia will recruit volunteers to serve for the duration of the war. Expect farms will be stripped of young men. Problem to feed military and populace with workforce of old men. women. and children. Outcome could turn on one good or bad harvest.

Willcocks left York, with considerable relief, soon after the session ended. He must get away from his nagging co-reformers so he could think straight. He'd been able to keep a lid on them. Barely. Their hot heads might come in useful later though. If things fell apart.

20 Mar

Returned to Niagara. Town full of militia recruits. Sense of optimism. Cannot join in those sentiments. All too aware of holes in border Americans can walk through. Or sail across. Worry increases daily. Which side should I follow? Have done pretty well backing Crown so far. but Americans could be in ascendancy. My contacts there suggest opportunities in the offing. Still undecided.

Rebecca

Tom had been back and forth to York over the past few months, visiting infrequently, but now he was back at Jones's for a stint, giving me the opportunity to see him.

The short-service militia he fought with at Queenston had been disbanded. Plans were now afoot to draft younger men into a Provincial militia to serve for the duration of the war. A tricky situation for Tom, given his spying remit.

"Are you sure you can spend this much time here?" I asked him after the third visit in as many days.

He grinned. "Enjoy me while I'm here. Once things hot up, you may not see me for months at a time."

My throat constricted. It was no matter for jokes.

"Jones has little work these days," he said, "and I've scrubbed every piece of type in his shop twenty times over. He's glad to be rid of me so I don't pester him for something to do."

My mind was running along other lines. "You could come to stay here for a while."

He looked at me sidelong and shook his head. "I need to stay in town. As long as I've got food and a bed, I'll do."

I tugged at the hem of his vest. "Have you grown again? I should have made this longer."

He brushed my hand away. "Stop fussing, Rebecca. I'm warm enough."

"Any word from Chief Norton?"

He shook his head. "Not for a few weeks. The last I heard, he was awaiting news from his scouts. They're following troop movements over in New York State. He hopes to get early warning of any attack."

"I'd almost rather something happened than endure this waiting."

"I can wait, thanks." He shrugged. "I'm supposed to be attached to the militia as a messenger. I always knew being a fast runner would come in useful. Besides… I can't shoot for beans."

We both laughed.

"I can stay steady under fire, though." He sobered. "Queenston Heights did that for me."

My stomach clenched and I caught his hand. "You can't outrun bullets."

"I may have little choice. But there… I'm less likely to be in the line of fire as a message runner, you know."

"Perhaps. But you're in danger on all counts as a Crown agent. You must take great care."

"Nobody notices me, Rebecca. It's why they picked me, you know."

That and your connections, I thought, gazing into his warm hazel eyes. His features might not be memorable to some, but I was not among their number. Nobody could duplicate his grin or his gurgling laugh. Should that laugh be stilled—I stifled those thoughts. "Come, I'll get you something to eat on your way back. It won't be much, mind, we've begun to ration food."

Tom

Tom left Niagara in early April, after Jones put up his shutters for the duration. With his portable press, he picked up small commissions, but spent most of his time in York's taverns, nursing his ale or cider and listening to local talk. York was a small place of under a thousand, although the traffic through it with regimental exchanges and itinerant traders made it seem larger at times.

He was one of the casual visitors himself, known sufficiently to be a familiar face, but not part of any circle. Sheaffe and Norton had advised him to keep a low profile, guidance echoed by Willcocks. This spying business was confusing, and he wasn't sure he could be useful. Nor could he be sure which side he would benefit most. At least he had a militia role that allowed him free movement, and an Army token from Sheaffe to prove his status as message runner, or he'd not be able to avoid being drafted into a "volunteer" battalion. He remembered stories of men pressed into the British Navy and thought they might employ the same tactics for a land war.

Willcocks was in York when Tom arrived, but left shortly thereafter. It was a relief, since Tom found it embarrassing to walk down the muddy streets at Jos's elbow while he declaimed his more controversial opinions in a voice barely short of shouting. His rhetoric was more inflammatory by the day. It argued against Tom's remaining inconspicuous—rather, it made him a target. But it had been Jos who was the object of attention after all, and Tom sank back into the background after he left.

It was only a matter of time. The Americans, bent on seizing control of British possessions, would not take their humiliating defeats at Detroit and Queenston without retaliating. Six long months and more had passed since Queenston. Spring had arrived, the ice was out of Lake Ontario, thus the time overripe for invasion. What better target than Upper Canada's young Capital, York?

Early on the morning of April 27, Tom collected his belongings in a leather valise, fortified himself with a hearty breakfast at his lodgings, and bade his landlady goodbye. He left the traveling press with her, promising to return for it soon. Bent on boarding the sloop for Niagara, he sauntered down to the docks. It was full daylight, the remnants of morning fog blown off by a stiff easterly breeze.

The view along the inner harbor was clear. Off to the east lay the greater part of the town and the Parliament buildings, backed by the bay where there was only swampy land at the base of the harbor-sheltering peninsula. The wind bit sharply so he turned to the west. Beyond the docks and shipyards near the harbor mouth and almost too far for him to make out, he spotted several ships. Could it be? He counted masts: twelve… fourteen… fifteen ships. They must be Americans. The British fleet was holed up in Kingston, defending the St. Lawrence River passage. Surely he would have heard if they planned a sortie to York.

As if to confirm his conclusions, puffs of smoke appeared on the shore opposite the ships. That must be old Fort Rouillé, a relic of the

French regime. He squinted to see better, but it was no use. They were too far to make out details. A passerby grabbed his arm.

"What's happening? Is it the invasion?"

Tom nodded. "Fifteen ships. Look to be landing troops out west."

"What forces have we?"

"Most are in Fort York. Light detachments at Fort Rouillé and the Western Battery, I think."

"What of reinforcements?

"General Sheaffe is still at Fort York. He'll send out more troops for sure." Tom drew himself up proudly. "I fought with his force at Queenston."

The man shook his head, unimpressed. "We're too few. Fifteen ships, you say? Why, they could carry over two thousand men. We've only a few hundred! I must get the family away." He scurried off before Tom learned his name.

He couldn't make it to Niagara today. His valise held only a change of clothes and a few small items but he was loath to abandon it. After a moment of indecision, he ran back to his lodgings, depositing the bag with his startled landlady. He urged her to assemble her valuables and either leave with them or bury them in her yard, then made his way back to the dock. The smoke from musket-fire had grown and moved closer. The regulars must have been pushed back as far as the Western Battery already. Were the militia engaged?

Frustrated, Tom headed for Fort York, joining others bent on the same errand. They were few. Most of the younger men were already with the militia despite the reluctance of many to comply with the new requirements. Those moving toward the fort were a few men of middle years unencumbered with dependants, who stayed to defend their property against marauders. Plus a few like him, whose attachment to the militia was a loose one.

"What ho?" he hailed a sentry at the fort.

"Ah, Strange, it's you," said the sentry. "I've to send you on to the command post."

Tom tipped him a salute as he proceeded into the fort. He was admitted to the General's rooms, but resigned himself to a wait in the anteroom while Sheaffe conducted his most urgent business. Low voices came from the inner sanctum where they would be poring over maps and discussing the defense of the town. He tilted the brim of his hat over his eyes and settled in.

At last, the door opened. One of the General's aides beckoned him to come in.

Sheaffe did not bother with pleasantries. "I need you to stay in York as long as you can, Strange. It may become necessary for our forces to retreat temporarily. I need an observer outside the fort to record the enemy's actions in the town. And," he hesitated, "if we must surrender, we won't give them their greatest prize. You must fire the new ship."

Tom stared. "The HMS *Sir Isaac Brock*, Sir? But… but it's just been commissioned!"

"If I'd had my way, it would have gone to Kingston with all the others. This is a good harbor, but a perilous bottle-neck for a single defending ship. We'd do better to have ships stationed at Burlington than here. But," he shuffled some papers on his desk, "there is no other choice. We cannot allow the Americans to have any major military asset. They may plunder small arms, muskets, cannon, but to let them have a capital ship? No, I cannot countenance it." He turned to look out the window at the troops on the green. Turning back to Tom, he said, "Go now, and do your duty. Watch everything that happens, and report when you can. This will not end here."

As Tom turned to leave, a loud boom came from west of the fort.

"That'll be the powder at the Western Battery," muttered Sheaffe. He looked up. "What are you waiting for?"

As Tom left, he heard Sheaffe say to himself, "… could prove useful."

It was easier to fire the ship than he supposed. The few people he saw were focused on some urgent business and paid him no attention as he boarded the ship. On deck, he found several tubs of pitch. He dragged them fore, aft, and amidships, heedless of spillage. That would merely help his cause. Next, he descended to the hold where he ransacked the storage bins for sailcloth scraps. These, he soaked in pitch and carried below decks to locations around the ship. One, he twisted around a loose rod as a makeshift torch.

He had to hunt for a fire-lighting kit. After searching several cabins, he found one in the ship's galley. It took several tries to get the torch lit. When it was burning steadily, he carried it round to the places where he'd left the soaked rags and lit each one. By the time he was finished, the smoke was near to blinding and choking him. He stumbled up the gangway onto the open deck and gulped a deep breath.

This was taking too long. People were going to notice the smoke. He ran from tub to tub, lighting each one. It was horrifying how readily the fire caught hold.

He must not stay to watch, though. Shouts came from the shore. He'd been spotted. There was no way he could climb down to the dock now. The townsfolk wouldn't be interested in explanations. He had no other option than to jump from the deck into the harbor.

Right after he did, a deafening roar came from Fort York. He had never heard such a blast and hoped never to again, but he knew at once what it was. All the powder in the fort's Grand Magazine had been set alight as cover for Sheaffe's retreat with most of the troops. Meanwhile, the *Brock* burned on.

Tom wasn't a strong swimmer, but put sufficient distance between himself and the now-blazing ship to avoid detection by those attempting to quench the flames. Billowing smoke from the ship, fast becoming a hulk, helped conceal him. He made his way to the east, to a low spot where he could climb out with less risk of detection, hoping he could explain away his wet clothing by saying he'd been one of those trying to stop the fire. In all the confusion, he passed without notice.

Only a few militia officers remained to negotiate with the Americans who were furious to lose their biggest prizes. Eventually, they settled to plunder only government offices. Upon the proclamation being read, the town descended into chaos. Despite official intentions, many private homes were looted by morning, the press at the *Gazette* destroyed, St. James Church damaged and plundered, and the Parliament buildings burned.

Tom watched, listened, and stayed as clear of the looters as he could. He made sure his landlady was well-barricaded in her house, since she couldn't leave. It was one of the few left intact. Not all looters had been invaders, and so he would report both to Sheaffe and to Willcocks when next he met with each.

The Americans did not stop long. They returned to their ships on May 1st and departed within the week, leaving chaos in their wake. Sheaffe and his troops had not yet returned when Tom finally left town on May 10th, headed for Niagara and some peace. He hoped Jos would be there already. They needed a serious talk about the direction of the wind.

May–June

Rebecca

I scanned the letter Robert had written to our daughters, considering what I would say in my turn. He wrote of the attack on York, what little we knew, and our renewed worries for our own safety. There was nothing left for me to say, bar a few words of greeting.

My pen needed trimming, and the inkwell was nearly dry, but enough remained for a brief note. I must grind more oak galls and look in the shed for a rusty nail to make a fresh batch. I shaved a little off the end of the goose quill with my penknife, and carefully cut a fresh channel in its tip.

> … I beg of you not to be overly concerned about the news of invasion. We're still safe here and the Lord willing will continue so. You must remain with the Mountain family until our borders are calm once again…

I tucked my note inside Robert's letter, folded the whole and sealed it with a scrap of wax. Robert would address it later and have it sent to Montreal with the next group of military despatches. There were few advantages to be had from his position as Chaplain to Fort George. This was one we were grateful for.

He was most tactful when he passed me the list of casualties at York. He could hardly have failed to note Josiah Burton's name among the dead, but said nothing. The news of Josiah's death distressed me, but at this remove, I found it hard to recollect the tender feelings I once held toward him. I had heard nothing from him since we parted, certainly no ill reports. I must hope he kept his promise to avoid transmitting his disease any further amongst his associates. On further reflection, I was relieved he had been spared the final stages of his illness, which were horrific in the extreme.

My apprehension at the nearness of the American forces grew daily. Fort Niagara was too close for comfort. We should leave town at the earliest possible moment. Lake Lodge was unlikely to be the location of a first assault. We must place our confidence in the small regular army force at the fort, supplemented by our local militia and the Indian warriors. The local militia, formed under the new regulation, had yet to be tested, but we hoped would prove valiant. Young men had signed on for the duration of the war, a measure we hoped would discourage the desertion so common in the early days. But the locals still needed to plant crops, so spring warfare was a chancy thing. In his rounds to other communities, Robert had seen a decline in the amount of land under cultivation. We worried constantly over the new crop—whether it would survive and provide sufficient food and feed for the coming winter.

On May 27th, I woke early, to gunfire. We had just moved out to Lake Lodge, and I wasn't yet used to the sounds of the farm, nor the lake lapping the shore right outside my windows. This sound didn't fall into either category, though. I would never grow used to gunfire.

I roused Robert and we busied ourselves with our morning

routines. The shots sounded distant, and we saw nothing untoward along the shoreline. I entered my stillroom to tie up some herbs gathered the day before, and Robert took a book out to the veranda overlooking the lake. It was warm, so I didn't fuss at him to take a blanket.

Soon though, as the mist cleared, Robert called from the yard that smoke was rising from the direction of the town. Not long afterwards, some men approached us along the lakeshore trail. One was our neighbor, Mr. Servos, bringing news from the town.

"We're going along the shore and warning people," said Servos. "Fort George is under bombardment from Fort Niagara, and looks likely to fall. The Americans have landed on our shores. You can expect baggage trains and wounded later today."

"Are we in imminent danger? Should we remove to somewhere safer?" Robert asked. His voice quavered, sending goosebumps up my neck. He cleared his throat and said in a more normal tone, "Is there reason for immediate concern?"

"Not yet. The Fort Major sent out a message they would bivouac near here if forced to withdraw. Wait until then before you move. But be prepared in case it becomes necessary." Servos moved off to rejoin his party.

"It's good I haven't unpacked much," I said.

"You may not need to. If the Americans are making a push, they may not come near here. I daresay they would go up the Swamp Road to the Indian trail under the escarpment if they intend to drive west, toward Burlington." The Swamp Road cut across the Niagara territory diagonally, heading inland.

My heart was aflutter all day, and my stomach churned. Every sudden noise startled me, and I looked over my shoulder at every turn. Garden chores were impossible, and I returned to the stillroom, the only place I could regain my calm.

Fort George fell to the American forces that day. Tom brought us the details.

"We got off lightly," he said. "The 41st lost four men in a cannonade, and a few more were wounded. I've just left the party carrying the wounded to the mill. Close enough for you to tend them, Rebecca, if you will. I hear their surgeon was one of the wounded."

I had already turned away from him, headed for the stillroom and my supplies.

Robert continued to pump him for details. "Should we worry for our safety? I don't want Rebecca to be in the line of fire."

"The men from the garrison were retreating along the Swamp Road…"

"As I thought."

"… and, if the Americans are tailing them, there is little to fear. At least for now."

"What of the Church?"

"I believe they evacuated the wounded men. They were going to try."

"And the townsfolk? Have they been harmed?"

"So far, the enemy seems intent on securing the fort and harassing the troops. The Fort Major believes they want to make a push overland to York and capture it before the fort is rebuilt."

Robert judged it too risky for us to venture into town while troop movements continued, and we waited over a week for news. Eventually, he decided he must assess the situation for himself. I urged him not to, but he was adamant.

Then Tom brought word. The Americans had taken Robert prisoner.

"I've been able to avoid them myself, but then I'm a fast runner," he said. "Now, you mustn't worry. They've rounded up all the men still in the town and are holding them in St. Mark's. I doubt they will keep the ones of advancing years long, especially not a man of the cloth."

"What do you think they'll do with the others?" I asked.

"I don't know. Send them as prisoners into the States?"

"You must have a care for yourself," I said. "I will go to town. I dare swear they're not imprisoning women."

"But Rebecca—"

"I won't have you put yourself in more danger. Not when you can serve our cause."

He argued some more, but finally agreed my plan made sense.

When I reached town, I learned that men of fighting age were to be sent way down the Mohawk River to Albany, the capital of New York State. They paroled some few on their word to take no more part in the war. Some others deserted to the American side. I was thankful to hear those were few.

I marched up to the church door and accosted the guards there. "You have my husband, the rector of this church. Let me see him!"

One man would have barred my way, but the other waved him aside. "Let her pass. What harm can she do?"

I left them behind me, arguing, and passed inside where all was chaos.

The American militia had dragged the pews to one side of the nave and piled the other side high with barrels and crates of supplies. They had made a rough hearth in one corner, the surrounding stones already blackened from the cook-fire.

A rough-looking man in a homespun jacket was guarding about a dozen men sitting or lying on the pews. He looked to be in charge, so I approached him.

"I'm here for my husband," I said.

He laughed. "Nobody's goin' nowhere, missus." He beckoned to his fellows and two more approached. They tried to shove me back toward the door.

I staggered but shoved back.

The commotion grew until an American officer approached.

"What's all this ruckus?" he asked.

"Pesky woman coming looking for a prisoner, sir," said the first guard.

I seized my chance. Maybe the officer would be less intransigent than his men. "You must let him come away. He's a clergyman, not a fighting man. I won't go without him!"

"Rebecca?" Robert's voice, very weak.

"Robert? Where are you?" I scanned the pews. Some were turned with their backs to me. I pushed past the guards and looked down at my poor Robert, lying on one of them.

He looked terrible. The few days imprisonment had aged him visibly. His graying locks were a shade paler, and his cheeks hollow. From his pouchy eyes, he might only have slept a few hours the entire time.

"My dear, we must get you home immediately," I said. I assisted him to sit up, then stand. He felt like a puff of wind might carry him off. I rounded on the officer. "Can't you see he's in no fit state to fight? He'll give you his parole, if you need it."

The officer hemmed and hawed, but finally relented. "I guess it's a waste of our time to keep him. I suppose we would have paroled him soon, anyway. Better for you to have to feed him."

I put one arm around Robert and helped him walk toward the door, slowly. We stopped while his release was confirmed, then walked a little more quickly through the town.

"Can you walk all the way home?" I asked.

"My pace may be slow, but it's a pleasure to move my legs. They penned us in. We were confined, but at least not chained."

Indeed, his steps soon quickened and he appeared to be the better for the walk. His fellow prisoners had apprised him of doings in the town and fort, which he relayed to me as we walked along the lake road.

"The bastions of the fort are heavily damaged, according to young Merritt."

"Won't it make their position harder to defend?" Truly, men's ways in war craft are an enigma.

He shrugged. "May it be so, I'm sure. I have little knowledge of such things." He lapsed into silence as we walked on.

Robert's spurt of energy during our four-mile walk back to Lake Lodge proved to be fleeting. I barely got him over our doorstep when he crumpled into my arms. He felt so frail against me, I barely kept him from falling. Tom was nowhere to be seen.

"Robert, my love, stay with me," I said. I willed him to respond.

After long moments, he raised his head and smiled weakly.

"Try to walk a few more steps, my dear."

I led him to his customary chair beside the fireplace and tucked him up with cushions and a warm shawl, for he was shivering despite the June heat. "Rest, while I get you a hot drink."

Hannah hadn't made a fire in the winter kitchen, with the weather so warm, but I knew one was lit in the summer kitchen. I crossed the few steps separating it from the house and found her there, setting bread to rise. The kettle hung from its hook over the fire, steaming gently from its spout. I spooned betony and lemon balm into a cup and poured boiling water over them, the scent wafting gently through the room. I added some chamomile and then strained the mixture into a second cup, finally stirring in some honey. That should be a sufficient restorative until I could prepare him a nourishing meal.

Robert had pulled up a footstool and appeared comfortable. He accepted the tisane gratefully and sipped at it while I sat near him.

"You gave me quite a scare," I said. "Are you going to be all right?"

He nodded. "I need some of your soup and a night of undisturbed sleep. It was a distressing experience, but at least I was released. Those poor fellows wrenched from their families, they're to be pitied most. And for how long? It could be months, or years."

"I'm selfish then, to have you back," I said. "And content to be so."

He gripped my hand. "But Rebecca… the American soldiers… I had not thought them capable…"

"Of what?" I asked anxiously, my imagination at fever pitch.

"Desecrating sanctified ground. They've dug rifle pits in our cemetery. Butchered carcasses on the gravestones. And stored ammunition in the church itself."

"Oh, Robert." Thank goodness it was only that. It could have been so much worse.

"I thought they would respect the church, but no." He shook his head. "First St. James in York, now our St. Mark's. I scarce believed the former news until I saw it happen here."

"It doesn't bear thinking of." I must try to raise his spirits. "We will concentrate on restoring your health, and then doing our best for our neighbors. And hope our forces may eject them from the region soon."

Jack

"It's too bad, I tell you." Jack shook his head as he reached for the toast. Damn, it was cold again. "Here we are, sat in this midge-ridden hole of an outpost while those lucky sods in the grenadier company are off as marines to take Sacket's Harbor."

"Sour grapes, Jack?" asked Dawson. "Afraid you've missed a chance for promotion?"

"And why not?" Jack spooned honey over his toast and bit into it, brushing away a cloud of insects. He hummed as the sweetness met his tongue and soothed his temper. "It would have been just the thing if only our battalion had been chosen for duty. Now we'll be picking bugs out of our breakfast here until we rot."

Dawson laughed. "You can thank the Vermont smugglers for that. Without them, you'd not have honey for your bread. Or beer to wash it down with."

"They're the only Americans I've set eyes on since Niagara. Are you sure their army is even in these parts?"

His detachment of the 100th had been kicking their heels on the Richelieu River for too many months, in Jack's opinion. Another detachment was seconded to the Navy for an attack on Sacket's Harbor, opposite Kingston, to stem American harassment of Lake Ontario's north shore. Jack felt the disappointment of staying behind, like a personal blow. The endless monotony of drill and patrol around the ramshackle fort and bastions at Ile-aux-Noix was purely cruel. He might never have a chance to test his mettle under fire. He now understood why men deserted their posts.

How exciting it was, then, to be roused, well before dawn on June 3rd by one of his men. Ile-aux-Noix, the backwater of all backwaters, was under attack.

Jack shrugged his tunic over yesterday's shirt and dragged his boots on. He made sure his sword was buckled securely, crammed his shako on his head, then exited his quarters at a run.

All was quiet within the fort save for the soft thud of feet in the grass. He could see the faint glow of dark lanterns carried by men of the regiment headed for the armed bastions that guarded the channels of the Richelieu River. He couldn't see ships in the dark, but heard the slap of the river against their planks and the creak of their anchor hawsers.

He gathered a few of his men and sent them, with a sergeant, to launch skiffs off the northern bank of the island, and fortify the opposite shore. He headed back to the fort, where he found his fellow officers huddled together for a low-voiced conference.

"Sent armed party. West bank," he said at a break in the talk.

"Good thinking," said Major Taylor. "Same for east bank. Two ships in western channel. Could be more in east."

"That arm is too shallow in summer."

"Not high summer yet. Ambush possible from either channel."

"Yes, sir."

"To your posts." The Fort Major laid his palms on the table and leaned toward his officers. "And by God, keep your men quiet until I signal." He turned to Jack. "Stevenson, get the second party out.

Soon be dawn. Surprise those Yankee bastards." He grinned. "They'll wish they'd stood abed."

"Can't wait for the fun to start, Sir."

They attacked the American ships at dawn.

Jack swiftly decided that "fun" was the wrong word to describe warfare. Engagement with a live enemy was completely different from target practice. He knew it must be so, but nothing could prepare a man for the cacophony of cannon fire in battle.

The Americans were surprised to find themselves surrounded but mounted a game resistance. Balls from both island bastions bracketed the two gunboats, *Eagle* and *Growler*, and showered the men on deck with muddy river water. Only a few did significant damage. The British intent was capture, not destruction. Meanwhile, the regiment's sharpshooters did their best to pick off sailors on deck.

"Form boarding parties," came the order.

Jack and his patrol swarmed the nearest ship, the *Eagle*, from their skiffs, scaling fore and aft while those on deck were distracted by the enfilading fire, as other parties did the *Growler*. The *Growler* got off several cannonades and the Eagle one, but these caused minimal damage to the fortifications.

On the deck of the *Eagle*, confusion reigned. Jack grimaced and sneezed as waves of smoke from black powder explosions cascaded over him from the cannonade and now from small arms fire.

Holding one arm over his mouth and nose, he drew his sword with the other and led his men as best he could. There was no hope of a coordinated charge on such a small ship, so each man did what he could to engage the enemy.

The Americans had little defense against the bayonets and muskets of the British soldiers. A few sailors carried pistols, but others only knives or cudgels.

Jack had to duck several times to avoid a blow or thrown knife.

He wasn't sure if it was ball or blade that nicked his left earlobe, only noticing the wound when he turned his head and saw blood all down his tunic's yellow facings. He spared a thought for the difficulty of removing bloodstains from wool serge, but his attention was brought back to reality when a roughly dressed sailor careened into him and he nearly fell overboard. Grabbing a nearby cable, he righted himself and fended off the sailor.

Finally, overwhelmed by the attack, both ships struck their colors and surrendered. It felt to Jack as if the whole action was over almost as soon as it had begun. Indeed, it had taken something under an hour from start to finish.

After the ships had been towed back to the island's dockyard and the prisoners were put under guard, Jack was detailed to question the American officers.

He found both men in a small cell usually reserved for drunken soldiers. They sat on a low bedframe, with shoulders drooping and heads down. Jack sat at a table placed outside the bars, with a sheaf of papers spread out before him. He took a fresh sheet and dipped his quill in the inkstand.

"Now sirs," he said, "your names, and that of your ships, if you please."

The two men glanced at each other and one spoke. "I'm Lieutenant Smith, in command of the sloops *Growler* and *Eagle*. This is Mr. Green, our sailing master."

"How many guns on each?"

"You can count them yourself."

Jack frowned at Smith. The man wasn't taking his captivity seriously. "All I need are straight answers." He cleared his throat and continued. "Your purpose?"

"To claim your fort, of course."

"Too bad you've lost your ships, then. They'll come in useful for us to defend against future attempts. There will be more coming from our dockyard as well. You'll be cooling your heels in a Montreal gaol."

"Better than facing the Captain," muttered Green.

Smith elbowed him and he subsided into silence.

Jack went through the full list of regulation questions, receiving mostly monosyllabic answers. Finally, he came to the end without gaining any significant information.

"The Fort Major will decide whether you'll be sent on to Montreal, or paroled and sent home to sit out the war."

Smith and Green appeared unmoved by this assertion. They stared blankly through the cell bars and over Jack's shoulder at the wall. He supposed they were still shocked by their capture.

Picking up his papers, he headed for the Fort Major's quarters.

"Ah, Ensign Stevenson, there you are. Come in. Come in." Major Taylor leaned back in his chair and looked Jack over.

"The reports you requested, sir."

"Thankee; thankee. Set them down. I've got some news for you. You'd have gotten it earlier without this little fracas." He waved at Jack to sit. "Thing is, the regiment has a flood of new recruits on the way, and what with one thing and another, there's some room for movement among the junior officers. You're one of the lucky ones to move up without purchase. So, Lieutenant Stevenson, how does that sit with you?"

Jack's eyes opened so wide he felt them in danger of bursting out of his head. "S-sir, r-really?" He flushed. He'd gotten over stammering years ago. But… *Lieutenant!* "Without seeing action, Sir?"

"Never fear. Duty off the field counts for something, too. And today you've added to your record enough to justify a field promotion and so it will read in my dispatch to headquarters."

It was almost too much to take in. He'd never have been able to put together the purchase on an Ensign's pay. His first action and his first promotion—all in one day. It had been a grand adventure.

Even more satisfying, a few weeks later, word of the action at Sacket's Harbor arrived. It turned out to have been a resounding fiasco, one Jack was now thankful to have missed.

Tom

Wallace's Tavern hummed with conversation, mainly from the occupation militia. A few locals had crept back into town, mostly older men. The Americans ignored these as being of no consequence. In their midst, Tom found Willcocks in a fusty corner where they could talk over the current situation without being overheard.

"You're still opposed to military rule?" asked Tom. "Even though we're at war?"

"I oppose despots of any kind," said Willcocks, pounding the table. A few heads turned, and he sat back, lowering his voice. "Anyone—civilian or military—who would arbitrarily overrule the Legislature. Resistance to bad government is a duty demanded of all loyal subjects. We must prove we deserve our independence by vigilantly defending our rights."

"You would challenge the rule of the King, then?"

"The King needs direction from the elected Legislature, as is the case in Britain. Here, we're ruled by local elites—petty tyrants—out to feather their own nests." He scowled. "Things have gotten much worse since the attacks on York and Niagara. You heard they've demoted Sheaffe?"

"Yes." Tom shrugged. "I can't say he distinguished himself at York. Didn't seem the man he was at Queenston."

"We could have worse commanders, and probably will. With the Americans holed up in Fort George, we're in a worse state than under Gore's regime. Why, the British Army considers a man to be disaffected if he was but born in the States. Ten times more so if he don't join the militia. But why would a poor man—like most in my riding, or Markle's, or Mallory's—why would he join only to let his family starve? It isn't right, boyo." His face darkened and his scowl deepened.

"What would you do about it, Jos? Many are disaffected."

"Under common law, all have their rights. Under military rule, none have rights. Upper Canadians have slavishly followed the military elite, and forfeited my sympathy thereby."

Tom's brow furrowed as he mulled over these words. "Jos, you're talking like you were composing an editorial. Can't you put it plainer?"

"I favor the rights of the common man over those of the privileged few. Is that plain enough?"

"Is it so black and white?"

"Clearer to me every day. The Americans have the right of it. More opportunity for a man of my beliefs, too."

Tom gaped at Willcocks, speechless.

Willcocks tipped his chair back and blew a cloud of smoke. "I can't support martial law as conducted by incompetents. And, with Parliament no longer in session, there are no opportunities to express dissent without being tarred a traitor."

"Jos! You would not—"

"Shhhh." Willcocks looked around the room before continuing. "I make no commitment… yet. I merely say I'm on the knife's edge in my allegiance. Who can say which way it will tip?" He pushed his chair back and took their mugs for more ale.

Tom feared for him. Were the British leaders right? Would he cap outspokenness with rasher actions? Actually desert to the enemy? That would mean arrest, or worse. He worried for himself, too, as a known associate. His conflicting interests in the matter gave him many a headache, but he must give Willcocks reason to believe he might be persuaded to join him. Too much eagerness would be out of character and could rouse Willcocks's suspicions. And he was doubtful in his own right. After what he saw in York, his confidence in the British as defenders of Upper Canada had taken a severe hit. On which side of the conflict did he truly belong? He felt a personal loyalty to Rebecca, but to the Crown? This spying business was more complicated than he thought.

Rebecca

It was getting so I couldn't tell which army was in control of the lakeshore, the front lines drifted about so much. Nearly every day, troops of different factions passed our farm. It was almost a mercy we had but few fields under cultivation this year, and those well away from the road. There was less to tempt raiding parties. Or so I hoped. Stores were running low. Both British and American armies were trying to live off the land, and I wasn't the only one worried about the coming winter. With most men in the militia, there was only limited planting and little hope for as good a harvest as last year. I hoped farms back in the interior were better off and asked Tom to reconnoiter for food while as "Thrush" he surveyed the territory for seditious activity.

We had committed to keep the safe room stocked, and should not raid it for our use unless we could make good what we took. In my role as midwife and healer, I must often part with some of our supplies to assist others, a practice expected of the clergy as well, so a double duty. My overarching concern was Robert—it was taking him a long time to recover from the shock of being taken prisoner and the insults to his church. He needed proper nourishment. I was hard pressed to maintain our table for that purpose. I resolved to use some of the safe room stores if I must, to keep him healthy. Meanwhile, I scoured the edges of our land for wild foods. Puffballs and morels, fiddleheads, dandelion greens and the occasional rabbit graced our table. I had not ventured on squirrel yet, but that might come.

One evening in late June, Tom arrived at Lake Lodge as the sun was setting. He slipped beside me onto the bench outside the summer kitchen where I was shelling peas. I jumped up, knocking the bowl askew, but he caught it with only a few peas scattered for the chickens to retrieve later.

"Tom, you rascal! You scared me half into next week!"

"Sorry, Rebecca. I've learned to move silently. Not everyone is as welcoming as you."

"I suppose our Indian friends have helped you there."

He nodded. "I have a story to tell about that." He picked up a few pea pods and helped me with the shelling as he told it.

"I was moving between militia outposts along the Twelve-Mile Creek and stopped in at John DeCew's house, up on the ridge near Beaver Dams, where a small detachment of soldiers was quartered. I was there when there was a great hubbub outside. A bedraggled woman came in. She blurted out an improbable story about a planned American attack on Beaver Dams. The officer in charge thought it some ruse but an Indian band confirmed her tale. They had met her and guided her to DeCew's house. She had already walked nearly twenty miles, from Queenston."

"In this heat?" I asked. "She must have been half-dead when she arrived."

"She surely looked it," said Tom.

"Who was she?"

"A Mrs. Secord, of Queenston. Mrs. James Secord, I think."

I shook my head. "I don't think I know her, but I would like to. It was a brave act." The great joke was she had prepared a story of searching for a lost cow, but never needed to use it.

"The soldiers weren't inclined to believe her at first but she held her ground. A good thing, too, for we were ready when the Americans attacked Beaver Dams. It was they who had the surprise, and we beat them soundly."

"You weren't hurt, I hope?" I looked him over, but there were no signs of bandaging, no surface injuries to face or hands.

"I painted up like an Indian and stood with them. I mustn't be identified by the Americans, not if I'm to keep on deceiving them." He grinned broadly. "It was a short action, and we rounded them up like cattle. The Indians did most of the fighting, there being so few soldiers. Most of the regulars are still up at the Forty-Mile Creek."

"It's pleasant to hear some good news. We've had so little lately." I rose, carrying the bowl. "There are plenty of peas and I have a rabbit stewing. You'll stay for dinner?"

"Of course!"

"Robert will enjoy your story. It will take his mind off his worries for a while."

But Robert had his own story to tell, and it wiped away my earlier pleasure.

"It has finally happened," he said, shoulders drooping.

"What on earth?" I asked.

"Willcocks. He and some of like mind have turned traitor, and joined the Americans. One of John Norton's scouts saw him enter Fort George yesterday and came to tell me." Robert sunk his head in his hands and groaned. "I always thought him a villain, but never this black a one. Honest dissent I could understand, at least, but this? He is a thorough blackguard."

I was as shocked as he, but noticed Tom made no remark. I looked at him quizzically.

"This has been brewing since Brock's death," he said. "When Sheaffe took over from Brock, Willcocks accepted his authority and found him not unreasonable. After the attack on York, when Sheaffe was discredited, Willcocks lost confidence in the British command. He sees more autocratic behavior and fears it may overtake any hope of reform in the Province. Reforms that would bring us closer to what the Americans already have. He's under pressure from some of his fellow legislators, and many of their constituents. So, no, I'm not surprised to hear this." He hesitated, then took a deep breath. "He had many contacts in the States, from publishing the *Guardian*. I suspect someone has made him an offer that fell on fertile ground."

Robert groaned again. "That man has plenty of Irish blarney to cozen the disaffected. Men who grumbled but remained loyal now have a standard to rally around. This will not end well. God help us all."

Someone with more temporal power, I hoped.

July

Jack

While still flushed with the glow of his new promotion, Jack received letters from both Maryel and Eliza. Maryel had taken to corresponding weekly, usually a welcome event. He tried to reply as frequently, but these past weeks had been preoccupied with additional duties following his promotion. This letter looked different, even before he opened it. The handwriting of the address was smudged, and the seal was on crooked. Maryel usually took great care over such details. He tore at the seal and quickly scanned the contents. Her normally prim hand had turned to a scrawl. The note was undated.

My dear Jack,

News of a terrible thing has arrived. Niagara is taken by the Americans! There is no possibility of news or letters reaching us. Eliza and I are frantic with worry. I know you can't do anything either. I just had to tell someone. Dr. Mountain counsels patience, but how he thinks it possible I cannot tell.

Do write to me. I need some assurance that all is well somewhere.

He turned to the letter from Eliza, which appeared to have been written in equal haste.

I implore you to write at once to Maryel, and add your persuasion to mine, that she not attempt a return to Niagara. I think it foolhardy, but she seems determined.

Now, here was a quandary. He had good news to share, but what if the thought of him in battle might upset Maryel further, though he was safe and unharmed? On top of the news from Niagara, it might only increase her fears. She would think more invaders would come up the Richelieu River at any moment. Devil if he knew what he should do. Maybe Hingston would know.

Willcocks

2 Jul

Entered Fort George last week. Joined Americans. Had enough of British tyranny. Time to overthrow the despots. They think I'm a traitor—simply for my ideas on reform. May as well have the game as the name. At least Americans appreciate value of democracy.

15 Jul

Received commission as Major in American army. Permission to form and lead unit of defectors. Will call it Canadian Volunteers. Locals who know the territory. Mandate: skirmish. forage. scout & raid. Harass neighborhood. Try to stymie blockade of Fort. Open routes for resupply. Black Rock of doubtful value. Lewiston? Fort Niagara?

23 Jul

Everything against us. Weather—searing heat or chilly deluge. Blockade severe. Privations in fort. Soldiers exhausted. Despite this. men trickle in. join my unit. Strange on board as runner. Shows promise in intelligence gathering. We'll show those Tory-loving fools who chose the right side.

Rebecca

Over the long, hot summer, the American forces rounded up many more men, sending them as prisoners of war into the States. Robert wrote to his daughters, describing the events.

My friend Mr. Merritt was taken prisoner in early July with many other respectable inhabitants of the town. He has since been released, on his parole not to engage in fighting for a year, but others are not so fortunate. I was taken up myself, briefly, but the American commander allowed that I was entitled to consideration for my age and position as clergyman, so I was put upon my parole, and suffered to remain in my own house.

I am sad to say that our Church was used as a prison before the men remaining in the town were transported to Albany, New York, over three hundred miles away from here. St. Mark's is now used as a barracks for the American soldiers.

When our army advanced toward Niagara, they formed a line about four miles from the Town, and our house was sometime the headquarters. Then I performed Divine Service to the separate divi-

sions of the army alternately, and visited the sick, who are very numerous. Your stepmother has been much engaged in treating those lodged at the grist mill on the nearby creek, which is pressed into service as a hospital. Our army expects to fall back when the winter sets in.

Lake Lodge was off the main road and a little distance from the Four-Mile Creek, but from time to time a small troop of soldiers passing along the lakeshore road ventured out to the lakeside. It wasn't always clear which side they were on. Militia garb wasn't uniform in the manner of the British Army, and most of the soldiers we saw appeared like our neighbors did when hunting deer. I can't say they acted neighborly, though—they raided the edges of my vegetable garden as they passed. I'm sure they might have dug up the entire patch if they hadn't been traveling quickly.

Our proximity to the grist mill was an ongoing worry. It figured in several skirmishes, and the fighting came as close to us as the Ball farm, with only one other between it and ourselves.

"Those shots last night sounded close," I said to Robert one morning.

"I walked out to the road at first light. Some of our troops have set up a picket at the end of our lane."

"I suppose I should be glad they didn't come up and demand billeting here."

"We should be more concerned about our crops and livestock, my dear. I doubt we shall be able to keep all our produce this year, even if we're able to harvest it."

He was right, and it wasn't only the vegetable patch that suffered. Individual sheep and chickens disappeared mysteriously until I had the presence of mind to lock them in the barn at night. But then, the fields of unripened grain closest to the road shrank suspiciously around the edges, as if being nibbled by phantom beasts.

"Gun-carriage horses," said Robert when I mentioned this. "Turned loose to feed at night."

It would be a wonder if we survived, at this rate. Other farms along the shore were raided, too. Our neighbors lost as much as we did, something all could ill afford. When we learned the Ball farmhouse had been looted, Robert insisted we bury the church silver and most of our own out by the barn, for safekeeping. We had already stored some of our valuables along with the preserved foods in the secret room and taken to eating with wooden forks and spoons. And then there was Robert's ruling passion: his books.

"I know it sounds selfish, but I'm thankful we moved my library here," he said over dinner one evening. "Though I have begun to worry they may burn as easily here as in Niagara."

"We must hope this is the safer location." I found it hard to be over-concerned about the books. Between the farm routine, tending to Robert, and my visits to the sick at the mill, I had scarce a moment to myself, let alone enough to read.

On my next foray into town, for Robert was not yet recovered sufficiently to go, I noticed the changes that had come over it. Not only were the streets patrolled by American soldiers, who insulted everyone they met, including me, but the very houses and yards appeared to have drooped in response to the battle. It had been a dry spring. Dust lay on the leaves where a fresh sheen should have been. Some kitchen gardens showed a bit of green, but more lay untended or worse, unplanted. If this held true around the district, it would be a hard winter. We had managed a fair harvest last fall, but what could be expected this year under foreign occupation? We might enjoy relative plenty at the moment, but starvation loomed in our future.

*

We celebrated the marriage of John and Catherine Norton on July 27th. Robert was especially pleased to both baptize and marry Catherine on the same day. There were so few happy ceremonies in these times of war that we treasured each one. We couldn't offer them a feast, but enjoyed a quiet afternoon of conversation overlooking Lake Ontario.

What a striking couple they made with their chiseled features and glossy black hair. They were dressed in traditional garb for the occasion, and I admired Catherine's beaded and heavily fringed gown. She appeared unencumbered by stays, for which I envied her. I envied her darker-toned complexion as well, which would not burn and peel as mine did. John Norton, too, was most handsome in his beaded tunic and leggings of soft leather, with fringed sash and feathered headband. He towered over us all. Magnificent.

Their wedding took place at Lake Lodge, in the upstairs chapel overlooking the lake. They had traveled from Burlington by boat. The church was inaccessible owing to the occupation, and Robert couldn't travel to the Mohawk chapel on the Grand River because of the frequency of raids by both armies.

"You are more important to us alive, my friend," said Norton, shaking Robert's hand warmly. "You do much to comfort the population. More than you know—or, perhaps, will acknowledge. I'd rather see you survive this war and continue your good work than I would any ten other men."

Robert colored a deep red. "My dear fellow, you mustn't say such things."

I smiled inwardly, but said nothing.

Robert recovered his composure and asked Norton what he heard of Willcocks. "We have heard only that he defected, the scoundrel."

"There's a great deal more to it, I'm afraid," said Norton. "Our network of agents has discovered…"

"Must we talk war on our wedding day?" asked Catherine.

"I fear we must, my love," he said, "although I would not wish to spoil your day." He removed his headdress, wiping his brow. "Perhaps Rebecca…?"

I hastened to the rescue. "Do you wish to see the house?" She nodded, and I showed her inside, all the while keeping an ear open to the men's conversation. I felt obliged to them that they did not bother to lower their voices. Catherine's remarks were general so it was a simple matter to murmur similar responses while listening to the men as best I could.

"Willcocks… trickle of recruits… Canadian Volunteers," said Norton.

"That blackguard!"

"… black-hearted a villain as… known… thought… mere gadfly… necessary evil in politics… shown us his true perfidy at last."

Thank goodness the windows were all open or I might have heard nothing. I lingered beside one as I showed Catherine my stillroom.

"Some causes he supported were worthy. I joined my voice to his on several occasions." Robert paused. I imagined him pursing his lips. "It did me no good with those in power." His voice trembled. "As if I, a man of God, a missionary for the Church of England, would betray my King and country."

"I never thought highly of Gore's judgment."

As Catherine and I made our way upstairs, I strained to hear more but their voices became indistinct. I led her through the bed-chambers. She remarked on the small privy chamber where I had installed a cabinet commode.

"It's too cold in winter to go to the outhouse at night," I said. "My husband has a weak chest, and I would not have him become ill because I failed to provide a simple convenience."

We compared household customs, which differed but little, then continued to the chapel from where I could hear the men again. They had apparently finished vilifying Willcocks's character and moved on to other matters.

"… word of more desertions, some to join Willcocks and his roving band."

"So, we can expect more raids?" Robert sounded discouraged. "The people suffer from both sides' raids, you know."

"An unfortunate consequence of war, sir. I wish it could be otherwise, but an army must provision itself."

"And the people must endure." He sighed. "It worries me that more local men are moving to Willcocks. With their knowledge of our territory, they can strike where and when they will. I fear for our lives and our livelihoods."

Beside me, Catherine stiffened. I put my arm around her, but to no effect. We slowly descended the steps to the veranda. The men stood as we approached, and Norton took his wife's arm.

"We'll be on our way," he said. "I must get Catherine back to Burlington by nightfall. We have yet to decide whether to remain there, or return to the village at Brant's Ford. But I will see you again, a few days hence."

August

Tom

Tom traveled back and forth through the blockade, running messages for both sides. Willcocks's new American unit harassed the British as much as they could, whilst the British went marauding along the American shore and around Fort George. He brought news of the latest raid by the British, and caught Willcocks at his dinner.

"Join me," said Willcocks. "I've a nice bit of beef here."

"Purloined?"

"Off some of those pestiferous Loyalists. I bagged a whole joint of a young steer."

Tom sat opposite him. "I could use a good meal. We got to Black Rock only to find the British had been before us. Not a sausage to be found in the stores there. The whole outpost was burnt out."

"The troops in Fort George won't like that. Weren't all the spare uniforms kept there? And the winter gear?"

Tom nodded. "They won't replace those soon, nor the food either. Short rations for those in the fort."

They clinked tankards. "Better out here for many reasons," said

Willcocks. "There's sickness in the Fort. Too near swampy ground it is, and full of fevers and agues. They don't care for the raids by the Indians, either. No more do I."

"Wishing you hadn't been so persuasive early on?"

"It would be easier if the Indians were fighting with us, not against us. We could use more on our side now."

Tom paused with a dripping morsel of beef halfway to his mouth. "We've lost the momentum, haven't we? We didn't push the British Army back as far as we could when we had the chance."

Willcocks nodded. "Unless we get reinforcements soon, this year's fighting season looks like it's ending in stalemate." He rubbed at the stubble on his chin. "The men left in the fort are no use. Sickly or lily-livered, it makes no matter. We do more to advance the cause than they."

"And the British pour more men down the peninsula. I was nearly taken on my way back from Black Rock. We're almost surrounded here."

"They keep promising us more men. Where are they?"

"Not coming from Sacket's Harbor or anywhere else on the Lake Ontario shore. British ships still rule there. We've a better presence on Lake Erie. Maybe they'll make a push from there." Tom worried at his lower lip. "I've better news closer to home, though."

"I could do with some."

"More of the settlers are ready to join us. Their farms have been raided by British troops to the point of destitution. Some have sent their families away so they can fight the British without harm to them."

Willcocks barked a laugh and rubbed his hands together. "Sure, boyo, that's the stuff. We'll welcome them and be all the stronger. What care we for more American troops when we have our home-grown men? The scum-sucking Loyalists will eat our dirt!"

Willcocks

17 ^{Aug}

Have at my command full one hundred and twenty men. Promoted to Colonel by General McClure. Markle and Mallory, both fellow legislators, are my senior officers. Eight juniors round out the command. A motley bunch, but knowledge of the territory is our advantage.

29 Aug

Skirmishing with Indians in woods surrounding the town. Too strong to take on directly, also have superior local knowledge to my men. They're less fearful than soldiers in the fort, but still find warriors tough opponents.

Rebecca

Norton returned within a few days, bringing Tom with him. When I asked after Catherine, he said she had gone back to stay with her family until he could rejoin her.

"We're here on Army business," he told us. "I've asked 'Thrush' here to lead a party to find and retrieve a cache of medical supplies buried on land closer to the town. I believe the farm is unoccupied at present."

Tom spoke up. "It's on John Secord's land. I think I know where. Not far from the end of the lagoon. There's pretty good cover around there.

"You'll be in danger of being spotted by Willcocks," said Robert.

"You must be extra careful," I said, "even if you paint up as a warrior. He would know you regardless."

Tom laughed. "I'm no fool, Rebecca. We've made sure he's elsewhere."

I shook my head. "You can't know for sure. And remember, some of our former neighbors have turned traitor, too. Have a care."

Norton interjected. "I will have him out of there as soon as we find the cache. Please, Mrs. Addison, it's crucial to our efforts. You have nowhere near enough medicines to see us through this year. Let alone longer."

"And then what?" I asked. "You'll bring them back here?"

"Yes. You can evaluate what we find? Make an inventory of what can be used?"

"How long have they been buried?" I asked.

"I believe it's less than a year." Norton's brow furrowed. "The surgeon in charge left word they were preparing the cache last autumn, before the ground froze. October or perhaps as late as November."

"Why didn't you bring him to locate it for you?" Robert asked.

"He succumbed to a fever after the evacuation of Fort George."

It was a long wait until darkness fell and their party set off. I packed Robert off to bed early since there was nothing he could do to help me. I had burned down a candle and a half and was squinting over the mending when the back door creaked and Tom came in.

"Did you find it?"

"Yes, and they shooed me off before I could get a good look." His face was streaked with warpaint and I sent him to the scullery to wash it off. Even after a good soaping, he ruined one of my towels. A small price for his safety.

He kept up a running patter in between swipes at his face. "We were close to the road at one point. Had to skirt the swamp by the Three-Mile Creek pond. There was nobody on the road then. But when we got to the farmstead, we had to wait awhile. There were scouts around the farmhouse, looked like they were looting. We didn't care to ask which side they were on, but kept to the shelter of the outbuildings."

He gave his head a final rub, leaving himself looking quite the scarecrow. "As I thought, there was a spot behind the cow byre, marked with a sandstone and a dead bush. It took two men to roll away the stone, and I glimpsed something in a hollow underneath. But then they sent me back here." He shrugged. "I don't suppose they'll be too far behind me."

Soon, I faced a dozen or more wax-coated packages of varying sizes laid out on my dining table. I scanned to see which were dressings and splints, and which medicines. The larger bundles were mostly bandages, and the smaller held medicinal ingredients. The latter, I carried to my stillroom for evaluation and I sent Tom to the cellar with the rest. Norton had already taken his warriors off, leaving Tom to assist me.

"I can't do anything more with these until tomorrow. You got the rest into the secret room?"

He nodded, yawning.

"Enough excitement for one day."

It was becoming more difficult for me to move about, so anyone in our vicinity who required my services had to come to Lake Lodge, or to the mill, at their own risk. I could not always reach the mill, although it had been occupied by British troops for weeks now. We picked up scraps of news from soldiers there, but relied mostly on Tom for updates. His visits were sporadic, though, so we often fell behind.

The British force, under General Vincent, had moved its headquarters forward from Burlington to Shipman's Corners on the Twelve-Mile Creek, and established outposts at the mill and further south, at St. Davids. This meant the American occupiers were holed up in Fort George most of the time. Willcocks's Volunteers were hemmed in more closely now, and restricted their foraging to farms nearest Niagara town, most of which were deserted.

They hadn't reached us yet.

There was a fair road along the east bank of the Four-Mile Creek, running from the lakeshore road to the hamlet of St. Davids, below the escarpment—the very road I had walked to Drusilla's quilting party, now much improved. This made communications and patrolling easy for the British troops, and their blockade more effective. Meanwhile, the American pickets had no such advantage and were often separated, the local ground cut by ravines, thickly wooded areas, and farm enclosures. They were cut off by water, too, with the British Navy controlling Lake Ontario and the mouth of the Niagara River. Re-provisioning their occupying force from the east bank of the river could only be accomplished under cover of darkness. With British patrols on Queenston Heights, even this was challenging. Supplies coming up the Genesee River were blockaded as well, and had to be transported overland to Lewiston. The few vessels trying to make their way along the American shore were intercepted, and the provisions seized for use by the British. This took some of the pressure off our limited stores, thankfully.

We still felt vulnerable. I started at every loud noise and Robert was almost as anxious. Our house directly overlooked the lake, and the bank was not high enough to prevent a sneak attack coming up in our yard.

Tom showed up one afternoon to find us unnerved to hear shooting not far away.

"What news?" asked Robert.

I stood behind him, hands clenched.

"A skirmish at Jacob Ball's farm." He caught his breath. "I came to warn you. The fighting is over and the enemy repulsed, but… our troops are picketed near the road, on your land."

Robert groaned. "So much for our oat crop then."

"If that's all we lose, I'll be thankful," I said. "But Tom, should we worry about more?"

"If you've still got valuables above ground, I'd bury them quickly. Our men are steadfast fighters, but they're owed months of back-pay and have little to lose but their uniforms and weapons. Anything lying around loose is a temptation hard to resist."

"Then it's fortunate we've already secreted what we have. I kept only a few knives for daily use and hid the others below."

"And jewelry?" Tom asked.

"Nothing but my wedding ring." I glanced at the thin band of gold. It would hurt to lose it, but if needs must…

"I must be off again," said Tom. "Errands 'Thrush' must run for 'Snipe.' I'll try to get back in a few days."

He embraced me and clasped Robert's hand and was gone as suddenly as he'd arrived.

Robert and I stood for a while at the door, and then turned back to our tasks, he writing a sermon and I preparing our evening meal. He opened one of our few remaining bottles of wine.

"We may as well have it now, rather than let someone else take it."

We lingered at the table, sipping the last of the wine.

Robert's brow was deeply furrowed with worry and I leaned over the corner of the table to smooth it.

He pressed my hand to his lips.

"The danger increases daily, but I cannot think of a place where we would be truly safe," he said. "Even if we retreated all the way back to England—which is impossible, given the state of war on both sides of the Atlantic."

"Try not to worry so much. We will face what comes, together."

Jack

In mid-August, new orders arrived for the 100th Regiment to rein-force York and Niagara. They were to travel light so the women must be left behind. There was severe distress among the wives and camp-followers, and many tearful farewells as they packed their gear for the trip back to Montreal from Kingston, where they had been recently quartered.

Jack found Hingston's wife overseeing the loading of her trunk onto a wagon and pressed a message into her hands. "Please, see that Miss Maryel Addison gets this. It may be the last I can send."

She accepted the commission, and he kissed her hands in thanks.

"Sam tells me you are expecting a happy event in some months. I wish you well."

Her hands fell to her rounded stomach, and she smiled back at him. "Thank you, Jack. We hope for the best. Keep your eye on Sam. He isn't cut out for field duty anymore, but try and tell him that." She climbed onto the wagon beside the driver, waving at Jack as they drove off.

How ironic it was that he should leave Maryel behind in Montreal as he had left her behind in Niagara before. Could they never occupy the same town for long?

Jack returned to his duty: supervising the loading of the baggage train. They would need to travel entirely by land, the number of warships on Lake Ontario having increased so troop transport by water was too risky. This meant wagon after wagon of ammunition, fodder for man and beast, and the various items of soldiers' kit that couldn't be readily carried over long distances. As it was, in a foot regiment, each man was heavily burdened.

The long march to York got underway before the end of August. They traveled on rough summer roads. Ruts from the spring mud hardened into grooves that never exactly fit either the men's boots or the wagon wheels. It was nearly as hot as July had been, but no man wished for rain. Better a rough road than one up to the axles in mud. Their luck held, for they were on their last day's march before York when the skies opened. The clay of the road quickly deteriorated into a thick muck that sucked at their boots, but they persevered and, shortly before dark, stumbled through the town to the gates of Fort York.

The fort was still being repaired after the attack earlier in the year, but there were dry tents for the soldiers and barracks for the officers.

Hingston gave Jack the welcome duty of delivering a ration of grog to the men. "We'll be moving on again soon. Let them have a few days to dress their blisters and feed up."

Rebecca

A knock came at the door late one August evening when we had finished our supper and removed to the veranda to enjoy the last of the light. It was a scruffy, curly-haired lad of about ten years. His elbows showed through a much-mended shirt, and he was barefoot. "Please missus, Ma is took real bad."

"Who's your Ma?"

"Clarrie Walters, missus." He shuffled his feet. "She says if you could come right quick."

But I was already moving toward the door, and my midwifing bag. I picked up a shawl lying on a chair near the door and called out to Robert as I left, the boy in my wake.

"Your farm is further along the lake, I believe?" I wanted to keep him talking, to occupy both of us on the walk.

"Yes'm. We're more'n a mile down the road west, t'other side, not on the lake." He sniffed and wiped his nose on his sleeve.

"How long has your mother been… feeling poorly?"

"Ma started complaining around midday. Said at first it was indigestion, but then she said the baby was on its way."

"And your father? Where is he?"

"Pa's been off these past two days, hunting. We ain't had meat for more'n a week."

"Your Pa's not with the militia?"

"No'm. He broke his leg real bad once and it didn't heal right."

I wasn't familiar with his injury, but then there were always new people coming into the district and I couldn't tend them all. Walters… Did I know the name? I looked a little more closely at the boy. Under those curls was his face tanned, or naturally dark-skinned? There were some colored people in Niagara, most of whom had arrived with the original Loyalist settlers. I knew, too, that a special militia unit formed of colored volunteers had fought with Brock at Queenston. This boy's father would not have been one of their number, though.

"Do you have brothers and sisters?"

"Rachel, she's a year older'n me, and Sammy, he's just a little-un."

"And your name is?"

"I'm Tim, missus." He lapsed into silence.

It took us about twenty minutes, I guessed, and we turned left into a lane bordered by a few bushes and the stumps of larger trees. A few dozen feet in, lay a few buildings made of chinked logs. Tim led me to one of the smaller ones, and through its low door.

Inside, once my eyes adjusted to the gloom, I could see a bed against one wall, with a woman lying on it. A young girl was tending a small boy on the packed earthen floor. The only light came from a small fire and a single tallow candle by the bed.

The woman was in distress, doubled over on her side and clutching her stomach. Even in the limited light I could see her color was not good. Her face was a darkish gray, her skin tone considerably darker than her children's. I assumed from this that her husband was of lighter skin, but these were passing thoughts, of no consequence. I must assist her birthing.

"Clarrie?" She gripped my hand when I took hers. "I'm Rebecca Addison. I'm here to help you."

She groaned and pressed harder on my hand as a contraction seized her. I shooed the children off to the other side of the room and examined her, lifting her shift to check her progress. She muttered something, and I bent closer to hear.

"It stopped moving."

"When?"

"Yesterday… No, day before."

My heart sank. They were all thin. Too thin. If they hadn't had meat for a week, what else had run too low?

"How far along are you?"

"Seven, maybe eight months." Clarrie cried out as another contraction hit. They were getting closer together.

I called to the girl, Rachel, to bring me some water and a clean cloth. I bathed Clarrie down, trying to cool her off. She seemed refreshed, and rested a moment.

Then, with a great cry, she pushed out the baby.

The poor wee thing was limp and lifeless. I did what I could, anyway. Carefully removed the mucus from its mouth, tried to puff a few small breaths into its lungs, but it was no use. I wiped it clean and wrapped it in a piece of cloth, and laid it on the bed beside her.

She turned her head toward it, then turned away, tears in her eyes.

"I'm so sorry." I massaged her abdomen gently, and a final contraction delivered the afterbirth.

Clarrie was weak but not bleeding overmuch, so I cleaned her up and left her with her children. I hoped her husband would return soon, but meanwhile her daughter was able to help.

I wondered how many other poor women would have to endure such events before the war ended.

September–November

Jack

The 100th moved swiftly from York, first to Burlington Heights and then into the Niagara region. September 16th saw the Regiment already bivouacked at the Four-Mile Creek, near Lake Lodge. They found the troops already quartered there to be suffering from illness, heat, and foul water. Agues and fevers abounded, and it wasn't long before many of the newly arrived soldiers fell ill in their turn. Jack was detailed to seek medicines from Rebecca Addison.

"Why, Jack Stevenson! Of all the people… And a lieutenant's insignia, too. My word, you're looking well."

He bowed with a flourish. "Happy to see you again, Mrs. Addison."

"You mustn't stand on ceremony with me, Jack. Call me Rebecca, please."

"Rebecca, then," he said with a grin. "I'm to ask for medical supplies. Especially laudanum." He flushed and fingered his collar. "Have you heard from Maryel?"

She tapped his arm sharply. "You volunteered for this duty, didn't you?"

He looked sheepish. "Well… yes."

"My dear boy, of course you did. I'll tell you everything I know. But, business first." She sighed. "If I had any spare laudanum to give, you may be sure I would. We did have some earlier in the year, but with so much sickness… Well, if you are willing, you can help me prepare a few other things."

He followed her into the stillroom, the fragrance of multiple herbs smacking him in the face and making him take a step back.

She laughed. "It can take some people that way. You soon get used to it. But I'll bring things outside so we can work in the fresh air.

Rebecca loaded Jack down with two bundles of twigs and small branches, two large bunches of dried herbs, and a small wooden box. She herself carried a large mortar and pestle, several sheets of paper, a ball of string and a roll of waxed cloth. They settled down on the veranda.

"You won't make me wait?" Jack asked. "Please, what news have you?"

She chuckled. "I won't torment you. My husband gets our letters in the Army dispatch packet, since he's Chaplain at the fort. We had one last week. Maryel is well, although pining for home." She raised her eyebrows. "And for you, too, no doubt. It's easy to read between the lines."

Jack grinned so hard he thought his face might split.

"Now," she said, "time for business. Head out of the clouds and pay attention, please. This is willow, for fevers and aches." She pointed out the yellowish-green twigs. "And this, cherry, for coughs." She showed him the others, smooth and gray. "I will give you one branch of each as a sample so you may locate and gather more if it's needed. Both grow near the mill. As for preparation, it's similar for both." She slit one branch along its length and peeled the bark from the inner wood. "It's easiest when they're young but can be done at any stage. Spring is best, when sap is first flowing, but they can be collected any time, except dead of winter."

She showed him how to strip the inner layer from the bark and gathered the scrapings onto a piece of waxed cloth. He imitated her process on several other branches until she was satisfied he knew the method. "You may either continue here, or carry the branches with you. It matters little." She gave him a second piece of waxed cloth for the cherry bark, and two lengths of string to bind the packages. "Both may be prepared by soaking in brandy for several days—in glass or glazed crock—then strained and mixed with a little honey. A few spoons of each should be sufficient, the willow for fever and aches, and the cherry for a cough. The tincture should keep several months."

"And what of the others?"

"The herb is horehound. A tea made with a handful of leaves and flowers, pulverized, soothes most coughs. In the box I have mullein flowers—also to be used in a tea for coughs. None is curative, but all relieve some part of the illness." She showed him how to strip the horehound leaves and let him produce another package of those. She spooned about a third of the mullein flowers into yet another packet. "I can't give you all of these. They have already flowered and I will have no more until next summer." She shook her head. "And I can't get poppy at all."

Jack was overwhelmed. "I had no idea there were so many details. I swear I've swallowed many a physician's potion with no idea of the contents."

Rebecca laughed. "Remember, add a drop or two of honey. If you have any. Most remedies have a bitter edge."

She waved him off. Burdened by his packages and bundles, he made his way back to the mill. Maybe these remedies would help some of his fellows. And he hugged the news of Maryel to his heart.

✳

Morale in the British and Upper Canadian ranks was low, made worse by the loss of the fleet on Lake Erie on September 10th, news of which reached the Niagara hinterland around the same time as the 100th Foot. Many had assumed from the beginning of the war that British naval superiority was unassailable, but the British fleet at Kingston and the American at Sacket's Harbor stared each other down in a perpetual stalemate, albeit with a slight edge for the British on Lake Ontario. Now, the British force had been soundly whipped by American gunboats on Lake Erie, and their commander—with the loss of an arm and a leg—reduced to a hulk along with his ships. This terrible news, and the strain of having the enemy holding their rear, led to gloom and consternation among the troops.

Disaffection in the ranks was rampant. On more than one occasion, Jack broke up quarrels over small debts, too long outstanding because of the continual delay in the Paymaster's office. The men were weary from inaction, and half-starved on rotten food. There were daily desertions—as many as eight or ten men a day went missing—but soldiers were needed so badly, that few were executed when recaptured, unless they had defected to and aided the enemy. They were merely clapped in irons for a few days, to think things over, and then returned to duty.

Jack found a handy tree stump, flat enough to write on, and overturned a bucket to use as a seat. He drew a sheet of hoarded paper from an inner pocket, and a stub of a pencil. Quill pens were a luxury he hadn't seen for some time, outside of Regimental Headquarters.

22 September 1813

Dear Father,

Hmm. Where to begin…

You asked for more details of military life. We have seen no new action, but have returned to Niagara. Affairs here are stagnant.

Life in camp is monotonous. Many are demoralized. Food is rotten, and pay is worse. Local farmers curse us for liberating their standing crops, but want us nearby so they can feel safer. There is much theft, so they have reason to complain. We don't flog the men for preventing their own starvation, for fear of more dissent in the ranks.

Naught exists to purchase even when we're paid, tho' I dare swear some merchants enrich themselves selling supplies to the Army. There is sickness in camp, but I am well despite the insalubrious atmosphere. I take my fiddle into the hospital to cheer the men. They enjoy the old tunes you have made so much of, and the newer music you sent me, by that fellow Beethoven. Some of his pieces are stirring. Perhaps in winter quarters I may gather a chamber group to study them more thoroughly.

Give my love to the whole family.

His pencil was nearly used up, and so were his ideas. He folded the paper and pocketed it, to include in the next post.

Willcocks

Willcocks beckoned to Tom to join him at the tavern's long trestle table and signaled the pot-man to bring more ale.

"Cider for me," said Tom, settling down on the bench. He cleared his throat. "What's new?"

Willcocks beamed. "You'll need to call me Colonel now."

"Congratulations, Jos. There's no holding you back." Tom pounded the table.

Willcocks preened under Tom's enthusiasm, patting his new epaulets. "Thankee, boyo, thankee. And what news from you?"

"Troops on the move, to winter quarters, I guess. Nobody sensible fights battles in winter."

"True. What else?"

"I've heard they need reinforcements at Kingston."

"What? So far east? Do you really think the army would abandon the Niagara Peninsula?"

"Word is out they may."

"Hmm." Willcocks was not inclined to take this at face value. Tom had given him useful information before, but this sounded too far-fetched.

"The commander-in-chief, Prevost, has a reputation for caution. Likes to keep his forces concentrated and intact."

"Is that so?" Willcocks rubbed his chin. "Almost exactly what Colonel Scott at Fort Niagara says. I thought him too hopeful, but..."

"The eastern end of Lake Ontario appears to be the key. If the American side wants to have a serious chance at Montreal."

"Our side, you mean."

Tom, his mouth full of cider, nodded assent.

"One of these days, the face-off between the fleets is going to break," said Willcocks. "We could cut off the whole of Upper Canada if we took Kingston. You heard we defeated them at the Thames River? Killed Tecumseh, too."

Tom shook his head. "Glad I'm not a General. I wouldn't want to have to decide where to put my troops. Not when there are such distances involved." He chuckled. "Not that I'm ever likely to be one."

Willcocks mulled over Tom's news, sipping at his ale. "If I pass this on, what odds Scott takes his New York militia down the lake, leaving us and a few regular troops to hold Fort George, while General McClure hunkers down in Fort Niagara?"

"Can they hold the country with a few hundred men?"

"I don't know."

"Well, it's more than my poor head can encompass." Tom drained his cider and wiped his mouth on his sleeve. "Any more recruits?"

"There are fewer to be had, but some trickle in." Willcocks leaned back in his seat, beaming. "All good fellows, shaping well as soldiers."

Tom stood, swaying a little. "My thanks for the cider. You can be found here most days?"

"Yes," said Willcocks, "most days, around this time."

5 Oct

What's the matter with Strange? Doesn't seem to know which side he's on. Ben Mallory insists he's playing us all for fools. Says he saw him snooping around McClure's quarters. Will bear watching.

Rebecca

Early October brought a cold snap, and a hard frost killed the few plants remaining above ground in my garden. I salvaged a few pot herbs for immediate use and the root crops would do as long as the ground didn't freeze. I could harvest them over the next few weeks for storage in the cellar. The air had a tang to it, biting at my nostrils like a cloud of tiny insects.

Robert had gone to the army outpost at the mill and I planned to spend the day in my stillroom. With the advent of winter and its inevitable ailments, I wanted to have a good supply of cough remedies and febrifuges on hand.

My good intentions were interrupted by the sound of feet pounding in the yard. The kitchen door crashed open to admit a flushed and panting Tom.

"Need... cellar... hide... now!" He hardly got the words out before stumbling toward the cellar door.

No time for questions. I grabbed a jug from the pantry shelf, filled it from the kettle hanging by the fire, and followed him.

He stood by the shelf-door to the secret room, sides heaving and hands gripping his thighs. "Following me… Suspects…"

"For pity's sake, breathe now, talk later." I put the jug down so I could open the door then pushed him inside and handed him the jug. "Calm down and make yourself some tea. I'll deal with whoever it is." I shut the door in his face and made sure all was concealed.

As quickly as I could, I climbed the cellar stairs and closed the door behind me. I breathed deeply and adjusted my skirts. I must take my own advice and appear calm, though my heart was racing. I looked around the scullery. No sign of Tom's entry bar a few stray leaves, but they were merely a sign of the season. And there was no time to clean them away in any case. For now, a pounding came at the main door. Willcocks!

Thank goodness he was alone. I had a reasonable chance of dealing with him myself.

"Where is he?" He stood on the doorstep, gulping air.

"Where is who?"

"Tom. I saw him come this way. He always runs to you."

"Well, he hasn't on this day. I've been alone here all morning." I stared at Willcocks, eyes wide. "What's going on?"

His brows drew together as he peered into my face. "You're sure you haven't seen him?"

He was so close I smelled stale liquor on his breath and backed away, offended. "I'll thank you for keeping your muddy boots off my clean floor."

He looked down at the prints left on the doorstep by his boots.

I sighed inwardly with relief that Tom's boots had left no betraying prints.

"I don't understand. I know he came this way." He continued to gaze at me intently, as if willing me to admit something. "You must have seen him." He scowled. "I know you're hiding something."

I gave him stare for stare. "You're mistaken."

He muttered to himself about bothersome women. With one last glare, he turned on his heel and strode away.

I closed the door behind him and took a deep breath, my legs turning to jelly. I reached the stillroom and collapsed onto a stool at my workbench.

Tom must now look after himself, without my help. Willcocks probably didn't believe me. He might lurk around the farm and return to check. I would have to be patient, at least until Robert came back from visiting the soldiers.

Around dusk, Robert returned, a puzzled look on his face.

"I met Willcocks in the lane," he said. "He looked like he had been ridden hard and put away wet."

I smiled. "Where did you pick up that expression?"

"I suppose I have been around the soldiers too long." He put his hat down. "He surprised me. I've never seen him as angry, even in Parliament. I thought for a moment he was going to strike me. But he restrained himself and let me pass." He smiled ruefully. "I know better than to accost a man with such a violent temper."

"I had a visit from him this morning. I never thought he'd hang about here so long." I lowered my voice. "We have a guest below. Tom."

"Was Tom…?"

"Shhh. Willcocks suspected something and was chasing him. It's a good thing Tom's such a fast runner. I think I persuaded Willcocks he hadn't been here, but I was worried he would stay close. I haven't moved from the house since."

We agreed we should pass as normal an evening as we could, and for me to take a dark lantern down to check on Tom after we had supposedly retired for the night.

But when I got there, I found only a cryptic note: *Expect me when you see me.*

Jack

*Our remove to winter quarters got us out of the swamps at least.
When we reached Burlington, we found many Indians from the
western tribes, bringing with them word of the loss of the great chief
Tecumseh. Sore news indeed… recalled to my duty and close with my
highest regard to you…"*

Jack didn't know if he was coming or going. No sooner had he finished his brief letter to Maryel than he was assigned to Colonel Murray's command, which headed back eastward across the Niagara Peninsula. About four hundred strong, they were dispatched to curtail the activities of the Americans still holding Fort George. Messengers had brought word to Burlington Heights of foraging parties from the fort harassing the surrounding farms.

"Ho, Dawson, you here too?"

"Aye, Stevenson. I am."

"You'd think they'd tire of marching us around like this. I know I've walked enough miles for several lifetimes, and me not twenty-five yet."

"If those bloody Americans would only go home, we could too."

"Do you suppose they'll be expecting us?"

"Who knows," said Dawson, yawning. "I'm sure I don't care, as long as they can't shoot any better than the last time we saw them. Say… doesn't your girl's family live near there?"

"Yes, a few miles from the town." He bit his lip. "I hope they weren't affected by the raids."

"You can ride to the rescue, play knight errant," said Dawson flippantly.

Jack cuffed him on the shoulder.

"Ow, that hurt! Save your blows for the enemy."

Murray's force was lucky. They surprised the Americans and drove them back into the fort with but few shots fired, then resumed their position at the Twelve-Mile Creek, which gave them a base to strike wherever there was need.

Small outposts were maintained at the Four-Mile Creek and St. Davids, as in summer, to provide scouts, pickets, and messengers to the main force.

Rebecca

It was a blow when, in mid-October, the British troops began their retreat to winter quarters. I may have deplored their raids on our crops and livestock as much as I did the same activity by the enemy, but at least their presence offered us a measure of security. After the incident with Tom, who had not yet returned, I was more worried about our safety.

And worried about Tom, too. What was he up to?

So, nobody could have been more surprised than I when Jack Stevenson strode up to our door one afternoon, whistling.

"Good day, Rebecca, I hope I find you well."

"Jack! I thought you were gone for the winter?"

"So did we. But word came the Americans were misbehaving, so some of us came back to rap their knuckles."

"You're cheery for a man who's leading out bands of skirmishers."

"Got a letter from Maryel," he said, patting his breast pocket.

"Really? We haven't heard in over a month. I don't suppose…"

He handed me a much-folded sheet that had obviously been read several times already. I scanned quickly down the page with its news of abortive attempts on Montreal by American forces.

"I suppose the garrisons at Montreal get regular word of all engagements, and Dr. Mountain has the trust of the commanders."

"That's what I think," said Jack. "It takes so long to get letters from one place to another that I wonder General Prevost can coordinate such a dispersed force." He grinned. "I'll wager General Vincent relied on that when he sent us back into the Peninsula. Prevost is known to be overly cautious, and to consider Upper Canada expendable. But we'll have none of that."

"It was bad enough waiting for letters to cross the Atlantic. I swear some of them cross two or three times now before finally making their way here." I smiled at Jack. "Thank you for letting me read your letter. I trust I didn't pry too much."

"It's no secret I'm smitten with her," Jack said, coloring to the tips of his ears. "And I think she's fond of me, too."

"You have my support, if you need it."

"I'm not here just for gossip, though. I have a trade to propose." He pulled a small bottle made of thick amber glass from another pocket.

"Laudanum!" I grabbed for the bottle but he held it out of reach, laughing.

"Only if you can spare more of your other remedies. And maybe some cooking herbs as well. To help disguise the taste of rotten meat."

If even the army was having problems with food supplies this early in the season, it didn't bode well for the coming winter.

"I don't have a lot of black pepper, but I can give you a little. I have plenty of sage and mint. Those might help a bit. I wish I could offer you rosemary, but it doesn't survive well here. Will those do?"

"Yes, marvelously. And I didn't mean to tease. I would have given you the laudanum anyway. I had strict orders to do so."

I laughed at him. "I've been around long enough to recognize a prankster. But I accept your apology."

"I warn you, I may be back for more of those pot herbs. The stew they brewed up last night was near inedible."

Willcocks

18 Nov

Strange appeared yesterday with news of British forces. At first, disinclined to credit him. Still unsure after suspicious incident last month. Positive he was prying where he should not, but have decided to watch carefully for now. He reports light troop presence nearby, but outposts maintained despite winter withdrawals. He estimates they will not move far in winter, nor be reinforced. I agree. Have discussed with militia commander. With my company to stave off Indian marauders Fort George may remain secure.

28 Nov

As I thought, a large part of our contingent removed with Scott to support forces at eastern end of Lake Ontario. Skeleton force remains in the fort. Unsure whether we can hold. Keeping Strange close for now. See how he responds.

Tom

Tom worked hard to convince Willcocks that Mallory had an over-active imagination, and any verbal slips were down to the need to watch his words around the British. He continued to provide valuable intelligence on British troop movements, enabling Willcocks to evade most skirmishes.

By now, his observations of the conduct of the war had deepened his cynicism to the point where he felt loyal only to himself. And Rebecca. He informed on one side to the other with abandon, and invented his own stories in the absence of firm knowledge. It amazed him when they swallowed his fantasies whole.

At one of their regular meetings, Tom laid his concerns on the table to allay further suspicion.

"I don't know if I can keep up the double-dealing. And I'm no longer sure of my contacts."

"I'm not surprised. I suspected you myself." Willcocks eyed him sidelong. "Not sure I still don't."

"It's almost impossible, Jos. If I had known what it would mean when you enlisted me…"

"Are you sure nobody on the other side suspects? What about Mrs. Addison?"

Tom frowned. "I never thought to deceive her. But it seems your suspicions convinced her I'm loyal to their side." He shook his head. "Their side, our side—always juggling words."

"Keep on as long as you can. We need all the intelligence we can get."

Tom nodded, eyes downcast, hopeful he was back on stable footing with Willcocks. It was hard to be sure.

Rebecca

I ventured more widely in the early winter than I had in summer. There were fewer daily tasks with the farm and garden in a dormant season. With the leaves off the trees and bushes, I could spot most hazards, including the two-legged variety, in good time to take cover or return home.

So, I roamed all over, gleaning what I could from the picked-over fields and woods. There wasn't the usual competition from livestock or deer, the soldiers having killed so many for food. We were fortunate to have maintained a few of our breeding stock from their voracious appetites. But we would have little benefit from them until at least next spring, and barely enough fodder to sustain them until then. Instead, I set snares for rabbits and squirrels, which were still plentiful. And plenty of nuts in the woods: butternuts, walnuts, hazelnuts—if we could beat the squirrels to them. I even found a few late berries and wild grapes before the first hard frost. So we were provisioned as well as we could be, better than many others, no doubt.

Tom was not the only tenant we hosted in the secret room. At irregular intervals, some courier would pass by and need a few hours' respite and some food. They never stayed long, and sometimes I didn't see them come and go, but found the evidence of their presence when I went down to check the room's condition. I did this weekly.

While I didn't know how or when I might send a letter to Sarah, it comforted me to put my thoughts on paper. Like everything else, paper was scarce so I chose my words carefully, not to waste it. Robert needed it more than I.

November 18, 1813

My dear sister,

It will be a hungry winter for many. I feel blessed to have knowledge to supplement our stores by foraging in field and forest, especially so since the competition from the armies is severe. Robert's daughters remain in Montreal, which means two fewer mouths to feed. We're in no danger of starving, and I hope to help others. Robert and I continue in good health...

No matter how casually I might write of our situation to Sarah, I acknowledged to myself the heightened tension and increased worry I felt. It had now been six weeks since Tom disappeared, and my fear for him mounted daily. Where could he be? Did he still live?

DECEMBER

Willcocks

2 Dec

What is wrong with our commanders? Don't they know we need regular supplies? New boots? Winter coats? Ammunition is low, too. Lucky we seized powder magazine in fort. Indians never stop harassing us. We need bullets.

5 Dec

I swear my gang of farmers is better trained than that mob of useless layabouts in the fort. They'd be better to run home to their mammies. It's down to them the place is so run down as to be indefensible.

7 Dec

Indians bad. Townsfolk worse. Treat my men—and me—like pariahs. Even those sympathetic to our cause. Refuse to share supplies. Turn away from us in the street. Some spit at my feet. Whatever comes, they deserve it.

Tom

Wallace's tavern was one of few remaining places where Willcocks's men were made welcome. Tom met him there in early December.

Tom stamped his feet as he entered the dimly lit taproom. "It's perishing cold out there."

Willcocks snorted. "You but state the obvious, boyo. Never mind, it's warm here, and the ale will help."

"Your message sounded urgent. What's happened?"

"A great deal of nothing, so far. But there are rumblings in the fort that McClure wants to withdraw."

"Withdraw? But why?"

"Too much sickness. Too many men unfit to fight. He worries the British might make a sneak attack and capture the lot. With the bulk of the army over two hundred miles to the east, and not making any progress there, he has a point."

Tom's jaw dropped. "I didn't know how bad it was."

"You've been out scouting amongst the British too long. I've watched our garrison slip into lethargy and despond. I don't think they could mount a defense if they were prodded in the arse with a sharp stick."

"But…"

"There's been news of a defeat to the east. McClure has always been wary of the British control of Lake Ontario. He would feel better grounded with his force, sad as it is, in Fort Niagara."

"If we abandon the west bank, it gives the advantage back to the British."

"I know." Willcocks slammed his fist on the table. "We'll be a laughingstock. I can just hear the snickers from the town." He drained his tankard and thumped it down. "I won't have it."

"What will you do?"

"Await a command decision. Then, we'll see." He gave Tom a sharp look. "Meanwhile, I want you close."

Did Jos suspect him again? Or was it only that he needed every man in case of attack? How could he alert the British to an American withdrawal with Jos's eagle eye fixed on him?

Rebecca

On December 13th, we entertained neighbors for dinner at noon, and dallied over the table until nearly dark, discussing the war. It was a rare occasion when we could enjoy a substantial meal in company, but the hunters had good fortune and we benefited by a gift of a deer's haunch. This was too great a bounty to consume alone.

Winter set in with harsh intent. The lake froze along its shore, and for a goodly distance out. While this meant our risk of direct attack was lessened, it also boded ill for a long, cold winter.

As we stood in the doorway, waving our guests on their way, Robert tugged at my sleeve.

"Look to the east. The sky!"

We all turned to see the sky over Niagara town lit near as bright as day.

Fire.

"The Americans must be leaving the fort," I said.

"If they are, they're making sure the British won't find anything usable. They must be burning their supplies."

"That glow looks overlarge for leftover supplies. Maybe the barracks are burning too." Or something worse, I feared.

We stood and watched for a few moments, but it was too cold to do for long. Robert wanted to approach the town, but I convinced him to stay at home. My fears for his weak chest in winter's chill, and at night, were too great.

"You aren't cut out for heroics, my dear."

He protested this, but I remained adamant.

Tom

Tom arrived at Fort George near dusk on the 13th to report on his most recent scouting mission as the last of the American soldiers withdrew. A sorry lot, mainly sick and wounded, who had been left behind when most of the able-bodied were sent to the east, now they would move back across the Niagara River. Most of them looked like they would never fight again. But where were Willcocks's Canadian Volunteers? Not in the fort, said a straggler. He thought they had business elsewhere.

As the last of the American troops disappeared on the road south, shouts came from the direction of the town. Tom peered across the broad common ground that lay between Fort George and the town of Niagara. The onshore breeze from Lake Ontario carried the smell of smoke—not unusual in winter—but as he moved toward the town, he saw open flames in many locations. The whole town was afire! He broke into a run.

Everywhere he looked, old men, women and children stood in the snow, or sat on pieces of furniture rescued from their houses. Yards were strewn with random items—boxes, dishes, clothing—

whatever people had been able to carry with them. Few tried to resist, and most were too shocked to lament. The cries Tom had heard were made by Willcocks's men, mad with drink, and putting the torch to every structure in sight. Houses, barns, sheds, churches. Nothing was left alone. Street after street of houses—most of them wooden buildings—blazed in the winter night, turning it as bright as day. He stopped in front of the Masonic Hall where Willcocks stood with his lieutenants, Markle and Mallory, watching their men ravage the town.

"Tom, boyo," said Willcocks, "you're here in time to see the fun."

Fun? Tom nodded, struggling with himself to remain calm. "I wondered not to find you in the fort, but now I see why," he said.

"We're getting our own back on these bastards," said Mallory, rubbing his hands together. His gleeful tone grated on Tom's ears.

"I can see that," said Tom. "They won't be harassing us any more then." His eyes filled with tears. He did his best to excuse it by coughing, as thick smoke drifted their way.

"No," said Willcocks with a sharp look at Tom. "They won't be doing anything here anymore."

"It looks like the men have things well in hand, Jos… Colonel. But… my report… there are British pickets not far from town and troops on the move just beyond them."

Willcocks nodded. He turned to his officers. "You'd better start rounding up the men, then. We should be away before the enemy arrives. Tom here can help."

Help these monsters? He'd as soon help the Devil himself. But his cover must be maintained, somehow.

Jack

Jack raised his hand to signal his troop to halt. Before them lay the town of Niagara, in smoldering ruins. The flaming brightness that led their forces from the encampment at the Twelve-Mile Creek had now mostly subsided to angry embers glowering a dull red across the snow-covered ground. The light sufficed to expose the heaps of smoking rubble and the disconsolate inhabitants who milled about in shock. The same dismal picture met the eye in all directions. He shivered at the biting cold, unnoticed during the march, but now penetrating his bones. The acrid smell of smoke made his nose twitch.

He spotted Tom Strange moving from group to group.

"I say, Strange, were you here?"

"No, but I was nearby, and came up while it was still underway." Tom's face and coat were soot-smudged and his eyes weary. There was a gash on his forehead and his hair was scorched to the scalp on one side. "It was that damned Willcocks and his band of marauders. These poor souls had only a half hour of warning. I doubt they could do more than drag on boots and coats and grab a few possessions. Those dastards put everything else to the torch."

"The devil they did."

Tom nodded. "I told them your troops were near and they moved off sharpish. I did what I could to help the weaker, but we'll have to find them shelter, and quickly."

Jack looked around. Where upwards of a hundred and fifty houses had stood, scarcely one remained. Dozens… no, hundreds of women, children and elderly men huddled together to share what little warmth they could. Pieces of furniture lay in the snow, some occupied by the aged or infirm.

"Would we could have gotten here sooner," said Jack, "but even on frozen ground, with light packs, it's over two hours quick-march along the most direct route."

"Don't berate yourself. I was much closer but could do nothing." He coughed. "One man against that pack of barbarians. What could I do?"

"Are they long gone?"

Tom nodded. "At least a half-hour ago. They left behind only the falling-down-drunk and a few wounded."

"We were sent as an advance force, to engage them if we could. Others are following by various routes."

"They left in great haste after a scout reported your advance."

"We hoped to intercept them, or at least prevent them from despoiling other settlements."

Tom shrugged. "I doubt your troops will find them, but they may protect others in their wake." He looked over one shoulder. "I see your men are providing assistance." He bit his lip. "I need your help with something."

"Come with me to the Major first. He'll want to hear about this from a witness who hasn't suffered such a shock as these poor folk."

Tom grabbed Jack's arm. "Wait. Can you take me to him as a prisoner?"

Jack stared. "Why would I do that?"

"Because I need to stay in Willcocks's good books." At Jack's questioning look, he elaborated on his position as double-agent. "Willcocks expected me to follow his company when they withdrew. I was the scout who alerted them. I feigned an injury so I could stay and help." He coughed again. "Somebody has to know, for me to keep up my role. I can trust you, can't I?"

What a crazy situation—so crazy it must be true. Besides, why would Tom lie to him? "Yes, you can."

"If you can treat me as a prisoner now, I can both report to your command and go back to Willcocks with a convincing story. But if ever I had doubts about where my loyalty lay, this has cleared them away. Even York wasn't treated so cruelly."

"I hope you know what you're doing."

After they reported to the Major, Tom was led off to cool his heels in a local farmer's barn along with the other prisoners. If Jack knew his man, Tom would escape soon and continue his risky business.

By now, two more detachments of the 100th had arrived. Jack joined them as they proceeded cautiously toward Fort George, which was abandoned but possibly mined. Their fear of mines was so strong that a burst musket cartridge shocked the troops into throwing themselves into the snow, after which they relaxed and could laugh at their groundless fears. Entering the fort, they discovered that, against expectation, the barracks and other buildings had been left standing, and a few tents also remained. The 100th grenadiers remained to guard the Fort while other troops were moved off to quarter at the Four-Mile Creek, or at Queenston.

Jack considered himself lucky to go to the Four-Mile Creek, where he might see the Addisons.

If there was one fortunate circumstance that dreadful night, it was that word of the forced march put the wind up the Americans.

They were in such haste to depart, they failed to blow up the forti-fications and powder magazine as intended by their commanders. Fort George was regained to the British flag, and once again housed British troops. The hapless townsfolk were taken in by neighbors on the surrounding farms, or were squeezed into the remaining space in the barracks and tents. The one remaining house in the town was uninhabitable until its broken windows could be boarded over. Next morning, they found the stone lighthouse intact, too late to shelter anyone on the night of the conflagration.

Willcocks

13 Dec

   Scouts report devastation and chaos among settlers and townsfolk. Most withdrawing from town site into countryside. Easier access when we attack again. Satisfying to see the town burn. I thought merely to torch public buildings. Might have given the men too much liquor. Once started. no way to stop. At least townsfolk won't be able to spit on me again. Their abuse more than I could bear. on top of all the slights and calumny already on my head. I will forget none of them. ever. May I live long enough to pay back every insult!

14 Dec

   More reports in on our wounded and those too drunk to escape— most made prisoner. including Strange. He wasn't drunk. maybe wounded in the melee. He's a crafty fellow and could escape. Might still be of use to us. but I have doubts about him. Mallory is jealous of our connection— may have spread false rumor. Trust is a chancy business. Can I trust anyone but myself?

Jack

Jack was appalled by the enemy's actions. For the entire town of Niagara to be burned and its inhabitants made homeless on a mid-winter night was an atrocity that could not be borne. This one action changed the character of the war on the Niagara frontier.

Jack's feelings were echoed throughout the troops and up through the command. "Let us retaliate by fire and sword," he heard Colonel Murray say to General Drummond as the assembled officers gazed on the smoking ruins of the town.

"Do so, swiftly and thoroughly," said Drummond.

With no more ado than this, a series of revenge attacks on the American side of the Niagara River were carried out with speed and precision. On the night of the 18th December, the flank companies of the 41st and 100th, under Colonel Murray, with other units in support, crossed the Niagara River, quietly putting ashore at the Five-Mile Meadows, three miles above the fort.

The midnight expedition proceeded with great caution. Orders were whispered, neither musket nor saber clanked, and the raiding party advanced with noiseless steps. Jack, among them, found it mighty hard to hold the cloth tight around his gear to keep it silent. They seized the Niagara sentries before they could give the alarm, entering the fort before a drum rolled or bugle sounded.

"Where is everyone?" Jack whispered to Irwin Dawson as they approached the main barracks.

"Dunno," said Dawson. "Asleep? Gone to visit their mistresses?"

Fort Niagara was seized before the American soldiers were fully awake. They attempted resistance and some eighty were killed or wounded. Over three hundred and forty men, the larger part of the garrison, were made prisoners. When a roll call was taken next day, fewer than thirty were found missing, escaped no doubt to join the General of their forces in Buffalo. A discharge from one of the largest cannon was the signal of success to General Riall.

There was much to be sorted through and gloated over.

"What a prize," Dawson said to Jack. "Look at this. There are thousands of muskets in this armory, plus powder and shot galore."

"I counted twenty-seven cannon on the battlements. The adjutant says there is a great store of clothing and equipment, food and drink as well."

"Those made homeless in Niagara will be glad of those."

The 100th spearheaded the attack and capture of Fort Niagara, with their advance party mentioned in dispatches. Jack came away from this action with nary a scratch, for which he was thankful.

Over the next two weeks, British troops carried out an awful vengeance on the American bank of the Niagara River. Villages all along were razed, from Youngstown near Fort Niagara through to Black Rock near Buffalo. And they didn't stop there. They pursued the retreating Americans to Buffalo, sacking and burning all in their path. Soon, Buffalo and Black Rock, deserted by their inhabitants, were smoking ruins. Anything that could not be carried away was ruthlessly destroyed. At Buffalo, only four buildings were left standing. At Black Rock, only one house escaped.

"That's for Niagara," said Jack. "And York."

"Rein in your delight, my dear fellow," said Dawson. "We have unleashed a beast that will not easily return to its cage."

"What do you mean?"

"Once we open the gates to this kind of retaliation and vengeance, where will it stop?"

"Well," said Jack, "I hear we're to be awarded battle honors for this campaign. I, for one, will wear them with pride."

Rebecca

We distributed supplies and medicines among the remaining townsfolk camped within Fort George's broken ramparts in the days following the fire.

Oddly, to my mind, the retreating troops hadn't burned the barracks or other buildings within the fort. On our first trip, I saw Tom, with a few others, in irons, being herded away from the remnants of the town. Should I follow, make a protest? I hesitated, unsure what was best.

"Did you notice, Robert?" I asked. "That was Tom among the prisoners." Something was very wrong. I couldn't believe Tom would turn traitor. Surely, he couldn't have been one of those who fired the town.

"Really? Seems odd, to be sure, but nothing will surprise me now," said Robert. "But it must be a mistake. I find it hard to believe he had a hand in this outrage. Why, he's one of Norton's agents."

My focus remained on Tom, receding along the river's bank. "It makes no sense, Robert," I said. "Why would the Army seize him? What's going on?"

He patted my hand. "Tom is a man of good sense. You mustn't worry so much."

"There's something peculiar going on," I said. Things I had noticed over the past year came together with an almost audible click. Tom was working for both sides. A dangerous game.

But now he was gone. I couldn't ask him to confirm my suspicions. At least he was still alive. Reassured on that point, I turned to more urgent matters. "We must take in some of the townsfolk as lodgers."

"The commanders might rather we not billet non-combatants at Lake Lodge, with the secret room and all."

I knew Robert was anxious to get along with the latest change of command. We had newly met Generals Drummond and Riall, but were pleased with what we had seen of them. Perhaps not so charismatic as Brock, but without the roughness of Sheaffe, and with sufficient intelligence to inspire confidence.

"I'm sure we can shelter them for a few days. Just until they can move elsewhere."

"We have been fortunate not to suffer so ourselves," said Robert. "And we have some comforts remaining to us. I am told I will receive a Captain's share of the prize money from the attacks on the Americans. I would not, in the normal course of events, wish to benefit from the harm come to others, but this is war." He hesitated. "Perhaps that was infelicitously phrased. But it's reassuring to have my reputation restored to its pre-war status. We can use the bounty money to assist the homeless."

"A significant advance from the dark days under Gore," I said.

"I'm told that troops have been assigned to replace the roof of St. Mark's. To be sure, this is so it can house stores and wounded until the Fort's buildings are restored, but it will prevent further damage. You know they burned St. Andrew's? Thank goodness we built in stone. The Presbyterians will need to build from scratch." He paused again. "I hope to see St. Mark's restored, if I should live to see the end of the war."

"Now, Robert." I shook my head at him. "You mustn't be so glum. We must pray the war will not last too much longer." It was hard to see how the town could suffer more after these latest events. Surely, we would be given respite, at least until spring.

"Do you notice," he said, "that for all the marching and battles, we end the year with no change in territory occupied by each side from when it started? How very odd it is."

I kept to myself the worry that another such year of looting and skirmishing might make the entire region uninhabitable for years to come, rendering borders meaningless.

1814

"The same energy of character which renders a man a daring villain would have rendered him useful in society, had that society been well organized."—Mary Wollstonecraft

"How can a rational being be ennobled by any thing that is not obtained by its own exertions?"—Mary Wollstonecraft

January–March

Rebecca

On the morning of January 4th, I saw to it that Robert wrapped himself in an extra shawl and pulled on fingerless mittens. It might make him warm enough to grip his quill pen, but to make sure, I brought him a mug of hot broth to thaw his fingers. All this so he could compose his semi-annual report to the Society for the Propagation of the Gospel in Foreign Parts. We had talked over the horrid scenes—so vivid in our minds—and agreed he must say something of them to the Society.

"I wonder what they will think," I said.

He signed. "Sad to say, I doubt my words will have much impact. Men in far-off London are more distressed by the European wars than by any colonial upheaval, no matter the effects on their missionaries and our flocks."

A short time later, he called me to bring more broth, and I read over his shoulder.

… during the last half year. the Enemy being in possession of Niagara. I cannot perform my duties as usual. The Town & Church are burnt… yet my house. which is about 3 miles from the Town. has escaped & afforded an Asylum to several unhappy Sufferers who fled from the flames. We hope for happier times. & to see the Church which was fortunately built of Stone. repaired... there are no marriages from May 2nd. 1813. to 1814. except for two Indian chiefs. The town was in possession of the Americans from May 27th to December 13th. 1813. and many of the inhabitants fled...

Robert examined his pen-nib with a pensive expression. "Should I say more about the Church?"

"If you doubt their interest, perhaps not."

He set down his pen and blotted the report. "That will have to do, then." He rose, joints popping, and turned to his bookcase, taking down a slim volume.

Assured that Robert was warm and settled by the fire with his book, I turned to my own letter writing. I brought my writing materials into the parlor where it was brighter than the stillroom. Candles, like everything else, were in short supply, and I made use of natural light whenever I could. It was chilly near the windows, and the view one of unrelieved gray, the water of the lake merging almost seamlessly with the featureless sky.

I sent word of the firing of Niagara to Eliza and Maryel, reassuring them we had not been harmed. With the enemy gone from the region, there was hope they would receive it soon. Then I settled in to write our news to my sister.

My dear Sarah,

Whatever dire report may reach you in London, please know Robert and I remain in tolerably good health, despite winter and wartime privations. Our neighbors have not been as fortunate. While our territory has been liberated by the Army, the departing Enemy fired the town. The remnants are an appalling sight. That despicable turncoat, Willcocks, was founder of the deed. We remain secure at Lake

Lodge, and do what we can to support those made homeless. It's pitiable to see so many brought low. What provisions were not looted were destroyed. We have appealed to the Army to give what help they can, though they can spare but little. We shall contrive, and I would not have you unduly concerned for our well-being. We're fortunate to have the respect of our neighbors and eager to provide what service we may.

The Army has begun a new fortification, with more advantageous sights on Fort Niagara. Until it's finished, many live under canvas. Come spring, the stalwart will doubtless rebuild their houses.

My longing to be elsewhere is tempered by the knowledge that it's little better anywhere in the Province. I'm happy you are in a place of relative safety and plenty. That is something to celebrate in such uncertain times.

Both sky and water had darkened now, and I must put aside my letter and get on with our supper. Such as it was, a cold rabbit pie, mostly carrot and a little onion, with a scanty short crust. My stomach was still growling when we retired for the night.

Jack

It had taken months to unsnarl the backlog of mail, but now the 100th Regiment was back at Fort George, and their communication lines clear, letters trickled in. Jack had one from Maryel from the previous summer, and two from family in Dublin.

One morning in February, he emerged from his quarters to see a lone figure standing on Brock's Bastion, gazing out over the ramparts toward Fort Niagara. Why would anyone brave such a bitter wind? He squinted, trying to identify the man. It was Hingston, dressed in only his Regimentals, motionless, with slumped shoulders.

Jack grabbed two fur-lined cloaks and, tossing one around himself, ran out carrying the other to his friend.

Hingston's face was bleak. He turned to Jack and held out a crumpled sheet of paper. It was a letter, dated the previous October.

Montreal, 9th inst.

To Lt. (Adj.) S.J. Hingston

Sir,

I regret to inform you that, on the 7th inst., your wife, Mrs. Winifred

Hingston, miscarried of a male infant and succumbed.

In your absence, burial was conducted with all honor, and you will find the grave in the care of the Rector of Christ Church. Your children have been taken up by Mrs. Murray, and are in good health, although naturally low in spirits. They beg to send their regards to you and wish you good health and a safe return to them at the end of the war.

Believe me &c

Capt. R.W. Robertson

Med. Corps

Jack swallowed hard. "Oh, my dear fellow…"

Hingston's voice was barely audible. "We had such hopes for a new life here. Now…"

Jack draped the cloak around his friend. "Come back inside. You will catch your death up here, and you still have your children to think of."

Hingston nodded and stumbled back down the embankment with Jack's arm for support.

Jack was appalled by this turn of events. Was this what it meant to marry? This ripping of the heart through dependence on the loved one? How would he fare if such a fate were to befall Maryel? And how would she fare following the drum? Was this how his mother's death had affected his father? These unanswerable questions made his head ache. He got Hingston safely inside their quarters, then returned outside with a pipe.

So far, Jack had been content to let his life proceed by happenstance, without a great deal of direction. He followed his father's wishes up to a point, and after that, orders from the officers above him in rank. The war had brought home to him the importance of purpose. Goals might not be achieved, but one should have them, he thought. And the goal of most importance to him, no matter the delay, was to win the hand of Maryel Addison. That meant not just a wedding, but all that came after. Hearth, home, children—too many unknowns to grasp all at once.

Supposing they both survived the war and could marry. What then? Where would they live? Would he get further promotion and have a longer Army career? What would he do if not the Army? He had little training for anything else. It might matter less in Dublin than it did here. He might fall back on music—there were many opportunities in Ireland for a moderately talented musician, either as player or instructor. Whereas here… music was something one made around one's own fire, or something one contributed freely to the community. As remunerative employment, it had not yet become common, unless as part of a traveling troupe. He didn't think Maryel was cut out for that kind of life. But was she cut out to follow the drum?

He was still mulling over his questions, and growing steadily colder, his pipe long burnt out, when Dawson found him.

"Good God, Stevenson, what are you about? Come along in and have a mug of something warm."

"I was thinking—"

"What d'you want to do that for?" Dawson grabbed his arm. "Come on, man, we'll throw the dice over a mug of mulled cider."

Jack allowed himself to be pulled into the comforting fug of the officers' mess where there was warmth, and friends, and drink, and fewer pesky questions to addle his tired brain.

Maryel & Eliza

Each morning that winter, Dr. Mountain braved the drifts of new-fallen snow piled high on either side of the doorway and blocking the light from the ground-floor windows, to retrieve the post. Most days he returned empty-handed.

Finally, in the last week of January, he returned with a packet of letters. He stamped his feet on the mat and shook himself to remove the snow. Not unlike a large, shaggy dog, thought Maryel, hiding a smile.

The packet contained what they had awaited so long. Letters from their father and Rebecca. Dr. Mountain had one from his colleague, Reverend Mr. Stuart, at Kingston. Finally, news, but little of it good.

As soon as they read of the disaster at Niagara, Maryel and Eliza agreed they could not stay cooped up in Montreal any longer. The Mountains tried to persuade them they were going into grave danger, but they were resolute. It took nearly a week to prepare, not least of which was locating a courier with whom they could travel, but they were ready to leave Montreal in early February.

The first leg of their journey was made by sleigh. They traversed the frozen lakes and channels around Montreal with greater ease and speed than either had experienced during the summer journey. Maryel could hardly believe the difference. It took a mere two days to reach Cornwall, a distance of seventy-five miles. If they could keep up their pace, they would reach Niagara by the end of the month.

But two days later, outside Prescott, disaster struck. The courier's horse went lame, and there was none other available. Those not taken by the Army had been eaten. Eliza negotiated with a farmer to allow his son, a sturdy lad too young for the militia, to accompany her and Maryel as far as Kingston and assist with their baggage. The farmer provided them with snowshoes, in case of fresh snow.

"The road is well-packed, so you may not need them," he said, "but I can't let you go unprepared. I doubt you'll find a horse and sleigh to hire before Kingston."

"That's a good sixty miles from here," said Eliza. "How long will it take?"

"If the weather holds, three, maybe four days."

"Are there farms along the way?" asked Maryel. "Or will we need to camp?"

"My boy here," he gestured at him, "he's been to Kingston and back, and knows where to stop. And if you get caught by a storm, he can make a serviceable shelter."

The boy nodded and gave them a gap-toothed grin. "Don't you worry, miss, I'll see you safe to Kingston."

In spite of all the military traffic along the north shore of the St. Lawrence River, it was hardly possible to dignify the route with the word "road." While the ground was frozen and the passage wider than the old single-file Indian trails, the going was challenging over alternately rocky and swampy ground. There were many soft patches in the swamps. Great care was needed not to break the surface and become mired in half-frozen muck. Only when they came to a frozen river could they count on a smooth patch, and often had to detour up-river to make a safe crossing.

"I can't feel my toes, sister," said Eliza.

"I wish you would not mention it," said Maryel, "for mine have been numb for at least an hour."

They made Kingston on the fourth day. The farmer's son left them at the Drivers Stables where they hoped to hire a horse, or join a party heading for York. On the second day, they learned of an Army messenger about to travel west by sleigh, who was willing to take passengers.

"Do you think it's safe?" asked Maryel.

Eliza laughed. "Look at the size of him. I think either of us could resist him alone, let alone together."

Maryel was glad their guide had been out of earshot when she saw how solicitously he treated them.

"I've a wife and daughters back in England," he told them, handing them into the sleigh. Despite his small stature, he easily hefted their bags in beside them, and covered their knees with a fur.

Snow fell most days and headwinds were icy. There was no hope of a fresh horse so they made only moderate progress. The horse, though fit, required frequent rest, and fodder was scarce. Better than walking, though. Maryel had never considered they might need to make the entire journey on foot.

Most days they arrived at a homestead before the horse grew overtired. If not, there were the dubious joys of making winter camp out of evergreen branches, the sleigh to one side, and underbrush to the other. Maryel wondered if her feet would ever be warm again.

At last they stopped to rest and thaw out in York where Mrs. Johnson had managed to get her house repaired and could offer a room. York was a pitiful shadow of what it had been before the American attack, The winter freeze had halted most construction, but there were some signs of renewal. It felt so good to sleep in a bed again, if only for a few nights.

Because of the naval activity on the lake, they were again compelled to continue overland, with frequent stops now they were in familiar country. They encountered more travelers on the road to share the journey with and arrived home as the ground began to thaw.

Rebecca

"My dears," I cried. "Whatever are you doing here?" I hugged each of them. "Come, sit by the fire for a good warm. I'll have Hannah fill hot water bottles. Over four hundred miles! And in winter!" Their cheeks were reddened and rough from cold and wind but their eyes were bright. "Robert… Where is he? Ah," as he came to the door of his office, "see what the winter has blown in, my love."

Robert embraced his daughters, kissing them soundly on the cheeks. "What a wonderful surprise," he said, but then turned stern. "You were supposed to stay away. Don't you know war is on our doorstep?"

Maryel laughed. "Why Father, that's exactly why we have come home. We decided you couldn't possibly fight a war without us."

He shook his head. "The world is coming to a sorry pass when daughters flout their father's wishes."

"Now Father," said Eliza, "you shouldn't tease us. Admit it, you're glad we're here."

"Yes, for my sins, I am," he said, but his smile vanished. "Now,

I'm sure Hannah will put together a larger meal than she had planned, and you look chilled to the bone. Rest now and we will talk over supper." He retreated to his study, leaving me to deal with the situation.

My initial excitement and pleasure to see them had worn off quickly. Food for two more mouths. That was going to be a problem.

Given the added demands of two more at our table, I was resigned to have our daughters returned to us. In truth, the depredations of the troops quartered around us were more of a challenge to our supplies than their light appetites. We must make the best of it, now they were here. I wrote a bit more to Sarah.

> Stocks of everything are low, not least because we help our less fortunate neighbors. Robert administers spiritual comfort while I struggle to maintain our health. I wish Eliza and Maryel had remained in Montreal, where at least they would have had enough to eat. It pains me to see them grow thinner. My own hands have more bone than flesh about them, these days. And Robert has not stopped coughing since December, though he attempts to conceal it.
>
> The question now is who will be left to see the end of the war? And yet, it could be worse, and may become so before the end.
>
> Few residents of Niagara town now remain. Several of Ralph Clench's relations were living until lately in his house, the only one left standing in town. Last week, even that house was burned, some said accidentally, some by arson. An added insult, with poor Ralph a prisoner of war. His family is now scattered.
>
> The firing of the Clench house gave me some sleepless nights, for Tom had been seen nearby. Rumor was rife that he was one of Willcocks's company, sent to finish the razing of the town. Gossip

ran wild on the possibilities. I held my peace, while I longed to see him and learn the truth. I couldn't believe him capable of such things.

ran wild on the possibilities. I held my peace, while I longed to see him and learn the truth. I couldn't believe him capable of such things.

Tom

Willcocks finally put Tom back on scouting duties, which Tom fervently hoped meant he was trusted again. He would still have to tread carefully, take care not to rouse more suspicion in the ranks of the Canadian Volunteers.

He sorely needed to contact the British again. Especially Norton, in case he hadn't heard about the new involvement of Indians living in New York State, some now scouting and fighting for the Americans. He planned to make his way along the Lake Ontario shore to Burlington, stopping if he could at Lake Lodge to see Rebecca.

Tom had reckoned without the persistence of one man.

Tom had crossed the Niagara River from Black Rock and made good progress along its low banks. As he crossed the Chippawa Creek, he caught sight of a gray uniform several hundred feet behind him.

Once he noticed his tail, Tom moved more cautiously. He adjusted his pace, slowing and speeding alternately, but the figure never came closer.

The pronounced limp of his follower convinced him it was

Mallory. Jealousy would be the death of that man. Tom meant to see that carelessness wouldn't be his own death. If he couldn't shake Mallory off, his plans would need to change.

April–June

Jack

It was a coin toss where he would end up, Jack reckoned. They placed bets in the mess about where they would be detached to patrol, and whether there would be any backup from local militia or Indian warriors.

"I'd prefer the Indians," said Jack.

"Why's that?" asked Dawson.

"They know the country best. And we know those we encounter are on our side. Say what you will, their American cousins haven't come over here to fight us yet. Whereas that rascal Willcocks is always trying to turn the locals to fight with him. And the warriors aren't always wanting to run off to plant or harvest or birth a calf or something on their farm."

"Good point."

"It looks like we're going to stay along the Niagara River, though, and not be shipped off to Lake Erie or back toward York."

"So, you can keep tabs on your girl. See no other redcoat makes off with her."

"You can keep your rude comments to yourself, Dawson!"

"You going to make me?"

Jack gave his friend a shove, only half in jest, and Dawson retaliated.

They were prevented from brawling by their mess-mates who dragged them apart. After some grudging excuses, their betting turned to which of them could win best of three in arm-wrestling.

Nerves were frayed and tempers short throughout the Army. The lack of reliable backup was a serious problem. They all knew there were only about three thousand troops spread over the frontier, all the way from York on Lake Ontario to Long Point on Lake Erie, a distance of some two hundred miles. Too few men for too many posts.

Most of the shoreline was undefended and settlements along it vulnerable. Willcocks's Company struck at will, burning even the homes of his former constituents. They knew the land almost as well as the Indians, and acted more savagely.

No man could be spared from duty and supplies were limited. Constant patrolling, insufficient food and seasonal swamp miasmas resulted in more illness in camp. Jack dreaded the sickness as much as any man, for there was no defending oneself from it. But there was no relief to be had, only the ceaseless round of duty.

Their regiment was stretched past its limits to garrison Fort George and the new Fort Mississauga—now underway at Niagara— Fort Niagara across the Niagara River, and Fort Erie at the river's opposite end, on the Upper Canadian shore. Detachments from other regiments were stationed along the Lake Ontario and Lake Erie shores, guarding key landing sites and provision depots.

The American fleet was a persistent threat. Troops stationed in York or Kingston could only give limited help if the war got hot.

"Half my patrol turned up on sick parade today," Jack said. "If that trend continues, we'll never mount a defense, let alone an attack."

"Careful the higher-ups don't hear you talk like that," said Dawson. "They might think you're sowing disaffection. Men have been cashiered for less."

Rebecca

I was still worried about Tom. It was far too long since I had seen him. Every time I went to check the secret room, I hoped to find a message, but as weeks drew out into months without word, my heart sank further. The room had its occupants—and I saw a few of them—but none had anything to tell me about "Thrush."

It pained me Tom had found no way to send word, but more that he might be ill, or even dead, and not be able to. Neither Robert nor I had an active role in the network of Crown agents—apart from maintaining their way-station and refuge—so our sources of information were limited. We couldn't appear too inquisitive of those of whose loyalties we weren't certain. I must contain my worries and carry on as usual. And, while both Maryel and Eliza had been let into the secret, they were sworn to speak of it to no one.

Tom was not my only worry. The demands of our neighbors and the agents on our stores, had brought them perilously low. We had depleted most of the reserve in the secret room. We would have to gather new shoots as early as the buds broke, and try to find a source of grain or flour.

I pressed Robert to request a portion from the Army, given our duties to the Crown, but he returned from that errand with empty hands.

"They are too low in supplies themselves to spare anything now," he said, head drooping, "although I did wring a promise from him that we are owed some rations and he will do his best to provide something soon."

Soon might well be too late. Meanwhile, I shorted my portions to ensure Robert and the girls maintained as good health as was possible.

Jack

The beauty of the spring morning failed to lift Jack's spirits as he trudged along the road from Fort George to the building site of the new fort. Not for him, the scents of opening buds and the fresh green on tree and bush. Nor was he at all affected by the trill of birdsong. He had been put in charge of a working party, and felt hard-done-by. That others of his rank had similar duties in the reinforcement of Fort George made no difference. He had a grudge with the world that day and was bent on nursing it.

The lighthouse that had survived the winter burning of the town had been demolished to make way for the new Fort Mississauga. The location was ideal: directly opposite Fort Niagara, and would enable bracketing fire from both forts on the Upper Canadian shore, should the Americans retake the one on their side. Meanwhile, all three were occupied by British troops, who thus controlled the river mouth.

Earthworks were well underway, the work of Captain Runchey's company of militia, made up of colored Loyalists and escaped slaves. Stout fellows, thought Jack, surveying their work. The wooden core of a blockhouse had been erected within the banks. His party was now in process of facing it with bricks salvaged from both the lighthouse and the rubble from the town's buildings. There was some competition for building materials, since a few of the townsfolk had started rebuilding already. Jack found this admirable, if premature.

Less pleasing, to his way of thinking, were the men in his charge on this day, and the officers who had assigned him this duty. One was a gang of malcontents and the other a pack of despots. He spared no thought his men might resent the duty as much as he did.

Only yesterday he had told Maryel he was posted to Fort Erie for he knew not how long.

"We knew we'd be separated sometime," she said. "We've been fortunate to have the time we've had."

Why was she being so reasonable? "Won't you miss me?"

"Of course, I will. I can't say I'd be happy fighting at your side, but it's as hard to wait and worry." She leaned toward him and kissed his cheek, giving him courage to seize her in his arms and kiss her full on the mouth. She was enthusiastic enough to send shivers down his spine, but when his hands roamed, protested that he must wait for more.

"What if Father came in on us?" She gave him one more hug and pushed him away. "I will be here when you return."

Would he have felt better if she'd wept in his arms? Or given him more than a few kisses? Perhaps not. But nothing pleased him lately. Maybe a few weeks on detachment would help after all.

He didn't relish the posting to Fort Erie, however temporary. The river's banks were low there, too susceptible to attack from Black Rock and Buffalo. Dammit, they were spread too thin.

He ticked the outposts off mentally as he supervised his men, pausing only to direct their work where necessary. Besides the four forts on the Niagara River and smaller outposts between Niagara and Fort Erie, there were detachments stationed at Burlington Heights, and guarding provision depots at the Twelve and Twenty-mile Creeks. York remained exposed, susceptible to attack at any moment from Chauncey's fleet. Port Dover, on Lake Erie near Long Point, was also in need of protection as there was a danger troops might be landed there and gain the rear of the army by the western road. Detachments had to be posted at Brant's Ford on the Grand River and also at Delaware to guard the advance of the enemy by way of the Thames. They must rely on Indian scouts and warriors to deter any attack between those posts.

It would make any man quake to consider their position. Not cowardice, but plain good sense.

✳

Despite messages sent to the high command, they got no reinforcements. Instead, in late May, representatives from the various regiments were called to attend assizes at Burlington.

Jack was sent to join the guard for prisoners charged with treason. A dubious honor, he felt, but better than sitting waiting to be attacked.

He borrowed a horse for the trip.

It was June, and warm. There was plenty of shade now the trees had leafed out, and the many creeks flowing from the scarp to Lake Ontario were easier to ford at this distance from the lake. The ground under the trees was blanketed with flowers, a trefoil white blossom dominating, with smaller clumps of yellow and violet. He could almost think himself in a springtime forest at home but for the different scent of the wildflowers.

Dawson had also been assigned to the guard, called from his post at Turkey Point on Lake Erie. They met on the west bank of the Fifteen-Mile Creek "Have you had trouble with raiders on the river?" he asked.

"Very little," said Jack. "Odd, with them in spitting distance of us. I suppose they're still wary after the winter burnings."

"Whatever the reason, they've been harassing the western communities all spring. We've had attacks all along the Lake Erie shore. That bastard Willcocks has been running wild, bringing destruction everywhere. Nothing is safe from his Volunteers. Public or private buildings—it makes no difference—they burn everything."

"Too bad he's not here to stand trial."

"He's on trial, even if he won't face the charges. He'll be a wolf's head after these assizes are done."

They arrived at Burlington to find a large gathering of military and citizenry, intent on holding trials for the traitors of Willcocks's Canadian Volunteers. The list of their crimes was lengthy and the judges in no mood for clemency. All, including Willcocks, were convicted of aiding the American forces and eight men present were sentenced to be hanged. Those not sentenced to death were exiled.

Willcocks himself, and many of his men, were absent from the trials, but were convicted as war criminals and sentenced to death *in absentia*.

By the following day, people were already calling it the "Bloody Assizes," though the executions were to be held later.

Jack felt uneasy at the ruthlessness of the judges and the general temper of those attending. To die honestly in battle was one thing. To be hanged as a traitor was quite another.

As he rode back toward Niagara, bearing messages for his commanders, he pondered the likely effect of the trials.

The death sentences may have put the fear into what remained of the populace: treason would not be tolerated. Britain meant to hold the Province and win the war.

But what of Willcocks? What Jack knew of the man suggested he would strike back harder and cause more pain and misery among his former compatriots. What had started out as something of a gentlemen's war in the days of Brock had become a bitter and spiteful conflict. The burning of farms, villages and mills on both banks of the Niagara—and the near constant raids on the Lake Erie shore—attested to it.

Tom

Toward the end of June, Tom found Willcocks at a farmhouse, deep in the Short Hills above the escarpment, where he had set up a temporary headquarters.

"What news, Jos?"

"Why, haven't you heard yet?" asked Willcocks, leaning back in his armchair.

"Heard what?"

"We're all traitors, boyo. Hung in effigy at Burlington. Along with eight poor sods who were hanged there and then." He pulled at his mustache. "The British Army swine have tried and convicted the lot of us. Sentenced to death for treason."

Tom's jaw dropped. "All of us?"

"Well, me for certain. And all my officers." He waved a broad-sheet at Tom. "You can check here. There's a long list of names. I didn't read the whole thing."

Tom scanned the list but didn't find his name. "Not here."

"Don't let that reassure you. There's no doubt more sentences to be handed out for any man they find working against them. But… since you're not on the list… yet…"

"You figure I can move freely still?"

Willcocks eyed him shrewdly. "As long as you can avoid suspicion. You're my most useful scout."

"It's getting harder around Niagara. My face is too well known. After they arrested me in December…"

"Good fortune you could escape."

Tom took that without blinking. Was Jos hinting at something? "What do you want me to do?

"Could you still get around by night? Shelter with sympathizers?"

Tom gazed at the ceiling for a few moments, moving his fingers and lips as if tallying a score. "Above the scarp, yes. Below, I'd have to stick to ravines, and there are fewer who would shelter me. But it should be possible."

Willcocks leaned forward and spread out a map of the region. "I've marked the most likely locations where a battle might occur. The more-detailed information we can amass about the ground on the western bank of the Niagara, the better."

Tom noted the locations. "This one is problematic." He pointed to a site near the mouth of the Chippawa Creek, a few miles beyond the Falls. "The settlers there are staunch Loyalists. I'll have to scout by night."

"Whatever information you can get will improve on what we have now."

"How quickly do you need this?"

"Every minute counts. I don't mind telling you, there's a major reinforcement on its way. Properly trained regular soldiers, not these half-hearted militias. We could be on the offensive by early July."

"I'll do the bank above the Falls first then. You'll be here for my reports?"

Willcocks nodded. "Until the beginning of July, yes. After then…"

They shook hands on it.

July

Jack

Well into June, the 100th Regiment were still awaiting their new recruits.

"I hope they arrive in time to give them some training," said Sherrard, in the mess. "The last were so green, I could have confused them with cabbages."

"Aren't they supposed to teach them to shoot before they send them out here?" asked Dawson.

"There's a reason they call them cannon-fodder," said Jack. That got a laugh.

"Well," said Sherrard, "we're bound to see action this summer, so if they can't shoot now, they'll learn fast or die trying."

The following month, these words came back to haunt them all.

On July 2nd, at the ferry landing across from Black Rock, one of the 100th's forward pickets watched as boat after boat of American soldiers debarked on the Upper Canadian shore and turned toward Fort Erie. They hastened to alert their flank companies, encamped south of Chippawa, and were sent on to bring up reinforcements from the Falls and Fort George.

Over the next two days, this contingent of the 100th was joined by Norton's warriors, the 1st Foot, an artillery brigade, and the Lincoln Militia. It still seemed too small a force for a pitched battle.

Jack heard talk that the main body of the 8th Foot had been ordered out from Fort York, and right enough, they showed up on the 4th. Most of that day was spent drawing up positions at Chippawa, considered as good a defensive position as any along the banks of the Niagara, with the river on one side of the battleground, and impenetrable swamps on the other.

Jack tossed in his blanket long into the night, thoughts racing. Ile-aux-Noix had been exciting, and the clearance of American posts along the Niagara River virtually unchallenged, but this? This waiting? This knowing that soon men would fire at your lines and you would be expected to shoot back? All very well when one had to respond to a surprise attack, or were yourself the ambushing force, like at Ile-aux-Noix. Quite another thing to know the enemy had landed on your shore, were bivouacked a short distance away, and one side or the other was bound to be first to engage their opponent, head-to-head. If not tomorrow, then the day after. His heart and stomach pounded in opposing rhythms, and he felt his bowels might turn to water. Hingston had warned him how it would be if they ever came to what he called a proper battle. Jack had pooh-poohed the idea then. Now he understood.

The morning of the 5th, word came of the surrender of Fort Erie by Major Buck of the 8th Foot, whereby the 100th lost a hundred and fourteen of its strength as prisoners. The messenger, a soldier of the 100th, reported that Buck's surrender had gone against his officer's recommendation, but he had been overruled because of excessive caution. This caused an uproar in camp and did nothing to promote confidence in their ability to withstand whatever engagement might ensue. Lieutenant-General Lord George Hay, Marquess of Tweeddale, the regimental colonel, who had joined them only the previous day, assembled his officers for a final briefing and did his best to encourage them.

"What is our total strength?" asked Sherrard.

"Around two thousand, all told," said Tweeddale. "About three-quarters regulars, the rest militia and Indians."

"Against how many?" asked Jack.

"Scouts estimate their strength to be about double ours." There was anxious murmuring at this, but Tweeddale gestured for silence. "Major Norton's scouts report them in gray uniforms. Like their militia."

The murmurs were now of assent, and Jack relaxed a little.

"You'll take up a position bordering the Niagara River and proceed with the 1st Foot on your right, to advance upon the enemy's position. General Riall hopes to take them unawares, after their celebrations."

"Of course," said Sherrard. "The Fourth of July. They'll be sleeping it off."

"Well and good, if we get an early start," muttered someone. Jack couldn't tell who.

But they didn't. It wasn't until mid-afternoon that orders came to march forth.

This was the moment they had been drilling for all these years.

The column would advance and then draw up ranks into a square—provided the terrain permitted it. If not, a double line so one could retire to reload while the other fired. The order of battle was firmly fixed in his mind, the orders he must give his men, his entire role in the proceedings. He gulped down the lump that had surged in his throat. Steady, man, steady. You've been under fire before.

As his column moved forward, Jack saw lines of gray uniforms come into view. The enemy had moved part of their force onto a ridge parallel to the river, and some into partial concealment around

Mr. Street's farm buildings and fences. His heart sank as he saw their numbers. Had the scouts underestimated?

Worse yet, these were no militia! It quickly became clear that, despite their uniforms, they were professional soldiers, a well-trained and disciplined force. He could tell by their movements over the ground. So could his fellows. A great muttering arose around him as the realization dawned. This would be no easy fight. For all their experience skirmishing, few among them had faced such a force.

The ground was limited, having been cleared between Street's Creek and the Chippawa River. It would have to be lines. Sounds of skirmishing that had begun in the late morning now turned into full volleys as the American lines drew up across from them. More and more of them emerged from the concealing wood.

The American volleys were well-placed and men dropped around Jack. For the first time, British forces in Niagara were facing a regular American army.

Riall ordered the 100th to charge.

Jack swallowed his fear and led his troop forward. To his right, he saw units of the Royal Scots on the same trajectory. The British lines formed and continued to advance, more slowly now.

The American artillery had their range, and so did their foot-soldiers. Between cannonade and musket fire, the 100th Regiment, in its position nearest the Niagara River, was cut to ribbons. There was nowhere for them to move but forward—hemmed in by artillery to their left, the 1st Foot to their right, and the 19th Light Dragoons to their rear. All suffered the same intense attack while attempting to respond in kind.

Jack's head pounded as he rehearsed his moves, over and over. Lines. Form lines. Loading procedure? Check. First rank fire, drop, fall back to load. Second rank, same. Guns pop. Smoke bursts, then drips from muzzles. Smoke hangs there, all around the field. Popping and buzzing. Canister shells finding the range. Musket rounds, too.

Men falling. Beside him. Behind him. Sherrard bleeding. He's carried away. Men screaming, groaning. Bullets buzzing. Near-constant buzzing. The incessant buzzing!

The smoke produced by both armies was so dense Jack could barely draw breath. He lost sight of men under his command, men he knew. How was he still standing? Men fell on every side. Shot flew around him like hail. He barely noticed when a ball grazed his left hand.

How could so many fall in so short a time? It was still full light, and could be no more than an hour since the order was given to advance. They must surely quit the field or be obliterated.

Ah, there it was—above the gunfire—a bugle signal, the retreat.

Jack gathered the survivors of his troop, and what others he could muster, and fled from the field, crossing the Chippawa Creek. Those at the rear pulled the planks from the bridge, leaving only a few logs for the trailing warriors to cross. But soon, the dense smoke of black powder fire was behind him and he could breathe again.

By the time night fell, he was so exhausted, he simply lay down with his boots on and sank into unconsciousness.

The following day, Jack learned the regiment had lost forty percent of their active strength, either killed or wounded. He was one of only four officers left standing. Some few of the wounded were taken prisoner; only a couple deserted. Wounded himself, in shock at the loss of friends, and weary to the bone, Jack managed to pen a quick letter that morning, one he addressed to Reverend Addison. He left it up to Addison whether he would confide the full details to Maryel. Who knew? He could be dead before the letter ever arrived at its destination. The impressions made in the brief battle were too overwhelming for him to assimilate quickly. Thirteen of his brother officers killed or severely wounded. It was inconceivable, but it had happened.

The enemy had yet to press their advantage, but another attack could come at any moment. General Riall had withdrawn the survivors over the Chippawa Creek, destroying the bridge, but there was no great impediment to a determined force. For all Jack knew, the Americans could be hot on their heels. Would any of his fellows have enough strength to load and fire a single shot?

As the day wore on and they trudged northwards toward the Falls, he wondered if he could survive the march, let alone another engagement with the enemy. By evening, he was soaked through in his woolen tunic and his head spun with fever. His hand, that he had barely noticed before, throbbed, reminding him of his wound. Blood still oozed from the base of one finger, where the ball had struck. Jack examined it through bleary eyes. From the pain, now excruciating, he thought there must be bones broken. He lay down to rest, hoping he might not have to rise again.

Rebecca

On the 6th of July, late in the day, a dusty Tom rode into our yard, his horse blowing hard, sides heaving. Tom! I had been working in the garden, but dropped my tools and ran toward him. "Tom! Where have you been? I thought you were dead!" I threw my arms around him as he dismounted.

It was a typical, sweltering July day. My dress hung limp and clung to my back. Tom looked as blown as his horse and took a moment to catch his breath.

"Not now, Rebecca," he said, pushing me away. "I'm on pressing business." He reached into his saddlebag, drawing out a packet.

"I must speak to the Reverend," he said.

It was cooler in the house where all the windows stood open to catch the breezes off the lake. I fetched a pitcher of water and some cups and Tom drank in great gulps.

"Don't choke now, foolish boy," I said, at which he laughed, spluttering.

Robert came out of his office and reached for a cup of water. "What is it, Tom?"

"I have messages and letters from the Army. There's some urgency." He took a deep breath. "There was a great battle at the Chippawa Creek, and our troops were forced to retire, in some disarray. I was sent first to Fort George, with a request to send up reinforcements, and to send word to Lower Canada for a fresh contingent of troops, if they can be spared."

He handed over the documents to Robert who shuffled through them and exclaimed. "There's one from that fellow Stevenson. You'd better call Maryel." He glanced at Tom, who shook his head.

"He's alive, but his Regiment…"

Maryel had been upstairs and came down at the first call. "Is there word from Jack?"

Robert smoothed out the sheet. "His letter is addressed to me. I'll read it aloud. It's brief."

Maryel pouted, but my arm around her shoulder settled her.

Robert cleared his throat and read:

"4 Mile Creek, from Jno. Stevenson, 100th Rgt near Chippawa, July 6th, 1814.

"My dear Mr. Addison:

"Of course you will have heard ere this of our unsuccessful attack on the Americans last evening. I can't describe to you the dreadful and destructive fire that was kept up on both sides for three quarters of an hour, much less the scene of carnage in the field of battle.

"Our regiment has been almost entirely cut to pieces. I know not except under the mercy and kindness of Almighty God how I escaped. Men were falling beside me like hail.

"I am slightly wounded in one of my fingers of my left hand by a musket shot."

"Oh no!" said Maryel, going quite pale. "I hope it's not serious."

"We can only hope and trust it isn't," I said.

Tom nodded.

"It was pure carnage. I hope I never see as bad again. What I saw horrified me."

I placed my hand on Robert's arm and squeezed it while he continued reading.

"We had including this trifling circumstance thirteen officers killed and wounded and one hundred and eighty men. Lieut. Gibbons who commanded the Grenadiers (Miss McNabb's friend) and Ensign Rea were killed and Capt. Sherrard received three balls in him, Capt. Sligh dangerously wounded in the groin, the same for the Adjutant, Lieut. Hingston. Lieut. Williams wounded in three places, Lieut. Vallantine in both legs, Lord Tweeddale in the thigh, Lieut. Lynn in both legs, Ensign Johnson in the shoulder, Lieut. Fortune in the shoulder and leg and taken prisoner, Ensign Clark in the foot."

"There," I said, "he got off lightly compared to those poor fellows."

Maryel said nothing, tears streaming down her cheeks.

"Thus you see what a miraculous escape the remaining four of us have had and how very grateful we ought to be. The enemy must have suffered severely as our own artillery was so well served. They must have been at least seven thousand men, I believe. We will leave this we are so weak, excuse this not sufficient explicit detail and the manner it's written.

"God bless you, adieu.

"Your son.

"John Stevenson."

Robert harrumphed. "Taking liberties, calling himself my son." He peered over his spectacles at Maryel, who blushed. "I suppose he has some reason." His tone was severe, but I spotted the twinkle in his eye. He handed the letter to Maryel, who clutched it as if to wring out an image of Jack from his unsteady handwriting, and pored over its contents.

More news trickled in over the next few days, along with a steady stream of wounded. There were tents and rough shelters in the town, but St. Mark's was the only place usable as a hospital, and we camped there to provide such aid as we could. Rows of pallets were laid out inside the church walls, and an area cordoned off for surgery, but all were under cover of canvas since the roof was only partially repaired. Most of the severely injured were shipped over to York where rebuilding was well underway. Those with minor wounds and fevers, or who were on the verge of death and could be moved no more, remained with us in Niagara.

John Norton made a point of visiting Robert and gave us more details than Tom had been able to. He and his warriors had been fighting in a wooded area on the western flank of the line and had barely made it across the Chippawa Creek after the retreating troops had broken down the bridge.

"We were lucky to make it away from the field," he said, shaking his head. "Our warriors are grumbling about the failure of the British commanders to give us notice of the retreat. That, I can understand, in the heat of battle. What is more troubling is that we were set against our cousins who live with the Americans. We have no special quarrel with them, nor they with us. Both are co-opted by the forces in power to aid in their battles. I fear my people will be less willing to join battle again. They've called for a meeting of our peoples from both sides to make a joint decision."

"You have already done so much," said Robert. "More than the Army may want to admit."

"They welcome us during a fight and are quick to praise our actions at the time, but I fear their goodwill and promises float on water and drift quickly from memory. To many, we're mere savages, and worse, competitors for the lands they want. This is as true of the English as it is the Americans." He paused. "I will use what influence I have to promote my people's interests, but it's little against the tide of colonial greed."

It was with this in mind—and the severity of the defeat just suffered—that Robert wrote to the Society a few days later,

> This part of the Province is again the seat of war. A battle was fought six days since within ten miles of my residence in Niagara. The English Force was obliged to retire. In consequence, the whole country is open to the Enemy, & nothing is to be expected but scenes of wretchedness & desolation.

In the face of such despair, I found it difficult not to lose hope myself. With every creek the Americans crossed, each fresh battle we lost, they came closer to our home. Our troops might fall back in good order, but here we sat with the lake behind us. There was only so far they could fall back before we were all pushed into the lake. Would we find ourselves on the battlefront before summer's end?

Jack and the remains of his company arrived back from the battle-field and most were housed in the St. Mark's hospital. The men rested there as best they could. Every woman with the slightest nursing skill was pressed into service among the wounded.

As Maryel tended Jack's hand, she tried to make conversation. I was changing the dressing on a chest wound nearby, and could not help overhear.

"We were too far away to hear gun-fire. Was it terrible?"

Jack raised his head a little. "What?" he whispered.

"The battle… I wondered… if you'd rather not…"

His head dropped back onto the pallet. He muttered, at first almost inaudibly, then rising to a high pitch. "Smoke and noise. So much smoke. Can't breathe. Near-constant buzzing. Stop buzzing!" He sat up and clapped both hands over his ears. "Stop buzzing!"

I turned at his cries and saw his eyes rolled back with only the bloodshot whites visible.

An army surgeon came over with a brown glass bottle and a small medicine measure. He poured a quantity of sweet-smelling liquid into the glass and persuaded Jack to drink it.

He took Maryel's arm and walked away a short distance with her, saying, "It often takes the younger officers this way. Sometimes they go into shock, and sometimes they feel guilty they survived. I'd say it's the fever talking in this one. Don't expect him to make sense yet. Finish with that dressing and get him to lie down and sleep. Let the laudanum do its work."

"Have I done him an injury?" she asked. "I couldn't resist asking him about the battle. He wrote to us right afterwards. His head must have been clear then."

"He should be fine in a day or two. Besides the fever, it was too soon to be talking. He needs to put the things he saw at a little distance. And then there's his hand." The surgeon rubbed his chin. "The ball merely scraped the flesh, but hit hard enough to break two finger bones and severely bruise the entire hand. All the field surgeon could do was put in some stitches." At Maryel's gasp, his tone became more reassuring. "I've set the bones. If you keep poulticing the wound, so it doesn't putrefy, he may regain full use of the hand."

Maryel exhaled deeply. "Thank you. I was worried about that. Wounds so often go bad." She looked up at the surgeon. "He's a musician, you know. I don't know if he could bear it if he lost the use of his hand."

He patted her on the shoulder, then moved off to deal with the next urgent case.

Turning back to Jack, Maryel finished changing his dressing, made sure his boots were off, and covered him with a blanket. He was already drowsy from the dose of laudanum and would soon be asleep.

I became aware of a background murmur of conversations and moans that had faded into nothing with my concern for Jack and

Maryel. My head was soaking, too, scalp prickling not only from the summer heat, but from tension, now released.

I sent Maryel off home. "You look like a bunch of wildflowers an infant has clutched too long in a grubby paw. I prescribe a washcloth, some cold well water, and an hour with your feet up. You can come back later this evening."

She was glad to take a break. "How you can keep going…"

"You're more affected because it's Jack," I said. "It's always worse when you care deeply."

"I could never do this to earn my living."

"You never know what you can do until you must," I said brusquely, pushing her toward the door. "You'll find yourself capable of almost anything."

✳

It wrenched my heart to see all these young men in such dire straits. And some not so young, either. But those of what I now thought of as tender years, appeared gray and aged from their ordeal.

The boy in the bed next to Jack was in a dreadful state. He had taken a ball in the arm which was shattered and must come off above the elbow. I wondered if he could bear it, but the alternative was gangrene and certain death. I sponged his forehead and persuaded him to sip a little tepid water.

The surgeon came by to examine him. He shook his head at my inquiring glance and said only, "Maybe."

It seemed selfish to rejoice that Jack was not severely wounded, but I did. His regiment was so badly cut up, they wouldn't be at full strength for some time. That didn't mean he wouldn't be called upon to fight again. Heaven knew we needed every able-bodied man in the field.

There was worse news to come. Tom brought us further word of demoralization among the Indians. "Many of them retreated to

Brant's Ford to lick their wounds. Some would give up their fight."

"That's terrible," said Robert. "After all our efforts to support each other, to lose them would be disastrous."

One more worry to add to my ever-lengthening list.

Willcocks

6 Jul

Great rout of English yesterday at Chippawa on Niagara R. My Company showed their excellence in battle. Proves to American commanders our value lies in more than raiding and skirmishing. We were delayed in crossing Chippawa Creek. Enemy pulled down bridge. Sufficient timbers remain for our forces to restore it pretty smartly. Our troops in possession of Ft. Erie once again. We shall hold it this time.

10 Jul

Advanced back to Queenston. tho' Riall holds all forts at river's mouth. on both banks. Indian warriors dispirited after the battle at Chippawa. Most of our small contingent of braves melted away. back to their villages no doubt. Some remain under Norton for the English. They're formidable on all grounds where we find them.

Tom

The British continued their retreat, harried by the Americans, until the former were settled in Fort George and the latter camped at Queenston. This position held for a few days while the Americans expected reinforcements. Both sides jockeyed for position until all Tom wanted was to know where he was supposed to report on any given day. He might leave camp in the morning and find it gone elsewhere by evening. Some additional troops arrived, but there was no naval support. Where were the ships? Tom was sent out on a scouting trip.

"All this skirmishing and maneuvering back and forth is wearing the men down," said Willcocks to Tom on his return from a scouting trip. "We're losing our momentum and they're losing their edge. And still no sign of Chauncey's fleet."

"I've news that might encourage them."

"By all means, let's have it."

"Our Indian allies have approached their relatives still fighting for the British, under a flag of truce. They propose that all of their people withdraw from the war."

"The British would miss them more than we would. Hmm… yes. That could work for us. Hearten the men a bit. Put it about, will you? It's better than nothing. Might stop the muttering in the ranks." He ground his teeth so hard Tom winced. "Let us have at them, damn it!"

✳

"We whipped them soundly at Chippawa, men. We'll do it again and again until they relinquish the ground!"

Tom joined in the calls of encouragement for Willcocks's stump oration, for form's sake. Jos surely knew how to drum up support among his men. Two full years now since war was declared, one since they had gathered as the Canadian Volunteers, and until now, they were the only company to enjoy nothing but success. Now that they had officially joined forces with the American army, they felt themselves invincible.

The new American troops had even unnerved the Indians. One in the eye for Norton, according to Jos, whose growing vindictive streak Tom found disturbing. It was ever more difficult for him to pass as an American. Everything Willcocks's Volunteers had done since Niagara's burning sickened him. Not that the British responses had been admirable. War was a damnable thing.

Willcocks wound up his speech to a rousing cheer from his men. He strode over to Tom and clapped him on the shoulder. "This is more like it, eh?" He rubbed his hands together, grinning. "We'll soon have those scrubby shag-bags on the run. You mark my words. This time next year, we'll be in charge here."

"Sounds like counting chickens to me, when we don't even have any eggs."

"Don't be such a Jonah, man. Anyway, now we have the regulars. We'll make mincemeat of the British scum."

"You don't have to convince me, Jos. We have to win battles."

"We're winning them all right. St. David's village found that out. Stone's men served them as we did Niagara, for denying them supplies."

"We loot. They starve."

"It's war, boyo."

✳

Two more weeks passed before the Americans made a decisive move.

"I hear we're to try for Burlington next," said Tom.

"That's the plan," said Willcocks. "But we need to watch the British. Monitor their movements. Get behind their lines if you can. I need someone I can rely on to check the situation."

Tom returned in the evening to report that the British, informed of the retreat by their scouts, had advanced to a position near the Falls.

"Now comes the test," said Willcocks. He grinned at Tom. "Tomorrow."

Tom had seen the extent of the forces arrayed against them. "It'll be a tough fight." How many more battles would there be?

Willcocks

26 ^{Jul}

Fiasco in a field near the Falls. Riall's forces moved out of their Niagara refuge. We advanced to engage them. Who ever heard of a battle running through the night? Darkness usually cooler, but not last night. Stink of powder blasts, smoke, blood, spilled guts, unwashed men still in my nose. Rough ground, mostly wooded. Even with a moon there would have been no seeing. Smoke from cannon shot and musket fire obscured anything at more than arm's length. Caught glimpses of familiar faces here and there. Mostly a shambles. This journal turned a bayonet aside— lucky chance. Dodged through rain of musket balls unscathed. Hundreds, maybe thousands, not so lucky. Fought to stalemate. No ammunition or powder or will to shoot on either side. Positive we had slight advantage, but ordered to leave the field! What madness was that? Let scurvy English think they've won the day? Run off like whipped dogs? No self-respecting Irishman could stomach it. Told my officers to resume raids on the locals still standing. Burn! Burn them all!

27 Jul

When we should renew the attack, at least maintain ground gained.

order comes to fall back to Ft. Erie, fortify for a siege. Further madness! Attempts to sway Generals otherwise failed.

order comes to fall back to Ft. Erie, fortify for a siege. Further madness! Attempts to sway Generals otherwise failed.

Rebecca

We received the first wounded from the night battle at Lundy's Lane early on July 27th. Tom was in the vanguard and drew me aside for a word.

"I must get back to my duties, so be quick," I said.

His face was smudged and worn and his eyes bloodshot. "I wanted the Reverend to know… Major Norton rallied some of his warriors but he doesn't know for how long." He shuddered. "I'm sure without them we'd not have held the field. It was like nothing I've seen, Rebecca."

"Surely it was madness to fight through the night?"

"You'd have thought so. But once engaged, it was impossible to stop. I don't know how anyone could see what they were shooting at. I couldn't see more than six inches in front of my nose. The smoke…" He coughed, a nasty ragged sound, and wiped his mouth on his grubby sleeve. "Be thankful you have never seen battle."

"Bad enough to see the results. Which is my chief concern right now." I embraced him briefly, then pushed him away.

He called back. "We held the field. It was a very close thing."

August–September

Rebecca

Was I nothing but a pair of hands? I knelt beside a man whose leg had been blown apart by a cannonball. There was no laudanum left, even for amputations. He screamed around the wooden gag placed for him to bite on until, at last, he fainted from the pain. After all I had been through, both in midwifery and this war, I was sickened by how little I could do to help his suffering. The surgeon had wielded his saw and cauterized the stump, and now it was up to me to pull this poor man through the shock. I say "man," but he was more of a boy, really. Most of the officers were under thirty years of age, some not yet twenty. This one was strong. If he survived the inevitable fever, he should recover.

It was bad enough when it was merely skirmishing. There were minor actions in our district almost daily. Major battles, like the rout at Chippawa and the night battle at Lundy's Lane, overwhelmed our ability to treat our wounded. They were evacuated back to Fort George for triage. We housed the overflow from the fort in the shell of St. Mark's Church. The military surgeons worked beyond their capacity and relied heavily on us—the women of the district—for everything up to major surgery. Thank God a line had been drawn there. I could face stitching up the most gruesome wounds, but not amputation. It might be necessary to save a man's life, but I couldn't do it.

Maryel was my mainstay with the seriously wounded. Eliza was handier with the convalescent. Her tendency to vomit at the sight of a putrid wound made her of little use in triage or serious nursing. Strange that Maryel was now the stronger of the two sisters. Before the war, she had been ineffectual, barely competent at routine tasks. Her sister had been more proficient in every way. But Eliza proved capable and reliable for preparing and administering medicines, bathing fevered brows, reading letters from home and changing dressings on minor wounds. Each pair of hands found its best use.

There was little to lighten the gloom of those days of endless toil and suffering, but Maryel found a few moments those August evenings to sit with Jack and help him exercise his left hand, healing slowly of its wound. I watched them from a distance. Occasionally, she pressed too hard on a tender spot, provoking him to yelp. I cocked an ear toward them, wanting to know how their courtship was progressing.

"Ouch! Careful!" He spoke to her in a reproachful tone. "You're supposed to be helping."

She laughed. I hoped he found it as funny as she did. After a pause, he laughed too.

"Fine then, abuse me all you like. I swear you are a callous nurse."

"But all nurses must be," she said, "or our patients would never leave our care."

"I would never leave your care." His voice was teasing, and she giggled.

"You, Jack Stevenson, are a terrible flirt. A rogue. A gambler. Would you gamble with my affections?"

"You're cruel about my talents, Maryel. I do have others."

"Yes, for drinking and dicing. Very edifying, I'm sure."

"For fiddling too, and piping. At least until these tendons were damaged."

"I'm sure you'll fiddle up a storm if you keep up the regime the surgeon recommends. At least the bones knit straight. Here, rub some of this salve into your hand. He said it would help, and Rebecca made it up especially."

"You're too kind to me. I don't suppose…"

"What?"

"I should speak to your father first…"

"Jack Stevenson! If you intend to make me a formal offer, this is not the time or the place!"

"Where and when then?"

"Talk to Father. Then we'll see. You know how he feels about Irishmen, though. So don't get your hopes up. Even if we have an informal understanding."

I smiled inwardly, knowing her father was resigned to the notion of their marriage. Hearing their exchange made me feel a little better about Maryel's future, at least if the war continued to go our way. And it looked, after Lundy's Lane, as if the tide had turned in our favor. If only it would end soon, before my endurance became entirely spent.

As the inflow of wounded eased, I pressed Robert to permit Jack to be moved to Lake Lodge, or at least to the mill nearby, with other convalescents, where Maryel could devote more of her time to him.

"I'd prefer her to be under your watchful eye," he said.

"With all the new cases in the church, I can scarce spare her a moment of attention. She's a woman grown, and I think has developed good sense. Besides, better have him here than at York."

He acquiesced, though it clearly went against the grain.

Willcocks

3 **Aug**

British generals reported victory at Lundy's Lane after we fell back. Pressing their advantage.

14 Aug

Yesterday's siege action left hundreds dead, mostly British forces. Huge explosion of powder beneath Fort Erie's south bastion when attackers breached fort. We beat them back. No sign of activity in their camp. Probably demoralized by losses. Good news for us. Anticipating reinforcements.

29 Aug

Rain making all ill-tempered. Scuffles between my men and New York militias. Their substitute commander not much use. His general left me in command, but he won't take my orders. Mayhem and disaffection rife in troops. Too many competing commanders in this fort. Still no reinforcements.

3 Sep

Plans for sortie underway. Can't command men who won't take orders. If need be. will go as volunteer. They'll need every man.

Tom

Among the press of men preparing for the sortie, Tom checked his gear thoroughly. He didn't want to fall because he lacked powder, shot, or had a faulty musket barrel. After cleaning it for a third time, he wondered for the fiftieth time how he had gotten himself stuck in a fort under siege. Worse, if he didn't show himself willing to fight, he'd lose his credibility with Willcocks forever.

Too many men crowded into the barracks. The stench was near overpowering. If reinforcements ever arrived, they'd have to build their own barracks—maybe two—to ease the overcrowding. Gunpowder, overflowing latrines, and unwashed bodies combined with rotting meat and soured vegetation to produce an aroma that would knock an ox flat. He might yet succumb to it himself.

Preparations made, he stepped outside for fresher air. Willcocks was there, leaning against the barracks and puffing on his pipe.

"Ready for action?" he asked.

Tom nodded. "It'll be a relief to get out of this damned coffin of a fort."

"Have a look at the ground out there before you get too keen."

Jos had a point. The field outside the fort was swampy. The earlier attack had trampled any possible cover. All that remained were mud and a few stumps.

Battle commenced with a few volleys and a short cannonade, then became fiercer. Both the sortie party and the siege troops were so muddied within a half-hour that few might tell friend from foe, apart from their relative positions. Again and again, they loaded, fired, reloaded, to little effect.

Tom took good care to aim high or low, although one could never tell precisely where a musket ball would go. The lines were never close enough for bayonet work, nor far enough to be out of range of the hail of balls.

Finally, after a brief lull, Tom looked full into the eyes of the officer opposite him on the enemy line.

It was Jack Stevenson.

No sooner had Tom recognized him than he fell to a fresh volley, as did those in his line. He felt his leg on fire and his head met the ground, knocking him out.

Jack

The bruised and battered 100th, still licking their wounds from Chippawa, and barely reinforced, were sent out again in mid-August to besiege Fort Erie. Their efforts failed dismally, and owing to command errors, their strength was reduced once again, this time by another fifth, mostly wounded.

It was not until the end of August that Jack was able to rejoin them, the surgeon having released him for return to duty. The 100th had been sorely cut up during their first attempt on the fort, and desperately needed reinforcements, even the walking wounded. Jack heard many stories of that action, the most appalling of which was the explosion of a powder battery right under the feet of the 104th Foot, with all but a few men killed.

The autumn rains had begun. Camp conditions were frightful outside the fort, and Jack could only imagine how it felt cooped up inside.

"It's hard to see how we can do anything but starve them out, in all this muck," Jack said to the adjutant.

Dawson agreed. "Half the men turned out for sick parade. It

wouldn't surprise me if more deserted." Despite the severe punishments that could be levied, many soldiers did desert, although most returned when the shooting stopped.

On the fourth of September, pickets in front of the British battery immediately outside the fort sounded the alarm. The Americans were attempting a sortie in its direction.

Jack was glad of some action again. At least it might make him warmer. His joints creaked after a restless night under an inadequate shelter, hastily constructed from sheets of birchbark.

"They've sent us out the militia," he said to Dawson. "Fodder for our cannon."

"The regulars think they're too good for us, is that it?" Dawson laughed. "I doubt it. My guess is they want the militia to wear us down so they can come out and clean up."

"Well, they can fight all day for that and get nowhere."

The New York militia were accompanied by the Canadian Volunteers. Jack spotted the infamous Willcocks in black side-whiskers and a colonel's insignia. He called for a volley from his men.

Just as he completed his signal, he caught the eye of the man next to Willcocks. It was Tom. What the hell was he doing there?

His men's aim was true. Both Willcocks and Tom fell. It was never easy to see men go down. And Tom was a friend, not an enemy. But his attention was wanted for the fight. It dragged on and on until a violent thunderstorm and outright deluge swamped the field and halted the action.

Each force gathered their wounded and dead. "This can't go on," said Jack. "If they don't pick us off, we'll drown."

"It's more a lake than a field. Even if we had tents, there's nowhere to pitch them," said Dawson. "The general must have some plan, but I swear I can't fathom it."

Tom

Tom awoke to excruciating pain in head and leg. What little light there was filtered through chinks in the log blockhouse, dimly showing pallets where other men lay. Their groans did nothing to help his headache, but he was most concerned about his leg.

"Help!" he cried. "Somebody, help me!"

"Wait your turn," said the man in the next bed. "No need to shout."

One of the fort's three surgeons finally approached his bed. "You're one of the lucky ones," he said. "Ball missed the bone, missed the artery, too." He probed at the wound on Tom's thigh, causing Tom to grip the sides of his pallet. "Clean wound, tore up the muscle somewhat." He re-wound the bandages. "You'll do."

"My head…"

"You took a blow to it when you fell under fire. Lovely goose egg but no serious damage." He felt Tom's forehead. "No fever. Rest will heal you up."

"What of Jos… Colonel Willcocks."

"Ah," the surgeon turned serious, "stone dead when they brought him in. Ball to the chest. Nothing to be done."

Tom lay back, his pains almost unnoticed after this news. With Jos gone, would his value as a double agent be less? He doubted his ability to continue with Mallory or Markle replacing Willcocks at the head of the Volunteers. They had always resented him and suspected his motives. Might he finally be free to return home?

But... What if the war dragged on?

Jack

What remained of the British forces at Fort Erie were relieved to get the order to lift the siege. On the 21st, they retired to Chippawa, a place Jack could not face with equanimity. He kept seeing his men and fellow officers falling under enemy fire. But they soon removed to Fort George.

The mess was afire with war news. Not only was Boney on the run in Europe, but the British had scored a notable victory against the Americans at Washington.

"Revenge for Niagara!"

"And York!"

"Why, how's this?" asked Jack.

"While you were off slogging through the Fort Erie mud, our forces entered the American capital."

"Aye, burned it, too."

"Only the public buildings, though. They should think themselves lucky."

"Their White House is burned black."

"Old Madison won't have liked that."

"Damned war hawk. Too bad he got away."

Jack could only shake his head at the news.

"And what takes the cake? Why, it was our most cautious General who authorized the attack!"

"Even better, they feared an occupation and burned their own shipyard."

And indeed, Jack learned, General Prevost had insisted the Americans had proved themselves uncivilized by their actions at York and Niagara and that retaliation in kind was called for. For a man most known amongst the Army as a prudent—sometimes overly prudent—man, who often hesitated to commit his men, this was an astonishing action. It was all just politics to Jack. Not comprehensible by the average man.

October–December

Jack

By October, the 100th had moved from Niagara to Queenston, to Chippawa. Their last major action came in mid-October, when the Americans made another attempt on Chippawa. Again, Norton's warriors played a major role, but it was to be their last action together. Momentum had turned. After that brief skirmish, the Americans withdrew to their side of the Niagara River, and did not return. Fresh reinforcements were sent to Niagara to relieve the veterans, and the 100th was slated to return to Lower Canada once more.

The bag that brought word of the new regimental postings contained a large bundle of letters addressed to residents of Niagara. Jack and some other junior officers took on the job of sorting them. Some had dates on them as far back as November and December, 1812. A few were addressed to the dead. A thick stack was set aside to be held until the whereabouts of the recipients could be determined for not everyone had returned to the town as yet. There were several for the Addison household, and Jack volunteered to deliver them.

"I hope there was nothing urgent in the older ones," he said to the Reverend when he handed over the packet. "There are three addressed to you and two to Mrs. Addison. None for your daughters."

"Two are from my sister in Heversham, in the north of England, and one from my brother in London." He broke the seals on his letters and quickly scanned their contents. Part way through the second letter, he sank into his chair with a moan.

"Sir... Father... whatever is the matter?" asked Jack.

"My father. He has died... No, no." He pushed Jack's comforting hand away. "It's the shock. He was an aged man, well past the three-score-and-ten the Bible tells us we're allotted. He had ninety-two years in his dish. Why, he has been expecting to die these past twenty years!" Addison wiped his spectacles on his handkerchief and put them back on. "My sister Mary has been tending him for most of that time. She went back to England... She came out here with Rebecca and my daughters, you know... Because he was ill and not wishing to leave his home and live with one of his sons or my other sister, Agnes. He suffered from sick headaches as he became older, and said they had too many children and their houses were too noisy and cramped." He smiled, a little sadly.

"I'm truly sorry for your loss. To lose a parent is a grief I share."

"Thank you, my boy, thank you. The truth is, my father was a vigorous man in his youth, and good with his hands, but as he lost their skill and dexterity, he became querulous and testy. He enjoyed ill health, as the saying goes. My poor sister... She delayed her own marriage to look after him, for he never would countenance another man taking over his household. I fear she has had a sad life."

"Will she marry now, do you think?"

"Why yes. She says so here. She says 'Against all reason, John Moon has stayed single all these years, and we're to be wed in February.' She will be fifty-four, and he a little older. I trust it will have been worth the wait."

Rebecca

The letter from Sarah spoke of family matters and I looked through it quickly before laying it aside to open the second. To my surprise, that was from Drusilla. I had all but given up hope of hearing from her again. This letter was dated last March and spoke of their receiving news of our calamitous year of 1813. After expressing her sympathy for the region's losses, and good wishes for our health and safety, she told me Quebec had been buffered from attack by General Prevost's concentration of troops there, as well as its accessibility by British ships. Her understanding was that the Americans had considered attacks on the interior more likely to succeed. I rolled my eyes at this remark. They had so nearly done so.

She went on to say:

> I have long regretted the rift between us, owing to my poor judgment, as I now realize. Our reconciliation at your wedding was too short-lived, then our duties called us in different directions. I am still bound by duty. My family is in poor health, and even if the war ends soon I cannot leave them unattended. Perhaps one day we may meet

again and resume our friendship, but I hope in the meantime our correspondence may suffice. Please write in return. I long to hear from you.

I sat down at once to compose a reply. I, too, hoped she could return to Niagara one day.

✳

The man at my kitchen door was Tom, sporting a week's growth of stubble and leaning on a stick.

"Should I throw you out, as the traitor folk say you are?"

"I'm no traitor, Rebecca. Will you hear me out?"

He took off his hat. I motioned him in. He sat with arms and chin propped on the back of a chair, and sighed as he did so. It sounded restless. Unsettling. I returned to the fire and stirred the contents of the kettle.

"Onion soup?" he asked.

I nodded. "Just needs a little longer." I gave it a final stir, then put the lid on and swung the crane back over the fire. "So," I said, "what have you to say for yourself?"

"You know I was playing a double game?"

"I suspected you were doing something extra-secret soon after Brock's funeral."

"Good thing my employers didn't know that or they might have found a reason to send you out of the Province."

"They needed me too much to do that. I wonder at their not informing us of your role." Did they not trust their own agents? "But I know you too well to believe you'd turn traitor.

"It sounds simple when I say I had to appear to be one thing to one group of people and entirely another to a different group, but that would be as easy as acting a part on the stage. I had to convince my enemies I was their friend, and do things that made me seem an enemy to my friends, while cheating my enemies out of their information but giving them information to convince them I was betraying my friends." He shook his head. "I fear some of the information I conveyed led to great harm to our neighbors in the district. And yet I was often under suspicion from Willcocks and his lieutenants."

Such a tangled web. "It must have been hard to bear."

"I had to make sure that my official contacts among our friends were always certain I was indeed a friend and had not betrayed them to the enemy. There was a constant pull between the two, for truly, no group can be entirely in error about everything, any more than it can be right all the time."

I recognized this as hard-won wisdom.

"Even poor old Joseph Willcocks, traitor that he was, had some merit-worthy ideas. Sometimes I wondered which side to favor. But I tried to stay focused on the fact that people had come onto our land with the goal of taking it from us. If I didn't do my best to thwart them, they might well succeed." He rubbed at his forehead, smudging it. "The hardest part was watching the town burn and letting it appear as if I'd been one of those torching the houses. After that, I knew for sure which side I was on." He frowned. "If the Government doesn't reward our Indian brothers, I will be ashamed. For what have we done but take their lands in the same way the Americans tried to take ours?"

I listened in silence. When I was certain he was finished, I turned back to the soup and ladled out a bowl. "Sit yourself round properly, Tom, and get outside of this."

I stepped into the pantry and returned holding both milk and cider jugs, with a loaf of bread under one arm.

I set these and a mug before him, saying, "Help yourself to whatever you want."

Tom busied himself for a few minutes, spooning up hot soup

and chasing it with chunks of bread and gulps of cider.

"That's the way, my boy."

"You haven't called me that in ages."

I sat next to him and turned him toward me, taking his face in my hands. "Never doubt this, Tom. We all love you, and are proud of what you did. You're as much a part of our family as if you were my son by birth, or had married Addison's daughter."

His eyes misted. "You've been so good to me, Rebecca. I always wished I was your son. I have always tried to be worthy of your love."

And there it was. I was almost afraid to ask. "You're going to leave, aren't you?"

"I must. This post as Crown agent… It gave me the chance to see more of the country. Now, I long to see more of the world. I have my trade. The outer reaches of our colonies can use a printer—eventually—and until then I may turn explorer, or fur trader, or continue as a Crown agent. Who knows? I may return, or I may not."

I put my arms around him and held his head to my shoulder. "I hope you will come back sometime, my lad, but that's as may be. Promise you'll write to me, at least. Gift me a share in your adventures."

He smiled through his tears. "All travelers write home, don't they? And you are my home."

✳

Having held me up through the years of wartime privation, my constitution now deserted me. Shortly after Tom's departure, I fell ill with a severe ague that threatened to settle into my lungs.

Robert found me swooning in my stillroom one morning. He and Hannah, between them, got me upstairs to bed, semi-conscious. All I knew was that I didn't want to lie down, and protested at their ministrations.

"Swooning? Me? I never heard of such a thing." I swung my feet over the edge of the bed, but when I went to stand, they would not hold me. It was Robert's turn to tend me, and my hollow cough echoed through the house.

For days, I either shivered under three quilts and as many blankets, or could barely stand the touch of a single sheet. My head ached constantly and so did every joint, including ones I never knew existed. Robert stayed by me most of the time, except when Eliza or Maryel dragged him away for his meals. He forced me to sip at warm or cool liquids, depending on the state of my fever. It finally broke, and the congestion in my chest eased, leaving me too weak to rise without help.

"How… long…?" My voice rasped from disuse.

Robert was sitting beside me, close up to the bed, my hand in his. I could barely turn my head to see it lying there limply. The touch of his hand as he smoothed the hair back off my forehead was as gentle as if he were holding a newborn.

"Full three weeks," he said. "I feared to lose you." He bent his head over my hand, and I felt the fall of tears. "I could not have borne it."

Three weeks? Truly, I must have been nigh unto death. No wonder I felt so weak.

Robert told me later, when I was returned to sensibility and on the mend, that he had never been so afraid of anything in his life.

"You have been such a rock—a pillar for us all to lean upon. To see you laid low… We did all we could think of to bring your fever down. Hannah brought cold cloths and bathed you hourly. I ransacked your stillroom—apologies, my dear—for possible remedies. I added willow-bark to the broth Hannah made and we got you to swallow as much as we could." His Adam's apple bobbed in his throat. I watched it, fascinated. Perhaps my senses had not quite returned after all. "I feared to use laudanum, after all your cautions about its dangers."

✳

They say healers make the worst patients, and it's true my patience was sorely tried by their cossetting. To my way of thinking, I recovered too slowly, for the season advanced and I should be up and doing. But they were firm. Robert went so far as to hide my clothes. I subsided and endured my convalescence as best I could. Maryel and Eliza were attentive nurses, and I was cossetted as I had never been in my entire life.

There was plenty of time to think. It was an uncomfortable luxury since I usually evaded any deep reflection on my life. Easier to go from day to day in service to others, focused on immediate problems and making such decisions as were necessary. Far harder to permit myself to think only of my concerns.

Now, though, such thoughts could not be contained. At first, I fought to do so. Gradually, they seeped back into my mind, prodding me to examine them. A repressed girlhood. Martin's brief love. My lost child. My father's cruelty. My mother's indifference. My sister's inability to help. Cousin Mary's kindness, supported wholeheartedly by my dear Robert. Right from the start, he refrained from judgment of my youthful indiscretion, and welcomed me into his family. It took me too long to recognize the pure love that entailed. Uncharacteristic tears leaked from my eyes as I thought of these things. I blinked them back, appalled at the weakness they signaled.

I had been an unformed girl, ill-prepared for the world's realities. Too long I had considered myself of little consequence, somehow less worthy than my peers. Now, after all that had happened, I felt only sorrow for my former self, and satisfaction at who I had become. I was on the mend in more ways than one.

✳

Maryel had been a faithful attendant during my illness, but she didn't want to be parted from Jack again. She insisted on following the drum. Robert remonstrated with her that she could well wait, at least until the new year, but she was headstrong and would have her way.

So, when the Regiment returned to Lower Canada in December, she followed in their train. No doubt the Mountains would welcome her back as a guest once more. It would not be for long, since Maryel and Jack planned to marry as soon as the 100th was settled at their next posting.

Robert's health had also been severely strained by the events of the war. He felt better on hearing of the official recognition of his efforts on behalf of the residents and soldiers of the region. Late in the year, the provincial assembly unanimously voted him £100 "in consideration of his work with the wounded soldiers of Fort George and the unfortunate inhabitants of the Niagara area." It was welcome recognition, and little enough in view of his labors and personal expenditures over the past three years. I thought they could well have done more.

We regretted our inability to travel to Montreal to see Maryel married, and that Robert could not conduct the ceremony, but he contented himself with the thought she would be among friends. He kept a few lingering doubts about the lieutenant's suitability for his daughter, which he confided to me, but said nothing to her while the Regiment remained in Niagara, for which I was thankful.

Those in our district had felt the war over once Fort Erie was regained, but news of battles on other fronts continued to trickle in. Newly arrived troops, no longer required in the fight against Napoleon, brought word of peace negotiations in Europe. Our conflict with the Americans, important as it was to us, was seen there as an annoying distraction from the main event.

Robert's duty travels were shrinking in scope—more clergymen came into the province and relieved him of some of the territory as the population increased. He had always intended to go home for a visit, despite his loathing of sea voyages, but never managed it before the war, and couldn't do so during it. His last tie to his old home was broken by his father's death. Now he would never return.

"Now the war is over, my love, we should plan a celebration," I said to Robert one morning over breakfast.

News of the peace negotiations in Ghent raised our spirits. Even word of Gore returning to his position as Lieutenant-Governor could not discourage Robert now. He had showed his loyalty so steadfastly during the war that Gore's earlier suspicions must be forgotten.

"We should," he said. "Perhaps at the turning of the year, if you feel well enough?"

I had thought Christmas might be a suitable occasion, but he reserved that to acknowledge the losses suffered by his parishioners and encourage charity among those remaining. So it was that, in the newly rebuilt Mason's Hall, we held a grand feast on the last day of 1814, to bring in the new year rejoicing.

Because of the repeated military actions and raids on local farms, we had to rely on hunters to provide meat for the table. Game was scarce, but they found a few fat turkeys and a young stag for the roasting. Each family contributed a small amount of produce, and the Army obliged with a barrel of flour which we made into bread and cakes. Mr. Tucker brought ale and cider so we made as merry as we could. After all, we were alive and the coming year would surely be a better one.

I still hugged the knowledge of the secret room and its store to myself. Robert and I had discussed them, and were determined the best use would be to distribute what food remained to those in most need as winter progressed. I hoped there was enough left to stave off starvation for all of us.

The Army provided musicians, and all who could, took part in the dancing. Their fiddler wasn't up to Jack's ability, but he scraped a decent tune. Robert stood up with me in the minuet, but he could no longer take part in contra dancing—it made him wheeze. For my part, I was not yet as steady on my feet as I would wish.

There were many toasts to local heroes and the King and the Prince Regent and anybody else we could think of. At the end of the evening, there was a final cheer.

"Damn all traitors and God save the King!"

PART 3
Aftermath

Chip
Rapids
Street C
Water
Lundy
Lundy Lane
Falls 150 feet
Bendor
Forsyths X
Johnston
Varney
Garner
Shannon
Burck
Muddy Run
Whirpool
M
Kerisuck
Thompson J. Lee
Robinson
Medoch
Nox
Cooper
Rose
Fr. Drummond
Davids
Page
Warner
Horton
Lambert
Queenston
Durhams
Stewart
Newark
Field
F. Ullman
4 Mile Creek
Black Swamp
Grantham
Cross Roads
Cudney
6 Mile Creek
Dupuis
Lawrence
I. Ball
9 Mile Creek
C. Law
McFarlane
Wilson
Ball
Pickard
Dickson
Servers
Fort George
Secord
Niagara
Cooks 2 Mile Point
2
4
6
8

1815

"Make women rational creatures, and free citizens, and they will quickly become good wives;—that is, if men do not neglect the duties of husbands and fathers."—Mary Wollstonecraft

"It is justice, not charity, that is wanting in the world."
—Mary Wollstonecraft

January–February

Jack

By early January, the 100th Regiment was quartered at Lachine, outside Montreal. It was only a brief ride into town, and Jack went there every day he was not scheduled for other duties. He got a fortnight's leave at the end of the month. On January 28th, Jack and Maryel were married by the Reverend Dr. Jehoshaphat Mountain at Christ Church Cathedral in Montreal. Jack's particular friends in the regiment, Lieutenants Samuel Hingston and Irwin Dawson signed the register as witnesses. Eliza was Maryel's only relation present, but Mrs. Mountain, and several other officers and their wives, attended the ceremony.

Maryel hoped to visit her parents, but that would depend on Jack's tour of duty. He didn't yet know whether the Regiment would remain in Lower Canada or be bound for some other duty.

Hingston and Dawson took Jack aside for a few words while Maryel was being feted by Eliza and the other women.

"Is she cut out to follow the drum, do you think?" asked Dawson.

"As much as any woman, I guess," said Jack. "Do you think we'll be transferred back to Niagara?"

"Hard to say," said Hingston. "Might even be to Dublin, or somewhere in England. But maybe the Crown will want to keep a military presence here for a while. Just to ensure the Americans behave themselves."

In their quarters that evening, Jack and Maryel enjoyed a late supper.

"You must promise never to twit me about marrying a younger man," said Maryel.

"As if a few months mattered," said Jack. "Besides, you'd turn about and say I wanted a mother, not a wife."

"It's odd," said Maryel. "At nineteen, I was convinced I would never marry. At twenty-five, some might have considered me unlikely to marry. Spinster of the parish! That was me. And all because of the war."

Jack laughed. "I never saw you as a spinster, not for a single moment."

"Oh, you…" she rapped his hand with her fan, obviously pleased. "Well, there's no going back now."

He caught her in his arms, laughing. "I wouldn't even if I could!"

Rebecca

At long last, the war was over. Rather, the wars, for news had recently arrived of the Treaty of Ghent, negotiated in Europe, and dealing mainly with the situation on the Continent where the depredations of Napoleon Bonaparte were of utmost concern. Our little colonial war was of minor consequence to the negotiators, and the European powers essentially returned the borders to those extant before the war. It made little difference to us—the Niagara River flowed between Upper Canada and New York State as it always had.

Hard on the heels of this momentous news, on a chilly February afternoon, a letter from Eliza arrived. This was of greater import to us, and Robert read it to me over supper.

"The marriage between Maryel and Jack went off very well, with our dear friend Dr. Mountain conducting the ceremony. I will share all the details when I return home.

"There are many new recruits to replace those killed or wounded in the late War, and I am becoming acquainted with some of them. There is one officer in particular, Ensign George Connolly, who is quite attentive and shares my views on many things, so perhaps even at the advanced age of 31 I am not beyond my last hopes of a family after all. Yes, Father, another Irishman. It is unavoidable. At least he is not one of these boy officers—he is of an age with me. But there—nothing may come of it in the end.

"After I see Maryel and Jack settled in their lodgings, I will make my farewells to our Montreal friends and return home."

How tantalizing. She wouldn't have mentioned Ensign Connolly if there weren't something more serious afoot. How lovely if she had found a compatible match. Perhaps I shouldn't, but I imagined her wedding in St. Mark's. It would make amends for our having to miss Maryel's.

I thought about how much less rocky their paths through life might be as married women. While I deplored it, a time when single women might be free from society's constraints had not yet arrived. Even competent women were better regarded if they had a husband, no matter how ineffectual he might be. But… I could not but wish both Eliza and Maryel happy.

He handed me the letter so I might review its contents. "I so wanted to be there," he said.

I reached for his hand, the one toying with his wine glass. It stilled under my touch. "I know," I said, "so did I. But it was wiser not to."

He rose and paced around the room, hands folded behind his back. "Will we ever see Maryel again?"

This surprised me. "Do you think the Army will be recalled?"

"I think it likely their presence here will be reduced. His Majesty's government will not wish to maintain its forces at a wartime level, now Napoleon is defeated."

"Would they be so confident the Americans would not attack again if they removed the deterrent?"

"I don't know. It will depend on how empty their coffers are. Once the threat of invasion of the mother country is over, money will be their chief concern. It's far from certain we're valuable enough to them to justify our continued protection." He took his handkerchief and wiped his spectacles, his familiar worried gesture. "I do not know if the Society will continue to fund its missions." He brightened. "At least I have a place here until all the reparations for wartime losses are distributed. And perhaps the community will still have a use for me."

"Try not to worry, Robert. All may turn out well."

But he stewed and fretted. It was his nature to do so, aggravated by reverses of fortune great and small, over many years. He came to me one morning with his quill box containing a single quill. "I must write to the Society, Rebecca, and look. The box is near empty."

Now it was my turn for concern. "I have too few geese remaining to kill one if we want to build up the flock again this summer. Could you be satisfied if I culled a few wing feathers for you?"

"That will have to do. I will try to keep my correspondence brief in the meantime."

I brought a mug of mulled cider to his desk and stood by while he reported on the state of the Church fabric and the town.

"… I have witnessed during the last summer Campaign, almost the saddest scenes of Distress which a Country subject to the Ravages of War can suffer. The English troops, however, by the blessing of Heaven, though greatly inferior in Number to the Enemy, have driven them beyond the Frontier…"

There was little point in going into great detail about the battles. They would have been reported long since in the English newspapers. He transcribed his *Notitia*—baptisms, marriages, burials—to close the report. Perhaps, if God smiled on us, this would be the last sorrowful missive he would need to write.

My thoughts strayed to our daughters. Would Jack be good to Maryel? If he was a less than satisfactory provider, she had drive and energy to make up for whatever he lacked. There might be a ready opportunity.: the Simpson couple had returned to Niagara and were already talking about opening a school for girls. That might satisfy any lingering wish for independence on her part.

If only both Maryel and Eliza could remain in Upper Canada, near to Niagara.

Tom

Tom found that his reputation in the Niagara region had suffered during the late war. So much so, he quit the area sooner than he had planned. That's what I get for serving my country, he thought ruefully. They say no man is a hero in his own land, but I never thought to be outcast either. Norton's words rang in his ears, the caution he had been so quick to dismiss when he became a spy.

He didn't regret most of his actions—they had been necessary and he took pride in his successes. The few times he had been called upon to act against his better judgment, like at Fort Erie, he put down to the exigency of war. He was happy not to have killed any friends. Or be killed by any of them.

From time to time, he pondered the puzzle of Willcocks, remembering both his passion for reform and his descent into treachery. Something wrong in Jos's head, he thought. And Rebecca was often in his thoughts, too, his separation from her his greatest regret. But she was alive, and that mattered most.

After spending the winter in York, he was no further ahead, scraping by on a few printing jobs. York was rebuilding, but too slowly to suit him. In late February, he set out for Montreal, hoping the roads would stay frozen under him the whole way.

His horizons had grown. Before the war, he had no thought of travel or exploring new places. Now, he seldom thought of anything else. Which was why he was headed for Montreal, that magnet for everything to do with the fur trade. There, he would find men who organized the exploration of the interior of the continent, still largely unknown. He hoped to exchange his cherished Army token for a letter of reference to support him in applying to join an expedition. Why, he might even meet the great David Thompson, who had traveled all the way to the Pacific Ocean!

March–June

Jack

arch saw the Regiment on the move again, to Fort William Henry at Sorel, where they took up headquarters, with detachments posted along the Richelieu. With its being their third posting to the region, the locals welcomed them back with open arms.

Jack found them lodgings in the town of Sorel, and Maryel labored valiantly to communicate with the landlady and cook in her schoolroom French, which was barely up to the task.

Toward the end of March, news arrived from London that the 100th Regiment had been selected to remain in Canada to take up land grants in a strategically located settlement near the confluence of the Rideau and Ottawa Rivers. The men of the mainly Irish regiment were mostly overjoyed—they would have few comparable prospects for land and independence at home. A few of the men were not so well-pleased, Jack among them. After discussing the matter with Captain Sherrard and Adjutant Hingston, he approached the Colonel, with their blessing. He was optimistic. After all, Lieutenant-Colonel George Hay, 8th Marquess of Tweeddale, was only a few years his senior, and should be sympathetic.

Tweeddale, well-primed by his staff, had no hesitation in granting Jack's request to take up his grant in Niagara. Jack would remain on active duty until the Army finished mopping up in the border communities, and the Regiment would work out its last tour of duty in Lower Canada before being disbanded. Jack still hoped for promotion, but knew opportunities would be scarce now the war was over.

He was delighted to learn from Hingston that he was on the list of invitations for Tweeddale's farewell ball, to be held in Montreal.

"It's going to be a grand affair," said Hingston. "The cream of Montreal society will be there. I've sent out upwards of seven hundred invitations. Our outposts will be down to skeleton staff. I pity the officers remaining on duty. They'll have a rough week."

"My wife will be overjoyed," said Jack. This was his lucky day. He must look for a card game this evening while his luck was in. Yes, that would be the thing.

Maryel gasped as Jack shook out the folds of pale green silk and spread open an ivory fan atop them.

"For me, Jack? Can we afford it?"

"I had a little windfall and wanted to get something you could wear to the Colonel's ball. It's next week. Can you get it made up in time?"

"I will do so or die trying!"

He laughed at her vehemence. "No need to go to that extreme, sweetheart. It wouldn't suit your corpse."

She rapped his knuckles with the fan. "Not amusing, Jack. But, oh… such lovely stuff."

"You'll be the belle of the ball. Then we can make plans for our new home in Niagara."

She jumped up at that. "He agreed?"

"Yes, my love." He caught her in his arms and twirled her around the room.

"No matter what else happens, Jack, right now I'm perfectly happy!"

✳

Now that Jack had more experience of the world, he regretted his estrangement from his father. He could swallow some of his pride. It might not taste too bad. But this would be a difficult letter to write.

> You will see by this that I have survived the War. As I don't anticipate further action, I seem likely to do so indefinitely.
>
> It's now two months since I married Miss Mary Eleanor Addison, daughter of the Church of England clergyman in Niagara. I am well-suited with my Maryel, as we call her...

He added a bit more about her, then got down to his other news. This was the hard part.

> At present, the Regiment is gazetted to remain in Canada, both in service of the military defensive objectives of His Majesty's Government, and to prevent floods of discharged soldiers from swelling the ranks of the office-seekers at home. I suspect the latter is uppermost in their minds, since they have made an offer of free land to sweeten the pill, an offer which few could afford to refuse. I am not one of those few. My prospects at home in Ireland would be slight, but here I am in good standing with the established community in one of Upper Canada's primary towns.
>
> You ask in your last if I will ever return to Dublin. It now appears likely I shall remain here. I am promised land in Niagara, thus my wife could be near her family as ours increases. Further than that I cannot say. I hope to see you again, one day.
>
> We have had our differences, and perhaps I was not a model

son. My understanding having grown since those days. I wish you will put our ancient disputes to rest, as I have.

That would have to do. Perhaps they might correspond more cordially in future.

Rebecca

Spring came early, lifting all our spirits. May's flowers were abundant and I made a point of picking some to brighten our table. The soothing aroma of lily-of-the-valley was reputed to signify peace and happiness.

My strength was now fully returned and I reveled in my herb garden. It was greening up nicely, and the rosemary plants I had carefully mulched last fall had survived the winter and were sending out fresh shoots. Even household duties seemed lighter somehow.

One morning after breakfast, Robert joined me on the veranda where I had lingered, looking out over the calm lake waters. He put an arm around me. "It feels like a newly born world, on such a morning." He kissed my cheek, an unusually public demonstration of affection.

I felt the color rise in my face. "Have you drunk from the fountain of youth, then? Such carrying on…"

"I am sure God will look kindly on me kissing my wife at my own front door," he said with mock severity. "And it's true I feel younger than I have for a long time. Ridiculous, when I am over sixty and every day closer to the Biblical limit."

"Maybe all the recent weddings have put you in a festive mood."

Robert was not the only one rejuvenated by spring and the end of the war. Weddings were in the air all over. Some were between widowers and widows—although a fair proportion of the widows were marrying bachelor soldiers. It was encouraging to see the sad events of the war being put aside for happier times.

Robert nodded. "I have just had requests for three more. I suppose next year it will be baptisms that fill my time."

We both chuckled. "Better than funerals, at any rate."

"Thanks be for that," he said.

In the packet of winter letters from England came one from Mary, Robert's sister, who I had come out to Upper Canada with nearly twenty years since, and who had returned to look after their aged father. We were pleased to hear that she had, at long last, married John Moon.

Eliza finally returned from Montreal, full of news about Maryel and Jack. We hung on her every word. Robert was especially happy to hear of their likely return to Niagara.

My news from Drusilla was mixed. I was horrified to hear of her recent losses: both her parents, her sister, and one of the twins had succumbed to a fever that sounded much like the one I had suffered. But there was some good news too. She planned to return to Niagara and take over the family farm. I looked forward to her return.

Now the war was over, letters flew between our rebuilding communities. One momentous day in early June, Robert brought me two particularly welcome missives: from Tom, in Montreal, and from Sarah, in London.

Tom's news was brief, but thrilling.

I was fortunate to receive an introduction to Mr. John Ogilvy, an agent of the North West Company, and thereby to Mr. David Thompson, an explorer of territories to the far West and sometime surveyor, first for the Hudson's Bay Company and later the North West Company. Mr. Thompson intends to take up a new position as surveyor for the Crown, and has kindly offered me a position in his employ. He had previously worked without an assistant but was impressed with my ability to reproduce a drawing he set me. He may also make use of my printing skills in producing maps of the areas he has explored. Some of which territory I may now see for myself!

Rebecca, this is the very type of work I had envisioned. I will keep a journal and write to you whenever I can. I know your good wishes will accompany me on my travels.

And then came the part where my tears welled up and I could scarcely read.

Your loving son,

Tom

After composing myself, I turned to Sarah's letter, which was accompanied by a package containing two new books.

I feel confident that this will now reach you intact. While the news from the Continent is dubious, our ships are no longer under attack by the French. Sister, I hope you will enjoy these volumes as much as I have. The author, "A Lady," has drawn such portraits of human folly as I know must make you laugh. We have all had such little laugh-worthy these past years as to make this most welcome.

I admired the covers of tooled red leather and leafed through the thick cream sheets. An elegant edition, to be sure. I hoped the contents would match the quality of the binding. Despite Sarah's praise, with such dull titles—*Sense and Sensibility* and *Pride and Prejudice*—I had my doubts.

DECEMBER

Rebecca

One chilly December morning, after our morning meal was cleared away, I settled in for some private time in my stillroom. Before starting my work, I re-read my latest letter from Tom, come yesterday. I shivered at his description of half-frozen swamps and the discomforts of portaging a canoe around rapids.

Frost rimed the window and I tucked my shawl closer against the drafts that filtered in from its edges. Some days, I thought I would never be warm again. As I sorted through the ingredients, and set out those I needed for cough mixtures and chest poultices, I could hear Robert's voice from his study. Calm and steady, it rolled out the weighty periods in sonorous cadences as he practiced his new sermon for delivery this Sunday in Advent. And, for a wonder, not coughing.

He had labored at the piece for several weeks. Feeling he must keep the needs of the less fortunate among us at the forefront of his parishioners' attention, he took a text from *1st Peter*: "And above all things have fervent charity among yourselves."

I let his words wash over me, caught by passages that expressed my feelings better than I could have. He spoke of mercy to all who had suffered. When he mentioned those taken prisoner, my throat clenched as I recalled my anxiety when Robert himself had briefly been imprisoned. My heart was torn for those who never returned to their families, or whose families had not survived to welcome them home.

At one point, there was a longer pause than he usually made when revising his work. When I turned my head, he stood in the doorway, a sheaf of papers in one hand, a pen in the other, and his spectacles crammed up on his forehead.

"I need an audience, my dear," he said. " I cannot feel the rhythm correctly without. I don't wish to interrupt your work…"

"Nonsense," I said. "I can continue later." I followed him back into his study and pulled up a chair beside him.

He drew down his spectacles and cleared his throat. "You may think some of my words too harsh." He continued, with more about reversals of fortune and exhortations to unspecified individuals to mend their ways, lest worse befall them.

I moved to read over his shoulder, noting some pointed phrases, "turn from their evil ways," "flee from the wrath to come," "just and deserved punishment," and "implore in fervent prayer with minds abstracted from every earthly consideration, His pardon."

Much of this was clearly aimed at those in power who always remained so despite the vagaries of fate. I found it surprising. Before the war, he had always been hesitant to confront those in power about their misdeeds.

"Perhaps you might moderate some of this?" I suggested. "Those sharp words will cut deep for some." And, I thought, prayer was of little use to combat earthly venality.

"No," he said, "I think it useful for those in power to be reminded while their memories are still fresh. I must speak out at least once, and this feels to me to be the right time, when all is still topsy-turvy from the war. I will conclude in a more forgiving tone, but everyone should be told the truth from the pulpit. Let those who are the most wicked amongst us take my words to heart and do better."

"It's a brave thing to do." Almost foolhardy, compared to his relative timidity before the war. But then, we were all changed by the privations and challenges of warfare and occupation. And we could all aspire to be better souls. I hadn't realized just how much he had changed.

We continued to review his text, and I suggested several places where he might make his point clearer, to which he agreed. We were finished before luncheon, and each returned to our separate tasks afterwards.

✱

The church was cold that Sunday, but the service was still well-attended. So far, the roof was still partly canvas-patched, and only three of the dozen windows had been replaced, so snow drifted in here and there. At least we had some benches, and most had brought cushions to sit on and keep a little warmer.

The congregation listened attentively as Robert read out the passages now familiar to me. My thoughts wandered a little, but when he got to his most-severe phrases, I noticed some sharply drawn in breaths. None that I could pinpoint, though. Luckily, Robert then continued in a milder vein,

"In my present discourse, I will inquire how this great duty of charity is recommended to us…"

This was my Robert's true character. Charitable to a fault. He urged hospitality, moderation in acquisition of material goods and charity as the road to heaven.

"The more we think on the prodigality of those stores entrusted more or less to man for the prudent and useful benefit of all, the more must we ever censure such lavishers of them."

This was hitting hard indeed. I wished he could read these words to the men in power in York and London, and be heeded. Perhaps he could at least influence the local situation.

According to those who had, those who had not were always undeserving. Always chastised, ignored, cast out. Always at fault even when they were the victims of wars they hadn't started, or shut out of the common good by private interests. I had myself felt some of this.

"Might not the kind assistance of some generous soul, to have stretched out their hand with relief at the critical moment of need, severed destruction from them and saved them to the community as good and honest members of society?"

Ah, Robert, if only there were more men of your stamp. I tried to picture a world where kindness was valued over power or riches, but it proved beyond my ability.

Those exiting the service appeared more thoughtful than usual and Robert took his time greeting each one, nor was there any rush amongst the attendees. At least for today, his listeners had taken his words to heart.

Christmas was two weeks later and we made such celebration as we could. We were still on short rations but those who could, shared something, and everyone in town had a good hot meal, on that day at least.

Robert and I celebrated the year's end with letters to family, and he to the Bishop of Quebec, regarding the church, his mission and, of course, his salary. Some things would never change. He made a suggestion I thought sensible: that he vacate his mission and concentrate on the region immediately around Niagara town.

Eliza and I both wrote at length to Maryel. We had received news at Christmas of her anticipation of a child in spring. Eliza was busy with plans to visit. While I longed to go in her stead, I knew she was eager to renew her acquaintance with Ensign Connolly.

I wrote to my sister, Sarah, concluding:

> I have now lived here nearly twenty years. Such changes as we have witnessed, I could never have foreseen. I am proud to have had a part in the colony's survival.
>
> I shall never return to England. I suppose I must call myself a Canadian now. This is the new appellation they give us settlers, derived from the French "Canadien." This land, with its extreme seasons, is rough and challenging, but has its beauties and comforts too. I am content to remain here. I find the thought of the changes to come exciting. Who knows into what this young colony may mature?
>
> Having gone through the greater hell that is war, I am reconciled to the past and looking to the future. I don't love those who have harmed me, but they can do no more harm. I made a straight path out of the ruin of my youth. And it is good, Sarah. I love and am loved. More, I am valued for who I am. That is perhaps the greatest success anyone can have in this life.

There. I set my pen down and leaned back in my chair. Around me lay the tools of my trade, their various scents blending into an harmonious whole. So I found my life to be.

Peace and belonging, at last.

Epilogue

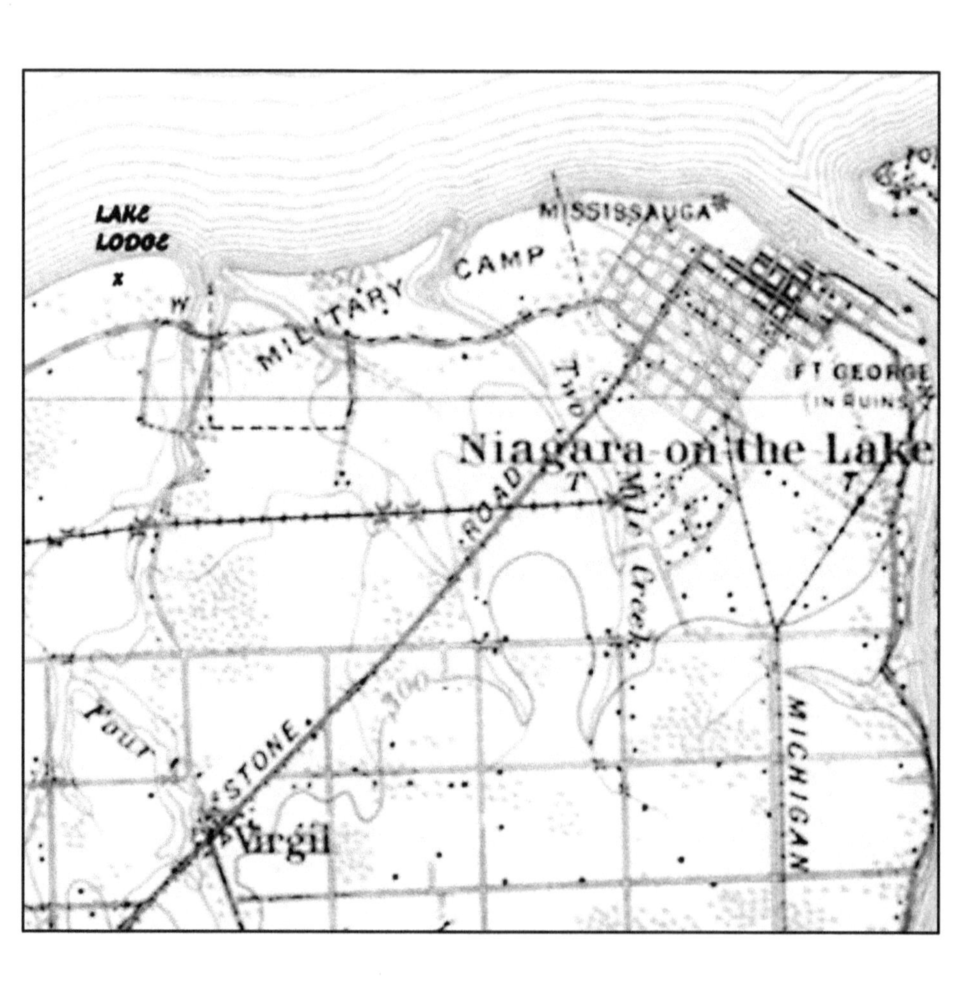

LAKE
LODGE
MISSISSAUGA
CAMP
MILITARY
Niagara on the Lake
FT GEORGE
(IN RUINS)
ROAD
Two Mile Creek
STONE
Four
Virgil
MICHIGAN

1850

"The beginning is always today."—Mary Wollstonecraft

"Friendship and domestic happiness are continually praised; yet how little is there of either in the world, because it requires more cultivation of mind to keep awake affection, even in our own hearts, than the common run of people suppose."
—Mary Wollstonecraft

Rebecca

I am a stout old woman now and a great-grandmother. Although eighty years old, ten past the Biblical allotment, I feel little different inside myself than I did all those long years ago.

We saw many momentous events in this young province. I knew General Brock—yes, Brock the hero. Or so they say. And Norton, and Willcocks, and so many others. Some were public figures, but some, like Addison, Strange and Stevenson, were my family and friends. All gone now, like fallen trees becoming loam in the forest.

Sometimes I find it hard to remember things that happened just yesterday, but those days shine crystal clear. To me at least. To others they may seem dull and dusty—something out of the attic—no longer fit for the parlor.

My grandchildren accuse me of living in the past, and my great-grandchildren want to move on to new, exciting things of their own.

But someday, somewhere, someone may want to know more about those early days. None of the books I have read do our history justice. So, I have told the story of that time, as we knew it.

Jack and Maryel had seventeen years, and eight children, before his early death, three years after my dear Robert, who faded away, worn by his long years as missionary, in 1829. Jack was what Robert had always thought him: a charming wastrel. He was a kindly man, but his aspirations always exceeded his accomplishments and his expenses his income. Maryel would have it he never recovered from the war, but I felt he relied too much on her strength. My fondest memories of him are reserved for his music, which brightened many a dark day. Maryel's children are grown, and their children too. By and large, they have done well and lead lives they are content with. Some live nearby, but others I have not seen for several years. We correspond regularly and that must suffice. I no longer desire to voyage by road, rail, or water.

Eliza married her Ensign and had her own family of four, but of their family only one daughter, one son and one grandchild survive. Eliza and George had a happy life together, though, and I am glad for that.

Tom still writes to me. His letters often take months to arrive since they must come by sea from Fort Victoria, more than two thousand miles away in the new colony of Vancouver Island. He keeps me apprised of his fortunes, though he no longer explores for the Hudson's Bay Company.

I am bent and a little deaf, but still alert and keen-sighted despite my four-score years. I share a comfortable home with Maryel in our apartments at Lake Lodge where my grandson John Connolly is the resident farmer. We are the only ones left who remember those days fraught with war and mayhem, but also with optimism and hope.

Some day, a descendant may come upon this story and read about our times. As all humans must be, we were imperfect, but perhaps our experiences may enlighten their own situations. For most people, I have found, share much the same trials and joys. May the future hold more joys than sorrows, for all my kin.

Everything ends. Wars. Lives. Stories.

Afterword

"Slavery to monarchs and ministers, which the world will be long freeing itself from, and whose deadly grasp stops the progress of the human mind, is not yet abolished."—Mary Wollstonecraft

"England and America owe their liberty to commerce, which created a new species of power to undermine the feudal system. But let them beware of the consequences: the tyranny of wealth is still more galling and debasing than that of rank."
—Mary Wollstonecraft

All the major characters in this work of historical fiction, except for Tom Strange, Drusilla Bell, and Josiah Burton, are based on real people.

Rebecca Plummer, of whom records say little beyond vital statistics, was the second wife of Robert Addison (MA, Trinity College, Cambridge). Addison was missionary to the Mohawks and rector of St. Mark's, Niagara, from 1792 to his death in 1829, having been sent to Upper Canada at the request of Thayendanegea Joseph Brant, by the Society for the Propagation of the Gospel in Foreign Parts. He was Chaplain to the Upper Canada Legislature and held several other posts over the years, including Justice of the Peace. Both of Addison's daughters married Irishmen, officers in the 100th

Regiment. Addison's elder daughter, Eliza, also married an Irishman, another officer in the 100th Regiment. Despite his dislike of the Irish, for reasons unclear to us, Addison was held to be a tolerant, open-minded man. For his day, he probably was. His voluminous library still exists and can be visited at St. Mark's Church in Niagara-on-the-Lake, Ontario.

I followed historical events as closely as possible—given the gaps in the records. And wherever possible, I have drawn information from primary documents, some of which I have taken license to adapt to this story. Addison's reports to the SPGFP and post-war sermon, and Jack Stevenson's letter after the battle of Chippawa, are historical documents. Public figures did much what they are credited with here. Some dates in Joseph Willcocks's Parliamentary career were altered to fit my chosen timeline. The reader should note that people of the Georgian era, while mannered, were a more earthy and open lot than their successors, the Victorians.

The personal events in the story are, of necessity, fictional. Private life, especially that of women, was not considered important enough to be recorded in the detail reserved for military and political events.

Quotes from Mary Wollstonecraft (Mrs. Godwin) were chosen to illustrate precepts that are as valid today as they were in the eighteenth century, when she wrote them. Many women of her day and in the years following took up her feminist ideas. May we all have the courage of our convictions that she did, to speak truth to power and stand up for our rights.

AS

2023

Acknowledgments

This book began as a conversation with my late aunt, Eleanor Proctor, sometime in the early 1980s. I caught the genealogy bug from her, and learning about early immigrant ancestors renewed my interest in Canadian history.

When I was growing up, the history curriculum focused mainly on British and European events, with a smattering of information on the European explorers and settlers in North America. The last year I took history as a subject in secondary school, we concluded with the causes of World War I. This was not long after Centennial Year, 1967, marking 100 years of Canada as a country. Word on the street was that we didn't have much history and what there was, was dull. Surely, I thought, there must be more than that. Well, guess what? There's a lot more to Canadian history than the years since Con-federation (although those have been packed with momentous and fascinating events). The part of our history that caught my interest most was the early days of Upper Canada, now Ontario, in which some of my ancestors had played a role. Never in the forefront, but intimately involved in the events of the day. I had a great time imagining their stories and weaving them into the larger stories they were part of. Did Rebecca do everything I attributed to her? Perhaps not, but someone took those actions, or ones like them.

It took me ten years to complete the manuscript. I had a great deal of help along the way. Early readers included Jean Farrall, L. Peach Akerhielm, Sarah Meral, and my long-suffering husband, Jim Nuyens. I work-shopped various parts of it with Paperback Writers critique group members Pam Isfeld and Mar Preston and with online critique partners Fionnuala Dominguez and Maria Vaughan. Classes on writing craft and editing given by Barbara Rogan and Barbara Kyle, and master classes from the Free Expressions group, gave me a good grounding as I developed the manuscript. I had the great good fortune to attend the Surrey International Writers Conference several times where speakers like Susanna Kearsley, Jack Whyte, Diana Gabaldon and Anne Perry added to my sense of how historical novels work. The Historical Fiction group at the Creative Academy for Writers (https://creative-academy-for-writers.mn.co), including Jenny Graman Lang, Brian Wyvill, Donna Conrad, Jacqui Paul, Janet Oakley, Sharon Michalove and Randy Lyman provided a safe spot to read excerpts, and some additional beta readers. I also shared drafts with my parents, Sonia and David Stevenson, who had passed their love of reading on to me. I was even able to show an early draft to my aunt Eleanor before her sudden death in 2018.

My thanks also go to Mike Werner, who showed me around Robert Addison's still-extant house, meticulously restored by his father, Ed Werner (of *Trivial Pursuit* fame), to the staff of the Niagara Historical Museum and St. Mark's Church, always helpful with my research, archivists at Library and Archives Canada and the Ontario Archives, and to John Petrella, who gave permission for me to reproduce his painting of the Addison farm. I originally planned to use that art-work as the cover for this book, but instead have made it the banner of my web-page.

Thanks go to my editor, Allister Thompson, and my book designer, Sherrill Wark of Crowe Creations, for their invaluable contributions to the final product.

Finally, my aforesaid long-suffering husband read and listened to several complete versions and provided housework and hugs in equal measure. I couldn't have done it without his support. Thank you, Jim!

About the Author

Adrienne Stevenson lives in Ottawa, Canada, on the traditional unceded territory of the Algonquin Anishnaabeg People. A retired forensic toxicologist, she writes poetry, fiction and creative non-fiction. Her work has appeared in many print and online journals and anthologies in Canada, the USA, the UK, Europe, India and Australia.

She is a member of two poetry workshops and an active fiction critique group.

Several of her stories have won prizes in contests held by Capital Crime Writers, Canadian Authors Association and the Ottawa Public Library. Non-fiction articles have appeared in *Byline* and *Anglo-Celtic Roots*.

Adrienne is an avid gardener and cook, a keen amateur genealogist, a voracious reader and sometime folk musician.

She may be found online at https://adriennestevenson.ca